WOLFSBANE
by
Craig Thomas

Jack Higgins said that Craig Thomas's earlier novel **Firefox**, was "in a class by itself."

Ira Levin called it, a "gripping, believable thriller."

Now, in **Wolfsbane**, the new Craig Thomas novel, he tells the story of a secret agent in World War II plunged into bizarre peril. Without his knowledge, he was marked for death. Trapped, he escaped.

Alone in a cold world where double agents did not hesitate to kill, he did more than survive. His name: Richard Gardiner.

He is the hero of . . .

WOLFSBANE

WOLFSBANE

Craig Thomas

BANTAM BOOKS
TORONTO · NEW YORK · LONDON

WOLFSBANE

*A Bantam Book / published by arrangement with
Holt, Rinehart and Winston*

PRINTING HISTORY

*Holt, Rinehart and Winston edition published August 1978
Book-of-the-Month Club edition Fall 1978
Bantam export edition December 1978
Bantam edition / November 1979*

*Grateful acknowledgment is made for permission to quote from
the following:*
"Old Friends" copyright © by Paul Simon. Used by permission.
"Burnt Norton," "Little Gidding" and "The Dry Salvages" in Four Quartets by T. S. Eliot, copyright 1943 by
T. S. Eliot; renewed 1971 by Esme Valerie Eliot. Reprinted
by permission of Harcourt Brace Jovanovich, Inc.

*Bantam Books are published by Bantam Books, Inc. Its trade-
mark, consisting of the words "Bantam Books" and the portrayal of a bantam, is Registered in U.S. Patent and Trademark
Office and in other countries. Marca Registrada. Bantam
Books, Inc., 666 Fifth Avenue, New York, New York 10019.*

*for
Ada
and
Wilf*

ACKNOWLEDGMENTS

My thanks to T. R. J.
for procuring the documents in the case.
My thanks also to Peter Payne,
who arranged a boating incident.

It was
A time of innocence,
A time of confidences.
Long ago . . . it must be . . .
I have a photograph.
Preserve your memories;
They're all that's left you.

—PAUL SIMON

1

TIME OF INNOCENCE

Time present and time past
Are both perhaps present in time future,
And time future contained in time past.
If all time is eternally present
All time is unredeemable.

—T.S. ELIOT, "Burnt Norton," I

1. A la Recherche du Temps Perdu August, 1944

Richard Gardiner had expected to be briefed by someone from F (French) Section, Aubrey himself or Hilary Latymer, who had picked him up at the small Kent airfield the previous day. Certainly the appearance in Aubrey's office of Michael Stanhope Constant, a career intelligence officer from MI 6, confused him and made him somehow resentful.

Latymer, observing him in the moments before the meeting started, sensed his discomfiture. Between Gardiner and him there had always existed an easy intimacy, and he now sympathized with Gardiner's dislike of the stranger. Yet at the same time he was aware that a recent distance had sprung up between them. He had seen Gardiner only twice since the Normandy landings, and on both occasions he had observed what he could describe only as a cold place growing in the man, so that he was more abrupt, less inclined to conversation, less comfortable with easy camaraderie.

Latymer supposed it had to do with the destructive overdrive into which Resistance groups like Gardiner's in Rouen, the "Ilium" group, had been pushed since the invasion.

Latymer had been Kenneth Aubrey's deputy at Baker Street in F Section of the SOE almost as long as Gardiner had been leader of the Rouen Resistance group. He was more used to the discomfort of the relationship between MI 6 and the SOE. Yet he, too, sensed more vividly the habitual contempt in which SOE was held by Constant as he studied from his vantage point against the wall, elbow propped on the mantelpiece, the tall, ascetic individual, formal in black coat and striped trousers, which complemented his cover as a civil servant in the Ministry of Food and which Latymer knew he always was careful to wear in uniformed company.

Aubrey, dapper in the uniform of a major in the RAOC, had claimed his own seat behind his desk after Constant had elected to perch himself in disdain on the edge. Constant, Latymer realized, was upsetting Aubrey, too. The man had the ability to chill the room, which Aubrey was always at pains to make warm, comfortable, suggesting the illusion of a common room from before the war. It was a bright, hot day beyond the window, but somehow Constant had the trick of darkening the room.

Latymer shook off the idle speculation. Instead, he studied the man from MI 6 carefully, as an intrusive, possibly destructive species. Aubrey, he could see, though in MI 6 himself until the outbreak of war, disliked him. From firsthand knowledge, Latymer assumed.

Constant was in his mid-thirties but appeared older, especially in the green eyes, which habitually expressed a watchful assurance. His chalky, narrow features were unlined, aristocratic in their molding and the hook of the nose; it was as if he were without experiences that aged him, or perhaps beyond such. Even the nasal drawl of his voice suggested to Latymer that they were transitory beings and that he, Constant, would continue forever. Yet, as the man unfolded his wares, leaning slightly toward Gardiner as the younger man sat stiffly upright in a hard chair, Latymer watched the voice catch Gardiner's attention, then his interest. The mission was important, it was obvious—less dangerous than important.

"The problem," Constant elucidated carefully, "is,

of course, very difficult, though I've no doubt you chaps in the field can appreciate it. But let me lay out the background for you." He smiled without pleasure or humor. "It arises from that tiresome individual Charles de Gaulle. He has an obsession that the Communists are planning to beat him to Paris and install one of their number in the Elysée instead of himself —a changeling in his crib at Bethlehem. He really should be told that his triumphal return to the capitol will fall a long way short, in sheer spectacle, of the Second Coming. . . ."

"You haven't told him yourself then?" Aubrey remarked maliciously, his mild blue eyes twinkling. Constant's thin nostrils flared for a moment, and then he continued, all irritation squeezed from his careful, studied tones.

"As you are no doubt aware, it is the supreme commander's strategy, and in this he is supported by the SHAEF Planning Committee, not to invade Paris. Too many divisions would be tied up, and the city might be destroyed in the fighting. The Wehrmacht will not give up Paris without a fight, because the Führer will not let them. Besides which, the V-1 and V-2 bases are SHAEF's first concern, and they are not in Paris.

"The Free French, and General Charles de Gaulle in particular, are mortally afraid of the Communists in Paris. There are, according to the latest estimates, at least twenty-five thousand Communists, well armed, in the Paris FFI. And most of the leadership is Communist, especially since the arrest of Lefaucheux in June by the Gestapo—and 'Rol' may have turned him in for all we know.

"I don't need to expand on the danger these chaps represent to de Gaulle. What he is afraid of is an uprising of the Communists *before* he himself can march into the city at the head of the Free French."

As Constant paused, Latymer lit a cigarette and glanced in Gardiner's direction. He caught his eye and shrugged and smiled. He knew what Constant required of Gardiner but would not by sign or gesture anticipate the revelation. The precursory remarks were

necessary. Paris did seem to hang by a thread, together
with the political color of the postwar government
of France.

Aubrey stared out the window, as if he had heard
it all before—which was true. He did not trust his
features to remain smooth as the man's affected patron-
age extended minute by minute, causing him to boil
slowly. Constant was an old adversary.

"You wonder, of course, what this has to do with
you," Constant proceeded. "And naturally, you are
suspicious of my frankness. There is no need for you to
be so. Let me explain. We are certain there will be
an uprising in Paris this month. De Gaulle forbade any
further arms drops in the Paris area on June the fourteenth to forestall it. But whatever de Gaulle wants
or does not want, he will be unable to prevent it.

"If that fact occurs, then it is in SHAEF's interest to ensure that the uprising has a chance of limited success. The supreme commander does not want
to enter Paris before the end of September. We must
see to it, therefore, that the Paris FFI, Communist
or not, has sufficient arms and ammunition to hold
out—to *weaken* the Wehrmacht without involving Allied forces. . . . You begin to understand, I hope?"

"You mean some kind of second front in
France?" Gardiner said. Latymer, knowing him,
sensed the effort he was using to keep excitement from
his voice. The significance of the mission was reaching
down into him, feeding the ego. Now he would not
ask even about the risks.

"Precisely!" Constant said, ironic applause in his
voice. Gardiner wrinkled his nose. It was evident to
Latymer from Constant's tone that it was his own idea
—whatever was to be told Gardiner—and that he had
probably taken it very near Eisenhower himself before
having to pass it on to someone who would introduce
it to the supreme commander.

"Indeed a second front," he proceeded. "If the
uprising were sufficiently strong, then the taking of the
V-1 and V-2 bases would become something more of
a formality, and we might even be across the Rhine

before the end of the year. As long as the uprising is not crushed in its infancy."

"Could I ask," Gardiner began, "could the Communists take over Paris before de Gaulle gets there? Is it a real threat?"

Constant shook his head and studied his fingernails.

"We evaluate that risk as not very real. The Nazis will not let Paris go—Hitler will not let it go. They will fight to keep it, even though they may destroy it in the process." Constant again shook his head. "A great pity if they did. Still, better statuary and stone than lives, gentlemen." Latymer, rubbing his chin, was aware that Constant's humanitarianism was nothing more than a gesture. "There has to be an uprising, and it has to be a real threat to von Choltitz's garrison of twenty thousand Wehrmacht and SS troops. Your task," he added suddenly, his eyes sharpening in focus, looking directly at Gardiner, "will be to estimate what supplies, in what amounts, the Resistance will need if it is to pose a serious threat to the Paris garrison."

Gardiner nodded. Latymer saw Constant suddenly as a skull on which the stretched skin smirked. He hated the ease with which he manipulated Gardiner. The significance of the job appealed to Gardiner's ego. It was the mythical single stroke which could shorten the war, and Richard Gardiner would be part of it.

Gardiner said, "The uprising is inevitable?"

Constant nodded.

"I'm afraid so. The Communists won't wait. The cry of '*Aux barricades*' will be heard in Paris before the end of the month." He smiled and added, "Which is why I have been unusually expansive in my briefing. You will go to Paris in the company of Alain Renaud, who is on 'Rol's' staff in the FFI and is a Communist himself. He will take you to 'Rol's' secret headquarters, 'Duroc.' What we require from you is a realistic shopping list from them and a realistic estimate of their present numbers, resources, and strategy." He leaned forward on the desk until Gardiner could smell the faint, expensive cologne. "You understand the seriousness of your task?"

Gardiner nodded.

"Yes—quite clearly."

Constant looked at his watch. Something in Gardiner's tone made Aubrey turn from the window, swiveling in his chair. Constant, having succeeded so well in enlisting Gardiner, masked his irritation at the evident insult, smiling with an attempted warmth.

"Good," he said. "Major Aubrey has all the details and your documentation. You have four days, no more. Then you will be collected, and we expect your little head to be full of the most interesting material." He smiled again, sardonically, and then added, "I'll leave you to the rest of your briefing then. Major Aubrey will give you the nuts and bolts, so to speak. . . ."

He bade each of them a good afternoon and left. Almost immediately Aubrey lit a cigar. He seemed released from his former mood, which he disliked but always indulged during meetings with Constant. He beamed as he blew out the first smoke, running his hand through his thinning, sandy hair. Latymer uncurled his tall frame from the mantelpiece, easing the cramp out of the arm on which he had been leaning, and offered Gardiner a cigarette.

Gardiner said, "Am I to swallow all that, sir?"

Aubrey appeared surprised, puffed at his cigar, and said, "I should jolly well hope so, Richard, my boy."

"Constant's assessment of the Paris FFI is correct?"

"Undoubtedly—why?"

"Perhaps it's just my dislike of him. . . ."

"I expect it is. You don't want to believe the man because he's such an evident shit. You were obviously under his spell five minutes ago," he added mischievously. Aubrey was almost blithe, and he blew smoke at the ceiling as he spoke. Latymer and Gardiner raised eyebrows to each other at Aubrey's unhabitual vulgarity.

Then Aubrey said, "Will you get out the sherry and the necessaries, Hilary? I didn't offer Mr. Constant anything to drink. He may have gone to Oxford, but he drinks sherry like a navvy drinks beer! However, even though I don't like him, let me give you two young'uns a piece of advice. If you want to go anywhere in the postwar intelligence service, remember it's people like him who'll be running the show."

Gardiner made a face at Latymer, who winked and said, "God forbid."

Gardiner added, "I don't want any more of this after the war. Just my articles, then the quiet life of a country solicitor. That'll suit me down to the ground." Latymer studied Gardiner as he said it; an unexpected sentiment, but he perceived that Gardiner was sincere.

"Shall I call in Renaud then?" Aubrey asked. "If we've sufficiently recovered our sangfroid after that visitation from Whitehall." He popped out of his chair, straightening his uniform blouse as he did so.

"In a minute, sir," Gardiner said. "What sort of mood is he in?"

"Who—Renaud?"

"Yes, sir."

"Hilary, you brought him here. Tell the young man."

"Belligerent, suspicious, impatient—all the things you might expect. You know him. He's risen high with 'Colonel Rol' in the FFI. He expects our assistance by some kind of divine authority." Latymer sipped his sherry and added, "Not a comfortable traveling companion. At best you'll be a pedagogue marking his essay."

Gardiner shrugged.

"It is important, isn't it, sir?" Latymer perceived the eagerness, the bloom of ego, like the switching on of some inner light.

"Yes, it is."

"Then let's have him in, and you can give us Mr. Constant's nuts and bolts."

"*My* nuts and bolts, if you don't mind, Richard. Mr. Constant does not bother himself with mere details, you know."

Etienne de Vaugrigard was unsettled as he waited for "Wolf" and "Wolverine." He had arrived late in the afternoon and had waited in a cool, uncarpeted corridor that smelled of dust, on the first floor of the tall, empty, narrow house that was part of a smoke-blackened terrace of a Bloomsbury square. He spent most of his time standing at a tall window, staring into the untidy, weed-filled garden. The man who had driven him to the house in an ordinary civilian car had left him, and he had let himself in. He had been to the house several times before, and the cool, musty emptiness was familiar to him.

There was a primitive kitchen, and he made himself several cups of strong coffee, yet he always returned to the corridor on the first floor, where his occasional footsteps echoed, to stare out over the garden at the sunlit, dusty space full of straggly yellow flowers and brick rubble. Once, in the early days of his association with the house, there had been a street there. Now, after the bombs, there were only the sunlit clumps of straggling weeds and the bricks heaped as if after child's play.

Etienne de Vaugrigard was Gardiner's second-in-command in the "Ilium" group in Rouen. His code name within the group was "Hector."

The two men for whom he waited arrived together, a little after six. De Vaugrigard heard them let themselves in, and the mutter of their voices washed up the stairs to the first floor like a small wave. Their footsteps were sharp in the empty, tiled hall; then he heard them ascend the stairs. When they came into view, he recognized the "Wolf" and his American companion. With a familiar sickness, he experienced the first of the reactions that assailed him during these occasions—impotent anger at the fact that though he knew their names, he was never allowed to use them. Instead, he paid deference to their code names. And he the heir to the Vaugrigard Armaments fortune and the factories in St. Denis that now turned out war materials for the Germans.

"Ah," the Englishman said. "Sorry you've had such a long wait, Etienne." He hated, too, the ease with which they bandied his first name as that of a subordinate. "Pressure of business while we free your beloved France, eh? I'm sure you understand."

MESSAGE FORM

PRECEDENCE (ACTION) ~~INFO~~ DEFERRED	DATE-TIME GP 200842/1430	CLASSIFICATION TOP SECRET	ORIGINATORS NUMBER G.7.

FROM G.7. WAR ROOM.

TO GRANTHAM S.26

Info

(1) COMPLETE FINAL DETAILS 39-144-2 POL/FR. IMMEDIATELY

(2) OPERATION "WOLFGROUP" MUST BE AT 12 HRS READINESS BY 12/4/42 AND 4 HRS BY 15/5/42

(3) AN "OPEN ORDER" BOOK IS AUTHORISED FROM WAR ROOM & SENIOR PROCUREMENT OFFICER WILL COMPLY

(4) PRIORITY OBJECTIVES REVISED :—

    a) ELIMINATION OF COMMUNIST FACTIONS IN RESISTANCE AND THUS THEIR POLITICAL POWER BASE IN POST WAR FRANCE.

    b) HARASS AND DEPLOY ENEMY FORCES IN WHAT WOULD APPEAR TO BE A "DOMESTIC" SITUATION

    c) TO ESTABLISH POTENTIAL LEADERS IN POST WAR FRANCE WHO TAKE THE WESTERN VIEW.

(5) STAFF APPOINTMENTS "WOLF" AND "WOLVERINE" URGENT FOR POLITICAL BRIEFING.

(6) INFO. ONLY. WHITE HOUSE HAS ADVISED PENTAGON TO ASSIST IN ANY WAY AND TO ASK NO QUESTIONS.

PAGE 1. OF 1. PAGES	DRAFTERS NAME & OFFICE	G7	
Encoded by G7	System EX/	OPERATOR 371 BARNES	DECODED BY GRANTHAM.

"I understand," de Vaugrigard replied in a murmur. His nerves grated together at the man's tone.
Behind him, the American smiled with a genuine, un-
masked pleasure at the discomfort of the young Frenchman. "Wolverine" was a man with a humorless face,
chiseled crudely, a large prow of a nose and a square,
unrelenting chin. His eyes were flinty, dead to light.
De Vaugrigard tried to calm himself, reminding himself that it was always the same in that house, with
these two. He must not become unsettled. He must
try. . . .

He disliked them intensely, so intensely that if he
were to retain any self-respect during their meetings,
he had to believe he was using them and not they him.
He disliked most of all the clarity with which they understood his need of them.

The office, which the Englishman unlocked, was
spartan in its furnishings and was sufficiently unused
for dust to have settled on all its dark wooden surfaces. The Englishman wiped a long finger along the
edge of the desk, inspected it, then sat down with his
back to the tall window that overlooked the garden. He
motioned Etienne to a deep, sagging armchair covered
in a chintzy material of hectic colors. The American
leaned against the fireplace, his strong fingers laced
across his chest, his hard eyes adopting a look of satisfied detachment.

"What do you want, 'Wolf'?" de Vaugrigard
blurted. "What is it this time?"

"Shouldn't you ask *who*, dear boy—mm?"

"As you prefer." He was sullen now.

"Not at all—as *you* prefer, surely?"

De Vaugrigard shrugged and held back his feelings from his features—satisfied with that tiny moment
of self-control, like a victory. Nevertheless, in the early evening light that fell from the window on his hand-
some features "Wolf" could observe the minute flaring
of the nostrils, the slightest flush to the pale features.
Etienne was angry and ashamed. "Wolf" was able to
goad him only because the young man's anti-Communist bigotry outran his dislike of his two superiors.

Etienne hated, and feared, the Communist party of France with the totality of his awareness, his background, and his upbringing. A deep and fanatical intellectual hatred. To him, the Communists represented the gravest of dangers of postwar France; together with his devotion to de Gaulle and his cause, his hatred made him perfect material for the "Wolfgroup." Etienne understood that—and hated the perfection of his usefulness to others, as if it robbed him of identity.

"What do you want this time?" he asked, looking across the desk from beneath heavy eyelids. He did the work the "Wolf" offered him with an eager efficiency. All that he disliked—so fiercely that he often felt a physical nausea when he left the Bloomsbury house—was the fact that he was entirely "Wolf's" man, *his* executioner. He hated that sense of being completely known; it was like some obscene and continuing intimacy, a marriage between them.

The Englishman steepled his fingers and smiled benignly. His face was planed smooth, with sharp edges at the jawline and the high forehead. His color was almost gray with the light behind him. "I want to offer you 'Colonel Rol' on a plate, Etienne—simply that."

There was a sudden heavy silence in the room. De Vaugrigard was ashamed of the dry hunger in his eyes, seeing it reflected by the man across the table in a satisfied twist of the lips.

Henri Tanguy—"Colonel Rol"—had been head of the Paris FFI since June and was the leading Communist in the city. The man, de Vaugrigard knew, wanted political power in postwar France, wanted no Gaullist government ever in Paris. Yes, de Vaugrigard wanted him.

"And Gallois, his chief of staff—and the others," the Englishman whispered like a tempter. Etienne smiled cynically, adopting a posture of assurance he did not feel.

"What do I have to do for it?" he asked, his voice tight. "Sell my soul?" Now the forced lightness came a little more easily.

"Not at all." "Wolf" smiled. "Not at all, dear boy.

All you have to do is to betray a man—as usual. Make sure that he falls into the hands of the Gestapo in Paris within the next couple of days."

"Which man?"

"You know Alain Renaud?"

"Yes. He worked with our group in Rouen for some time."

"He is in London at present and returns to France tomorrow night. He must fall into the hands of the Gestapo as soon after that as possible."

"Why?"

The American spoke before "Wolf" could reply. He was still standing behind Etienne, leaning against the empty fireplace. His voice was harsh with contempt and confidence. He, like de Vaugrigard, seemed impatient with the feline tactics of the Englishman, but for a different reason. His contempt sprang from his obscure sense of de Vaugrigard as some kind of traitor, however useful. "Wolverine" hated Communists, but he disliked and mistrusted Europeans also. He bullied and bulled his way through every such meeting at the Bloomsbury house.

"Because there's going to be an uprising in Paris before the end of the month which, if it succeeded, would put a Commie in the Elysée when the war's over."

"This month?"

"That's what I said, friend."

"How—do you know?" De Vaugrigard felt himself choking.

"We *know*. Never mind how. We know."

"You see," "Wolf" began, "why we need Renaud captive to the Gestapo. He will break under torture; even *you* know enough about him to be reasonably certain of that. . . ." Etienne nodded slowly. He was swallowing compulsively from a dry mouth. He felt himself in some light, anaesthetized trance. "So—Renaud will tell the Gestapo where to find 'Duroc' and the names of the sector organizers, the arms dumps—everything."

Etienne was suddenly cold, as if some bag of

iced water in him had burst, flooding his body. He felt his hands quivering on his thighs.

He was afraid of the moment—*the* moment of his life. It was what he had waited for, ever since the shadowy "Wolfgroup" had recruited him, as a prominent anti-Communist, in 1941. He had done his work, whatever they had asked of him, all the time silencing his vestigial conscience with the promise of the one stroke—the deed that would affect the war, affect the world after the war.

He had been responsible for the destruction of forty-three men in three years; he had no idea of how many other agents were employed by the "Wolfgroup." He had only a shadowy idea of its aims and purposes. He did not care. A self-assumed sophisticate before the war, he now lived an immature life, seeking daring and boldness as signposts of his experience or fulfillment.

In a moment of flickering, compound time, he saw faces, names—people dead because of him, every one of them a dangerous fanatic working only for the ruination of his country and his hero, de Gaulle. He knew how much the general feared the kind of uprising the American had spoken of. All those other deaths, then, had been in the nature of a prelude. This was his cataclysm.

He felt warmth in his loins, like a sexual arousal. He looked upon "Wolf" almost as an ally. And "Wolf" saw the electricity of heroism, of self-posturing, alter the shape of the young man's body in the chair. His shoulders were subtly squarer, the head thrown slightly back, the half profile presented. There was for the Englishman a cold pleasure, the prerogative of the manipulator, at the back of his mind. De Vaugrigard was now shaped as he wished him.

He said, softly and insinuatingly, "There is one other matter, before we get down to the brassier tacks of this little operation—which we have called 'Quick Red Fox,' by the way. Renaud will be accompanied by an English agent when he returns to Paris. The betrayal of that man is also required in case the Gestapo begin to suspect that Allied Intelligence is behind the whole thing and don't for that reason do what we wish. . . ." De Vaugrigard nodded without real surprise. "It is unfortunate, of course, but verisimilitude is of the essence here." He lowered his voice and said without a trace of inflection, "The man is your group leader. Richard Gardiner is the man you must also betray to the Gestapo."

Gardiner was arrested with Renaud at the Café Tabac in the Left Bank's rue de la Montagne while they waited for the Paris FFI to contact them. He drank gassy beer and watched the Parisians drift in and out of the dark café—and the chain of betrayal achieved its final link.

There was no possibility of escape. He had seen that from the moment the men in the stylized black raincoats had blocked the light from the doorway and the noise of splintering wood was evident behind him as the rear entrance was kicked in and three more men spilled into the café's interior. Renaud was frightened; Gardiner had seen that in the first moment of surprise. There was no moment of shock; he passed directly from passivity to fear. Gardiner dismissed him, weighed his own chances—and found them hopeless.

There was one moment as they were bundled out into the lancing sunlight of the rue de la Montagne, a narrow street that ran twistingly down from the Panthéon toward the rue des Ecoles. Gardiner knew the Left Bank well enough to understand its capabilities as a refuge of safe, blind warrens. He squinted against the sudden light of the noon street, then acted. He feinted a slip, lurched against the guard on his left, freeing his right hand by the sudden innocuousness of the movement. Then he jabbed for the eyes with stiff fingers. The unbalanced man screamed, high and terrible like a wired rabbit, and fell back into the doorway of the café. With a second swift blow, Gardiner struck the other escort's genitals, feeling his fist drive into the soft mass. He wasted no time in hitting him again.

He began to run, down the slope of the street, hearing a voice calling after him. Then two shots puckered dust and stone chips from the wall near his head. He skidded on a patch of wet from a street-cleaning truck, and his cheek dragged painfully against rough stone, his hands clutching the wall for support. Then he pushed away from the wall, accelerating again, surprised faces turning to him, bodies making a passage for him, dressed as he was in French clothes, fleeing from the Gestapo. The blood drummed in his ears, the inward decibels rioting, and his chest heaved as if it threatened the rib cage.

There had been others, of course, posted at either end of the rue de la Montagne. Even as he cannoned into the smooth material of the big man's leather coat, felt the knee drive for his groin even though the man was off-balance, he sensed that this was no chance arrest. The whole thing was much too expensive in Gestapo manpower.

Which meant Renaud. They wanted Alain Renaud, a man with secrets to tell them. A gun butt struck him. He keeled toward the pavement.

The man whose eyes he had ruined had to be taken to the hospital. The man he had punched in the groin had recovered sufficiently to walk down the street to where he lay on the ground and to kick him three times, each action accompanied with a grunt of effort and pleasure.

Gardiner was barely conscious when they bundled him into the waiting car. As they drove to the Avenue Foch, he kept passing out and briefly regaining consciousness. Each time he opened his eyes, he seemed to see, foggily, the frightened face of Alain Renaud, unmarked by violence, and to understand that the man would talk, would tell the torturers in the cellar everything they wished to know.

Before the car stopped and he was dragged out, he had slipped into a steadier unconsciousness, as if seeking some fugitive ease before the Gestapo began their work.

During the days in Fresnes Prison, as his body attempted to forget pain and his nailless fingers in the dirty bandages seemed less clumsy as they grappled with cutlery and the chipped mug in which they served the vile ersatz coffee of the place, he became aware that the endless, mindless four days in the cellars of the Avenue Foch might conceivably have been worse. Much worse.

It had become apparent, perhaps on the second day, that Renaud had told them sufficient information for them to believe that Gardiner's mission was of some significance but of no direct threat to the German garrison in the city. He believed that Renaud had told them something close to the truth. Therefore, their treatment of Gardiner, as newly arrived and ignorant, might have been a secondary concern while they concentrated on Renaud.

As "Wolf" had anticipated, the Gestapo realized whom they held and wanted to make sure they extracted everything held by the screaming mind that slowly retreated from them. They suspected an uprising by the FFI, and the opportunity offered them by the betrayal of Renaud made them greedy, and forgetful of Gardiner. His identity as "Achilles," the leader of the Rouen group, was either unknown to them or of more long-term interest. Nevertheless, with the efficient sadism that distinguished them from the more casually brutal SS or SD, they tortured Gardiner, wrung the sponge for any moisture it might hold.

It might have been on the third day, some time on August 7 or 8, that Renaud died under torture. Gardiner was never told directly, but the body's agonized response to the intensified sufferings inflicted upon it informed him that Renaud was dead and that he had not told them all they wished to know.

It was perhaps another thirty-six hours before his torturers understood with reluctant fury that he could not give them the answers and that Renaud had been his only contact with the Paris Resistance. He craved death by that time, wanted the Gestapo to end their interrogation with a bullet in the brain. Instead, he was transferred to Fresnes, sensing, in the small bouts of consciousness as he bobbed like a cork on the surging pain, the recriminatory fury of the men who had learned nothing from Renaud before he died. Gardiner presumed the body had been buried, with all the others since 1940, in the cellars of the Avenue Foch.

The womblike, silent darkness of the cell in Fresnes was welcome after the hard light and the rational moments of eyes close to his, the smell of food stale in mouths whispering against his face—sharper than the smell of his own vomit and urine. He retreated from what had been done to him. In the darkness he slowly healed. He touched the wounded places of his body but kept clear of the wounded places in his mind and the memory of pain. There was no amnesia to be gratefully embraced, but he was able to still memory by an effort of will, separate mind and body so that each painful movement on the narrow, filthy cot did not remind him of the last few horrific days.

It was the morning of August 11. Outside, it was not yet light, and he wondered, for a moment, what had woken him. He craved sleep and turned on the cot, digging his head into the pillow, which smelled of hair oil and sweat and fear and hopelessness. Then, far below him, three or perhaps four floors of the prison, he heard the slamming open of cell doors and an unidentifiable metallic screech, as of some alien bird. He shuddered. It might have been one of his own screams as they had pulled out his fingernails. The bandaged hands throbbed by an act of memory, and he gritted his teeth.

A pattern emerged even though he tried to ignore it. A door would open, and then the metallic screeching would be heard. Then a silence, and then another door and the screeching noise. He even began to be able to detect the small increases in volume as the sounds approached. He concentrated on ignoring them, considering instead the fitful illuminations of his reason.

He had been betrayed, and by someone who knew of Renaud's arrival in Paris—knew also the time and place of the rendezvous with the Resistance, knew who he was and the importance of his companion. Now it was only by channeling the pain into the narrow perspective of revenge, however distant and however hopeless, that he could ease the terror and agony of what had happened to him.

When the door of his cell banged open and the metallic screech stopped, he was surprised. He had been drifting into sleep again, clutching revenge to him like a child's comforter, a night-light to keep back the dark. He turned his head, puzzled, and saw the SS guard in the doorway, his face wrinkled in a sneer. He realized that he was huddled on the bed, hands protecting his genitals, fear on his face, his lips automatically moving in a wordless plea. There was another figure behind the guard, fat and not in uniform, leaning over a coffee trolley. He heard, distinctly, the noise of the hot liquid filling the mug.

The guard, stepping to him, prodded him with his gun and said, "Get up." His English was adequate, snarled and confident. "Coffee. For your journey, Englishman." There was a smile on his face, and something that seemed eager for the shock of realization by Gardiner.

"W-what is it?"

"Coffee—you understand? You don't like coffee?" He turned, as if to leave the cell, and Gardiner clutched the gray sleeve of his uniform. The SS man shrugged the wounded hand away, and it fluttered back to rest on the edge of the cot.

"Where am I going?"

"You want to know that? Better not to ask!" the German said, moving to one side to let the fat man pass the chipped mug of black, bitter coffee to Gardiner. "Drink!" the guard ordered.

Gardiner coughed as the liquid scalded his throat; then he said, "Is everyone leaving?" He had now to explain the noises he had tried to ignore. It seemed important. He brushed one bandaged hand across his hair, as if to smarten his appearance before this proposed journey.

"More than two thousand."

"Two—thousand?"

He had heard the rumors, naturally, in Rouen, passed from group to group like a message of defeat or an incitement to action. The trains—leaving for Auschwitz and Buchenwald and Bergen-Belsen and the other places. He shivered with knowledge, and the hot coffee spilled into his lap, scalding him through the thin trousers. He looked down stupidly, as if he had urinated—perhaps afraid that he had done so, like a frightened child or animal.

The guard said, "You know then?"

Gardiner nodded. From the two prisons, Fresnes and Romainville, thousands of men and women of the Resistance had been taken to the freight station at Pantin, just behind the Paris stockyards, to the cattle cars and the last journey to Germany.

"Christ . . . Christ . . . Christ . . ." he heard himself saying again and again.

The guard said, "Get up!"

He sat there. It was only when the guard slapped him across the face, repeatedly, that he realized that he was listening to the cry of his own voice, something rusty and unused and frightened as it mounted and became a thin scream. He was dragged from the bed, the thin stuff of his shirt ripping in the guard's grip. He smelled the guard's breakfast still on his breath and the hair oil he used. Then he was leaning against the door of the cell, and men were filing past him down the corridor. As if from a great distance, he heard the cup break on the floor of the cell. He looked around stupidly, mouth open, to see where it had smashed. The guard pushed him out into the corridor, into the stream of men, and he fumbled one foot before the other to retain his balance. He heard someone swear in French and by some instinct looked down. He had urinated with fear. He could smell himself.

By the time he got out into the prison yard the women prisoners who were to travel that day had already been herded into the buses and taken to Pantin. It was a little after sunrise. The sky was heavy with gray clouds, and there was a chill in the air—at least it seemed chill to Gardiner as he stood in his torn shirt and wet trousers, waiting to be herded onto one of the green and yellow buses.

There were a great many SS guards in the yard and hundreds of prisoners. The place was crowded, yet almost silent. There was little tangible sense of fear, only a pause, a sense of release from the gray walls around them. The sense of the future was absent, the emotional temperature low. Only the present existed, and they were outside, and the sun was coming up and trying to struggle through the clouds. It was as if they had learned the same trick of the mind at the same moment. Even Gardiner was able to forget why they had been herded there. He stretched his face to the air, a plant seeking the sun.

Someone spoke to him in French, but he did not answer. It was as if he had forgotten the language. There was only the gray sky above him, the distant sharp barking of names and commands harmless as the calls of foxes, and the shuffling noises as feet pressed toward the buses.

An SS man roughly moved him in the direction of one of the vehicles. He stumbled, then drifted with the tide of men. His face was blank. Pain, suffering, hunger, thirst, recrimination—all had been erased.

Once inside the bus, he continued to stare out of the window, upward at the sky. It was through his nostrils that awareness returned. He could begin to smell the bodies around him, smell the prison smells and the new odor of fear, as the gears grated and the vehicle began to move. He kept his eyes on the thinning clouds all the way to Pantin, but his other senses allowed reality to seep into him like an ague until the vacant stare was nothing more than an escape.

He felt the rough cloth of a man's jacket against his arm, heard the muttered fear of other men behind him, smelled the unwashed bodies and the waves of terror—smelled his own drying urine on his trousers. His wounds caused him pain, especially in his hands and back.

He stumbled out of the bus, and the cinders of the freight station crunched beneath his feet. A guard pushed him into line, and he lumbered forward with little more volition or intent than that of the shove in the back. Other men obeyed the same blind stutter toward the cattle cars coupled together in the siding. It was a walk of perhaps two hundred yards from the bus, yet it seemed to drain him of the little energy he possessed. Reluctantly he summoned last reserves, the use of which would leave him spent. Even so, he lurched with weariness against the man in front of him.

The man displayed no anger and no pity. It was a collision of air against his skin, a fleshy wind which had nothing to do with him.

Before they boarded the train, there was the final indignity of being searched. Gardiner, through fogged awareness, sweat in his eyes now that the sun was beating down on him from a sky being dried to a washed pale blue, admired with irony the thoroughness of the SS. Even though the file of men had come straight from Fresnes and Romainville and possessed nothing of any value, they were still searched efficiently and with the maximum humiliation.

Gardiner was forced to strip—he heard a muttered comment on the wounds across his back, the burns and bruises and the cuts—and stand naked while an SS *Oberleutnant* with a narrow dark face and thick eyebrows studied the heap of clothes. He grimaced at their filthiness, perhaps especially as his gloved hand touched the stained, fouled trousers, then looked up and smiled as he saw the humiliation in Gardiner's face.

"Put on your trousers—little boy," the German said. Then he pointed to the shirt, and an *Unteroffizier* removed it to a huge pile of clothing heaped near the waiting train. Gardiner watched his torn and filthy shirt in disbelief, thrown onto the dump. He had heard that the SS collected everything, even old clothes, that they computed the value of rags, hair, bone. . . .

He wanted to laugh. It was insane. The world's ragpickers, the terrible SS. . . . Just men with dirty carts crying out for rags. The *Oberleutnant* slapped his face when the laughter was no more than a lolling grin, and he was pushed half-naked into the black interior of a cattle car. It was like being shoved into an oven. He remembered immediately one brilliantly hot summer before the war, hiding in a corrugated-iron chicken shed from his brother, and the choking heat which had finally driven him out. He had been thankful, almost, to be ducked in the river for stealing Stephen's best fountain pen and filling it with black currant juice. . . .

He looked up as other bodies, slippery with sweat, pressed against him, forcing him to the back of the car. The roof was rusty sheet iron. His first breath inside the car seared his throat. He was suddenly aware of the repulsiveness of sweaty contact. He could see, over cropped heads like a broken skyline, the top of the door and other heads bobbing up into the doorway. The world outside was a ragged bar of blinding light.

He was slowly pressed against the far wall so that the rough, splintery wood tugged and scratched at his wounded back. He winced with the pain, winced, too, at the stifling pressure of bodies. Within a minute it was almost impossible to breathe. His head lifted to the rusty, boiling roof, and he sucked in the fetid air greedily. When the SS decided that the car could hold no more, the door was slammed across the head-broken line of light, and they were in cooler darkness, a coolness that at once became hot and stifling as the mind's illusion slipped from them.

There was little noise, little movement. It was that which struck him most forcibly as the dead, endless time passed. It was as if he and the others had accepted the animal roles suggested by the car. Gardiner understood the final and absolute condition of hopelessness: to stand like a beast, empty-minded, merely breathing.

Silence. The occasional slither of sweat-covered bodies, the shuffling of feet, the punctuation of streams of urine into the tin bucket in one corner. When they moved, to let someone use the bucket, his back was pressed against the wood, sharply and agonizingly. And then again the silence.

They waited for perhaps the whole day. One or two of them noticed, as if with a supreme effort, that the light had faded and it was night outside. There was a drop in temperature inside the blind car, but they hardly registered it, so dizzy and light-headed were they by that time, so parched of even the memory of water or cold. Many of them, including Gardiner, refreshed themselves by licking the sweat from their own and each other's bodies.

They refused to believe, at first, that they could hear a locomotive cautiously approaching. Then Gardiner's back was rubbed across the side of the car, and he heard through his renewed pain the grinding of buffers, the grate and clank of couplings. There was a pause, as if each of the hundred men in the stifling dark held his breath. Then the car lurched, and the train began to move out of the Pantin freight station. Though they could not know it, it was almost midnight on August 11, and the train, carrying twenty-five hundred captured members of the Resistance, had begun its journey to Metz and the German border.

When they moved, Gardiner was shaken by the pain and by a sense of relief from a light-headed dream in which the figures in the car had become the drifting mariners of a great painting, struck in the attitudes of hopelessness. They were the survivors from the wreck of the *Medusa;* he had begun to believe they might descend to cannibalism, so potent was the delirium of the dream.

Then he heard it, as other men heard it—sad, ridiculous, and defiant. Despair gave power to their parched throats. The rise in temperature had subsided. Now they seemed cooled by movement. The night air reached them in puffs and drafts from the rotten woodwork of the car.

It was the "Marseillaise." One or two voices picked it up; then suddenly they all were singing. Men were smiling and crying, leaning against one another now in a comradeship each had before shunned. Now the weariness and wetness of bodies no longer mattered. The din inside the car was incredible. Gardiner cried as he sang.

It was dawn before the train halted, a mere forty miles from Paris, in a smoke-filled tunnel on the main line to Nancy, at Nanteuil-Sacy. Unknown to the prisoners, the track had been dynamited for a length of sixty-five yards by an FFI commando unit. A message had been rushed from Paris by bicycle before the train's departure, and it had arrived in time.

Because of the risk of attack, the SS backed the train into the tunnel. The initial surge of ecstasy that followed the whispered inspiration that the track had been blown soon subsided, and the blind, coughing men in Gardiner's car realized that the presumed attack on the train was not about to happen. They understood that the FFI commando must be waiting for reinforcements.

For two hours the SS kept the locomotive pouring black smoke into the tunnel, so that the men began to think they were intended to suffocate. They were sick over the floor and one another, and the mood in the car began to mount, emotional mercury, toward panic. Gardiner, through a smoke-clogged consciousness, through waves of nausea, began to calculate.

There was one chance and only one. The men around him clung to the fading hope that the Resistance would attack the train and free them. Gardiner understood that it would take only three or four men to dynamite the track, but unless a great many more arrived to attack the train, the track would be repaired, or. . . .

His one chance was that the SS would find another train and transfer the prisoners. In the tunnel or in the open if the SS opened the doors, he would make his attempt. Resolved, he began to breathe more shallowly and to fight down the nausea. He would have only seconds, and he would have to run as never before. He prepared himself, closing his senses to the urine and vomit and bodies and fear. He had to live. Buchenwald and the other camps had retreated in his imagination; all that was left was revenge.

The train lurched forward, and daylight showed through the cracks in the car's walls. Then he heard the shouted orders, and the doors of other cars slid back. Gardiner tensed himself, and the light and sweet air suddenly flooded the car. Men's lungs grabbed at it as they stumbled, retching and coughing, into the sunlight. They looked around them, expecting death or perhaps hoping for rescue. None of them seemed to possess the instinct to run. It was a pity. Had many of them broken from the column that was forming, then he might have had cover for his own escape. The comradeship of the song and the night was broken for him, and there was only himself to consider now.

He fell into line, attending to the scene around him. He knew the area south and west of Paris well enough to know roughly where they were, saw the loop of the river Marne below him, the high sides of the cutting where the track had been blown, and the trees dropping away to the river. On the other side of the track were open fields white with daisies. It would have to be the trees.

The guards were spread out every fifteen to twenty yards on both sides of the track. He could see, ahead, the rear of the train the SS had found—another cattle train. He sensed the returning hopelessness of the men in front of and behind him, but less vividly than the touch of the cool morning air on his skin. He avoided looking at the sky and the sun. They reached the stretch of exploded track, and part of his mind admired the efficiency of the operation.

But the reinforcements had not arrived. Wherever the commando was hidden, probably across the Marne, they must be watching hopelessly as the prisoners were transferred.

Suddenly there was shooting, and he saw a man fall not ten yards from the car. His was the dash of panic, of mindless fear. Gardiner was opposite one of the guards as his eyes flickered away from the line of prisoners toward the intruding noise. The scene had been so ordered, so like a herd of animals moving. . . .

Gardiner leaped at him, striking him across the throat, beneath the chin strap of his helmet. The SS tabs on the collar bulged in his vision, and then the man began to fall away. Gardiner wrenched the machine pistol from the loosening grip and leaped over the body as it sagged to the tracks.

There were shots whining over his head as he stumbled down the slope. There was no hesitation now, no awareness of danger coming through the spine or the shoulder blades to stiffen or slow him. He was beyond being killed as blood pumped in his ears and his heart strained.

Faintly he heard whistles and shouted orders and more shots. He understood that he had reached cover only because a bullet gouged a white patch in a trunk as he slithered against it, then drove on into the shadows beneath the trees. He could not stop, even though he felt a fit of coughing beginning in his chest and his legs threatening to give out, betray him. He drove on, head back, arms pumping, almost dropping the encumbering machine pistol, its strap slapping at his arm and side.

Bullets whined through the trees, and birds cried and flew up through the branches. He glimpsed something scuttling from his path, and then the ground lightened and the poplar trees vanished on either side of him. There was only the river ahead.

He paused for a moment, dragging in lungfuls of air, trying to still the exhausted shaking of his body. The SS would spare only a few men from the guard detail, at least until the prisoners were safely installed in their new cattle cars. He had perhaps a few minutes.

He listened like an animal, forcing his mind into his ears, squeezing the other senses flat and dead. Faint shouts, and already the slamming of doors. Five hundred yards away. He looked back behind him. There was no flicker of unusual shadow within the trees, but he could not be certain. Sunlight only emphasized the darkness beneath the leaves.

He looked at the river. Despite the narrowness of the valley at that point, the current of the river seemed sluggish, insufficient to carry him at any speed northwest, away from the cutting and the train and the SS.

No alternative. He slid down the steep bank, and the cool water lapped around his thighs. He walked out into the current, feeling it stronger than he had assumed, for which he was grateful. His feet lifted from the river bottom, and he rolled onto his back, kicking weakly with his tired legs. He began to drift, slowly it seemed, but pleasantly after so much effort, with the sky and the fringe of leaves and the sides of the cutting, which he could just see drifting slowly— a figure in a punt, drifting on the sluggish Cam. The memory came back softly, dreamily, so that he wanted to close his eyes, anticipate the flicker of light and shade from the branches above him.

He snapped awake. He was drifting too far out into the river. With a few strokes, he guided his body back toward the shore. Checking, he saw that he had drifted only a couple hundred yards. Anyone coming onto the bank from the trees would see him immediately. He trod water, shook it from his ears, and listened.

Nothing. No doors slamming. The crowd of men and women had been loaded aboard the new train. He trod water awkwardly, as if weeds clasped his limbs, and felt the desire of the present moment overwhelm him and tears prick at his eyelids—he would wait until they came. . . .

He had thought of moving in one line only, downriver. He looked across at the opposite bank. He had to make it. He fumbled the gun over his shoulder, but it slipped away into the water as soon as he began swimming. He let it go. He came out of the shadow of the trees into the sunlight, and his strokes became swifter, more positive. He had to cross the river before he was seen. He ground his teeth together, his head swinging from side to side as he breathed, his tired arms pumping feebly at the restraining water.

He lost track of time and distance. All his awareness had retreated to his arms and legs, trying to move the dead lump of the torso through the resisting water. Four limbs and a laboring chest were what he was, heaving through the water, feeling the tired current drag at him. He dared not look at the opposite bank —it might even have been slipping away from him.

A tired leg dropped in the water, sinking like a dead weight. His foot touched the gravel of the riverbed. He tried to stand and fell forward into the waist-deep water, coughing and spluttering. He tried to roll onto his back, but the water closed over his face. He splashed at the water, but it would not go away. It closed like the doors of the cattle car, final and solid like wood or steel. He could no longer struggle. . . .

Something grabbed at his arm and pulled. He felt the shoulder muscles protest, tried to shake the grip of the thing away. His chest and thighs scraped briefly on the gravel; then someone was holding him upright.

"Come, *mon ami*—we have no time to waste!" the Frenchman said.

Gardiner pushed, but his legs buckled. He felt himself dragged for a few yards before he blacked out.

He rested in a safe house in Nanteuil-sur-Marne until he was sufficiently recovered to be smuggled down the line of Resistance groups to Meaux, then Senlis, Neuilly, Beauvais, Gournay, and Rouen.

There had been five of them, the original commando who had blown the railway line to Nancy and who had then had to watch, helpless and desperate, as the prisoners were transferred, on the other side of the Marne, to the new train, and their reinforcements had failed to come.

They took him to a farmhouse outside Nanteuil, where he was hidden in a hayloft from German patrols, fed and clothed and his wounds treated. His wounds won him their respect and sympathy, yet without ever closing the distance between them. The distance that existed because, despite their belief that he was "Achilles," leader of the Rouen group, he was an Englishman and two thousand and more Frenchmen and women had been on the train they had tried to stop. Not one of them had escaped.

Also, he himself was withdrawn. Though he listened to the broadcasts from London and began to understand the general progress of the Allied campaign, it was a war of which he was no longer a real part. There was a distance like thick, soundless glass between history and himself, between others and himself.

After a week he allowed himself to be ferried down the line like a parcel to be collected and opened on his arrival in Rouen. He felt his days of running and hiding, eating, sleeping, the faces of strangers and the steady scent of hope pass him by in a dream of which he was no real part.

There was only one reality, a narrow pinprick of confusing light. He had been betrayed, and he wanted revenge. He had no idea of the origin of the betrayal —probably inside Paris and perhaps intended only to net Renaud; many people in Paris must have known the date and time of contact.

He knew that he was likely to be recalled as soon as he made contact with his group, shipped back to London, at least behind the Allied lines. There he could begin the task of retracing the path of his betrayal. Therefore, until that opportunity arose, he allowed himself the patience of something inanimate.

The Allied armies were close to Rouen by August 26. It was a dull day, the afternoon sky oppressive with summer storm, the air rough and tangible against the skin. There was little trouble in getting into Rouen itself, to the suburb of Sotteville. He drove with a local farmer in an antiquated van, chickens clucking loudly in the rear, the whole vehicle smelling of droppings and dusty feathers and vegetables. He was relaxed, though aware. Tension had returned the previous night with the knowledge that he was so close to safety, but he had stilled it during the morning, and now he functioned with professional competence.

He was dropped in the center of the suburb, in a quiet back street, much of it reduced to the level of the cobblestones. Warily he began to trace his steps from the dropping point to the safe house. It was less than half a mile away.

The German garrison in Rouen was preparing to pull out, that much was evident. They paid him no attention, and he knew the Gestapo and the SS would have no time for arrests and interrogation. He was just a Frenchman, shabbily dressed, part of a scene through which they passed. He was not stopped once.

He came into a quiet square with a small church. The safe house was two streets away. He began to cross the road and heard the engine of a small Renault fire. Casually he inspected it. It was not Gestapo, and he ignored it, his hands thrust into his pockets to hide the plasters over the fingers, his gait shuffling, purposeless, head bent as he seemed to stare at the cobbles across which he walked.

The noise of the engine leaped at his awareness, suddenly loud and near. When he looked up, the car was almost on top of him, and he saw quite clearly through the windshield the faces of two men he knew. Their code names gleamed in his thoughts—"Nestor" and "Patroclus," two of his own group. Danger stuttered to attract his attention even as he instinctively raised his hand to greet them. . . .

The eyes of both were intent, riveted. He sensed hands on the wheel of the car, determined. He tried to back away and saw the car's nose swing with him.

Then he was flung through the air, and the body screamed at the impact, screamed again as it struck the cobbles, and he was hurled into a black pit. For a moment the two faces with riveted eyes haunted him, looking down on him from the edge of the pit. Then they were gone.

FILE TITLE INVESTIGATION "HERETIQUE".

O.A.S. ACTIVITIES IN PARIS AREA

DOSSIER Nº 14 QTM 66

SUBJECT DE VAUGRIGARD, ETIENNE. JEAN-MARIE. ARMS MFR.
SUPPLY OF FONDS/ARMS — METROPOLITAN FRANCE

Initiated by HEAD OF SECTION U.P.9.

ALLENTRIES MUST BE DATED ON THIS COVER AND INITIAL NOTED
BY THE INITIATING OFFICER, BEFORE TRANSFER TO CENTRAL
FILING PARIS.

Note 1. ANY OTHER ACTION ONLY APPROVED BY A VARIATION
CERTIFICATE (VG12) SIGNED BY THE MINISTER.

		1	2	3	4	5	6	7	8	9
A	BIOGRAPHICAL	2/3/59	13/7/59	9/1/60	15/2/60	14/7/60	3/9/60	27/4/61	15/1/62	7/3/62
B	FINANCIAL	11/11/59	22/3/59	6/8/59	3/10/60	16/6/61				
C	POLITICAL	3/9/59	4/2/60	20/4/61	20/5/61					
D	SUMMARY OF EVIDENCE AND INDICATIONS	2/10/59	20/4/60	12/4/61	7/9/61					
E	RECOMMENDED ACTION	F.50	F.52	14/2/62						
F	ACTION TAKEN	14/3/62								
G	RESULTS.									

NOTE

ALL DOCUMENTS, TRANSCRIPTS, PHOTOGRAPHS, ETC, PLACED IN THIS
COVER MUST BE MICRO-FILMED AND STORED WITH TAPED MATERIAL
UNDER RETRIEVAL CODE EJMDV 14 QTM 66

Time Mark		
	INT	I assure you of that. You are in the corner, after all, Monsieur. And you have brought yourself there.
	SUB	I am loyal — I have been loyal for ten, twenty years — since the war.
	INT	We were all loyal than Monsieur.
	SUB	Not as I was —you— yes, I shall tell you. This fabricated material you have here — it cannot outweigh the services I have rendered France in the past — I was a member of the "Wolfgroup". You have heard of it I imagine ?
●31.15	INT	Perhaps. Is it relevant here?
	SUB	You know that it was partly because of the "Wolfgroup" that the General was able to succeed in France after the war —
	INT	Ancient history, monsieur. It cannot be admissible —
	SUB	It has to be — it has to be — I betrayed Frenchmen on behalf of De Gaulle and London — you understand — on behalf of two men in London, I betrayed Frenchmen — on behalf of the General.
	INT	The names of these two men ?
	SUB	▓▓▓▓ ▓▓▓▓ COMPROMISE RISK— NAMES DELETED—FILED UNDER 333 DOSSIER (REF: 333/12/62) UNDER DISCONTINUED PREFIXES WOLF AND WOLVERINE
	INT	I see. Proof would not be forthcoming of that particular operation, I am afraid. It is not of any importance.
	SUB	It has to be. I even betrayed my group leader, the man Gardiner — he was part of the betrayal. And I tried to kill him later, when he escaped from the Gestapo. I betrayed a friend for General de Gaulle. What more do you want as evidence of my loyalty ?
●32.03	INT	Most of this is now unimportant, monsieur. However, perhaps you had better tell me about it. Confession is good for the soul, so they say.

Tr. by   SECSEC/219

Interrogator
Ckd. by   3 HoS/OP9.

The Minister of the Interior   14.9.62

M. le Minister,

<u>Ref: O.A.S.File 14QTM 66</u>

1.   I draw your attention to the enclosed section of transcript from the above File.

2.   We shall have no problem in convicting the man de Vaugrigard on the O.A.S. charges pending. However, I recommend postponement of all proceedings against him.

3. De Vaugrigard's wartime connection with the WOLFGROUP, until this time unknown to any section of the SDECE , is of crucial importance, since the leaders of that Group between 1942 & 1945 (names deleted from the transcript and filed under a 333 CODE ref: 333-12/62B to which I request you make reference) have a vital connection with the NATO Joint Intelligence Committee 'Utmost Security' breaches we know to have taken place during the past two years.

4.   I recommend opening a file on Richard Gardiner, the man betrayed by de Vaugrigard, with a view to his employment as an agent of the Security Service, <u>without his knowledge or consent.</u>

5.   I further request an urgent meeting to discuss a possible scenario.

                          Your Obedient Servant,Sir,

                          Head of Security UP/9

No immediate action other than :—

1. AXE FILE to be opened on Richard Gardiner.

2. Six month time limit on feasibility study of all possible scenarios

                          E.M.R.
                          21/9/62

AXE
FILE N° 1360982/45

 R **F** MINISTRY OF THE INTERIOR

M. Le Minister.

I enclose the completed AXE File 1360982/45 on RICHARD GARDINER, which gives as complete an account as is possible of the man's post-war life and career.

It has taken a great deal of time and work as you will see from the choicer pieces I have placed at the front of the File.

1. Since the identities of WOLF & WOLVERINE are known to us, they provide us with targets we have known in another context for a long time.

2. Our Subject would need to be brought to France — the Tourist Office could send leaflets ,etc.unsolicited.

3. A complete scenario for the Operation,codenamed — WOLFSBANE —could be with you next week.

H

HoS UP/9

Action approved — open File : "OPERATION WOLFSBANE", to commence when subject placed in proximity to Dupuy, and triggered.
E.M.R.
28.4.63.

NAME *GARDINER, Richard*   RANK *Cpt.* NUMBER *213095*   DATE *27 March 1946*

Whilst still 11 lbs. underweight, he has made a remarkable recovery
from his ordeal.   Strength and stamina good, certainly above average.
Vision & hearing unimpaired, tactile sensitivity of hands & feet
improving and appear virtually normal.

Mentally, there may be difficulties.   In layman's terms, he appears
to have erased his recent experiences, and cannot be induced to 'bring
them into the open' by the usual therapies.   His nightmares, etc., are
however now more rare.

There is a small risk of some sort of breakdown but the probability
seems less with the passage of time.   His strong personality and
ability to identify with and relate to changing circumstances allows
him, it is felt, to suppress his feelings and responses to a remarkable
degree, in a deliberate and controlled manner.   This would partially
explain the rate of recovery.

DISABILITY PENSION NEITHER REQUESTED NOR AWARDED

Signed *BJ Fowler*   Rank *H/Col.*

F68/57/219.

DORSET POLICE

<u>BRIDPORT</u> **Station**

FULL NAME <u>RICHARD GARDINER</u> DOB <u>30-7-21</u> OCCUPATION <u>SOLICITOR</u>

ADDRESS <u>THE OLD SMITHY BECKET LANE NORTH MILTON DORSET</u>

Place of Arrest <u>GARTH FORD</u> Arresting Officer <u>761 PC WILLIAMS</u> Date Time <u>2104/1627</u>

FINGERPRINTED	No		PHOTOGRAPHED	No

PARTICULARS OF CHARGE

THE ALLEGED OFFENCE WAS COMMITTED SUBSEQUENT TO A MINOR COLLISION INVOLVING VEHICLE BFO 196, THE PROPERTY OF RICHARD GARDINER, WHEREUPON HE DID IN A PUBLIC PLACE viz. GARTH FORD USE THREATENING AND ABUSIVE WORDS AND BEHAVIOUR, WHEREBY A BREACH OF THE PEACE WAS LIKELY TO BE OCCASIONED CONTRARY TO SECT 5. OF THE PUBLIC ORDER ACT of 1936.

Reported in answer to Bail (38(2) and advised by Chief Constable — in writing — No FURTHER ACTION DPHa/327/6 dated 20/4/57 Refers. 143 P.C. Jobling

Person Charging <u>761 PC WILLIAMS</u> Stn. Officer <u>138 Sgt Lawson.</u>

Bailed in the Sum of £ <u>25</u> to <u>BRIDPORT</u> ~~COURT~~/POLICE STATION

I, <u>RICHARD GARDINER</u> of <u>THE OLD SMITHY NORTH MILTON DORSET</u> acknowledge to owe our Sovereign Lady The Queen, the sum of £ <u>25</u> upon condition that I, <u>RICHARD GARDINER</u> shall personally appear at <u>BRIDPORT</u> ~~Court~~/ Police Station on <u>30th APRIL 1957</u> to answer the Charge under <u>SECT 38(2) of M.C.A. 1952</u>

<u>Richard Gardiner</u> Signed

<u>138 Sgt Lawson</u> Stn. Officer

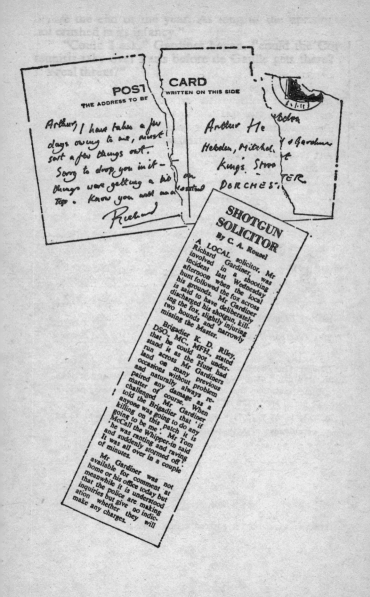

...pe the end of the year. As tough as the spread
...t crushed in its infancy."

"Come I say," Gardiner said. "Could the Cru...
t....something back before he thinks gets there?
....eet Street...

POST CARD

THE ADDRESS TO BE · WRITTEN ON THIS SIDE

Arthur, I have taken a few
days owing to me, must
sort a few things out.
Sorry to drop you in it—
things were getting a bit on
top. Know you will mad....

Richard

Arthur He...........bden
Hebden, Mitchel.....& Gardiner
King's Stree.....
DORCHEST.....

SHOTGUN SOLICITOR

By C. A. Rowsel

A LOCAL solicitor, Mr
Richard Gardiner, was
involved in a shooting
incident last Wednesday
afternoon when the local
hunt followed the fox across
his grounds. Mr Gardiner
is said to have deliberately
discharged his shotgun, killing the fox, slightly injuring
two hounds and narrowly
missing the Master.

Brigadier K. D. Riley,
DSO., MC, MFH., stated
that he could not under-
stand it as the Hunt had
run across Mr Gardiners
land on many previous
occasions without problem
and naturally always re-
paired any damage as a
matter of course. When
challenged Mr Gardiner
told the Brigadier that if
anyone was going to do any
killing on this patch it is
going to be me ". Mr Tom
McCall the Whipper-in said
"he was ranting and raving
and suddenly stormed off.
It was all over in a couple
of minutes.

Mr Gardiner was not
available for comment at
home or his office today but
meanwhile it is understood
that the police are making
inquiries but give no indic-
ation whether they will
make any charges.

IN PLAIN
ADDRESSEE33/A 6178 HOS UP9
989513 X DST FOREIGN VISITORS SECTION
SERIAL 23.456. TIME 1437
HOLIDAY BOOKING IN NAME RICHARD GARDINER MADE 2 MAY 1963 STOP
CAR TOURING HOLIDAY STOP VISITING BRITTANY AND DORDOGNE STOP
FULL ITINERARY TO FOLLOW STOP
IS THIS WHAT YOU WANTED STOP

 R F   MINISTRY OF THE INTERIOR

HEAD OF SECURITY UP/9

TO : "WOLFSBANE TEAM"

a. Operation "Wolfsbane" is now "go".
b. Gardiner's arrival at LA BAULE confirmed for AUGUST 12th.
c. Dupuy installed through de Vaugrigard as temporary waiter
   at HOTEL BOULEVARD DE L'OCEAN.
d. GREEN ALERT EFFECTIVE IMMEDIATE. Surveillance teams to be
   established with immediate effect.

                                        HoS UP/9

FINAL OPERATION ORDER FOLLOWS WITHIN 6 HRS.

2. A Family Holiday
August, 1963

Already there were figures moving on the beach, erecting huge sunshades or deck chairs, or spreading towels; there were one or two prebreakfast bathers. Sunlight splintered off the wrinkled sea, and the gleam of sand hurt the eyes. There was only the mildest of breezes. Richard Courteney Gardiner, on the terrace of the Hôtel Boulevard de l'Océan, left his newspaper unopened and watched La Baule slide effortlessly into the business of another hot August day. For a few moments the oppressive presence of his wife and the attentions of his two sons were absent, and he enjoyed the luxury of an empty awareness, the merely sensuous registration of movement, figures, sound. A waiter hovered briefly, and he shook his head, indicating the empty chairs at the table. He began to feel that his motoring holiday in Brittany might exceed his slim expectations.

He knew that he had wanted a holiday away from his family, but he had been reluctant to suggest it. He had compromised—a touring holiday, a succession of good hotels with swimming pools or beaches to satisfy his wife and the boys, and for himself the hours behind the wheel, the absence of conversation as his wife dozed or read and the boys hesitantly taught each other chess in the back of the Rover, and the daughter of friends, Sarah, brought with them in the role of *au pair* to the boys, contented herself with the glamour of her first French holiday.

His wife and the girl joined him, and reluctantly and with irritation, he pressed his attention to the present. He felt a sharp and irrational anger at the scraping of his wife's chair, at the cigarette she was already smoking—even at the bodice of her low-cut beach outfit and the evident sensuality of her figure. Sarah's small breasts and slim hips were still girlish in the bikini she wore beneath a beach coat. She hovered for a moment, then sat down silently, hands clasped between her thighs, eyes regarding the tablecloth. Gardiner did not look at either of them as he said, "What would you like?"

"Just fruit juice and coffee," Jane Gardiner replied. Gardiner looked at the girl, who nodded in agreement.

His eyes remained expressionless, masked by the sunglasses, as he summoned the waiter. He saw his two sons, both serious and intent, coming toward them, the traveling chess set held between them like some precious burden. He ruffled the dark hair of each absently, smiled formally, and then looked up at the waiter.

He was a man in his late thirties. He was standing between Gardiner and the view, the sun at his back, and his head was haloed with light. The Polaroid lenses of Gardiner's glasses showed him the man's features in shadow. He saw the man's nerves, the tic of an eyelid, and he saw the smudges of ingrained dirt on the man's collar. He had been out of work or was habitually careless about his appearance. His face was thin, dark, yet sallow, the eyes narrow, the mouth petulant, full-lipped. He appeared old in experience of the unsuccessful, even the sordid.

Because Gardiner felt so detached, he ignored a sudden pluck of subconscious recognition and dismissed the man's evident nervousness, ordered breakfast, and proceeded to read his paper. The waiter scuttled away. Gardiner, once only, told himself that he did not know him, the cool appreciation of the man's appearance fading. He turned to the cricket scoreboard.

When they had eaten and Jane was smoking another cigarette and drinking a second cup of coffee, he said, "Well, you two—want to go sailing this morning?" There was a forced enthusiasm in his voice that seemed to communicate itself to Timothy and Giles. They watched him out of dark eyes as if judging whether they should indulge him or not. There was a long silence. He had not bothered to consult the girl.

Eventually Timothy, the elder, said, "Can we finish this game first, Daddy? I've almost beaten him."

"You haven't!" Giles snorted.

"OK. Finish each other off; then we'll pop down to the yacht harbor and see what's for hire. You'll come, too, Sarah?" The girl, startled from the crumbs of her croissant, looked up and then nodded silently. Gardiner looked at his wife, saw the sense of satisfaction brought about by the general lack of enthusiasm for his idea, and added, "What plans have you this lovely day, my dear?"

He studied the beautiful, chiseled features as small emotions chased and flickered like camera shutters. Then the face became smooth, a melting into self-assurance that began at the green eyes. She brushed a lazy hand through her blond hair and said, "The beach, I should think—unless you'd like me to come sailing with you . . . ?"

"I'm sure you'd be bored."

"I'm certain of it."

"Darling. . . ." His eyes indicated Sarah. She smiled.

"Of course." She stubbed out her cigarette and stood up. "I'll get ready for the beach." She bent her face to the table, and Timothy and Giles bestowed small pecks at her cheek; then she was gone. Gardiner watched her move across the terrace, registering her body, noted the head held challengingly high, and recalled the time when he had desired her so greatly that the feeling was palpable, choking like smoke in the throat. . . .

He dismissed her, watched his sons as hands hovered for the mate, the childish kill, and then returned his attention to his newspaper.

The waiter, whose name was Alfred Dupuy, registered the departure of Jane Gardiner with scant attention. His eyes, and his awareness, were concentrated on her husband. The bent heads of his two children were dark blobs beneath the umbrella's shadow, and the slim body of the girl, which another time he might have studied with satisfaction, required no concentration. But the man. . . .

Impossible.

Alfred Dupuy could feel himself sweating even as he watched the oblivious Englishman reading his newspaper. It was that obliviousness that disturbed him, rubbing his shallow self-possession raw. He could not bear the tension of the apparent lack of recognition, not when he had been so certain, and almost at once. The indifference, it had to be assumed. . . .

It was as if Richard Gardiner had not recognized him at all. He had prayed for that ever since he had learned that he and Perrier had failed to kill "Achilles" when they ran him down in the quiet square in Rouen, as he crossed the street—had prayed intermittently for nineteen years and had prayed the previous night, awake and sweating, after seeing the English family across the hotel dining room. Then, he had not been able to believe it, though it was the first scene in that waking nightmare that had never left him for nineteen years.

He and Perrier—what they had done to Gardiner —why had Gardiner never come back for them after the war? He had seen the man's face through the flyspecked windshield of the van, had seen the shock of recognition in Gardiner's eyes, the moment of hatred and fury that had surfaced through the fear—he *knew*.

Borrowed time—always borrowed from somewhere, from someone. Gardiner would come back. He had known that for him, a situation had never been finished, never been irreversible—Gardiner never let go of things.

He's come for me, he must have. . . . He formed the words precisely, as if solemn and spoken aloud, and they orbited in his thoughts. There was no other way that he could understand or consider. He was unable to believe in chance, and while each hour of the previous night had creaked past like an endless, marching column of haggard moments, he had come to what he thought was an understanding of the situation.

Cat and mouse. Gardiner's old game, the way he had seen him play before. Contempt for weakness, ruthless, arbitrary in his decisions—that was he. Dupuy knew him, only too well—knew what he would do, given the slightest chance.

He shuddered. Standing at the table from which he served coffee and tea, he watched the man pretending to read the English newspaper, his eyes hidden behind his sunglasses. Dupuy could read the expression, even though he couldn't see the eyes. He had come there because he knew that "Patroclus" was working there. . . .

The Englishman was taunting him now, playing with him. . . .

He had to act. . . .

He felt cold with the thought.

When Gardiner left his table, the form of the waiter, who suddenly turned his back, flickered at the corner of his eyesight. He looked across at Dupuy, and a vague recognition muttered like distant thunder. Then he forgot it and passed into the cool of the hotel foyer. Sarah and the two boys trailed reluctantly after him.

Soon after he completed his duties at breakfast, Dupuy made a telephone call to Paris, from a tiny, almost-bare room in the attic of the hotel. It was hot and airless up there, even with the window open. He sat on a hard chair, the telephone strained on its lead to the small coffee table with the marks of rested cigarettes around its edges. It took him several minutes to obtain the extension he wanted, and when he did, he was nervous of the voice at the other end of the line. A blind panic had prompted him to make the call, and at once he began to despise the impulse.

Etienne de Vaugrigard, to whom he had gone seeking work, had found him only this menial summer employment in La Baule. The lever he had sought to apply, that of their mutual past and perhaps their mutual guilt, had functioned inadequately. De Vaugrigard seemed unsurprised, though contemptuous and aloof, as Dupuy explained the reasons for his call.

" 'Achilles' is here," he said, his voice breathless and quiet in the hot room, his free hand pressed down on the table to prevent its nervous palsy. "He is staying as a guest at the hotel, with his family."

"He recognized you?" the voice asked, its tone quickened by an interest that was disguised but not feigned.

"I—I am not sure."

"Why have you rung me, Dupuy? All this was nineteen years ago, you recall? He never came back before. Of what interest is it to me now what our former ally is doing during his vacation?"

"You—you know why!" Dupuy blurted out.

"*I* know why?" the voice challenged him.

"The—orders. Orders. . . ."

"Go on."

Dupuy was silent. Then, cowed, he said, "You —gave me this job. The only one, you said. . . ."

"I did not request reports on your guests during the summer."

"But him—in the whole world, he is *here!* You don't understand!"

"Understand what?"

De Vaugrigard had been "Hector," second-in-command to "Achilles" in Rouen. It was obvious. The orders, those he hardly now dared mention—orders that must have come from him. They both knew that —*knew* it!

"Why is he here? Why didn't he come back after the war? He saw me! Mother of God, I saw him looking into my *head* when we ran him down!" His voice sobbed, and for a while he was silent, oblivious of the man at the other end of the line, in his sumptuous Paris office. Then he asked, as if of the room, "What shall I do?"

"Have you saved enough to be able to leave your employment?" Etienne de Vaugrigard asked sardonically.

"A little. . . ."

"But you are greedy, in direct proportion to your laziness. Therefore, you will remain at your post."

"But—I. . . ." The confession was blurted, indistinct. "He is a very frightening man."

"Was. Remember that. You say he does not recognize you. Very well. Pray that it remains so and keep out of his way. You believe that he saw you. You were mistaken. Not your only mistake during those years."

Dupuy was suddenly angry. He had a quick, sudden image—a face bright with recognition, then pale with fear, then the wing of the Renault striking flesh, and the awful blackness for a moment when the body lurched up onto the hood and rolled across the roof. . . .

"I saw his face—he knew it was me," he said dully.

He had never been certain that de Vaugrigard had organized it. Perrier had forced him into it, and the implication had been that the word had come from Paris, from high up. Gardiner had been betrayed and knew it; now he had to be killed. He captured almost perfectly that moment, felt the prickle of tears he had felt then. They had to kill "Achilles."

"So?" the voice said, cold and brusque, as if there had been no implication on de Vaugrigard's part. "I know what happened, and I know why you are afraid, perhaps." There was little sympathy in the voice. "But I saw Gardiner many times, in the army hospital, even after the war in England. He never spoke about it." A sense of confidence entered the cool voice. "I don't think he even thought that he had been betrayed in Paris or in Rouen. Do you understand what I'm saying?"

"Yes."

"Good. If you are worried, keep out of his way!"

There was a click, and the receiver purred in his ear. He took it from his cheek, stared at it, then replaced it. A fly buzzed in the airless room, crossing vividly through a slanting bar of sunlight.

He was on his own. The man at the other end of the line, the millionaire de Vaugrigard, would do nothing. What had he expected him to do? Nothing. He had not ordered Gardiner's death, and he wasn't afraid.

Dupuy could see Gardiner's face again through the windshield. He knew—at that moment, he *knew*.

And must still know.

Gardiner knew that his wife had embarked upon another affair. She wanted to go shopping in La Baule that afternoon, even though he had suggested that they all go to the beach together. The excuses were feeble and transparent. She had met the man at the casino the previous evening and no doubt on the beach that morning.

In itself the circumstances of her infidelity did not disturb him. It was the lack of concealment of her eagerness that irritated him. Not angered—that was too far in the past, and he had achieved a shallow certitude that he was not to blame and that there was no recapturing the early days. He did not question the relationship—or lack of it—anymore. To have done so would have courted a dangerous introspection, which had betrayed him more than once in the past. It was her fault, all of it. Unbridled appetite.

When the boys showed reluctance to do anything except assemble a model airplane kit they had brought from Dorchester, he turned on them angrily and turned also on the girl because, with her silent patience, she was little more than part of the furniture of their holiday. They were surprised at his anger, yet he felt that they sensed its cause, and the nakedness their knowledge gave him injured his ego, and he left them, the whole lot of them, grateful only that in their still, hot bedroom Jane had made no display of her body as she dressed for her assignation. She had done that, in the past, and always it had incensed him, muddied his feelings, and tarnished his sense of detachment. At least not that.

He took the Rover from the hotel car park and headed out of La Baule on the road to Vannes, heading north. He did not notice Dupuy, still serving lunches, even though the man's eyes were riveted upon him as he passed through the foyer.

Once out of the town, he drove with little sense of direction, forcing the attention into the mechanical functions of the body, into hands and feet, even into the hot leather of his seat.

At Guérande he turned, on impulse, eastward on a minor road, heading for the Grande Brière, the fen country crossed by drainage canals and margined and bracketed by dikes lying north and east of La Baule. At first the flatness of the countryside, the white cottages, and the slow cattle all dulled the awareness. It was perhaps an hour before he realized he was becoming steadily more angry, that the car journey was an irritation in itself, designed as it was as an escape from the stifling hotel room and the proximity of his wife. He could not escape his memory, his prognostications, and these seeped back into the apparent and superficial calm he had maintained.

Before long the scenery along the D 47, as it skirted the Grande Brière, became unrelievedly flat, dull—reduced in scale until it was a toy landscape, a painting done by someone with little taste and a cumbersome sentimentality. He stopped the car, pulling onto the side of the road, and got out.

He leaned on a fence at the side of the road and tried to watch the slow progress of cattle across a pasture. His eye and mind were distracted for a few moments by the sight of a flat-bottomed punt moving gracefully along the canal half a mile away. But the stooping, rhythmic figure with the pole was too insect-like to demand attention. He turned his back on the scene and studied the empty road and his car.

The car was new, and such as he might be expected to possess as a partner in the firm of Hebden, Mitchell and Gardiner, solicitors. He was forty-three, successful within the somewhat narrow confines of the

legal practice of a country town, and his wife had
money of her own. The Rover was dusty and travel-
stained, and its appearance seemed an apt comment on
his life. Substantial, comfortable, with a hidden power
—yet somehow made ordinary, dull.

He wanted to blame her, and usually he could.
She was the first to be unfaithful. His lips twisted at
the quaintness of the expression. She was the first. She
had told him, in the days of their blind, hating quarrels, how cold he was, how indifferent to her. Incapable, of loving, of tenderness.

He drove the thought away, flicked at it as his
hand flicked away an insect near his ear. He had
drifted, he admitted, into the brief, ungenerous affair
with the girl Diane, as a mirror image of his wife's
infidelities. He had intended his holiday as a break
that would see the end of that liaison. He had not had
the courage to break cleanly, to dismiss the girl who
was twenty years younger than he. There was a young
man, he believed, a traveling salesman of some kind.

With the images of his brief entanglement with
the girl fading in his mind, the anger seemed also to
die. The girl had driven out the wife at least, he
thought. The day was hot, and behind him the lush
grass gave out the murmur of insects. His back was
hot, and against his sides there was a dampness beneath the arms of his cotton shirt. He rebelled against
the situation suddenly, against the image of his futility
it seemed to encapsulate. He got back into the car,
switched on the ignition; the tires squealed on the road
as he let out the clutch.

He followed the signs on the D 47 to Herbignac,
and then he left the hamlet on the N 74, heading back
toward La Baule. There was something contemptible
to him in the way he had lost his wife to other men;
something now more contemptible in his running from
the knowledge of infidelity. He had always been a man
in a car, driving furiously away from the bed, the assignation.

He had no intention of vulgarly surprising his
wife in the arms of her lover, seeing the man's head
looking over his shoulder at the sound of a door open-

ing, looking along the ridiculous white perspective of the buttocks. . . . Perhaps she was astride him, the dominant position she often indulged. . . .

He gripped the wheel of the car fiercely and pressed down hard on the accelerator. Hatred, envious loathing, helped to emphasize her culpability, the completeness of her responsibility for their situation, the collapse of their lives. She was to blame even for the pettiness of his sufferings, which disappointed him.

The car's speed crept up satisfyingly. Fifty, sixty, sixty-three, sixty-eight. . . . The traffic was heavy, though moving freely. Tourist traffic, a few heavier vehicles. He ticked off the cars he overtook, beginning to envisage the faces that glanced at him, oncoming or sliding past the window, as a sequence of defeated opponents.

He understood what he was doing. He had not invited it or willed it, yet he understood it. He escaped into the present moment, utterly—entirely unconcerned at his progress, its consequences, the hot cry of the tires on the tar of the road. . . .

He did not kill anyone. Afterward, even soon afterward, when they strapped his wrist and saw to the knee in the hospital in La Baule, he was grateful for that, that the people in the oncoming Mercedes had been shocked but uninjured. That satisfaction remained with him.

The gray Mercedes came at him, leaping to occupy the gap of road he had entered as he overtook a slow Renault van just north of Guérande. He squeezed the brakes, hands suddenly wet on the wheel and the tremor of reaction beginning in his leg—he thought he might slow in time. The driver of the van, comically bereted and wearing a striped jersey, had been irritated at the foreigner's imperious use of a French road and had accelerated. Gardiner could not regain his own side of the road, and the Rover's offside wing crunched along the flank of the Mercedes as its driver heaved the wheel desperately to take him onto the narrow strip of dusty grass at the side of the road. Gardiner was sandwiched for a moment as the impact threw him back against the van; then the wheel escaped his slippery palms, and the big saloon lurched for the far verge of the N 74, thrusting its blunt nose down into the ditch. By the time the front wheels began to revolve over emptiness, the engine squealing like a hurt pig, his hands were in front of his face. His forehead struck the windshield, which did not shatter, and he felt his neck heated by the wrench on his muscles before he passed out.

Afterward he could not decide whether he was conscious or not when the disorientation began. He was hurt, but out of the car now, and there were voices coming from an impossible distance, and hands fluttered out of his sight like glancing wings. He could see only the hot blue of the sky directly above him.

There was the expectancy of more pain. A strange dislocation of the awareness. His head hammered, but the pain was dying to a mutter now, and his knee hurt, and when he lifted his left arm, there was a stab of pain in his wrist. It did not seem sufficient. He did not understand. He felt that the hands inspecting him were fumbling not with the blue cotton shirt but with the rough material of a jacket. He smelled the acrid, rich scent of a foreign cigarette. He expected the hardness of cobblestones beneath his shoulders, along his legs.

He heard the siren of an ambulance, sliding nearer. There was a redness obscuring his vision, and he assumed that it must be blood from a cut on his forehead or face. A shadow bent toward him, wiped at the redness with something, and a voice asked him questions. A French voice. He saw the Mercedes coming toward him again, and he mentally braked. Yet the angle of vision of the memory was higher; he was standing upright, walking across a space of cobblestones as the car came toward him. He saw two faces through the windshield, vague, penciled sketches rather than human faces, and he saw the intent, staring eyes of each.

Another place, another accident.

Cobblestones.

Rouen.

"Oh, Christ!" he cried out in protest as they

lifted him toward the ambulance. Someone apologized, assuming he had hurt him.

He was being forced to regurgitate the past, the past he had buried so successfully for so many years.

He knew who the waiter was.

Etienne de Vaugrigard, as a consequence of Dupuy's call, made a telephone call of his own that afternoon, soon after returning from a heavy business lunch. The prospective purchasers, the government of an emergent African nation, had toured the St. Denis factories the previous day; a lucrative arms deal seemed sealed. Yet the euphoria of business success —he always liked to attend to major contracts himself during their closing stages—was dispelled even as he dialed the Paris number he had been given and whose owner he could not trace. The capacious office, thick-carpeted, highlighted with ornaments, rich with decoration, was solid, comfortable—now suddenly possessing an insubstantial modernity of tubular steel and glass, a thing he had tried to avoid when choosing the furnishings.

He got through almost at once.

"He hasn't made any kind of move," he said bluntly, feeling the tongue thick in his mouth, a dull instrument incapable now of the assured, suave pleasantries that littered his lunchtime conversation. He was hot despite the air conditioning.

The man at the other end of the line spoke French. He said, "We expected that, Etienne." De Vaugrigard winced at the use of his first name, usage which seemed to strip away the padding of deference with which his life had become surrounded. "I have my own sources, Etienne, and I know that Gardiner has done nothing—that he took no notice of Dupuy. However, it would seem likely that Dupuy will force himself upon the Englishman very soon. As we anticipated."

"Why do you always include *me?*" It was intended as rejection, yet it seemed like a plea.

"You are involved, Etienne." The voice was inhuman. Etienne found the man incomprehensible, the one who called himself *l'Etranger*. Ridiculous and—yes, sinister.

"It won't work!"

"No?"

"I told you—it was nineteen years ago. He's buried it all deep down in his mind by now. Got on with life." He was sweating, and he realized he had balled his silk handkerchief into a damp little lump in his fist. He dropped it on the desk in revulsion. "I've seen him since then. He had no suspicion. . . ."

"That is not what you told me previously, Etienne. Nor is it true. Dupuy will bring the tiger out from beneath the sheepskin. I am certain of that. I, too, have been studying M'sieur Gardiner. If he is threatened—then. . . ."

"Yes." Something in de Vaugrigard had collapsed like a weakened cliff, sliding into the water. His voice was older than his fifty years. "You are sure it—will work?" He had wanted to ask after his own safety, could not stoop, not so far.

"The price of failure is higher for you than for me, Etienne. We must both—pray for success." There was not even contemptuous laughter in the voice.

"Yes."

As if reading his mind, the voice said, "I have promised you will be safe, Etienne. So shall you be. Good-bye."

The phone clicked, then purred in de Vaugrigard's ear. Slowly, as if it were heavy, he replaced the receiver, then resisted the temptation to pick up the crumpled handkerchief and mop his brow, as he caught sight of his reddened, strained features in a mirror. Instead, he slumped back in his leather chair and stared at the ceiling.

There was little doubt that *l'Etranger,* as he wished to call himself, was SDECE—French Intelligence. And that he was playing some especially murky game which somehow involved Gardiner. De Vaugrigard could not feel culpability at that involvement, just as he had dismissed guilt for Gardiner's treatment at the hands of the Gestapo years before. Feelings rarely lingered with him; as he admitted, only the gratification of controlling de Vaugrigard Armaments had lasted down the years.

L'Etranger had come to see him concerning certain funds that had reached the OAS, together with small arms unaccounted for in the records of his companies. And terrified by the consequences of his actions, he had babbled the whole story of the "Wolf-group," his loyalty to de Gaulle, even to the betrayal of his friend Gardiner. And he had named the "Wolf." And sprung, it seemed instantly, his own trap.

He stared at the portrait of his wife, Geneviève, next to the silent digital clock on the desk. His face wrinkled in dislike, as if she were in some obscure way to blame for his predicament.

He had been betrayed by de Gaulle, as had the army in Algeria. He had helped, yes. But this? This kind of—*humiliation* of terror?

Unsettled and dispirited in self-esteem, he visited the Faubourg St. Honoré flat of his young mistress, parking his large black Citroën near the Madeleine, before he returned to his family house on the Avenue de Madrid. When he reached home, late in the evening, his wife had already retired. He took a bottle of cognac into the library and sat staring at the solid rows of gold-lettered volumes that had belonged to his father.

Dupuy stared at the gun. His right hand was clenched around the butt, the left curled tightly on the barrel. It was an old Luger, a prize of war. He had kept it as little more than a memento of the past. He had cleaned it occasionally, and there was a full clip of ammunition on the coffee table in front of him. He sat in a hunched, almost reverential position.

Why he had decided to kill Richard Gardiner was clear to him; it was something he must do. An imperative. Through the rest of the morning and the afternoon, he had sat in the airless room, the clouds of cigarette smoke reluctant to diminish, the battered tin ashtray full of crumpled stubs yawning in his staring eyes as if it threatened to swallow him.

Gardiner would kill him. He knew that, with utter certainty. It was only a matter of time before he was recognized. *Kill or be killed.* He liked the narrowness of it, the definition it gave to the surrounding objects of his life.

Bigger, with the gun. Yes—he admitted it. Comforting blued steel, as he caressed it. Sharp feelings from the old time; he was younger again, and his head was clear. He did not blame Gardiner for having come to La Baule, having stayed at that hotel. Not now. Now he would kill him.

The young policeman who interviewed him while they stitched his knee and strapped the wrist was hostile, arrogant. Evidently he disliked tourists, especially English tourists who drove recklessly on French roads. Perhaps, Gardiner reflected with some small unencumbered part of his mind, it was only because the people he had almost killed were Germans that he was not arrested and charged. As it was, he was warned not to leave La Baule and that he would undoubtedly be hearing from the police the following day when a fuller investigation had been carried out.

When he left, it was immediately as if he had never been in the chill little room where they gave him a cup of coffee, his trousers torn from cuff to thigh and pinned, his shirt sleeves rolled up, and his head thudding. Two stitches in the cut and a patch of wadded plaster covering the left side of his forehead.

He tried to grasp a minute of peace in the empty room, as if sensing that he could no longer open the door on the same world he had left on entering the room. He hated the French driver in the beret and the jersey; his revulsion at the immediacy of his own past required an object of focus.

He had been in a military hospital for eight months after they had tried to kill him in Rouen. He left it, to convalesce at his mother's home in Devon, a month before the war in Europe came to an end. When he was sufficiently well, he resumed his studies at Cambridge. Qualified, and understanding precisely the motives behind his actions, he had joined the firm of solicitors in Dorset, married a wealthy young wom-

an of rigidly conventional county stock, bred two children—and buried the past and his former self.

He clenched the one good hand—the wrist of
the other pained him as he attempted it—in fury that
the mental equilibrium of years had been shifted like
so much ballast by a single occurrence. He hated his
past. Grateful it had not killed him or permanently
crippled him, he had lost all interest in it, all desire to
revenge himself on whoever had betrayed him—even
on the mechanics, Perrier and Dupuy, who had driven
the car under orders.

Dupuy. The waiter with the dirty collar and the
rough hands that had seen too much menial work.
"Patroclus." He squeezed the past out of his mind, his
teeth grinding loudly in the silence of the room. His
strength, over the years, had been measured in the success with which he had been able to forget and ignore.

A lurch of his stomach like nausea. The image
of the Renault van. He lifted his head as if to bay at
the ceiling, his eyes shut tight, his mouth working,
his breath coming like that of an exhausted runner.

Which he was, he recognized. Always running.

Now, having to run again. Get away from Dupuy,
before he brought back the dreams. Dreams of fingers'
ends and fists and clubs. A white light and the questions. Urine-soaked trousers and thirst. And pain ev-
erywhere, in his back, and legs, and head. Cobblestones and Rouen.

The room stifled him. He tugged his jacket—
no, someone else's, slung across his shoulders as he had
walked limping between the ambulance men into the
hospital. To warm him, he supposed. He put the jacket
untidily back over the chair and let himself out of the
room.

Someone gave him a number to ring, and he
called a taxi. When he was dropped at the Hôtel Boulevard de l'Océan, he went quickly to his room, afraid
he might confront Dupuy if he lingered in the foyer or
went into the bar.

Jane Gardiner returned in sufficient time to change
for dinner. When he explained what had happened—

he was still dressed in the torn trousers and the blood-stained shirt—she was initially shocked. However, she seemed grateful for the reluctance of his explanation and the aura of introspection with which he seemed to have surrounded himself since lunch. She ordered his dinner sent up to the room and took Sarah and the boys down to the dining room. When she had gone, the memory of her being in the room was as insubstantial as the last of her perfume on the still air. Alone again, he breathed calmly, attempting to relax, aware that there was still tension in his frame, as if braced to resist some shock.

Soon after his meal was delivered, the telephone rang, startling him. He picked up the receiver with a sudden dart of his hand and gave his room number; a voice he did not recognize, speaking good English, said, "M'sieur Gardiner. I—have some information concerning your wife. . . ."

"Who is this?" He was aware of the blurted words, wishing to recall their frightened tone.

There was a brief silence, as if the speaker were taking stock of his mood, then: "A friend. I have information concerning your wife's—*affaire* with a certain member of La Baule society. . . ."

At first Gardiner could not answer.

"What—are you talking about? What is my wife to do with you?"

After a pause, the voice said, "You have no interest that your wife is unfaithful to you, m'sieur?" The tone was leeringly confidential.

"I don't care to hear it from you," Gardiner said tiredly. He assumed that the caller was a putative blackmailer. Ridiculous.

Yet he realized he would have to meet the man. Otherwise, there might be trouble, scandal that drew attention to him, or some means of forcing him to stay in La Baule—even Dupuy's attention. . . . He had already resolved to leave La Baule as soon as the Rover was repaired. He said, "Very well. We must meet—but not at my hotel. Where?"

"That is more sensible, m'sieur. I would have had to mention the photographs soon. . . ."

"Very well!" Gardiner said urgently. It seemed clear to him at that moment that he had to recover the photographs, had to pay off the blackmailer, whoever he was. He suspended examination of his motives. It had something to do with safety, he knew. Like the pattern of his life since the war. *Safety.* He said, "Where? When?"

"Tonight," came the reply. "In La Baule-les-Pins, near the Parc des Dryades. There is an empty villa, set back a little from the street. Turn off the Avenue de l'Etoile at the squash club, into the rue des Epinettes. The house is number forty-six. You have that?"

"Yes." Gardiner's voice was a whisper in the empty room.

"Good. Until tonight. Shall we say eleven o'clock?" The telephone clicked, and Gardiner instantly put down the receiver. He slumped back in the chair, and his eye caught the crumpled edge of the bedspread where his wife had sat to roll on her stockings, the head scarf in blotched bright colors draped over the back of a chair, a cigarette end smudged with pink lipstick stubbed into a crested ashtray.

He hated her for being caught out, for placing him in the hands of a blackmailer. She was making him behave stupidly, weakly. But the blackmailer threatened his anonymity. He had to see him, settle it. Get the pictures, hand over whatever was demanded.

He seemed to be sinking into a morass of weakness and was unable to help himself. It was simply that he had to escape Dupuy and his past. He couldn't bear the dreams again, the choking rages that had tormented him in the military hospital. Not again.

At ten forty-five he turned the hired Peugeot into the rue des Epinettes. It was difficult to drive the car, even with an automatic shift. Yet he persevered with the pain in his wrist because he had to keep his appointment.

His wife had gone to the casino, presumably to meet her lover, soon after dinner. The fact that she was, in his estimation, not worth one moment of the weak, fearful agitation in which he had picked at his dinner and then arranged to hire a car did not weigh with him. The completion of some deal with the black-mailer had assumed a symbolic proportion in his mind. It would be like closing the lid upon his past, on the box that had spilled out his world's evils.

The villa was half hidden behind a dejected tall hedge, holed like dark lacework and unkempt. The tires crunched on dusty gravel, and he pulled the car around to park it behind the hedge, opposite the porch. He got out stiffly, rubbing his knee gingerly to relieve the stitched discomfort. Straightening, he surveyed the facade of the villa. It had obviously been built in the heyday of La Baule as a new seaside resort, toward the end of the previous century. It was pale in the bright moon, ghostly rather than solid, ornate and decayed. It had evidently not been lived in for many years. Windows were boarded up on the ground floor—some of them at least—and in the corners of the porch were still some of last autumn's leaves. Heavy old trees leaned toward the house, giving it a Gothic unreality.

He climbed the three steps to the porch and touched the front door. It swung stiffly open. His first footsteps echoed in the hall, and the boards creaked. He called out, and the sound of his voice died some-where away at the rear of the villa. He wondered, fearfully, if the man might not come.

There was a door open, and the light from a passing car glanced across the portion of wall he could see. Ugly blotches of old wallpaper. It was a drawing room, it seemed, overlooking the front of the house. He looked at his watch, seeing he was early.

He pushed open the door and stepped into the room.

There was a shadow by the window. He was re-lieved rather than afraid; then he saw, in the light flung by the headlights of another car passing along the rue des Epinettes, the face of the blackmailer.

Dupuy. The waiter with the dirty collar. The face behind the windshield.

" 'Patroclus'!"

A moment's silence, then the flat crack that magnified in the room to a roar, and the spit of orange flame as the man fired the gun he held at his waist.

3. An Old Game

Gardiner stumbled as he turned instinctively, and pain shot through the stitched knee; the wrist hurt as he braced his body against the door. He was deaf for a moment after the shot, and he moved as if in an alien element into the hall, grabbing for the banister at the foot of the wide staircase. He heard the boards creak under his weight as sound returned, and his breath rushed in his ears. He went up the bare flight of stairs, dragging his injured leg behind him, adrenaline surging in his blood, his heart laboring with shock and fear.

Yet already it was as if something were moving more slowly in him, something emerging from a chrysalis. Dupuy was the blackmailer, and he wanted to kill him—*kill him*. It was as if he had been hit by the wildly fired bullet, the pain of fear was so tangible.

He flung open the blank door to a bare room and ducked behind it. His back was pressed against the peeling wallpaper. The moonlight was coming dustily through the single tall window.

The man downstairs had not fired again. He pressed his damp palms against the wallpaper, feeling it turn clammy, inhaling the musty, dead air of the room, trying to calm the body's clamor.

The face of Dupuy returned again and again,

flickering like imitation movements from a flicked series of still pictures. In the passenger seat of the Renault, downstairs, and younger up at the farm near Rouen.

Dupuy had been precipitate—something told him that, and he wondered why. Dupuy had not meant to fire at that moment. Yet the old code name had startled him, and the sudden movement by Gardiner.

He wanted to cry out to Dupuy, to protest his harmlessness. He wanted to take hold of the last nineteen years like clothing and wrap himself in them; they seemed insubstantial, as if the pale moonlight had affected them. His breath sobbed in his throat, though his breathing had become calm.

He felt the acute physical symptoms of drunkenness or delirium, a wrenching pain in chest and stomach, the sense of leaning out over some dark gap. . . .

And then he laughed, an explosive noise which seemed to expel not only breath, but the sense of nausea. He felt thinner, almost skeletal. He began to shiver in the returned silence, ears strained to listen; reaction, but he sensed it as transformation, hideous and sudden. When his body was still, he sensed that it was different, changed to something other than himself. A cold rage; a pure iciness of understanding.

Dupuy was afraid of him, afraid of the revenge he must have thought would come in 1944. Kill or be killed, the law he had blindly obeyed.

Dupuy was already dead, even before he began to ascend the staircase. He shuddered with the resolve.

The fact that "Patroclus" had a gun pleased him absurdly. He would kill him with his bare hands. He began to laugh loudly, the sound chilling through the empty house. He called out, "Dupuy, you bloody fool! Yesterday I didn't even recognize you! I've spent nineteen years forgetting you! I would have run away—yesterday! Now you're a dead man—unless you can kill me first!"

A weight paused on a stair that creaked. Gardiner's ears, concentrating the moment he choked off the final word, heard it. Then he heard the shuffle as the man moved off the betraying wood. He laughed again, a sharp, barking noise. He tested his knee, then grimaced as if at weakness he could not pity. Tensing himself, he moved from behind the door. He passed down the wide corridor, opening door after door on either side with as much noise as he could.

"Come and play!" he called. "Come and find me!" He laughed again, and remembered his brother and him as children playing hide-and-seek in the big old rectory. A high, boyish laugh seemed to answer him, and he shook his head as if to clear it of muzziness. The memory was hampering now. It did not belong either to the war or to the years after. He recalled instead the sunlit square and the agony as they tried to lift him; the pain cleansed him. It drove him to extract recompense.

Dupuy fired a shot. Gardiner doubted whether he had even reached the head of the staircase. Whistling in the dark.

Gardiner ducked into a bedroom. Here there was the smell of empty linen drawers and lavender, fossilized. There were the shapes of a bed, old, four-posted, and of huge darkwood wardrobes. Perhaps the last refuge of some ancient female who had inhabited the house. He waited behind the door and listened. Another stair creaked, and then nothing. He wondered how well Dupuy was relearning the old lessons. Had he removed his shoes yet?

Gardiner bent down and unlaced his suede shoes, took them off and slid them away from him. Then he tested the sprained wrist, grimacing as he tried to clench his hand. He cursed the weakness, then bent down and felt for the shoes. Swiftly he removed the lace of one and tested it, snapping it taut again and again. He knotted it in the middle and tied one end of the lace around his forefinger, in case the grip failed. Then he froze the sprained hand into a fist so that it clenched one end of the lace. He gripped the other end, raised his hands over his head until they touched the wall above him, and waited.

Silence. Then a door, banged back on its hinges, to surprise him. Silence again, trembling with relief and the spasm of fear.

Four bullets, perhaps six or seven. He did not know the type of gun. Gardiner realized that he had repossessed his former identity, redeeming "Achilles" from burial in his own mind and his postwar persona. It had been as simple as peeling an onion, and without tears.

Now was *then,* a house in France and a man with a gun. The skeleton of a world, the mere bones of a human experience.

The footsteps had established a pattern now—mouse shuffles toward each succeeding door, then the banging of the door as it opened, then silence. After long minutes Gardiner was able to pick out the explosions of breath, muffled though they were, after each new empty room. Soon the noises became louder, more routine. Gardiner had opened all the doors along the corridor. Dupuy was being lulled into a routine that would dull his awareness, finally betray him.

Mouse steps, then the slow creak of a door. Gardiner relaxed slightly.

He waited.

Air moved against his cheek, and he heard the tiny noise of a woolen sock in contact with rough floorboards. He did not move. The door began to open very slowly. Gardiner waited, aware only of the lace stretched tautly between the clenched hands. Dupuy's head appeared.

One further step. Gardiner saw moonlight glint on the old Luger and waited. Uncountable seconds later Dupuy moved. In the moment of less sure balance as he stepped forward, Gardiner heaved the door against him, squashing the man against the wall. There was a cry of pain and then the mute struggle as the lace tightened across the throat with its bobbing Adam's apple.

By a desperate effort of will, Dupuy managed to drag Gardiner across the room behind him. But the lace did not slacken for a moment, and he felt consciousness slipping from him. He scrabbled at the lace, already buried in the folds of flesh of his neck, scratching his skin into bleeding lines. The moonlit square of window wobbled in his vision, and he lurched toward it. Then the pain was looser in his throat, and he tried to drag in air. Then he tried, suddenly, to put out his hands, to stop the idiotic descent of the body even as his mind registered the crashing of the dirty glass, the cool air, and the pricks and stabs of the shreds of glass in his face and hands. He tried to scream in the moment he broke his neck on the flagstones at the back of the villa.

Gardiner looked down briefly at the lifeless body heaped on the terrace, as if in satisfaction, and turned to leave. His body remembered the next movements; his mind seemed to be impelled upon a familiar course. He bent to look for his shoes, and a fierce pain gripped him, paralyzing him and making him cry out. His stomach was tied in knots, burning as if it was tarred rope set alight. He vomited, and when he was done, he was shaking uncontrollably, as if some spell or drug had worn off.

He realized what he had done, and it terrified him. Panic welled, and he was afraid of being found, of the noise of breaking glass, of the police. . . .

Afraid of himself, as if he had escaped some awful moral vacuum.

He shrugged on the shoes, not waiting to relace the left, shoving the lace in his pocket; he became irritated to frenzy with the difficult tight knot around his forefinger as he tried to free it. His wrist hurt now, and his knee threatened to collapse. He limped his way down the stairs.

The door banged behind him, and he slithered into the driver's seat of the Peugeot, the key fumbled into the ignition.

The engine fired at the third attempt, and he revved far too much, the gravel spurting from beneath the rear wheels. He pulled the car around in a tight circle and drove straight out into the rue des Epinettes, headlights ablaze.

He drove as quickly as he could back to the hotel and the safety of his room.

He had to lie rigid on the bed, arms at his side, legs stiff, until the fit of shaking deserted him. He lost

sense of passing time, only dimly aware of the toilet
flushing in the next room as one of his sons used it.
The noise was hundreds of miles away and in another
world of experience.

He felt himself to be more than one person—at
least two, but he could not be certain. There might be
more figures, half-formed personae crowding into the
dank little room of his brain. There was the self that
had embarked upon that holiday, shivering with fear,
sweating and chilled alternately. That person was not
indivisibly the same as the one who was afraid of the
police or the discovery of Dupuy's body and his tire
tracks and fingerprints, yet he had the dim sense of being the same as the person who was afraid because the
past had come back and assailed him with a gun. That
was a younger man, growing younger even as he sought
to define him, all the way back to the broken young-
old man in the succession of hospital beds and wheel-
chairs which squeaked out onto terraces when the days
were warmer—the young-old man becoming reconciled
to a restoration of manhood as he began to be able to
feel the rough material of his pajamas against the legs
that had been dead of feeling for so long.

And there was the other one—the person who
had leaped on his back in that house in the rue des
Epinettes, seemed to burst from his body as if from a
useless chrysalis. Gardiner the killer, the leader. The
man he had run from to Dorchester and the safe
country practice and the dull friends and the pomposity
and coldness of his middle years. His sense of himself
as a multiple image went that far back.

The worst thing was that he was fascinated by
what that Gardiner had done. It had been years later,
but threatened, he had been able to kill, coldly, con-
fidently. An unhealthy glamour seemed to crowd
around that forgotten self, and he raised his hands often, staring at them in the moonlit bedroom, feeling
the shoelace taut across the palms, the bite into the
heels of his hands as it bit into Dupuy's neck.

The first gulp of the whisky he poured when he
finally moved from the bed made him gag, and he put
down the glass with a heavy sound. It was as if the

earlier Gardiner, which he now accepted as lurking somewhere in him like a virus or a cancer, had rejected that way of being put aside. Because he had used drink once before, in the effort to renounce. . . .

He went to the window and for a long time stood in silence. His skin became responsive to the external temperature rather than to the heat of thought, and the beach across the promenade was silver in the moonlight. A thin white mustache of foam showed where the tide was turning. *Yes,* he thought, again and again, *it is like a cancer. It is eating me.*

He shivered, yet it was a milder spasm and might be attributed to the cool air coming through the windows, idling the net curtains against him. He understood.

He turned suddenly, as if someone had come in. Looking at the bed, making out the outline of the depression where his wife had sat, the patch of her scarf, her clothes over the back of a chair in one corner. It was as if those fragments were all that remained to him of nineteen years. Suddenly he wanted her there, with the deep pain of a child requiring maternal comfort, an embrace that would exclude the rest of the world, even banish thought—but she was not there. She was with her lover.

The quick ease with which he invested the thought with malice caused him to breathe painfully. Then he turned back to the window. His hands were clenching and unclenching; his body could feel Dupuy pressed against him in the violent pederasty of murder as he strangled him. The memory trembled through him—the quick last shudder of the bodies in the moment before they parted and he heaved the dying man through the window he had struggled to reach.

He lit a cigarette with shaking hands. The smoke calmed him surprisingly quickly, and he found his mind turning, naturally, to the contemplation of his future. He had to leave La Baule as soon as practicable. Self-preservation.

Rouen. A lit, garish thought. He had to go to Rouen. Dupuy and Perrier had run him down, intending to kill him, in the cobblestoned square in Rouen.

Someone else had ordered them to do it. And before that, he had been betrayed in Paris. By the same person.

He welcomed the decisiveness of the moment, its momentousness. He exhaled noisily. A kind of reversal had been accomplished—then was now, now then. He did not try to understand it, but he did embrace it.

He would need a *carte d'identité* and money. He had to disappear completely. Without trace. If he left his wife without money, then let her lover keep her until she was repatriated with his sons. Pleasure from the thought, as if he had drunk something potent.

Cancer.

He dismissed the idea. Inevitable, he admitted. He had adjusted, painfully, to the postwar world, to what was termed normal life, because he had almost died. But he knew himself. The violent outbursts of temper, the drinking, the coldness to his wife, the abrasive relationships with partners he seemed somehow to—frighten . . . ? Gardiner was "Achilles." He knew that.

He had seen others like himself during the war, and he had never considered his own nature in the light of theirs. He should have.

He wanted revenge.

The key lay in Rouen, with the former members of the "Ilium" group. Some of them must be there, sufficient to tell him where Perrier had gone after 1945. His pulse quickened. The girl would still be there. She lived in the area before the war, on a farm. She would know.

He stubbed out the cigarette end and undressed. He wanted to be able to pretend sleep when his wife returned. Naked, he slipped beneath the sheet, than ran his hands over the body as if in the act of inspection. Running to the fat of middle age. But not badly. He wasn't old, thank God.

He lay staring at the ceiling, remembering August 1944—each moment of each day. He was asleep when Jane returned, drifting into sleep perhaps half an hour after lying down, satisfied that he had recalled every incident, perhaps every thought, of those past days.

Gardiner dismissed his wife and children from every calculation he was in the process of making. In the moments while he waited for the police to interview him in his room, he allowed the lurid images of her copulation, of the heavy, sexual happiness he had seen in her eyes when she had awoken, to die; he found that it no longer rankled. He had been able to watch the parade of her naked body before the mirror, when she thought he was not observing her, almost with equanimity. And for that reason, too, he embraced his new future.

"You were dreaming again last night," she had said as he shaved. He had looked up into the mirror, seen her face behind him in the doorway, and noticed the lines of worry at the corners of her mouth and eyes. Some vestige of concern.

He shrugged it away and said equably, "Was I? I hope I didn't disturb you, darling." The acid emphasis at the end removed her from the doorway with a flick of her blond hair.

He knew he had been dreaming and supposed that, too, was a part of his transfiguration. He had been frightened again, in a half-waking moment, but his body had still been dry, and the sheet was hardly ruffled. He had been murmuring, obviously. Jane had long ago stopped asking about his nightmares, long before the dreams themselves seemed to have stopped.

A moment of recollection, he sobbing in her arms, against her cool skin, his face wet with perspiration— he dismissed it. Part of a buried life.

The boys were excited by the arrival of the police in the hotel during breakfast. He had sent them off with plenty of small change in the care of Sarah. Jane went to swim.

Gardiner, sipping at his coffee, heard a knock at the door.

"Come in."

A small man in a tan suit opened the door, bowed

with a miniscule nod of his head, and closed the door behind him. He crossed the carpet, smiled, and sat himself opposite Gardiner in the chair Gardiner had arranged. They were framed by the dazzling whiteness of the net curtains at the window. A breeze from the balcony stirred the curtains.

"M'sieur Gardiner, it is kind of you to make yourself available for questioning. As I explained in the dining room, we are investigating the death of a waiter at this hotel, a man called Dupuy. . . ." Gardiner nodded at the recital, and the little man snapped, "You knew him perhaps?"

"No—I don't think so," Gardiner replied carefully, trying to still the little vein of excitement that seemed to have opened in his temple. He was studying the man, and he had to struggle to control the obviousness of his interest. "I'm sorry—er . . . ?"

"Inspector Costain, of the prefecture." He took out a notebook, as if reminded by something in Gardiner's manner that it was an official inquiry.

Gardiner said, "Perhaps I knew him by sight, but not by name. Is there something unusual about his death?"

Costain nodded. His dark features were rough-skinned, heavy for such a small head. His eyes had a spaniel brownness, a watchful patience. He would make a determined opponent, and Gardiner realized that the time he possessed for complete freedom of action was short. The policeman was treading on egg-shells at that moment, questioning holidaymakers about a murder.

"*Oui.* He was thrown out of a first-floor window last night—and he was choked almost to death before that."

"I see." Gardiner pulled a face. He could feel himself again as a multiple of himself, drawing the postwar self about him like a cloak, remembering its pomposity, its *ordinariness*. "How do you think I can help you?" He smiled inwardly. He might have been speaking to a nervous client.

"This is routine, you understand, m'sieur. We are questioning all the guests in the hotel. . . ." He paused for a moment, then added, "Everyone who was out of the hotel last night, that is."

"Oh. Was—did the man not die here then?" Costain shook his head, and his eyes watched Gardiner's face carefully, as if seeing beneath the surface. Gardiner, unnerved, adapted his nervousness to surprise. "Sorry. I naturally thought it took place here. I don't know why."

"You can account for your movements, m'sieur? It seems perhaps strange that you should hire a car, having been injured a little in your own. You did not wish to rest last evening?" He looked down at Gardiner's knee. "How is your leg?"

"Rather stiff. Yes, I did hire a car. I just drove around, I'm afraid. . . ."

"You were seen? You went into a bar perhaps?"

Gardiner shook his head, then watched Costain scribble for a moment in his notebook. He said, as if dictating, careful of his tone, "I'm afraid not."

"Why drive at all? You were recovering your confidence perhaps? Was that it? Your wife was not with you. We have spoken to Madame Gardiner in the lobby. . . ."

Gardiner saw the moment slipping from him, and he grasped it.

"I see. No, Inspector, my wife was not with me last evening. She went out—to meet someone. . . ." His lips compressed, and his eyes became bleak. The little pulse of excitement still beat in his temple, and he was aware of some objective part of himself studying his performance. Carefully he lowered his gaze and shuffled one foot irresolutely. He held his breath, waiting.

"I see. Yes, Madame Gardiner supplied us with a name, in confidence, of course."

"I do not want to know it," he said freezingly, catching perfectly a moment of past reaction from years before. Two spots of color glowed on his cheeks, and he appeared to regret his confidence to Costain. "To you it may not mean very much . . ." he began, then trailed off. He let one hand quiver slightly, then moved the other to still it.

"I—forgive me, m'sieur. I have to ask, however.

Is there anyone who can say exactly where you were and what you were doing between eleven and twelve last night? You returned to the hotel at about twelve-fifteen. Correct?"

Gardiner shook his head slowly. It was as if he were absorbed by another subject. "I suppose it was," he said. Then, more firmly: "Yes, it was about then. I'm fairly sure."

There was a silence in which Gardiner's confidence seemed to begin crumbling, and the silence roared in his ears. He was unenlightened as to the effect of his story on Costain. Then the policeman stood up.

"My apologies, M'sieur Gardiner, for asking you all these questions. You are staying in La Baule for another three or four days, I believe?"

"Yes."

"Good. We have some checking to do on this man Dupuy. We shall try not to trouble you again."

He shook Gardiner's hand firmly, and then he was gone. Gardiner looked at the door for a moment or two, then stepped out onto the balcony. He remained there until his wife returned to the hotel for lunch and came up to the room to change.

He stayed out on the balcony, watching her through the shimmer of the idling net curtains. She seemed grateful that he was silent, yet also disturbed by the possible state of his knowledge. Only once, as she stood at the mirror to brush her hair, did a former self feel a catch of breath. He turned to look out over the promenade and the beach, and the emotion died in him. He observed with pleasure this new control of feeling and reflected on the quality of his performance for Costain. He was relearning old skills, as he had relearned an old aptitude in the house on the rue des Epinettes.

He followed her and the children down to lunch. He ate his way through the Breton leg of mutton and white beans almost without conversation. Jane Gardiner, intent upon preserving the silence, which betokened ignorance, and her composed image in the eyes of other guests, mentioned neither the policeman nor his questions.

After lunch he forced Jane to take Sarah and the boys to the beach, promising to join them when he had checked up on repairs to the Rover. He had no intention of doing either. When they had gone, he sat in the hotel lobby for a while, behind his copy of the *Daily Telegraph*.

It was four o'clock when he finally drove to the yacht basin at the northern arm of the shallow bay. The journey took him twice as long as it need have done because he went through the old, laborious work of checking for a tail. He was relieved but unsurprised to find that he was not being followed. Once at the basin, he made inquiries concerning a dinghy to be hired the following day, but no actual booking. He wore his dark glasses all the time and presented himself as a Frenchman with a casual interest in hiring a small boat. After establishing that persona, he wandered about the basin, studying the boats and the people working on them. Sunlight glittered off the still water, gleamed from the bright hulls and chromework.

It took him more than an hour to find what he required—three possible boats, each of them thirty-footers or larger and each of them owned by individuals who had not used them recently. Two of them were berthed near boats whose owners were on board or who were in the town at that time. Only the third boat was berthed alongside other boats with absentee owners. The third boat received the greatest attention; he put his shoulder to the door, broke into the cabin, and inspected its equipment and stores.

The thirty-footer carried a Bermuda rig that he could handle alone; its charts were up-to-date and covered the required areas of the Brittany coast; there was food in the cupboards and water in the tanks. The boat was fueled, and he assumed that the owner was expected in the immediate future. It was too tempting to resist, nevertheless. He paused only for a moment to wonder at the helplessness of committing himself to a journey by sea if his method were to be discovered; then he decided. At high tide that night he would steal the yacht.

He replaced the broken lock as best he could,

smearing grease over the white, newly exposed wood. Then he wandered with apparent purposelessness back to his car.

Before the shops closed for the evening, he bought a stout haversack at one store and an anorak and waterproof overtrousers from a sports shop. He regretted leaving such signposts, but there were no warm clothes or waterproofs on board the yacht.

It was on the journey back to the hotel that he realized that he was being tailed. Someone in a fawn Renault had picked him up, probably in the street near the sports shop. It did not look like a police car, but he knew he had little time left, much less than he had hoped.

The tail had unsettled him, even though the Renault had driven past the hotel car park, on down the promenade. When he reached the safety of his room, he urgently wanted a pen and paper. He had to make a list of names, some kind of talisman for the next few days. Each member of the old group. His mind struggled to recollect every name. Occasionally he put a thick line through a name—the man or woman was dead before the betrayal. He noted the details beside each name—color of eyes and hair, weight, the name of a street, occupation, distances. . . .

What if the fawn Renault had been at the marina, seen him there, looking for a boat?

Another name—this time the height, the age clear.

What if . . . ?

Stupid romanticism, escaping to sea, like a boy in a book.

He had to go that night, and he needed funds and a means of escape. Under pressure of certitude that he was being watched, the boat became a chimera, something not to be trusted. Yet he had no alternative solution.

He was standing at the window again, leaving the list for a moment to clear his mind. Below him a woman in a swimsuit crossed the road, and a fat lady on a bicycle wobbled to change direction, ringing the bell furiously. The idea that came to him was as-

sociated with cool summer nights and a blackened
face, perhaps, or rough workman's clothes, riding
through the countryside around Rouen, carrying mes-
sages, checking on components of an operation, or
meeting a drop. . . .

He was pleased, though instantly aware that it
was only half a plan. *Was the boat now only a bluff, a
discarded card?*

Then the sandwich board in the foyer, which had
given him the idea of the boat. It was the remainder of
his scheme. He knew how he could murder himself.

*One problem—Jane had to be out of the hotel,
with her lover, when he left.*

When she came in, he sensed a returned bravado. She must have met the man on the beach, even
though her sons had been with her. She made no remark about why he had not appeared. He saw in the
way she undressed for a shower that she was confident
again, flattered and wanted by the young Frenchman.
It would not be difficult to engineer a quarrel. She
simply needed to feel threatened.

As she soaped herself in the shower, having
drawn the curtain when he had appeared in the bathroom, he took off his shirt and washed his face. Then
he lathered it carefully, inspected the blade, and began
methodically to shave, luxuriating in the steam that
rose from the hot water, partially clouding the mirror.
At every stroke of the razor, the water in the shower
streamed in a soothing background. As he cleaned
his chin of the lather, he said, "The car will be ready
tomorrow—we'll move on then. I want to get down
into the Dordogne as quick as we can. It'll mean a lot
of driving. You won't mind that, will you?"

There was a silence, only the swish of water. He
scraped carefully at his upper lip, not glancing toward
the shower. Then he heard the curtain rings chatter
back, and she said, "Why do we have to leave in such a
rush?" There was the smallest hint of nervousness, of
disappointment which she could not quite squeeze
from her careful tone.

"I've had La Baule," he said, careful with the
cleft in his chin. "You and the kids have had enough

of the beach and lazing around. My turn for some enjoyment, eh?"

"I don't see why we have to leave tomorrow, that's all!" she snapped.

He waited for a moment, then said, "What's the matter—not sad to leave your lover, are you?"

There was an audible intake of breath. Still, he did not turn toward her. Gardiner had mentioned the unmentionable.

"What do you mean . . . ?" she began.

"There you are then," he cut in, snapping his head around so that he looked at her for a moment, then went back to his shaving, the last few spots of lather. "Nothing to keep us here."

"What did you mean?" Her voice was stronger, recovered.

"About your lover? Why, haven't you had time to find one yet?"

"You bastard!" she replied. "What the hell do you mean by that?"

"You know very well what I mean. It's just that, although I usually refrain from comment, it does seem reasonable to me that you should contrive not to indulge your libido while we're on a family holiday. Don't you?" He eased a false sweetness into his voice as he said, "If only for the sake of Sarah and the boys."

"Christ! They wouldn't notice if I was making love to someone on *their* bed, unless I rolled over and broke one of their precious models!" She was angry at him, but there was something in her that still seemed to wish to avoid the blunt directness of the confrontation.

He said, "Quite possibly you're right. However, with the exception of changing for dinner or the beach, I do wish you would manage to keep your knickers on for a fortnight at a time."

She swept past him, towel around her almost virginally. As he glanced up into the mirror, he saw that her face was set and frightened. She was angry and bewildered, too. She could not take him for granted at that moment, like a safely extinct volcano, and the idea disturbed her. She was remembering, he knew, the old jealous outbursts, and perhaps even before that, when he might have considered himself to blame. Physical violence—even that, before she had been able to consider that he no longer cared, no longer objected.

"You . . . have a mind like a sewer," she breathed, pausing at the door of the bathroom. She was short of breath, as if after exertion.

"Quite. And you have the morality of a sewer rat, my dear—we make a lovely couple. . . ." Without turning to look at her, he picked up the thick white towel and began to wipe his cheeks. Then he let the water out of the basin, amusing himself with the analogy to his marriage and to the last nineteen years. Just water running away, leaving nothing but a gray scum. All the while he could sense her anger, her hatred. Then he turned to look at her, and she hitched the bath towel more securely around her breasts, as if threatened. "Well, my dear. Do what you want tonight, for tomorrow we drive. We're leaving in the morning!"

There was a long, tense silence as they glared at each other. Then she turned away, biting the full lower lip, chastened and degraded. He had no sympathy for her, only a pleasure in having engineered the situation successfully. Now, damaged in self-esteem, she would determine to spend this last night in La Baule with her French lover. He had spoken the unspeakable and made her into nothing more than a tart; for that, she would make him suffer. When she returned that night or the following morning, she would expect to fling her infidelity in his face, her ego restored, her sense of her desirability returned to her.

To ensure that she telephoned her lover and made the necessary arrangements, he took Sarah and the boys down to dinner early, where he was affable, even lighthearted, with the girl and the other guests at nearby tables. As if, he admitted, he were taking his leave of a part, apologizing in advance for his plan to rob them of their French currency. For he had also solved his currency problem.

He ate crêpes, homard à l'Americaine, and Rennes

pralines, drank most of a bottle of Muscadet, and lingered over his coffee. When Jane joined them halfway through the main course, she was carefully made up, stiff and silent in her seat. Already he witnessed the return of sexual confidence. Her lover had been flattering, eager apparently.

She left a little before eight-thirty, kissing the boys briefly and ignoring Gardiner.

At two minutes after midnight he knocked on the door of the manager's suite on the hotel's first floor. There was a muffled sound from within, and he pushed open the door. The manager showed a slight surprise at his appearance, but got up from the sofa where he had been listening to Charles Trenet from a record player, put down his drink, and said in English, "M'sieur Gardiner, is it not? What can I do for you?" He came toward Gardiner without suspicion. "What is it—is something wrong?"

Gardiner took the razor-edged cheese knife, which he had pocketed at dinner, from the pocket of the new anorak and pressed it against the protruding stomach of the manager. The small man's eyes bulged comically, yet he seemed to be aware principally of the tallness of the Englishman rather than of the knife.

Gardiner said, "You wouldn't want to end up like a piece of the rather inferior Camembert you serve downstairs, would you, m'sieur?" He pressed the point of the knife against the stomach so that it pricked through the man's waistcoat, touched the flesh.

The manager winced, closed his eyes, then opened them again. Gardiner saw that he was sufficiently afraid. The manager said, "What do you want?"

"Apart from a small float, I presume you keep the currency from the *Bureau de Change* here, in your safe?"

The manager was incapable of lying. He nodded. "Yes," he said.

"Good. Shall we?" He prodded the knife into the stomach, and the little manager swallowed. As he turned to lead Gardiner, he caught sight of himself in a full-length mirror on one wall. He looked fat, and frightened, and ridiculous. Gardiner allowed him to bend

before the safe, holding the knife at his throat, where
it was irritated into a rash by the stiff edge of his
collar. A pudgy hand fiddled with the combination of
the small safe built into the wall of the room but un-
disguised.

The door of the safe opened, creaking slightly,
but not as loudly as the man's stifled breath creaked
in the silence. The manager could hear the clock on
the mantelpiece quite distinctly. Then he was handing
the bundles of francs out to the man with the knife
and beginning to feel the questions thrust upward
through the rush of panic and reaction he could sense
in his body. He handed Gardiner dollars by mistake,
and Gardiner put them back in his hand, then snatched
them again.

"All of it then!" he snapped, as if angry with
himself. "Quickly!"

The manager fumbled the neatly stacked bundles
out of the safe, the small, sharp knife never moving
from the side of his neck. Gardiner bundled the
money into his anorak—dollars, sterling, marks,
francs, lire. Then, quite suddenly, the safe was empty,
and the point of the knife was very sharp against the
manager's throat. He dared not turn his head. It was
no more than a moment before the knife was gone and
Gardiner hit the little man across the side of the head,
just behind the ear, with his flattened hand. Soundlessly he slid to the floor, curled in a fetal position like
some small hibernating animal.

Gardiner put the knife in his pocket, then took
the unconscious form by the armpits and dragged
the manager of the Hôtel Boulevard de l'Océan across
the room. He back-heeled the bedroom door open
and dragged the body to the bed. Then he knelt down
and pushed the manager under the bed. He tidied the
bedspread, straightened his anorak, and closed the door
behind him. He locked it.

The hire car was in its place in the car park, an
ancient bicycle, the property of a desk clerk on duty
until the morning, in its trunk. He drove toward the
yacht basin. There was little traffic, and the journey
took him less than ten minutes. He drove straight to-

ward the outskirts of the town and the Pointe de Pen-
chateau.

The road which had bordered the beach curved
around the low, rocky point here. The retreating tide
still covered most of the rocks—no sand would be exposed before his time expired. Across the water he
could see the lights of La Baule, glittering and unsub-
stantial now. He unlocked the trunk of the car and
took out the bicycle. He carried it across the road and
down the worn steps onto the rocks. It was slightly
risky, leaving it there for perhaps more than an hour,
but there was no alternative. He placed it against the
seawall, a mere ten feet high but sufficient to hide the
bike from eyes on the road. He waited while a car
went noisily by, the din of a car radio fading behind
it, before going back to his car and taking the haversack from the back seat. Into this, on top of his change
of clothes, he had stuffed the money from his anorak.
Leaving it, too, was risky.

He searched for some minutes until he found a
deep and narrow crevice in the rocks. He thrust the
haversack into it, out of sight.

Standing up, he dusted himself off, feeling the
wetness of the newly uncovered rock on his knees. He
went back to the car, turned it in the road, and returned the way he had come, until he was opposite
the yacht basin. He parked, locked the car, and left it.

The yacht basin was unguarded, as far as he
could tell. There was a fence and a locked gate. He
climbed over the gate, dropping soundlessly on to the
other side. The drop was small but seemed to take an
age, as if something had slowed on film, and his mind
raced through a hundred memories, nosed a hundred
scents of his past, before his feet touched the earth.
He understood it only as a dossier the body collated
in a microsecond. He went into a cushion crouch, and
as he straightened up, it was as if he were seeing himself differently. He looked across the glittering water at
La Baule—a million miles away perhaps. Then he
made his way swiftly to the thirty-footer he had selected.

The tide was ebbing quickly, and the boat, dark-colored, low-hulled, slopped ungracefully in the idle power of the tide. He climbed on board and went straight to the stern. For his purposes he had no need of the small auxiliary motor or to rig the boat. The ebbing tide would take him out with it—a short journey, he had calculated. He would use the motor if necessary, but he considered that he had time to position himself where he wished without it.

Muffled rock music from a café or dance hall. He cast off and took the tiller after having thrust the boat away from its berth, sitting in the lee of the tiny cabin. The boat, one he would have liked to have been able to afford in his previous existence, was nothing more than a tool now. The lights of the town were behind him as the current plucked at the boat. The sky was alive with stars as he turned his face out to sea.

To starboard he could see the small lighthouse at the mouth of the river he had crossed on his way to the point. His single point of reference, as he gazed to starboard, was a clutch of lights, sliding behind the rocks of the point, seemingly suspended. He knew the course of the pleasure cruiser, had seen it traversing the bay, back and forth, the previous night—midnight dancing, food, and wine. His mouth grimaced at the remembered notice in the hotel foyer, and he wondered whether his wife and her lover might be on board. He rather hoped they would.

The minutes passed, and he moved with the tide on his appointed course. The lights slid from behind the rocks and the music from the band on board the cruiser could be heard across the dark water. The chain of lights was a blurred necklace at first, slowly enlarging to individual lamps of many colors. The music became louder, and he recognized the melody—an old waltz, which might have belonged to the period before the war, to his youth. The warmth of the summer night became real to him for the first time, and a part of his mind idled with the music even as he computed the distances and the point of convergence.

He saw that he was not exact and fired the auxiliary motor. The tune washed from his thoughts as the motor coughed, then stilled. He fired it again; it coughed, asthmatic promise, then silence. The music louder, and the churn of the screws audible. The passage of the boat thrumming through the hull of the yacht. He cursed, looking up at the point of moonlit sea already glowing with light from the cruiser, and then fired the motor again. It erupted, spluttered, then settled to a steady note. He slumped back in the seat with the sudden forward movement of the yacht and then clasped the tiller to him, steering the yacht toward the intended point on the gleaming surface of the bay. Perhaps only seventy or eighty yards.

He watched the cruiser carefully. He had to make it appear accidental, and he feared the watchfulness of the crew. Guests passed, heads and no more, along the rail on the port side. The cruiser loomed; then he heard the megaphoned cry, even as the music stopped and something harsher and more modern took its place. Then a cone of silence beneath the bows, and he was sharply, deeply afraid as the cruiser towered over the yacht. The ship's hooter bellowed, and the music had stopped, and there was the faint cry of a distorted human voice, inadequate as a bird's call. The bow wave of the cruiser seemed to slip away from him, the dark knife-edge in the water rearing above him, seeming to bend aside. . . .

He stood up in the boat, then dived into the water on the side farthest from the great bow over him, pulling down into the water even as the first shock of the collision juddered the tiny yacht. He pulled down frantically, blood rushing in his ears until drowned by the deafening sound of the screw passing above him. He began to be buffeted by the cruiser's passage. The great dark shape passed over him, canceling the gleam of moonlight. He noticed, oddly, the sting of seawater in his stitched knee and then only the threatening lungs as they seemed to swell beneath the rib cage. He had to get deep.

There was a precise, stark moment when he realized he might die. The sound of the screw was a hideous din, and the water plucked at him, pulling him upward, tearing at his limbs. He was unable to swim in the maelstrom—he had miscalculated. Then he was fighting for his life, spun like something without gravity at the mercy of a great wind, whirling in the dark water which churned about him.

Then there was an absence of thought, a suspension of time passing. Feebly he struck out, heading for the surface, but without volition or urgency. He had exhaled, and he felt empty, light, and buoyant.

His mind, some part of it, warned him, and he realized that he had become disoriented beneath the water. He was striking *down*. Nothing but darker water ahead of him, and he rolled clumsily so that the faint starlight gleamed ahead of him. He had no sense of up or down but struck—because now the blood cried for oxygen and the limbs were heavy and the brain was beginning to spin and fumble—ahead, toward the faint light, hoping that the increasing light was not a mere illusion.

His head broke the surface, and he choked in great lungfuls of air, swallowing seawater at the same time. The cruiser was already changing course, trying to retrace its path. There was hardly any wreckage of the yacht in sight on the disturbed water. He heard muffled shouts, the giving of orders. There did not appear to be any music. He forced himself to swallow for a last time and to push his head back beneath the alien water. He was drained and forced himself to strike out, beneath the water, in the direction of the point.

When his head broke the surface again, the cruiser seemed no farther off. He dove again, understanding, only very distantly, that the cruiser was following a reciprocal course and that he might be in danger of being overrun again. He could do nothing about it, only bob to the surface again, his lungs crying for relief, his body weary of the strange, difficult element into which he had led it. He was heavy on the surface, as if maintaining a precarious hold on a ledge, about to slide off into air and darkness. He could not be sure whether or not he was in danger of losing consciousness. He remained on the surface for a long time, the cruiser appearing to have stopped engines. He saw the lighthouse again as he trod water.

With each stroke he felt the current of the ebbing

tide drag at him, as if pushing him back out to sea. Losing a sense of time passing, he seemed engaged in a continuing, frenzied beating of the water with his arms. Later he knew that he must have almost passed out several times and that he had rested often, but always the swim to the rocks of the point came back to him in the same way—arms beating feebly, as if keeping an enemy at bay, body losing purchase on the ledge of water. He struggled in two separate periods of time. Aware of himself now, reminded by the lights of La Baule and the sweep of the lighthouse beam, and aware of himself also crossing the river, toward the bank and away from the train. It was 1944. Two persons fought and became sealed in some strange way, fused together; the years between vanished, squeezed by effort from the aching muscles and forced from the frantic mind.

When he pulled himself onto the rocks, he was spent. He vomited, seawater and half-digested food spilling weakly from his mouth as he lay with his head hanging down into a hollow, the water of a rock pool inches from his bleared eyes, his feet still in the retreating tide. He shivered with exhaustion and relief.

Much later, when the tide had left his feet, as if it had thrown him up onto the rocks at the full and he were some stranded aquatic creature, clumsy and slow-moving, he turned on his back and laughed. Weakly, wetly at first, then forcing the sound to express his defiance. When his breathing returned to normal and the wet clothes were uncomfortable to renewed senses, he undressed and dried himself with a towel. He dressed swiftly in the least English-looking suit he possessed, leaving the money in the bottom of the haversack, beneath the anorak and the other wet clothes. He looked out into the bay once. It must have taken him a long time to recover—there was no sign of the cruiser or any search for him.

He cycled, via the back streets of La Baule and country roads, to the port of St. Nazaire. There he boarded the early-morning train for Paris, having checked the bicycle at the station.

FROM   Head of Intelligence
TO   Foreign Secretary
DATE   12th February 1962

MEMO   Series 62/DEF/134

DIGEST OF LATEST INFORMATION & INTERROGATION DOCUMENTS TO
REACH ME FROM OUR SOURCE 'ANATOLY' HAVE INCRIMINATED, WITHOUT
DOUBT, GEORGE BLAKE   SIS AGENT.

IMMEDIATE ARREST FOLLOWS.

FROM   Head of Intelligence
TO   Foreign Secretary
DATE   3rd February 1963

MEMO   Series 63/DEF/ 89

REPORTS FROM HEAD OF STATION MOSCOW, CONFIRM ARRIVAL OF
PHILBY ON SOVIET SOIL 27/1/63 , FOUR DAYS AFTER LEAVING
BEIRUT.

Extracted for post-operational ref.
by Head of Intelligence
4th November 1963

the debate eventually ending at about 4.0 am.
followed by a couple of hours sleep.!

15th JUNE 1963

Worked on papers most of the morning before
routine weekly meeting with P.M.
At 3.00 pm "C" came to see me for my decision.
There appears to be a fourth "Judas" in NATO and
"C" tells me that Washington concurs via Source
"Franklin".

I do not like private police forces and Wigg
would have a field day if my decision came out
– but if this is an "inside" affair the fewer people
that know the better. I gave "C" the go ahead
and agreed the appointments of Aubrey and Latymer
to command 504.

The funding of the operation had been troublesome
but the P.M. advises me to go ahead and write it
down under "research". His precept appears to be
do it first – and explain to the Treasury later –
that is if they find out!

Had dinner with members of the Overseas Trade
Mission but after an all night sitting I must
have been a very dull guest and had it not been

4. Affairs of State

The river was an oily, sliding gray under low clouds, clouds that were flecked across the belly from the rising sun, heavy and swollen on the lip of the city downriver. It was very much like a winter morning, after the overnight rain. Hilary Latymer, not having slept for another night, had left the house in Cheyne Row and had walked to the Chelsea Embankment. His features, too, were wintry like the day, raw and drained. Light from the lamps on the Embankment colored his face garishly as he continued his unseeing patrol.

Behind him the elegantly furnished eighteenth-century house that they had bought with Victoria's money was cold and silent. He had thought about selling it, then immediately stamped on the thought as if it had represented some kind of betrayal. He had sent the one servant that Victoria had employed for years, their cook-housekeeper, away to her relatives in the north. There was no dismissal, merely that for Mrs. Wetherby to be present, with her silent sympathy and doglike, pained eyes, would have been too much of an irritant. He preferred to eat at unusual hours, mostly cold scraps if he ate at home at all. Empty of other human beings, the house was bearable.

Coming down to the Embankment had not been a good idea, he decided. Yet he could not bear the house at all after a sleepless night—the silent rooms, the drawn curtains, the furniture that announced Vic-

toria wherever he looked, until the daylight was strong
in every room. The harsh flickering of the striplight in
the kitchen scratched at his nerves.

Only once before, when his brother had died in
Normandy in 1944, had he felt anything like his present appalling misery. Grief pressed down on him, lim-
iting his horizons of feeling. He had thought of resigning his post, yet he held back, as if dimly aware of the
utter emptiness of his days if he had no work to occupy
at least part of the brain.

Hilary Latymer, at forty-six, was by inclination a
placid man. He was unused to intense states of feeling.
His detachment had made him a good intelligence officer during and after the war. His brother's death
had been learned, and suffered, at second hand and in
wartime. With Victoria, it was as if he were dying.
Without the comfort of drugs, deadening the awareness, the sense of being a dead thing held somehow
upright by pointless sinews.

He needed something, he realized, in order to escape from his own devils. Someone else's demons to
pursue perhaps, a cancer in the body politic, driving
out thoughts of the vile, inoperable thing eating at his
wife's brain. Mentally he was trying to breathe very
shallowly these days, as he waited for his wife to die.
He was treading a thin crust of feeling.

On the Embankment he turned, the trees bordering the grounds of the Royal Hospital above him, and
began to retrace his steps toward the empty house in
Cheyne Row.

He arrived at his office before eight. He had
picked at a breakfast he had cooked himself but had
fled the house as soon as he decently could, taking the
tube to the City. In Old Jewry he entered a side door
which led to anonymous offices above a small private
bank, Gairstang's, and a uniformed porter checked
his pass, then nodded him in. Above the bank, which
handled some of SIS's Banking Section funds, principally those for operations in Europe, were the offices
of Latymer's new section of SIS.

He glanced into the duty room and saw Biggar

with his feet on the table, two empty beer bottles in the wastebin, and the air thick with bluish smoke. Biggar opened one eye lazily, nodded, but did not speak, and Latymer closed the door behind him. He went slowly up to his own office, next to Aubrey's up three steps from the main renovated suite of offices which had only a few weeks before become the home of SO–4.

The office was cool and dark until he released the blind. He had worked late the previous night, and there were still papers on the desk, a sloppiness in security that he now felt he had committed to assuage some personal resentment. He had felt himself bound to his work last night and had tried to blame it for what was happening to him. The attempt had been unsuccessful, and he had been left finally with the empty Chelsea house and the bottle of malt whiskey which he had halfheartedly endeavored to finish. Then the huge empty bed and the smooth sheets and the lack of sleep. He had begun, eventually, to imagine that he could hear her breathing next to him in bed—a harsh, rasping sound. A recollection of the early weeks, before they had taken her into the nursing home near Oxford. It was as if the bedroom were a recording device and he had willed it to play back.

He sat down at his desk, rubbing his hands down his smooth cheeks, and stared at the photograph he had maintained on his desk by an effort of will—Victoria, smiling but unposed, with mountains in the background. Norway, only three years earlier. A tall woman with a good figure, fine-boned in the face, a rather large nose, fine gray eyes. . . . He held his fingertips to his temples for a long moment, as if containing his thoughts.

SO-4 had been established at the beginning of Victoria's terminal illness. He had transferred to it under Aubrey from the Joint Intelligence Liaison Department, having worked with Aubrey ever since the war in one or another of SIS's departments. Aubrey had pressured him into accepting this last transfer; the comforting illusion was to be that new and more demanding and sensitive work would offer some sort of palliative, a drug. It had not worked. Already Latymer knew that Aubrey was beginning to have to apologize for his performance, to reconsider his decision.

He stood up and went to the window, looking down through the tinted glass at Old Jewry, at the self-effacing facades of the buildings across the street. He wished it had been otherwise—there was a nagging disappointment that he was not as greatly esteemed within the service as formerly. He did not blame Victoria or himself. It merely saddened him that he was not as *efficient* as he once had been.

Because after Philby and Blake there was another. There always was, it seemed. After the resignations—and in one case the removal of a personage from the ranks of the SIS by means of a car accident —there was now a double within NATO, the wider sphere. A double undoubtedly British and the evidence suggesting he was a member of the SIS. In the House questions had been asked when Philby went over, questions that presupposed another man, who had warned Philby as Philby had warned Burgess and MacLean. The foreign secretary had done his utmost to calm such rumors while at the same time causing the head of Intelligence, "C," to stir the ant heap with a stick and witness who ran for cover or out into the sunlight. And then—step on them.

And, Latymer reflected, SO-4 was the stick and the crushing foot, for this time there would be no trial and no eventual exchange. The "mole" would die. And SO-4, as watchdog of the SIS, had no other brief than to find that "mole," whose sphere of operations was the NATO Senior Joint Intelligence Committee.

Latymer observed, with the detachment or helplessness—he could not decide which—of an outsider, that time was running short. The Americans and the French were both clamorous that the leak be stopped. Leaks which had been confirmed only recently by a highly placed double, code name "Franklin," inside Moscow Center. "Franklin" was anonymous, but evidently one of a handful of KGB officers turned while resident on service abroad. "Franklin" confirmed the leaked material covered weapons reequipment, dispositions of troops, attitudes within NATO—and, especially, the worsening relationship between de Gaulle's government and the rest of the NATO alliance. But "Franklin" was unable to name the source.

Latymer swiftly tired of the profitless regurgitation of data, sat down at his desk again, opened a drawer, and removed a bottle of whiskey and a glass. He examined the bottle and the clichéd act, considered the condition of his nerves and the tiny pulse already beating in his temple—and poured a drink. He swallowed the liquor greedily and with a shame that seemed to assail the nostrils like stale sweat or grime.

He put down the glass and crossed to the mirror on the wall. A soberly dressed individual stared out at him, still almost boyishly slim, the full head of hair brushed back from the high forehead beginning to gray. Chiseled features, almost delicate, the curving nose, the blue eyes. Not sharp now; slightly fuzzy, marked with dark stains beneath. A hollow man looked out at him. He felt dirty in body, as his wife had confessed she did when she had first learned of the tumor.

He shook his head at his reflection, aware even as he did so that he was attempting to transmute guilt into rueful disapproval.

Before he could regain his desk, Aubrey opened the door, and his head, pinkly shiny above the two gray wings of hair, appeared. He seemed to take in the slope of Latymer's shoulders, the glass and bottle, even the photograph of Victoria, at one glance; then he said, "In my office, if you would, Hilary. I want to arrange our story before Deputy gets here."

The head disappeared, and Latymer felt he had been caught in some shameful act. Shrugging, he followed Aubrey's rotund figure along the corridor and into the larger office of the department head of SO-4. Unlike Latymer's own office, which had become an arid, sterile place even in a few short weeks, this was warm with the personality of its occupant. Everything was impeccably tidy, but a spider plant trailed across the top and down the front of one tall gray filing cabinet. The curtains were heavy, richly patterned in golds and browns, and on the desk two small pieces of jade —a horseman and a small Buddha, set at either of the front corners of the desk. They seemed to highlight the aesthetic and ascetic in Aubrey.

Aubrey was dressed in a black jacket and striped trousers like the archetypical civil servant he considered himself to be. Though Latymer entered almost immediately behind him, he was already looking out the window, back to the room.

"Close the door, Hilary, would you?" he said, and Latymer, who would have done so, felt he was being treated like an errant schoolboy. Then the little man turned from the window, stared at Latymer quizzically and without apology, then said, "You've not slept." Latymer shook his head. "You'll be precious little use to me—and no use at all to Victoria—unless you sleep. . . ." Latymer knew that Aubrey was deeply distressed at his wife's illness, but he regarded his grief as irrelevant, even impertinent, and therefore hid it.

"I know," Latymer observed, shrugging, an unhabitual gesture which Aubrey noticed with distaste. "Not that my professional uselessness will be any new turn of events."

Aubrey wrinkled his nose.

"I don't like self-pity, Hilary—don't bring it in with you again."

"Sorry."

Aubrey stood on the other side of his desk. He possessed, like many small men, the ability to appear belligerently bigger than he was. Latymer sensed him bristling; then Aubrey took his hands from his pockets, sat down at the desk, and smoothed the two wings of gray hair.

"Sit down, Hilary. I want to be clear on our scheme before Deputy gets here."

"Quite."

"These weekly tutorials are becoming rather a bind, don't you think? Have you your essay to hand?" Latymer smiled, conscious he was being charmed from his depression. "It really is very naughty of the KGB to penetrate us quite so successfully—one feels quite raped!" Latymer laughed aloud at the image. "Mm. What have we got?"

"Not very much, I'm afraid. . . ." With a sharp,

though momentary, regret, Latymer felt himself
drawn effortlessly into the world of his peculiar profession. It was as if he were leaving Victoria alone in a
dark room. He went on. "I've been running over the
timetables of committee meetings from which material
has been provenly leaked. It gives us all four of our
suspects, assuming the usual gossip in rooms and corridors, and the subcommittees which would have pro-
cessed a lot of the stuff. The sheer volume and diversity
of the material confirm one of our four and no low-
grade personnel—but not which one."

Aubrey shook his head. In the sharp blue eyes
there was a momentary pity; then he said, "I see—not
very encouraging, mm?" Aubrey was sympathetic, but
disappointed—in Latymer.

"No."

"Still, it can't be helped. If the CIA won't give
us access to 'Franklin,' we can't do much more than
work in the dark. And the fact that 'Franklin' is a totally *anonymous* source as far as we're concerned is—
most *irritating*."

"They're not likely to tell us while our little friend
the 'mole' is still in business."

"I agree. But the CIA won't use 'Franklin' to obtain a complete breakdown of leaked material unless
it passes across his desk. Heavens, the man, whoever
he is, can't have more than two or three years before
he's tumbled. What could he do that's more important
than this, eh?" There was a silence for a moment; then
Aubrey said, "I have an idea, which we will broach
with Deputy when he gets here."

"Yes?"

"When is the next meeting of the full committee
in Paris?"

"Thursday."

"Who is to attend?"

"All four of our men."

"Mm. I thought so. Very well, we shall be more
drastic. Questions will be asked of us soon, Hilary. We
are the new blue whitener in the service, and we *have*
to get rid of the stains! We shall prevent one, if not
two, from attending and concentrate our efforts on the

other two. If it doesn't draw anything, then we go to work on the other two. Agreed?"

"Yes, of course."

"It's a pity we can't do a nice little bit of spadework at this end, and up pops our little 'mole,' blinking in the sunlight. I'd hand you the spade to beat him over the head. Now, instead, because we think it all happens in Paris, we shall have to run some sort of operation. What we want is something juicy fed to the committee, which is bound to be reported back; then 'Franklin' can keep his eyes open for it. Whom can we trust?"

Latymer, intrigued despite the sudden fits of indifference that seemed to come like the stuttering onset of narcosis, thought for a moment, then said, "Jorgensen. The Norwegian. He's a full member of the senior committee, and he worked with SOE during the war. You recall he's worked for us since the war?"

"Yes. We'll use him then. Something juicy—is there time to put it on the agenda?" Latymer nodded. "We'll think about it then. Something going on inside the Arctic Circle, I shouldn't wonder. Up near the Soviet border. Now declassified for NATO dissemination. Would that be in 'Franklin's' area at all?"

"You know it would."

"Mm. It *is* a pity! I do so hate operations—all the paraphernalia. The men, the nasty guns, the timing—ugh! It really puts us on the level of the CIA. But I see the necessity. Our little 'mole' is eating up the ground beneath our feet. Our whole NATO Intelligence credibility will be a myth if we don't stop him. And not to mention the French kicking up such a stink because they are thinking of pulling out of NATO—and then making an unholy fuss because our man is giving the Soviets firsthand accounts of the fuss they're making! Really, it is too ridiculous for words—especially since it is only a matter of a few years since the French were busy as bees being penetrated themselves. It really is most unsporting of them not to extend a little sympathy to fellow sufferers. 'Martel' made them put their house in order, and now they want to show the rest of NATO how pure they are by making a moral crusade against us."

Latymer smiled. "We'll get him, Aubrey." He had projected himself, almost without decision, into his work for the moment. It was much easier to take it all seriously when Aubrey was present. In dialogue it had solidity, was in three dimensions.

"I do hope so," Aubrey said. "Otherwise, we shall look such clots, shan't we?"

Latymer got up to go. Aubrey watched him, then seemed to recollect something. As Latymer pushed open the door, he said, "Oh, by the way. I had a little note yesterday, via the usual channels. Richard Gardiner is dead."

"What?"

"Yes. Some kind of accident, I believe. A great pity. He was on holiday, you know, in Brittany." Aubrey shook his head. "Only one thing mars the natural decencies. He's supposed to have killed a man!"

Latymer closed the door and came back into the room suddenly. His face was drained of the liveliness and health induced by Aubrey's bonhomie. He said, sitting down, "Killed a man—who?"

"Ah. Now that is indeed an interesting item." For a moment, before he looked up, Latymer suspected Aubrey of some bizarre lapse of taste. He was wrong. There was a slight smile on Aubrey's lips, but a bewildered pity in his eyes. Probably his voice had imitated the manner in which he had received the news, which must have come from the department which, among its other tasks, monitored the world's newspapers. Aubrey went on. "During the past two days there has been a very apparent loss of newspaper interest in the case."

"Blackout?"

"No more than second-degree—however, interesting all the same."

"We haven't asked for it?"

"Why should we? Gardiner is—*was*—a citizen of the United Kingdom, pursuing his lawful occasions. He hasn't worked for us since 1944."

"Correct. Then why?"

"Don't ask why—ask who?"

"Who?"

"Who did Cock Robin kill—'Achilles' last victim?"

"Who?"

"A waiter at the hotel where he was staying. A certain M'sieur Dupuy. Does that mean anything to you?"

"No. Does it to you?"

"Perhaps. There was an Alfred Dupuy in the 'Ilium' group. His code name was 'Patroclus.' Recall him?"

"The name, yes. I think so—but not the man. Is it the same man, do you think?"

"Name and age fit. I went down to the warehouse to look at the old records. Do you know, old Carstairs is *still* down there, pen poised to await the day he can write the full history of SOE?" Aubrey shook his head. "He looks as dusty as the piles of bumf down there —I wonder if he feeds from the stock?"

"Don't mock those records, Aubrey. Our pasts are in there. . . ." Latymer's face clouded, and he said quickly, "Why did he kill him? They're certain of it —the French police?"

"I haven't checked. Thought I'd have a word with you first. Of course, it's of no interest to us professionally. But I was very fond of Richard, and so were you. Did you keep in touch?"

"For some time—not recently, though. Victoria quarreled with his wife."

Aubrey clicked his tongue as if regretting the inevitable complications women introduced to human life. A bachelor himself, he was suddenly thankful he would not have to face the blank desertion that Latymer would encounter when his wife died.

"I see," he said quietly.

"How did Dupuy die?"

"A cord around the throat, then a swift exit via an upstairs window. One of the tried and trusted methods. A shoelace probably. Oh, there was a gun near the body, and Gardiner stole the contents of the hotel manager's safe, at knifepoint, before he disappeared." There was the shadow of a smile on Aubrey's face, a schoolmaster hearing of a former pupil's success later in life and allowing himself a modicum of self-congratulation for academic groundwork firmly laid.

"It was him then," Latymer said. "But—why the hell . . . ?" Then an idea struck him, mentally winding him for a moment. He said, "Then nineteen years of trying to forget all about it has come to nothing—just because he met Dupuy." He paused, then added, "Dupuy must have been the man who betrayed him. You realize that? The past must have caught up with both of them."

"Poor devils."

"How did Richard die?"

"Oh, making his escape by yacht. He was in a collision with one of those dinner-and-dancing jolly boats—midnight cruise across the bay." Then Aubrey stared at the ceiling, his hands in his pockets. He ignored the cigarette case held out by Latymer, who lit a cigarette. He heard the lighter grate, then the spurt of gas. He saw the bluish smoke drift into sight, rolling under the ceiling.

He said, "What an awful, awful shame. You're quite right, of course. He must have identified Dupuy as one of the men." He sat up suddenly and stared at Latymer, whose eyes seemed to be considering the crease in his trouser leg. He said, "I saw him only the once, you know. After they transferred him to hospital over here. He wouldn't tell me anything about Paris or Rouen. I couldn't even debrief him. It was—quite terrible, the way he seemed determined to forget. He was determined to blot it out. I always wondered what happened. . . ."

"Not that it mattered to us," Latymer observed dryly. "There was never any problem with the Rouen group since it was abandoned as an operational force only a few days after he was run down." His voice hardened. "The little bastard! Why the hell should he run Richard down?"

Aubrey shook his head. "Is his wife back in England?"

"You—think I ought to see her?" Latymer asked, understanding the duty of the moment and experiencing an awkwardness of which he disapproved.

"I think that would be a very good idea—do that, would you?" Then Aubrey shrugged and added, "Now leave me to compose my thoughts, and I'll call you when Deputy arrives." He waved his hand, dismissing Latymer.

Michael Stanhope Constant, as deputy "C" and effective second-in-command of the SIS, was less inclined than ever to conceal his arrogance of mind and temper; he was prepared to enjoy Aubrey's discomfiture and Latymer's sullen silence. The scheme that Aubrey began to propose—neat, logical, and face-saving—irritated him because of its very existence.

He arrived a little after ten, and Latymer was immediately summoned.

Constant was seated in Aubrey's chair, and Aubrey had placed narrow armchairs for himself and Latymer on the other side of the desk. On this occasion, Latymer noted, Aubrey had introduced the sherry bottle, despite the early hour.

Constant, despite an evident reluctance, was impressed by the operation proposed. Unlike Aubrey, who was much more apt to enjoy paperwork and committee-style espionage, Constant relished the flair that a quick mind could bring to a field operation. This piece of saturation surveillance appealed to him, and he applied himself to the details with an alacrity that Latymer had not expected.

"I can divert Lavender," he offered, sipping cat-like at his sherry. He was referring to his compatriot, Deputy C1, whose responsibility was for the oversight and analysis of inbound intelligence, unlike Constant, who as Deputy C2 was operations manager. "It shouldn't be difficult. He and I should have our monthly planning meeting the day before he goes to Paris —I'll have to fall ill, but make the meeting urgent. Then he'll have to stay home. What do you suggest, Aubrey—a little gastritis?"

"I think that would do very nicely, sir," Aubrey replied blandly. Latymer watched him enjoying the encounter with Constant.

"Good. Who else do you suggest?"

"I think—Allom. He's head of Ciphers, and he attends the full senior committee meetings only once or twice a year, even though he is on a couple of the smaller subcommittees. He would have to work hardest to collect as much as our 'mole' seems able to pass."

"Good," Constant said, nodding and finishing his sherry. He put down the crystal glass carefully, in the exact center of the green blotter. "That leaves us with Lidbrooke and Melluish. One of them is to attend the full committee, the other the Eastern Bloc Coordination of Intelligence subcommittee. Yes. Anything juicy to offer them?"

Aubrey said, "I think so—do you want all the details, sir?"

Constant shook his head. "No, I shouldn't think so. Just make it an 'Eyes Only' memo, in retrospect." He linked his fingers behind his head, leaning back in the chair. Though older, he was, remarkably to Latymer, still the man who had unwittingly sent Gardiner to the cellars of the Avenue Foch and to the square in Rouen. With a sudden flood of feeling, Latymer disliked Constant intensely at that moment.

Constant said, "I'm sure that 'C' is most afraid that it's Lavender. He has, of course, the taste of thirties Cambridge, and he was well acquainted with Philby for years. Also, he's not a career intelligence officer. A former Foreign Office special adviser is a suspicious breed in itself." He laughed, a short, barking sound without humor. Aubrey smiled noncommittally. He knew that Constant and Lavender were suspicious of each other and that Constant would be pleased to discover that Lavender was the sought-after double. It would leave him in an unassailable position as inheritor of the office of "C" when Sir Dick White retired.

"Quite," Aubrey remarked. "Very well, Deputy. We'll make it Lavender and Allom to sit this one out. Saturation surveillance on the other two while they're in Paris and after they get back. I take it you'll want to review the matter in . . . ?"

"Give it two weeks. If nothing happens, then we'll try something else for the other two."

"I take it you'll sign the appropriate chitties for phone taps and the like, Deputy?"

"Naturally," Constant replied, his airy tone dissipated. He leaned forward on the desk, elbows resting, arms flat, fingers still linked. "But there must be no slipups, no suspicion by any of the four that we are investigating them. I want this little mess cleared up before it begins to stink."

"I understand, Deputy."

"I hope you do, Aubrey. This is an emergency as far as NATO Intelligence is concerned. The Americans are screaming for action; worse than that, ever since the French put their intelligence service to rights so ruthlessly in the last couple of years, they are quite unbearable!" He paused, then added, "Besides which, we don't want SIS used as the whipping boy if and when the general decides to leave NATO flat!"

When Constant had gone, Aubrey ordered coffee and appeared to relax visibly.

"Well, what do you think of that, Hilary?"

"Of Deputy?"

"Everything—down to the last flicker of his nostrils and the tiniest inflection of his voice. What a masterly performer, eh? He's absolutely wetting himself in the hope that our man is Lavender, who's far more astute than Constant in many ways and is blessedly without his overweening vanity—and might get the top job when 'C' goes to pasture!" Aubrey laughed. "I can see an image of myself in him," he confided. "As I was when I left SOE and came back into this show. You went off to Cambridge for a while. But I had everything worked out, especially an assessment of my own capabilities. Then I worked for eighteen months with Deputy in SO-One, the action gang. By the time that was over I found myself trying to be everything he was not. Consequently, I am very highly thought of, but very rarely promoted!"

Latymer smiled. There was no need to commiserate. Aubrey was a man who had learned contentment with his rank. He said, "Who is your money on, Aubrey?"

Aubrey tucked his thumbs into the pockets of his

waistcoast and leaned back in the chair he had recaptured after Constant's departure.

"Ah, my money? Melluish is the obvious bet—former head of Moscow Station, where he could be easily got at. But he's a very strict and upright man, is Mr. Melluish. A lot of the Scots' nonconformist temperament about him. He might be unable to bear the burden of guilt, which he would undoubtedly contract if he went over to the other side. And he isn't ambitious, uxorious, or homosexual—what did the Russians do to him then? He'd have to be persuaded he was doing *right*." Aubrey shrugged. "Perhaps he has been?" He paused for a moment, then went on. "Lidbrooke—a flashy character, reckless, one might say life-loving. He would think it an awfully good wheeze to work both ends against the middle. As assistant head of SO-One, he would be a good capture—right up at the sharp end. Mm.

"And Mr. Allom, whose wife drinks and whose daughter married a Ghanaian up at Leeds University, having to go through the formalities to legitimize the fruit of forbidden passion. Poor Allom's life is a bloody mess, but he's brilliant and dedicated."

"But he doesn't have the ideological commitment?"

"Do we? No, you can't demand of others loyalties we often wonder about ourselves. He does need money, but as head of Ciphers he ought to be collecting sufficient. After all, I believe his wife drinks only an inferior sort of gin. . . ."

"Then—Lavender?"

"Who can say? As Tungay says of David to Mr. Creakle, 'Nothing known against him—there's been no time'!" He laughed aloud, then said, "All right, let's get this show on the road, as I believe they say at Langley. We'll want a number of Patterson's men for this one—most of the beaters we've used before, I think. They'll be discreet. I'll order them—you get hold of a full schedule of the committee and subcommittee meetings for Thursday."

"What shall I do about Richard Gardiner's wife—widow?"

"What? Oh, get that out of the way as quickly as you can, would you? I'm sorry about Richard, but we have something more important on our plate at the moment." He held the telephone in his hand and looked up from dialing. "I suppose there *is* a certain heady delight connected with action; I feel as if we've been sitting on our bums doing absolutely nothing for weeks!"

Latymer was still smiling as he reached his own office.

The man who had introduced himself to Etienne de Vaugrigard as *l'Etranger* sat at his desk in a small office in the Quai d'Orsay, the French Foreign Ministry, dictating quietly into a tape recorder. The office was one which he had acquired with his official rank in the French civil service. He had another, more anonymous office in his role as a functionary of SDECE, French Intelligence.

The tape was intended as protection, yet even as he moved his lips, he knew it all sounded just as if he were making a speech for the defense or a plea for clemency before a court. Perhaps, he reflected, it was the only way the words would ever emerge. His masters in SDECE had sanctioned his bizarre maverick operation to employ Gardiner, to trigger him by using Dupuy, one of the men who had tried to kill him in 1944. They had not even objected when Dupuy had been killed. . . .

They had agreed to postpone the investigation and undoubted arrest of Etienne de Vaugrigard until the operation was completed—or until it had manifestly failed.

"It was the most fortunate of accidents," he said in the room innocent with midmorning sunlight. The window was open—he could almost smell the river, and the traffic across the great bridge was audible to him; certainly the tang of August dust from the Paris streets was sharp in his nose. "To be told about the 'Wolf' and the 'Wolverine' by a man afraid of his silly little games with the OAS now that they had been found out."

He sighed. It sounded so flat, unconvincing. Not at all like the leap of insight he had made, the daring scheme that had seemed fully armed even as he formed its haziest outlines.

When he spoke again, he said, "Gardiner is now in Rouen, proceeding with his investigation, which will lead him to de Vaugrigard. . . . Of course, de Vaugrigard has been promised protection. . . ." He cursed. His mind was wandering. This was not a progress tape, but something else.

Insurance? Is that what he craved?

Frightened then?

He needed the tape.

"The two men who are our operation targets are dangerous to France, much more dangerous than Etienne could ever have suspected. This operation has been approved despite the current governmental opposition to NATO—it is for the medium term, even the long term, that their removal becomes important. . . ."

Yes, he thought, *it is because of de Gaulle that I have to make the tape.* He shook his head, and the tape whirred on, recording the muffled traffic and the drumming of his fingers on the desk. *Because what I am doing is a kind of—potential treason?*

Stupid.

Etienne knows about treason, he thought savagely. *Twisted sense of loyalty, and Renaud goes to the Avenue Foch, and Gardiner with him. Twisted again, and he supplies the OAS with money and guns to fight back at de Gaulle, hero turned traitor. . . .*

If France withdraws from NATO? He wondered whether he had voiced the thought and made as if to rewind the tape, then relaxed in his chair, smiling.

"If France withdraws from NATO and stays out, then this operation will be disapproved by my masters, even disowned. Which is why I am making you, little spool, bear such heavy and such unconnected thoughts."

The tape next picked up the sound of his laughter. In the smaller outer office an assistant looked up from a sheaf of papers, winked at another young man, and went back to his work.

Gardiner's house was a converted mill. Once inside, however, the conversion left Latymer with no sense of its past occupation. A modern coolness, even sterility, possessed the long lounge on the first floor, its windows overlooking the Dorset countryside. He was assailed by an almost feminine intuition that it was a room in which Richard Gardiner had ceased to live a long time before.

Apple-green carpet, brown-covered suite, low tables—a room waiting for occasions. He felt almost as if he were attending Gardiner's funeral in a tasteless modern funeral parlor and half expected piped hymns to issue from the walls or the hi-fi equipment on the uncluttered shelving.

Jane Gardiner was self-possessed about the meeting. She seemed indifferent to his initial murmurings, waving him to a seat. The view was suddenly behind him, and the room became more arctic than before. Jane sat opposite him, on the other side of a low table, smoothing her narrow green dress over her knees. It was silk, Latymer thought. She was dressed to advantage, and he disliked her for that.

"It—came as such a shock," he asserted diffidently, possessed by awkwardness.

"Yes," she said. "Would you like coffee?"

He was about to refuse; he wanted to be rid of her for a moment, while his preconceptions adjusted or were buried. He nodded.

"Thank you."

She was little more than a few minutes. He stood up, looked out the window, despising her, but having the innate justice to sense that he had prescribed a role for her which she could not have supported; even had she appeared as the tearful and repentant wife, he would have suspected the honesty of the portrait. He slouched before the picture window, hands in pockets, as if asserting some role within himself.

Jane Gardiner wasn't a likable woman. Victoria had said that, and imperious as she was, she was warm toward people at first. One had to rebuff or rebuke Victoria to earn her poor opinion.

He did not want to think about his wife, not even

her opinions, and shrugged her away, concentrating on the carpet and white walls, their history smoothed out by plasterers, until his hostess came back with the instant coffee.

Almost the instant she was seated she said, "Why have you come here, Hilary?"

He looked up at her, putting down the cup. Coffee tickled in his nose from the little splutter of surprise. Her face was raw with challenge, the eyes alight. So she must have faced Gardiner often, he thought.

"I wanted to pay my respects. No, that sounds too pompous. I wanted to know whether you were all right."

"Thank you for that."

"I'm sorry. I sense I'm intruding."

"Perhaps. I don't suppose you mean to. Not many people have called, you know. Richard's stuffy partners, one or two of his boating acquaintances—they probably came for the drink or a description of how he went down with colors flying while the band played. . . ."

She seemed to cut herself off with an effort. She looked self-betrayed. Latymer was surprised at the intensity of his dislike.

"I see."

"Do you? You're one of his friends, of course. I'm wearing my armor visibly this year. You know, of course, that I was having another of my interminable, incessant affairs at the very moment he died. Yes?" Latymer shook his head. "You don't seem very well informed, Hilary. I'm surprised. But I won't bore you with the details. I don't suppose it will surprise you, any more than it would surprise Richard's other friends. Some of whom would welcome the opportunity of replacing him between his sheets. . . ."

It was said without arrogance or self-compliment. Latymer stared at her, his milky coffee growing a skin, as if willing her to reveal a weakness in the hard mask, some gleam of emotion behind the self-possession. Perhaps so that he could sympathize with her. . . .

"I—knew, of course, that Richard and you were not happy together. . . ."

"Not quite true. We enjoyed some of our quarrels. However, Hilary, that isn't your concern."

"No."

"What is?"

"Just——making the gesture, I suppose."

"Ah." She seemed pleased by his honesty, as if a schoolmistress whose pupil had recited something well learned.

"That's about it, isn't it?" he said suddenly. "You and I, not really giving much of a damn."

"Perhaps."

"Can I be of practical help, then, in his affairs, money, the boys . . . ?"

"Arthur Hebden, the senior partner—he's taking care of the business side of things. The boys are with my mother in Cheltenham. They'll be going back to school early this term; there's an arrangement in cases like mine—no, I don't think there is much for you to do, Hilary."

"You'll stay on here?"

"It's mine now. And Richard was heavily insured."

She seemed determined to present nothing of softness, nothing he might catch hold of, regard as *proper*. He wondered how hard she really was, what had attracted Richard Gardiner in the first place. She might well be that hard, that withdrawn. Gardiner could be like that; like to like?

"You'll be comfortable then?"

"Thank you, yes."

He no longer wanted the coffee, which had cooled. She seemed pleased at his confusion. He said, because he could not get up and leave at that moment, having made such little impression on her, "What exactly happened? Can you tell me?"

"Professional interest?"

"I don't know, to be honest. What about the man he is supposed to have killed?"

"I never knew anything of that. The French police asked me about him—I could tell them nothing. They told me that he was a wartime acquaintance. Something to do with that part of Richard's life."

"This was Dupuy?"

"I think that was the name—yes."

"You know that Richard was betrayed—tortured.

Then someone apparently tried to have him removed altogether. . . ."

"Something of it. He never talked about it. He dreamed about it sometimes—but he'd never talk about it in the mornings. I stopped inquiring a long time ago."

"Yes. This man was a waiter at the hotel?"

"Apparently."

"Why did Richard go to meet him?"

"I've no idea. Auld lang syne?"

"Perhaps."

Latymer was soothed by being obliquely in control of the conversation now; it was a professional inquiry, mere routine. Broken bones of emotion and hostility no longer stuck up through lacerated skin. Smooth. Like the walls, behind which the rough mill still existed.

"He robbed the safe and stole a boat. Was he a good sailor?"

"Yes—at least, he should have been. He spent enough time in the last four or five years with the boat he bought. Which I shall now be selling, naturally."

"What was the weather like that night?" He asked the question because his mind had suited itself to familiar grooves. A logical progression, in one way.

For a moment recollected pleasure. But unshared with Gardiner.

"Fine—a lovely summer night."

"Where were you at the time?" He felt himself being distracted; something else, he had meant to ask something else. But she created emotions in him that got in the way. With her lover. . . .

"I was on board. Isn't that rich? I wonder the French police didn't suggest I bribed the captain—" The eyes challenged him, daring him to condemn her.

"No, not that—say what you said again. A fine summer night, was that it?"

"Yes."

"The boat? Was your boat illuminated?"

"Of course. A pleasure cruise. . . ." She smiled, almost to taunt. *Pleasure.* . . .

"Was there a wind?"

"None. We—were on deck. A calm night." She seemed seized by something that would reassert control, shock him. "I didn't even see his boat, didn't hear anything until it was all over. Just a slight tremor in the deck. . . . And it was over."

Reactions flooded Latymer's awareness, but he rejected the mess of information.

"He was a good sailor. You said. . . . Did he want to die?"

"I—hadn't thought of that." She considered. "Perhaps. He had killed a man. He was strange that evening, as if drawn up tight in himself. . . . I don't know."

Latymer wanted to get out then. Quickly. The woman confused him. He saw, in a moment, that it was all an act: the hardness, the glinting armor of unfeeling—nothing like the truth. But he did not have time to spare on her now. He said, getting up, "If there's anything I can do—at any time. . . ."

She stood up.

"Of course."

They knew that they would not meet again. She smoothed her dress over her hips, formalities over.

He went down the stairs, and she let him out. She took his proffered hand, lightly and without meaning, and then the door was closed behind him. He got into his car, sat for a moment, excitement welling in him. Then he started the car and drove off. Unaware that she was watching him from the picture window, his cold coffee gray in the delicate cup she held in her hands.

Latymer rang Aubrey from a public call box outside Dorchester. When he was put through, the excitement in his voice was evident.

"I've just spoken to Jane Gardiner. Richard is supposed to have collided with a cruise yacht illuminated like a Christmas tree on a fine night in a calm sea. Do you realize what this means, Aubrey? Richard's still alive. He just wants everyone to think he's dead. I'll stake my life on it!"

2

THE ANGER
OF "ACHILLES"

We shall not cease from exploration
And the end of our exploring
Will be to arrive where we started
And know the place for the first time.

—T. S. ELIOT, "Little Gidding," V

Thus the high born son of Priam pleaded for mercy with Achilles. But there was no mercy in the voice that answered him. "You fool," he heard Achilles say, "do not talk to me of ransom: I wish to hear no more speeches. Before Patroclus met his end, I was not disinclined to spare the Trojans ... But now not a single man whom God brings into my hands . . . is going to live; and that holds good for every Trojan who lives. . . . Yes, my friend, you too must die. Why make such a song about it? Even Patroclus died, who was a better man than you by far.

—HOMER, *The Iliad*, Book 21
(translated by E. V. RIEU)

5. French Connections

L'Etranger picked up the secure telephone on his desk, in response to his secretary's instruction, and listened to the code identification at the other end.

"I see. Your men are in place? You have briefed the Grodin woman—what was her reaction?"

"Truculent—bloody-minded. But she'll do as she's told."

"Can she act the part well enough?"

"Tough as nails. She'll do. I wouldn't like to have met her on a dark night around 1942—at least, not wearing field gray." There was a chuckle at the other end of the line.

"Where is Gardiner?"

"Hôtel de St. Ouen—one of the shadows is booked there, just in case."

"Good. I've spoken to the local inspector. No questions to be asked. I must admit, I'm pleased with the way in which Gardiner dealt with his identity and his disappearance from La Baule."

"Clever bastard, isn't he?"

"He is. I'm beginning to respect him more and more. As soon as he's been to see Grodin, you check back with her, then get to Paris as soon as you can—take over here."

"Sure, Chief. See you."

L'Etranger put down the telephone and opened a drawer in his desk. Time to commit a little more to tape. He smiled. Gardiner was a man one could easily admire; in doing so, he was aware of admiring his own brilliance of mind.

He pressed the record button.

The Hôtel de St. Ouen in Rouen in the rue de l'Hôpital was situated on the right bank of the Seine. Richard Gardiner stood looking from the tall, narrow window of his third-floor room, obliquely along the street toward the cold, uninspiring facade of the Church of St. Ouen, a nineteenth-century addition that appeared to him as the work of some clumsy plasterer, hiding a mosaic or a frieze. He was smoking a cigarette after eating breakfast in the dining room and preparing himself for his visit to Vivienne Grodin, still living at the farm in the Seine Valley west of the town, one of the wartime headquarters of the "Ilium" group. As her father's only child she was now the owner. The old man had been dead for many years, and Gardiner was glad of it. The old man was strangely sacrosanct in memory.

He had driven out to the fruit farm in the car he had hired in the name of Jacques Remy, whose face stared muzzily back at him from the *carte d'identité* he was currently using. Remy was a fictitious character, but his face was the face of a man he had seen on the Paris metro and whose wallet he had stolen in the rush-hour crowds. It was a simple matter to alter the typed details so that they applied to his alias, but he was unable to alter the photograph with its embossed stamp crossing one corner. Therefore, all the men whose *cartes* he had acquired appeared much as he did himself. For Remy, he had grown a mustache which altered the shape of the mouth, and his hair was a little darker. He had found on those occasions when he had used the *carte* that close scrutiny was entirely absent. The man in the carhire office had had to be pressed to do more than glance at the khaki fold of pasteboard in Gardiner's hand.

Gardiner thought about Vivienne Grodin. She

had once been the mistress of Renaud, who had died in the Avenue Foch; once Gardiner had been her perfunctory lover. Yet she had relatives in the group. He was uncertain of her reaction to any request for information. He recalled her as a girl of twenty-two; she had been tough with the slow, definite toughness of her peasant background. She had taken orders, chosen the men she slept with, and developed a capacity for independent thought and action. It was that last quality that threatened the smooth progress of his plans. She was capable of proving an ally or an opponent.

During the days in the scruffy pension on the Left Bank, after his hours of haunting the metro for faces that resembled his own—a grotesque, nightmarish journey it had seemed at times—he had begun to limit the horizons of his revenge. A crazed capacity and desire for violence had come to him in the aftermath of Dupuy's death—he understood how easy it would have been to kill the little hotel manager or anyone who might have challenged him at the St. Nazaire station; now that had abated and burned with a colder, more regulated flame. He wanted Perrier now, the other man in the Renault that had broken his body like matchwood, and the man who had given the order for his death. They would suffice.

It had to be justified revenge and the sense of something left unfinished. In these terms, he disguised his nature from himself.

The cigarette burned his fingers, and he smelled the coffee from a shop across the street as his senses re-awoke. He would accept the risk. He had to talk to Vivienne Grodin, and he did not think she would know about Depuy.

"Au 'voir, M'sieur Remy." He passed the clerk and was smiling by the time he stepped onto the pavement outside the hotel. The smell of coffee was stronger—he could see the roaster rotating in the window of the shop-cum-café. There was a pleasing atmosphere of unhurried tourism in the street. The traffic was light, and in the shadows on that side of

the rue de l'Hôpital there was retained the illusion of early-morning freshness. The water from the cleansing cart was still evident in the damp patches on the pavement.

He drove out of the town, following the D 51 as it threaded its path through the industrial suburbs along the right bank of the Seine. Then scrubbed residential developments, hotter it seemed than the old town, dry and dusty with use. Traffic increased. Factory chimneys thrust into a sky already becoming hazy and colorless, and his attention was retained only by his recognition of change. It was somehow unpleasant, the admission that something loved had changed; a body, known and explored, changed by some accident, broken and put together differently. There was no sense of the irony of his part in the destruction. It was Allied bombers that had done the damage.

He passed through Croisset, then Val-de-la-Haye, where Napoleon's body had rested on its journey from St. Helena to Paris. He recalled members of the group who had begun by hardly noticing the place, especially the column to commemorate the event, but whose need for such a tangible evidence of their country's credibility had deepened through 1941 and 1942 until the village had come to possess an almost talismanic effect upon them.

The slopes on which the fruit trees clung were right against the road as it followed the Seine, on the edge of the forêt de Roumare, in a clasping loop of the river. He turned off the main road, and climbed toward the farm—white-washed, red-roofed, tiny above the valley slope, enlarging to human dimensions as the car ascended the rutted, dusty farm track. He inspected his feelings and sensed the ruts of the road beneath his feet or through the jolts of a bicycle saddle. He smiled.

It was no homecoming, but the farm still possessed some of its elemental power suggestive of rest and safety, even of the quick, necessary encounters with Vivienne in the hayloft. Neither he nor any others of the group had ever brought outsiders to the farm. He had lived for several months in the house itself; he could visualize it, knowing that it would not have changed significantly. It had become his head-quarters in February 1943, a season of iron ruts in the road and thick rime on posts and fences and pasture—bare trees. He had moved into Rouen itself in 1944. Yet it had always continued to function as an important staging post for drops and later for the small, single-engine, high-winged Lysanders to land or as a hideout for members of the group when the Rouen Gestapo performed one of their periodic, ritual acts of cleansing in the old town.

He parked the car outside the gate. Through the heavy, laden greenness of fruit trees he could see the farmhouse. He passed through the gate and thought about Dupuy, but only now in his identity as "Patroclus," the boy who had hero-worshiped "Achilles." There was a sudden sadness as he remembered a conversation with the boy as he tried to explain what had happened to his father and mother.

It was not that Gardiner would have turned back at that point. In fact, he pressed the thoughts down, expunging the memory which had been evoked as he crossed the orchard, the grass rustling around his shoes, the pink rump of a pig disappearing behind a tree; they had chased a pig once, he and the boy and even Perrier, and dressed it in a captured German uniform as much as they could. Then they had tied it to an apple tree and marched past it, arms outstretched in the Nazi salute. The boy had tried to paint a swastika on the pig's rump. . . .

He shunned his memories, sensing their power, the freedom with which they moved here in their own element. His shoes scuffed on the dusty track. He knocked on the door.

For a moment he did not recognize her. She had never been beautiful—thin-faced, dark-eyed, a long nose. She had put on weight now, ample breasts swelling beneath the black dress. She dressed in an almost forgotten style. She might even be married, though her name was still her father's name, so they had said in the village. She greeted him, and the voice still belonged to Vivienne. He said, "You don't remember then?"

A slow recognition, dismissed. She said, "Can I help you, m'sieur?"

Gardiner watched the mouth open into a round hole, and the eyes fill with something akin to fear. There was a delay of recognition. She had to see beyond the new mustache, then adjust to the past to provide his proper context.

"Vivienne," he said warmly, preparing his role carefully. He smiled as he might have done had he really been only a visitor, his object mere nostalgia.

" 'Achilles'. . . ?"

He nodded. He watched her face intently. It seemed for a moment as if she had expected him, but not at that moment; then she held out her arms and took his hands firmly. He dismissed the idea as a mistake. He laughed—there was, surprisingly, a genuine pleasure, something come back out of the past that was not unclean or violent. It was not love, but something like the camaraderie of the past, of living together at the extremes of experience. It was good to see her.

"Vivienne!" He kissed her cheek, tasting the face powder as something strange that he did not associate with her, feeling the roughness of the skin.

"What are you doing here—Richard?" She struggled with his name. "Richard."

"I'm on holiday!" he said with conviction. The role was easy to play; he wished to play it. He would count the cost of using her, making her betray confidences and men's lives, later. This had to be done in this way, as if to compensate for spending the last year of the war in hospitals and for not having come back before this. He added, "Touring! I left my wife and children in Rouen and came out to see you." She was still holding his right hand, and he felt a tremor run through her which he assumed was shock or relief. She led him into the big living room of the farmhouse.

It was as he remembered it. The old furniture, heavy and graceless and highly polished, the deal table scarred with work, the stone floor partially covered with dark faded rugs and pieces of carpet. She said, "It—it has been so long!" She motioned him to a chair at the table. "Sit down—coffee?" He nodded, taking in the room still. Its contours reestablished their old familiarity. It *was* pleasant; as long as he continued to behave as he had, it would not be awkward or dirty.

He watched her move toward the kitchen with the slight sway of a big woman, the economical slither of someone used to labor that continued from birth to death. He called out, looking at his soft hands, "You're not married then?"

"No!" she called back. A moment's hesitation; then she laughed. It was as if she, too, were relearning an old role. "Who would have me? All the men in this area know I used to kill Germans for a living— who would not be frightened?"

He laughed.

When she brought in the coffee and sat down, her face was more open, the sharp eyes softer, more humored. They talked—only moments of awkwardness while she inquired tentatively after his injuries in 1944; then recollection achieved its own momentum. They talked through the remainder of the morning, until she prepared a lunch of bread and cheese. There was a bottle of young, strong wine, and he understood that it, too, was in tribute to the past. Only one part of his mind stayed alive to his purpose, and he was satisfied that she had had nothing to do with his betrayal. Then he relaxed. There was no need to point the conversation; it would arrive at the necessary destination, given time.

The bread was fresh and warm, sticking to his palate so that it had to be washed down with the wine. He watched her, just as she watched him. She spoke of her sister, Marie, who had married Georges from the café in Hautot-sur-Seine, a couple of kilometers away—Georges he remembered, surely? He nodded, smiling, and raised his glass—it had been tin or enamel mugs before.

Sunlight spilled into the room through the small

windows. The shadow of a man, looking out across the orchard from beside one of these windows, flickered in his mind for a moment. As if it reminded him, he settled to the less pleasant work of memory.

"What about the others?" he prompted. "How many of them still live near here?"

"You want to see them?" she said quickly. He shook his head.

"No, just idle curiosity. What about 'Patroclus' or 'Nestor'—how are they? Do you hear from them?" He asked the question lightly, looking at the last of the wine in his glass, swilling it idly around.

"No. . . ." One eye had watched her face. Dupuy's code name had caused a tightening of the skin around the mouth, but nothing in the eyes.

"Not 'Nestor'—I suppose he went back to Paris . . . ?"

There was a moment of silence; then she said with a mechanical lack of inflection, "Yes—we heard from him, Marie and me, once or twice. He had begun a small business, fruit, I think, because he said it had been the farm that had given him the idea."

He nodded.

"My family and I are thinking of ending our holiday in Paris—you wouldn't have an address for him, I suppose?"

"I—I don't think so. . . . I can't really remember. Perhaps it was on the Left Bank, and he was very proud of the shop because it had his name above it. There was a photograph of him standing outside, showing the sign. François was very pleased with himself, and already putting on weight!" The laughter was not quite real. He nodded.

The moment was past now, and he concentrated on disguising any tracks he might have made toward the information. They talked for perhaps another hour before he left, and both of them seemed more relaxed. When they parted, he kissed her on both cheeks, and she returned the light pecks firmly. They had never spoken of their relationship, a part of their mutual past that had slipped over memory's horizon. He waved to her through the trees as he reached the gate.

When he was gone and she could no longer hear the car, she collapsed in her chair and laid her head on the table, her cheek quivering against the rough wood. Her mouth worked in a hysterical, silent relief, and her eyes were wide as if she were witnessing some horror.

She had performed the task appointed to her. She did not know how well, but she had done it. And she knew, without doubt, she had sentenced François Perrier to death.

The man who had come to see her a month ago had told her everything. She did not know him, and he did not give his name—but there was the insidious, insistent recognition that he was French Intelligence. She could not be sure, of course, because she had seen no papers, but she knew. The task he had given, and the understanding that she had no real alternative, had made everything simple and naked. Only in a moral sense was it appalling.

Perrier had betrayed Gardiner. Gardiner would come, looking for Perrier. She was to point Gardiner toward Paris and Perrier's shop. She had been horrified, even twenty years after, at the bald narrative of duplicity and betrayal. When Gardiner had indeed come, she had inhabited a little room of fear inside her own room until he had asked, and she had told. Then she wanted him gone, because he appeared still as he had been before, her leader from the old days, softened a little by time and affluence.

Even now, with her head against the rough, comforting wood, she thought with pain of the memories he had brought back, as if he had known she was betraying him.

It was a long time before she went slowly back to her tasks, and the two men, father and son, who worked for her went unnoticed until they finished their day's work. She tried to learn the art of forgetfulness—but his face was still vivid to her when the man came to speak to her in the evening. It was not the same man who had rehearsed her in what to say. This man, paunchy and with vivid eyes closed in lines of fat, asked her about her conversation with Gardiner and seemed satisfied with her replies. When he had gone, she realized she could begin to forget.

Later that evening she went to visit her married sister. She did not mention "Achilles."

Aubrey had set up his Paris headquarters in an apartment leased by the embassy in the rue de Castellane which lay between the Madeleine and the Boulevard Haussmann. He went no nearer the embassy than that, though it was close, in the Faubourg St. Honoré. Both Lidbrooke and Melluish would use the embassy facilities during their stay in Paris, and he had no wish to meet them by accident in a corridor of the building. By the same token, he intended avoiding the NATO building.

Latymer had brought with him the files he had drawn from the warehouse in London and which related to the "Ilium" group.

Now, sitting in the apartment, he had made his decisions. Aubrey could run Operation Guesswork, and he would try to trace Gardiner. Both he and Aubrey owed enough to Richard to try to stop him from what Latymer knew he must be planning. In Latymer, there was a puritanical streak, narrow but evident. He was a civilized man, and he believed in the wrongness of Gardiner's actions; Dupuy might have been self-defense, and Gardiner was still not over the edge of the flat moral earth. Latymer might yet save him.

He did not consider his motives too deeply. He left them at the bottom of his consciousness. They were confused and muddy, and he decided, though normally fastidious in self-analysis, to let them be.

When Aubrey returned from his initial briefing of the Beaters, stationed in an empty warehouse near Les Halles and owned by the embassy through an extended lease—Latymer never remembered the address—Latymer said to him with an assumed blandness, realizing as he did so the imperative nagging at his stomach, "I want you to give me a certain freedom of action for a few days, Aubrey."

Aubrey, helping himself to a midday sherry, inspected the label on the bottle, recognized the firm with the current FO contract for "Embassy Victualling, Wines and Spirits," and seemed satisfied. Then he turned his head and smiled quizzically.

"Yes?" he said. "I thought you were keen to come in on this affair?"

"I was. But not to see it through."

Aubrey sat down opposite Latymer, silently raised his glass, and said, "Oh. Don't tell me you only came for the nightlife. I shall be disappointed."

Latymer shook his head. The nerves seemed to be tapping at his stomach like cold fingers.

"I want to look for Richard Gardiner."

Aubrey seemed unsurprised, and his head wobbled like that of a small bird eating and as if in some kind of compact with Latymer. Nevertheless, Latymer uncomfortably sensed that Aubrey understood something about him that he had not wished revealed. Aubrey said, "I don't quite see things with your moral squint, Hilary. But I suppose there *is* an obligation. . . ." He sipped at the sherry. "We sent him to Paris in the first place." He appeared to be talking to the ceiling. "I don't understand it after all this time—Richard is a reasonable man!" He was almost pleading.

"But we can both deduce what he's planning," Latymer said heavily. The flutter in his stomach had hardened into a ball. It was as if he had been frightened that Aubrey would forbid him. Now that did not seem likely.

"Yes." The sunlight from the long window spilled onto the shoulder of Aubrey's gray suit as he moved in his chair, focusing his attention on Latymer. Once again the sharp, appraising stare, the tiny nod of acceptance, then: "Yes, I suppose we do owe it to him, to try to stop it." Then he burst out, the patch of sunlight sliding across his chest as he moved, "But it was nineteen years ago . . . ! Damn it, why can't he forget?"

"He's been forced to remember it all again. Nineteen years wiped out for him. He can't forgive that." Aubrey looked sharply and nodded. "We both know what kind of man he is." Latymer could not suppress a shudder. "Richard was not a—*kind* man. . . ." The phrase was hopelessly inadequate.

As if embarrassed, Aubrey said, "Do you think that the last nineteen years have been a kind of fiction for him then?"

"I don't know. I don't think so. He was trying to adjust. Did it. But something's come back from the dead now, and it isn't interested in being a county town solicitor any longer!"

"I suppose you're right. Where will you begin?"

"Rouen, I think. Then here in Paris, with Etienne de Vaugrigard—he might perhaps know where the rest of the group is now."

"Very well. I'll run Guesswork from here. Everything's staked out, and you're not really needed. I wonder whether I'm not letting you go on this thing just to spite Constant . . . ? But I can't spare you any help."

"I understand." Latymer's eyes suddenly blazed. "I can understand it, you know, Aubrey! I can understand, dimly, the power of the past over Richard Gardiner. It has the satisfying element of mystery, and it's tied up with the people we once were. It's an escape, you know. For him and me."

"Mm. Do you think he *prefers* being the man he was?"

"Perhaps he does. He—amounted to something then."

"Yes. But what hope have you of finding who was responsible for what happened to him?"

"I don't know. But Richard doesn't know either perhaps. Not yet. If I can get to him first. . . . He'll have gone to Rouen or to de Vaugrigard, I think. I'll try both." His hand rubbed his thigh. "I just don't know *who*. . . . He was one of the most successful leaders we ever imposed upon a group. He wasn't material for betrayal."

"I wish you luck. Sincere good fortune." Aubrey looked at his watch. "I should think the first session of the Senior Joint Intelligence Committee has adjourned for lunch by now, and I suggest we do the same. Jorgensen will bring up 'Snowshoe' this afternoon. . . ." He smiled. "There'll be opportunity for our man to bring the subject up this evening. There's an informal cocktail party for the chairman. He's being posted back to Washington."

"Van Lederer's done a good job," Latymer remarked idly, standing up and putting on his jacket. "Whither General Eugene Van Lederer? Saigon?"

"I shouldn't be at all surprised. Come, let's eat, Hilary. I have reserved a table at a little place I know. . . ." Latymer smiled, content in some strange way, and allowed himself to be ushered out of the apartment.

Lieutenant Colonel Nils Jorgensen of Norwegian Army Intelligence ate his salad lunch slowly. He was not partial to the heavy, oily dressing, but it was not the food alone that failed to please. It was the memory of that house in Fulham and the little man he had known in wartime Intelligence, Aubrey, that robbed him of appetite. It had been two days ago when they had concocted "Exercise Snowshoe," a fake term for a fake operation in the Finnmark the previous winter, around Vadso and the Veranger Fjord. The details were sketchy, but even the summary, which would be all expected of him that afternoon, was explosive. "Snowshoe" was the name supposedly given to the training of British SAS officers and men in arctic conditions, including secret night landings from a nuclear submarine and sabotage of radar and naval installations. The exercise was supposed to have prepared a small force for long-range penetration down the Finnish border, even into the Kola Peninsula as far as Murmansk—in time of war. The training had taken place inside the agreed limit between Norway and the Soviet Union forbidden to foreign troops.

In his general report to the committee, Jorgensen would introduce this bombshell. Since the operation did not exist, the Russians could not know of it. And if there was a "mole" on the committee, then it was too fat and tempting a grub not to be digested, stored, and regurgitated for the information and use of Moscow Center. With reluctant admiration, Jorgensen admitted that Aubrey had provided a very tempting meal.

Which did not make the whole thing any more palatable. It merely made Jorgensen, who had spent most of the war in the Norwegian mountains as a member of the Resistance, long for past simplicities and an enemy as declared as the invading Nazis.

He ate slowly, and his conversation with those around him in the fourth-floor dining room of the NATO building was desultory. He was a normally reticent man whom they respected, and his behavior was neither misinterpreted nor condemned.

He was glad not to be sitting near either Lidbrooke or Melluish.

Latymer, though surprised at the lack of hesitation in Aubrey's acquiescence, suffered the small waiting time with impatience. A sequence of routine procedures resulted in a telephone call to Etienne de Vaugrigard, whom he had known with some little intimacy during the war and had met some three times since. He was invited to dinner. The family had just returned from their holiday at Deauville, where Etienne owned a small villa. They would be delighted to see him—eight o'clock, black tie. Latymer smiled at the continuation of Etienne's stiff formality. He had never been able to *like* de Vaugrigard; even as a young man he had possessed an arrogant, unyielding temper and a stiffness of bearing. Like the general he had idolized. Growing older, and the phenomenal success of his business, had not softened him.

He provided himself next with a telephone directory of the Rouen area. He checked with the local police that the Vivienne Grodin shown in it was the woman he remembered and decided that if de Vaugrigard were unable to help him, he would take a train or hire car to Rouen the following day.

In midafternoon Hawthorne from the embassy called in at the apartment, bringing a report from the London end of Guesswork. It stated that none of the likely contacts for the "mole" had left the city. A close surveillance of the Soviet and other likely East European embassies was being maintained. It was as much as Aubrey had anticipated. The contact was in Paris.

While he waited for Aubrey to return from the warehouse in Les Halles, Latymer worked his way through the Paris telephone directory, attempting to match names with people in the files of the "Ilium" group—and regretting that from the faded text of the files the past had risen like smoke. A fire was burning, and its name was Gardiner.

From time to time he remembered Aubrey's words about the "mole," and they seemed to apply equally to Gardiner. He had said, "This one, if he feels threatened or cut off, will do the maximum damage possible before we catch up with him and put him down. He'll know that we won't arrest him, or make his treason public. . . . He could do anything—anything at all!"

The cocktail party began early. Most of the afternoon session had been taken up by Jorgensen and "Snowshoe." Its announcement had been greeted with shocked silence, then vivid and vocal disbelief. It was a hard-line exercise, so many of the security delegates said. The committee was baffled as to its usefulness, troubled by its anti-Soviet blatancy, and intrigued to know more. Jorgensen felt more and more that Aubrey had placed him in a most unfavorable light and regretted the involvement of his country, through himself, in such a ridiculous deception. If the Russians made a formal complaint or took some kind of covert action . . . ?

He defended his position in as tight-lipped a manner as was possible, implicating the United Kingdom as Aubrey desired, and then, squeezing his lips into a bloodless line and folding his arms, he refused to say more.

The smaller groups at the cocktail party were obviously still considering the implications of a military exercise by British troops in the north of Norway as Jorgensen waited for someone to approach him on the subject more directly. If Aubrey's "mole" was present, he could not afford to pass up the opportunity.

There was a general bonhomie to which each man responded as the drinks flowed. They were saying farewell to a chairman each of them respected, U.S.

Army Intelligence General Van Lederer—a big man with heavy features, a straightforward lack of tact and nicety that made him an efficient chairman of committee, and a blunt respect for the men who had served with him.

When he spoke to Jorgensen during his circulation of the groups in the room, a large bourbon in his hand, he was intrigued, and the gray eyes gleamed—but he seemed intrigued by Jorgensen's reticence as much as by the information he had imparted. He said, "Hell—I don't know what the British are up to with that crazy sort of provocation. What if the Russians found out?" He swallowed at his drink, smacked his lips, and added, "Hell, they ought to get rid of this post facto clause in the rules of this committee. We should've cleared something like 'Snowshoe' before it got off the ground or sat on it. Who cleared it, I wonder? Our two British friends don't know a thing about it, not by the surprised faces they put on this afternoon!"

"Quite," Jorgensen murmured as the general passed on to another group. "I knew nothing of it myself until recently," he added with a sour attempt at a smile.

Jean-Jacques Haussman, the senior SDECE member of the full committee, watched Colonel Jorgensen carefully for perhaps ten minutes after he had finished his conversation with Van Lederer. He thought he understood what was happening. For that reason he watched the two Englishmen carefully, without appearing to distract himself from the conversation with Helvigsson, the Icelander, and Protti of Italian Military Intelligence. He considered Jorgensen's performance as having the slightest air of unreality, especially now that he appeared to avoid conversation, as if waiting for a chosen partner. Lidbrooke or Melluish, Haussman thought. And that meant a British "ferret" operation; "Snowshoe" was a blind, concocted probably by Aubrey to smoke out the "mole." Which would explain why the other two, Lavender and Allom, were not present. Two at a time.

He was certain that Lidbrooke and Melluish, like the rest of the committee, had been taken in. It was only because he had spent most of his postwar career in the counter-intelligence section of the SDECE and was trained to a pitch of concentration on human beings that he suspected anything. Having interrogated perhaps thousands of men and women, he knew the signs of a lie.

It was perhaps an hour later when Lidbrooke approached Jorgensen. It was the moment the Norwegian had been waiting for, yet when it came, it was a surprise, and he experienced a watery feeling of nausea in his stomach and a vague, infinite regret. He had to concentrate very carefully on the tone of his voice and the stance of his body to avoid giving himself away. Lidbrooke, after the introductory pleasantries, said, "God, Nils—that was a bloody bombshell you dropped this afternoon! I almost wet myself at the idea . . . !"

Jorgensen managed a small, weak smile and rubbed his forehead, mumbling something about feeling hot and perhaps opening the windows a little wider. Lidbrooke, smiling sympathetically, adopted a conspiratorial look.

"You know, they're not supposed to do things like that?"

"Who?" Jorgensen said abruptly.

"The SAS—and my masters. I'm supposed to know about things like that—you know my position, Nils. Don't you think I ought to have been told about this lunatic thing?" Jorgensen nodded. "Who sanctioned it, Nils? Have you any idea who thought it up?"

Jorgensen shook his head and said, "I don't, Derek. I was given a summary of the material, all names removed, and told to pass it on to the full committee. It had just been downgraded for dissemination by our security chiefs." Jorgensen found himself suddenly calm. He was playing a role he had practiced, and that had a certain narcotic effect. Also, he was beginning to enjoy the baiting of Lidbrooke, was able to think of him as a discovered double agent. He studied the green eyes, the fair hair which curled over the collar of the suit; the slightly flashy clothes included a wide-striped shirt and a yellow tie.

He knew that Lidbrooke was a flamboyant operator—a very successful field agent. Jorgensen knew his power as assistant head of SO-1.

The slight smile on his face seemed further to incite Lidbrooke's curiosity, and he said, "You can't tell me anything, Nils—just between ourselves?"

Jorgensen could sense the urgency of the man but could not be certain of its cause, anger or treachery. He shook his head.

Lidbrooke added, "Well, I'm going to make a right bloody stink about this when I get back to London. I'll take it to the top, if necessary. Bloody fools, living in the romantic after-shave of imperialism! Who the hell are we to go pissing about up in the Finnmark with SAS men and a nuclear sub? Christ! What a mess it could have been! Do we know whether or not the Russians know?" Again Jorgensen shook his head. "Bloody fools!" Lidbrooke snapped again, then downed the remainder of his drink in a single gulp.

When he wandered away, Jorgensen saw him in earnest conversation with Melluish, who seemed to be on the end of a verbal outburst similar to the one he had borne. He shook his head and wished Aubrey luck. Lidbrooke's interest might be professional or sprung from a dented ego.

Jean-Jacques Haussman watched the exchange between Jorgensen and Lidbrooke with interest. He, too, privately wished Aubrey luck—and looming behind his private wishes was the growing anger, self-righteous and even unreasonable, of the Quai d'Orsay, the SDECE, and even the Elysée, at the reports reaching the Russians from the center of NATO. Lidbrooke, he concluded, had taken the bait, hook and all.

Etienne de Vaugrigard had always regarded his mistress's apartment in the Faubourg St. Honoré with a certain clandestine excitement. It was not so much that it contained the secret sexual part of his life, the young woman elevated from the offices of Air France on the Champs Elysées; rather, it was the fact that he had come to use the place for that other secret part of his existence—the OAS and his financial connection with it.

Two men sat with him now in the apartment. It was almost seven, and he expected to be back at the Avenue de Madrid house in time to welcome Hilary Latymer at eight. At the moment, however, another Englishman occupied his thoughts.

François Perrier sat with his cousin, Henri Janvier, "Plastique," a Congo mercenary, a former member of the Foreign Legion who had operated in Indochina and who was now, on occasion, a sabotage expert for the secret forces of the OAS in the Paris area. Perrier, the member of the "Ilium" group who had driven the van which ran "Achilles" down, was there fortuitously, connecting de Vaugrigard with the man he needed—"Plastique."

Perrier had been part of the OAS for years, a low-importance errand boy and occasional driver, depending on which was required. He had prospered in his fruit business, sold it, and moved into the wholesale side of his trade. Yet, de Vaugrigard suspected, there was something left over from a former life, as with himself, though he did not make the comparison readily, something that chose to coalesce around the symbol of de Gaulle's betrayal of France and the army in Algeria. Perrier, like himself, had funded the OAS, but in a lesser fashion, and involved himself personally with low-risk enterprises—recapturing the feeling of Rouen and its times perhaps.

Janvier was different. He was tied to the OAS by the money it paid him, and by nothing more. After Dien Bien Phu and his march to safety through the jungle with the other pitiable units that had remained uncaptured or wiped out, he had turned away from all idealism, all appeals to any better nature he might have. The Congo had allowed him to practice his facility with explosives, and the OAS campaign in metropolitan France was simply another backcloth against which to play a mercenary role. If anyone could kill Richard Gardiner for him, it was Janvier.

For that is what de Vaugrigard had decided to do. The idea had come to him simply and entire. In the bed in the next room, waking from a stupidly crazed, sweating dream, and after the girl had turned over and resumed her sleep, he had known what he must do. The distrust of *l'Etranger* had suddenly thrust itself like a cold plant through the earth, telling him that his own life was in danger, that the man from SDECE would not protect him from Gardiner.

And the solution had been simple. A convincingly violent OAS outrage in which Gardiner just *happened* to die. It would not be traced back to him. Of the consequences of his known association with the OAS —he refused to think about it, enclosing himself instead in this chill passion to rid himself of the Englishman.

De Vaugrigard knew he could frighten Perrier into helping him; the man would be afraid of his own skin, just as de Vaugrigard admitted once more, with distaste in his mouth like drunken sleep, vile and bitter, the similarity between himself and the fatter, more vulgar Perrier. But it was "Plastique" he needed, and that meant money. He said, "We agree then? One hundred thousand francs. . . . Not a small sum for the death of one man, eh?" He smiled at Janvier. It was an unreturned gesture. He watched the lined, mustached face, unmoved, though the eyes flickered slightly at the sum mentioned.

"He is a very dangerous man then?"

"Perhaps. I want him dead, and it must look like an OAS thing—you understand? He dies by apparent accident. Which is why I need you." He looked as if in apology at Perrier and added, "Perhaps you could impress upon your cousin what this man is like, mm?"

Perrier, apparently pleased to be making some contribution, said, "Henri, this man is a good killer. As Etienne. . . ." He looked swiftly at de Vaugrigard, who smiled to encourage the use of his first name, resenting it only secretly. "As Etienne says, if he wants revenge now, and he has already killed one of our Rouen comrades, then it's him or us."

"Not me," Janvier observed. "He doesn't know

I'm alive." He sounded blunt, uninterested, but de Vaugrigard understood it as a minor exercise of power. Perrier's face fell. Then Janvier added, "However, if he is worth the price, then he is a dead man."

"Good," de Vaugrigard said. Perrier was evidently relieved. He had been almost perpetually afraid since de Vaugrigard had told him of the death of Dupuy. His was an image of de Vaugrigard's fear, enlarged. Etienne hated him for it and was subtly gratified at the same time. "Good. I will not ask for details— the money will be paid to you how and when you wish." Janvier nodded. "Half this evening. But there is very little time. The man must be in Paris by now. I want him dead within the next forty-eight hours— understand?"

6. The Lady of Situations

Aubrey was still up when Latymer returned from the de Vaugrigard house. The little man had removed his collar, and his shirt was open at the throat. In his scarlet suspenders, he looked peculiarly untidy, even vulnerable. His slippered feet were up on a stool. He was sipping meditatively at a whisky and soda, and a heap of discarded sheets of flimsy lay near him on the sofa. He looked tired and frustrated.

"Did you have a pleasant time?" he asked with an acidic edge to his voice.

"Very pleasant, thank you. The de Vaugrigard family have a very good cook at present." Latymer slipped off his dinner jacket, loosened the bow tie, then poured himself a whisky. The ice clinked loudly in the tumbler, intruding on the expectant silence.

"I'm *so* glad!"

"What's the trouble, Aubrey—drawn a blank?"

"Indeed we have. I begin to wish I'd assigned you to oversee Guesswork and given myself the task of saving Richard Gardiner from his own worst excesses. . . ." He swallowed some whisky and added, "It would seem that Lidbrooke and Melluish have developed an infatuation for each other's company, or their sense of insularity is much greater than usual."

"How come?"

"They haven't left each other's sight all night! After the party at NATO they went to a restaurant, then to a nightclub—all on SIS expenses, of course—and then they went to bed!"

"Together?" Latymer, sitting in an armchair and stretching his long legs, could not resist the remark.

"Not according to my sources. However, they may be being very discreet about that."

"No drop?"

"Not so much as a toffee paper. No—Lidbrooke isn't clever enough to fool the Beaters. The drop must be in London, even though Paris is more likely."

"What about the Russians?"

"Nothing. Nor the Czechs or the East Germans or the Poles. Everyone's being impeccably innocent. You'd think there wasn't a Center man in Paris, it's so quiet." He looked at Latymer. "What did you find out?"

Latymer shook his head.

"Not a great deal." Aubrey appeared disappointed. "Etienne de Vaugrigard doesn't like the general, he's self-satisfied, smug, overwealthy, and a prig, and I'm sure he has a young mistress stowed somewhere Geneviève won't find her—but he doesn't know a thing about Richard. He's had no word from him, nothing. He didn't even know about Dupuy, which I suppose is not surprising." He picked at cigarette ash that had fallen on his trousers. Aubrey, as if reminded, lit a cigarette himself and pulled an onyx ashtray to his side.

"I see. And you don't like Etienne very much either—eh?"

"True. The son seems much in the same mold, and Geneviève is the classic aristocrat who married money, feels grubby because of it, and really ought to have been handed over to Citizen Robespierre years ago!" He smiled at Aubrey's smug expression. "Yes, I'm frustrated, too. I shall have to go to Rouen tomorrow to talk to the woman Vivienne Grodin."

"Oh, dear. These moral crusades *do* run out of steam very quickly, don't they?"

Latymer raised his glass, acknowledging the hit. Then he said, "The daughter was different—Françoise. Beauty among the beasts, rather."

"Ah."

"She's nineteen," Latymer observed. "And has taken to calling me 'Uncle Hilary,' if you must know." His face darkened as if with memory for a moment.

Aubrey, aware of the direction of his thoughts— Oxford—said quickly, "I see. But there's nothing then?"

"No. Except confirmation that Richard won't stop now until he's evened the score. Etienne talked about him during the war. Not a pleasant picture or a man a young lady would take home to meet Mummy. But we know that very well for ourselves, mm?"

"Quite." Aubrey mused for a moment, then looked at Latymer with a strange, intent expression. "You do want to follow this up, don't you?" Latymer opened his hands, shrugged. "Do you or don't you?" He seemed to be willing Latymer to answer in the affirmative. Latymer nodded.

"Yes," he said. "I think I must. Richard will kill himself over this. He can't get away with it—and I must stop him trying."

"Good. In that case, you may continue with your inquiries. Alone, of course. Personally, I don't think you have a hope in hell of stopping what was begun in La Baule or even in the Avenue Foch. It has the smell of a certain unpleasant kind of destiny about it." He shook his head.

"I shall talk to Jean-Jacques Haussman, I think.

Tomorrow, after I've seen the woman. He might be able to help—unofficially."

"Able—but willing?"

"I think so. Well, perhaps. He belongs to the same period, to liaison with SOE and all the rest of it. One of yesterday's spies, like ourselves. And we keep in touch. I think he might help, yes."

"Good."

"What of you? One of the other two, is it?"

"I'm not sure. Lidbrooke went for Jorgensen like a ferret down a hole—after our 'ferret,' as it were. But it could have been hot air or righteous indignation. 'Snowshoe' should have reached his ears in the normal way." Aubrey plucked at his lower lip, shifted his feet on the stool. "I just don't know. He *could* have been turned and we wouldn't necessarily have known. Keep him asleep for years, bring him out when the time is ripe. Who knows?"

"Post-Philby?"

"I should think so. Post his original resignation anyway. After all, dear, charming, urbane Kim was their prize, their star." He smiled, sadly. "And when he went supernova, it was too good an idea not to have someone else very close to the top, perhaps in line of succession."

"Mm. But why use him at all?"

"Proof of usefulness. There are always doubters in the Center setup, you know that. Prove your double is capable of the sort of thing you claim or we won't authorize these ridiculously high payments he's demanding. That sort of thing. Or just the utilitarian approach that also characterizes the Center. We have a double, so he must be employed. It's part and parcel of dear Kim's reasons for failure. He had to carry on spying on his way to the top. That and the gross ineptitude of some of the people who inhabit those plush little offices in Queen Anne's gate."

Aubrey finished his drink and stood up.

"Are you retiring?" Latymer asked.

"I think so. My job has a certain urgency, dictated by others. Otherwise, I would stay up and listen with you to the music you undoubtedly intend to play. . . ." He moved to the door of his bedroom and added, "Don't have the volume too far up the scale, will you? I haven't brought my earplugs."

When the small noises in bathroom and bedroom had stilled, Latymer idly inspected the collection of phonograph records in the teak cabinet against one wall. Most of them were not to his taste, but he found two records of excerpts from Bach cantatas and sat listening, the volume low, for more than an hour. It was one-thirty when he finally went to bed, the somber passages running in his head uncomfortably. Bach, he sensed, had taken him closer to the real, the oppressive, and he was sorry he had not drunk more or less.

Aubrey had switched the telephone through to the extension in his bedroom, and its noise woke him, but not Latymer. Aubrey's blue eyes blinked in the sudden light of the bedside lamp like those of a child. He rubbed at his thinning, tousled hair and looked at the traveling clock. After three.

"Yes?"

It was Rushton, one of the Beaters, on night surveillance of Lidbrooke.

"Mr. Aubrey? We've just followed Lidbrooke from his hotel to an apartment house on the Left Bank. Rue Soufflot, behind the Sorbonne, near the Panthéon?"

"Yes. Go on." Aubrey had come fully awake, as if a strong scent, animal and pungent, had come to him.

"He took care that he wasn't followed, but we managed to use the two-car dodge to keep on his tail."

"Yes!" Aubrey snapped. "Whose apartment?"

"We don't know, sir. There are six of them in the building, and we haven't approached the concierge yet."

"Good. Leave it. I'll be right down."

Aubrey put down the receiver, dressed swiftly, and went down to the ground floor. The door opened onto a small courtyard blank with drawn curtains at the windows. He had not bothered to wake and inform Latymer.

He started the car and rolled it quietly through the

archway into the rue de Castellane. The street was deserted, the orange glow of streetlamps making pools of shadow. He wound down the window, and the cool night air flowed into the car. Pleasantly.

He drove past the huge, oppressive bulk of the Madeleine, which housed a somber and affecting interior that always impressed him, and down the rue Royale, past Maxim's, to the Place de la Concorde. Even at three in the morning red lights glowed as cars braked and minced across the vast expanse. He eased his way across the square, turning left into the Quai des Tuileries.

He crossed the Seine via the Boulevard du Palais, to the Left Bank. It took him only another five minutes to locate the rue Soufflot.

There were a number of cars parked in the street, but he picked out two shadows in a parked Renault and parked as close as he could. Rushton got out and came toward his car. Aubrey opened the passenger door, and the heavy man slid into the vacant seat.

"Which one?" Aubrey asked.

"Over there—number twenty-six." Aubrey followed Rushton's pointing finger. A blank, light-stoned facade, many windows open, the shutters folded back against the brick. No lights. Anonymous. It appeared promising, and Aubrey nodded to himself as if to confirm the thought.

"What have you done?"

"Names from the board, checking now with the embassy night staff—and kept our eyes open."

"No one else has arrived?" Rushton shook his head. "No lights on. How long before they went off?"

"Maybe half an hour—no more."

"Mm." Aubrey retreated suddenly into a concentrated abstraction. To Rushton, he seemed a great distance away; he had worked for Aubrey on previous occasions and settled to wait for the little man's emergence from his mood. Then Aubrey said, "What papers have you on you?"

"Police Judiciaire, Vice Squad, SDECE, Customs —the usual range."

"What's your French like?"

"Not bad if I play stooge."

"Good. Then I think that sometime soon we'll be having a word with the occupant of that apartment. Which one, by the way?"

"We think it's the front one, top floor. The pattern of lights agrees with someone arriving when Lidbrooke did. . . ." He paused and then removed the mask of professional detachment for a moment. "Do you think it's him, sir—Mr. Lidbrooke?"

Aubrey looked at Rushton solemnly and said, "I don't know. I just don't know. This doesn't look good anyway, whatever his explanation." He waved his hand at the street outside the car, the sodium lamps flaring in the soft darkness, the blank, unlit wall of the apartment building.

"I suppose it's got to be someone . . ." Rushton murmured.

"It doesn't *have* to be anyone!" Aubrey snapped. "It happens because they choose treason."

"Yes, sir."

Aubrey looked at Rushton again. Like most of the Beaters employed by the SIS, often paralleling the functions of the Directorate of Security (MI 5), he was a closed personality. A complete and entire functionary, without power of decision, without the expansion of personality of those who constructed policy or who enacted field operations. It was almost strange to hear him express a human reaction. Aubrey said, "With SO-Four, more and more of your work is going to be like this, you know."

Rushton nodded. "Great," he said tiredly.

"Mm. Now, when Lidbrooke leaves, we'll go in and see the concierge. Vice Squad, I think. That always has a nice ring to it. Then we'll have a word with our mysterious occupant. Man or woman, by the way?"

"We think it's a woman, but there are probably two flats on the top floor, and we don't know which is which. One's a man; the other's the woman."

The conversation subsided. It had become to Aubrey rather like sitting next to a statue, and he wished he had woken Latymer and brought him in the car. It would have been easier on the temper to have discussed music or even Lidbrooke. He did not know what Rushton thought of either subject; he suspected, however, that Lidbrooke was admired by the Beaters in general because most of them were field agents of one kind or another, and Lidbrooke ran the action department, SO-1, under the urbane and ineffectual Kennedy-Shaw—head of SO-1 only so long as Lidbrooke carried him.

Lidbrooke left at six-thirty, after it was light but while the rue Soufflot was still deserted. The gutters flowed with the cleaning stream of water, and the air was still fresh. The sky was pale, the bellies of the few small high clouds lit with pink. It promised to be another fine day.

Rushton roused Aubrey from a waking doze in which he was examining Lidbrooke's career in the SIS and finding very little that was suspicious and few occasions when the man might have been turned. He watched, his body slumped as far down in the seat as possible, as Lidbrooke walked down the street to where Rushton explained he had parked his car. As he turned the corner, Rushton signaled the black Renault, and the engine fired almost immediately. Aubrey saw Horton's face briefly as the car passed them; then it turned the corner into the rue Paillet, the brake lights flickering for a moment, then vanishing.

Aubrey nodded, and they got out of the car and crossed the street. As he glanced to the left, the Panthéon, forbidding and grandiose, loomed at the top of the rue Soufflot. The street and the Place du Panthéon, in daylight, possessed a flinty appearance, as if there were nothing in their composition but stone. It was the absence of trees, Aubrey supposed.

The concierge was in her booth inside the green-painted door. Aubrey, who had taken a police ID card from Rushton, knocked on the glass, and the old woman with a squat, unsmiling face looked sullenly out at him. A black cat nestled on her aproned lap, and she wore thick stockings and dirty carpet slippers.

"What?" she asked, opening the door of the booth, having delayed to stoke the small fire she kept going even in August. A waft of heavy, stale air seemed to creep over her shoulder and assail Aubrey's nostrils.

"Police," he said swiftly. "Vice Squad." His French was hurried, slurred, colloquial, and Parisian in accent. "We want to interview one of your tenants."

"What for?" The woman's eyes had narrowed craftily, a peasant cunning in her face.

"None of your business!" Aubrey snapped. "Just stay out of the way—but don't disappear. I may want to ask *you* a few questions!"

The woman's attention to his un-French clothes vanished as she felt herself threatened.

"It's none of my business . . . !" she almost whined.

"The man who left here—who was he?"

"I don't know, m'sieur!" Now she was whining, her body adopting a suppliant posture, her hands clasping one another across the heaving bosom of her apron.

"Why didn't you ask him?" Aubrey snapped again, a look of contempt on his face, his blue eyes uncharacteristically cold and shallow. "Are you getting a rake-off from what goes on here?"

The woman started to snivel and to protest her innocence. She said, "I tell them the rules, I warn them about the police . . . !"

It was obvious to Aubrey that there was at least one prostitute in the apartment house. He hoped it was not the woman in the top-floor flat. He dismissed the concierge with a stony glance and headed up the stairs, narrow and uncarpeted, his feet and Rushton's heavy step echoing coldly. The building seemed to possess a dampness, a musty smell, now that they were inside. He heard the noises of waking and a toilet somewhere in the building being flushed. A man's voice flared briefly, admonishing a child. The sound of slapped skin and a tiny cry. There was the smell of coffee and the stale smell of meals from the previous night. Aubrey wrinkled his nose.

On the top floor two dark-brown blank doors confronted him. He knocked peremptorily at the flat which overlooked the rue Soufflot.

A woman neither young nor pretty, but evidently French, answered the door. Aubrey held out the ID card and said, "Vice Squad. May we come in, madame?" He saw the ring on her finger, which she clutched at his form of address, as if reminding herself of it.

"What do you want?" she asked, backing away slightly. She was perhaps five-feet-eight, an inch taller than Aubrey. Yet she appeared at a loss and frightened, as if she did have something to hide.

Aubrey came through the door, and Rushton followed, closing it behind him. The thing that struck Aubrey forcibly, even with his first glance at the room, was its transitory nature. No one lived there, which appeared promising: a drop or a safe house. It had the smell of such a place, the dry, stale mustiness not erased by the very temporary presence of two human beings. It still clung to the walls, to the closed and grimy windows, and to the few scraps of furniture.

"Who was the man who left you ten minutes ago, madame? Your husband?" There was a contemptuous twist of disbelief to Aubrey's mouth; he enjoyed his portrayal of a man of less sensitivity and intelligence than he himself; a kind of histrionic slumming for the ego was how he always regarded such impersonations.

"Y-yes," the woman said. "Why?"

"We know he is not your husband, madame— he is English, and he is in Paris for a few days only. Please do not lie to us. What is your relationship with him?"

From the evidence of her eyes, their rapid movements, the woman was thinking furiously. Then she said, "You're not French—those clothes you're wearing, they're not French either!" There was something challenging about her voice that intrigued Aubrey. And she seemed to welcome having settled something about him that had previously puzzled her. She was a professional or something very similar.

"You are an expert on the fashion sense of the Paris police, madame?" he asked with a smile intended as sardonic. Then he said to Rushton, "Rostand, search the place."

Rushton opened the door to the tiny, cramped kitchen, then to the bathroom and the one bedroom. Aubrey had a glimpse of sheets pulled back and rumpled. It possessed no necessary significance. He returned his attention to the woman. He did not know her—it was unlikely he would—but there was a nagging sense about her that she had expected him or someone like him, though not perhaps at that precise moment. He picked her handbag from the table and spilled its contents onto the stained tablecloth. Then he sifted through the items. Nothing—but on this occasion all she would possess would be a verbal report from Lidbrooke for Moscow Center.

He looked at her *carte d'identité*. He thought he knew the name.

"Madame Rollin. The same name as the journalist who writes such powerful articles against the American involvement in Vietnam, eh? You are not related, madame?"

The woman hesitated just long enough for him to understand that she was lying; then she shook her head and said, "No, I have nothing to do with that Catherine Rollin. May I have my *carte*, please?" She held out her hand, and Aubrey reluctantly returned it. Then she said, "Why do you come here? What do you want? I am not a whore, and you have no right to invade my privacy like this!"

Aubrey registered a sense of making up for lost time and lost impressions. She was overreacting now, but it was just a fraction too late. She had been too cool at the beginning. He said, "You do live here, madame?" She nodded. "We can check, of course."

She hesitated, and with apparent nervousness she bit her lower lip. It was a sensual mouth, and arrogant, and it did not lend itself readily to indecision or fear. Nor did the dark eyes. And there was a confidence about the slant of her body. He could not quite believe in her. He suspected that Latymer, though more susceptible than he to this kind of powerful, dominating woman, would have the same reservations.

She said, "I—have the lease. I use this place from time to time." She hesitated; then it blurted out, the supposed truth. Aubrey considered it quite a reasonable performance. "I—you know that I am married. I cannot meet—someone—at any place my husband might use. I use this place, to entertain a friend. . . ."

"And he is the man who just left?"

"Yes," she said in a small voice, and then she looked up at him, her eyes brighter with tears, but her mouth adopting a defiant pout. She was not ashamed, it told him.

He said, leading her with a sense of amusement, "And your husband is unfaithful to you, and he no longer loves you. And this other man—he loves you?" She nodded. "He is English. How often do you meet?"

"Whenever he is in Paris—perhaps once a month. . . ."

"Here, like this? Every time?" Aubrey commented with a sense of using a knife on the woman, whose arrogance was beginning to irritate him. His performance was better than hers, and that also irritated him. It was not such a good and satisfying game after all. He waved his hand in the direction of the dirty tablecloth and the poor scraps of furniture—a pair of decaying armchairs, a bare sofa, two upright chairs for the table.

"The rent is cheap," she said. "Now—what do you want here? In *my* flat?"

He looked at Rushton, standing behind her, and the big man shook his head. Aubrey said, "I may need to talk to you again, madame. I have your address now. Your real address, that is."

"My husband?" she said quickly.

"You will have to trust me to be discreet, madame. Rostand, come!" He nodded to her and left the room, Rushton looming behind him. He heard the door of the apartment close and saw the frightened face of the concierge as they reached the ground floor, a prisoner in a glass cage. He glared at her.

"You did not tell me that Madame entertained her lover here!" It was as if he had been embarrassed. The old woman cowered.

"But, m'sieur. . . ." Nothing was her fault.

"You fool! I want no trouble from women like

her—they can always cause trouble, you understand? How long has she had the lease, eh?"

"I—perhaps a year or more."

"How long has that man been coming here?"

"What man?"

"Don't be more stupid than you have to be, you old cow—tell me!"

The woman's craftiness dissolved in fear, and she said, "Almost from the beginning, perhaps once a month, sometimes more. He does not stay during the day, and he lets himself in with a key late at night. I do not know who he is. Madame is married. . . ." The latter was a bonus, offered by way of conciliation. Aubrey sneered.

"You are the madam! If I can get you on a vice charge, I will! I'll be back with more questions—understand?"

She nodded, and he turned on his heel and went out into the fresher air of the rue Soufflot. There was a smell of coffee and breakfast and rubbish out there, too, but not so insistent. As they crossed the street, he said to Rushton, "We'll take both cars, since she may have seen both. You wait around the corner, and I'll send a relief as soon as I can. But nothing on this street at the moment. She's Catherine Rollin all right —and Lidbrooke is mixed up with her. What the hell he thinks he's doing—if he's doing anything other than being a traitor—I can't imagine. A bloody, bloody shame!" He did not look into Rushton's face but walked straight to his own car.

Aubrey was slumped on the sofa when Latymer returned to the apartment from Rouen. The name of François Perrier had been supplied to him by Vivienne Grodin, just as she had been instructed to do if inquiries were made by any Englishman concerning Gardiner. Aubrey's face was gray with fatigue, and the blue eyes were dimmed with concentration. He looked ill or drunk, certainly troubled in thought.

Latymer poured himself a drink and was about to recount his day when Aubrey said, "Sit down, Hilary —I've got to talk to you, or I shall burst!"

Latymer poured two sherries, handed one like a solicitous doctor to Aubrey, stared for a moment at the numbed, sacklike posture of the man, then said, "What's up? You look as if the whole thing has blown up in your face."

"It's Lidbrooke—has to be." He pulled a mournful face.

Latymer understood the expression. It was not that Aubrey held any special brief for Lidbrooke as an individual. The man had a certain flair, but he was far from irreplaceable. It was merely the confirmation of the fact that there was a "mole."

"Why him?"

"He's mixed up with Catherine Rollin. . . ."

"The journalist? Fearless fighter for the oppressed and the Left—always supposing there's no difference? God, that's a little obvious, isn't it using her as his contact?"

Aubrey's face darkened, and he snapped, "What the hell do you mean, it's *obvious?* It's bloody devious, Hilary! Bloody devious."

"I suppose so."

"You suppose so? The only thing that's odd is the fact that we haven't seen him in her company before!"

"She was downgraded to category D as a suspected foreign courier months ago! Deputy 'C' himself agreed to it. So we weren't watching her. She's not serious, Aubrey—*wasn't* serious. How long has this —association been going on?"

"A year. Damn it, more than a year! And if he's innocent of treason, what could he be doing having a sordid little affair with *this* woman? Good God, aren't there sufficient women in Paris for him—women in whom we have had no interest whatsoever?"

Latymer ignored the testiness of Aubrey's reactions, the formality of his description of Lidbrooke's supposed crime. He considered the information and could discern only a strangeness that it should be Lidbrooke. He said, "*Is* he entangled with her in any other way?"

"I saw bedclothes pulled back, but that could mean something or nothing. He visits this pokey, sordid little flat every time he's in Paris. And no doubt makes the drop, or simply relates events, every time. Whether he does it while hunched over the lady's nakedness or while they merely sit in armchairs toasting the Politburo with Russian vodka really would not appear to matter a great deal!"

"How did he meet her—is there any cover at all?"

"I don't know. I haven't asked him. I'm waiting on investigations into her movements, as from now. She guessed we weren't Vice Squad...." Latymer laughed at the improbability, but Aubrey merely glowered and added, "So she may tell him, she may not. In any case, she may well run for cover. She's being watched, and it may be a long business." He looked up at Latymer. "One of these self-possessed, cold madams, the kind that always make me feel uncomfortable...." He stared into his memory, scrutinizing her image, and added, "She wasn't a very good actress, Hilary. I think that annoyed me as much as anything."

"You're still watching Lidbrooke?"

"Naturally."

"What moves has she made so far?"

"Gone back to her flat in the rue George V—a very nice little place, according to Evans, who's parked along the street. And since then she's stayed in. We can't know what calls she's made, but if she comes out, then we follow her. Her husband is a businessman—advertising, I think. I believe London cleared him of any involvement with Madame Rollin's suspected activities. So we shall be hanging on here until there's confirmation of some kind. That should please you?"

Latymer nodded.

"I am rather pleased. I know the intended victim's name...."

Aubrey, with surprising venom, said, "God, I wish I was playing around with yesterday like you, Hilary! The present has the smell of decay about it!"

Latymer, relying heavily on wartime acquaintance as well as on more recent favors, was able to persuade Jean-Jacques Haussman to assist him. He was able to convince him that Gardiner would kill, and kill again, unless he were stopped. Haussman, checking discreetly with La Baule, assured himself that the likelihood of self-defense existed in the death of Dupuy. Therefore, he assigned some of the men under his control to trace François Perrier. They found his former shop, then the wholesale business, before Perrier left his office for home.

He was dragooned by their presence, and his own fear, into assisting them. A guard was placed inside the house, and surveillance teams set up around his home in the suburb of St. Germain-en-Laye, in a street of pretentious new houses that had come within his pocket only a couple of years earlier. His wife, who seemed to belong to a past era of his life and to have been left behind like a fossil, was frightened by the presence of the SDECE men. The wait began.

When the telephone rang, Aubrey was sitting alone in the apartment, reading, by the light of a single standard lamp, papers that Hawthorne had brought from the embassy. The papers contained little beyond a rather haphazard account of surveillance on the Rollin woman over the past two and a half years.

Catherine Rollin had, at the beginning of that time, made an extensive tour of Eastern bloc countries. She had therefore been the subject of a routine alert and handled by the SFC (Suspect Foreign Citizens) section of the Beaters. She had written a syndicated series of articles on her experiences and then had traveled in Cuba and Latin America and still later in North and South Vietnam. There was no proof of any enlistment by Moscow Center or any East European intelligence service. She had been marked as a "Potential," awaiting further proof.

As the telephone shrilled in his thoughts, Aubrey looked at his watch. Eleven.

"Yes?" There was no sense of tiredness in his voice, only a consuming impatience.

It was Rushton again, back on duty and leading the nightshift team watching Catherine Rollin.

"She's running, Mr. Aubrey." His voice was without inflection.

"Where?" Aubrey's voice was small in the room, which seemed suddenly to have expanded, fuller with dusky shadows thrown by the standard lamp.

"Right into the Czech embassy, sir. She was admitted five minutes ago."

Aubrey sat with the receiver held limply against his cheek, tugging the flesh out of shape. His eyes were dull, his lips set. Lidbrooke was a dead man.

7. Concorde

Richard Gardiner had been watching the house for most of the day. It had not been difficult to find; that pleased him since he could begin almost at once to study the behavior of its occupants. He had very deliberately conceived the death of François Perrier as a species of hunt. He had not considered the method of execution; he knew only that he wanted the man to be afraid. He did not want him to suffer the quick kind of death of Dupuy, whose culpability had receded in death. For Perrier, who had driven the van, there had to be terror.

It was not obvious that there was at least one other man watching the house until the minutes just before darkness, when the long day and the anticipation of relief betrayed another man. More than one, he confirmed half an hour after sunset, and perhaps more inside the house.

Perrier had come home alone a little after six, driving the big black Citroën straight into the garage. Gardiner had been intrigued by the bald, stocky man in the expensive suit as by a stranger; then Perrier had fumbled for his keys in his trouser pocket, and the slump of the shoulders had leaped nineteen years. It was "Nestor." He watched him enter the house.

A girl came out of the house a little after seven, collected at the sidewalk by a youth on a motorscooter, his hair long and fair. The girl, in a red miniskirt, sat sidesaddle on the scooter, which sounded like a much larger machine until its noise died around the corner. Other than that, there was no sign of life about the house, set back behind a sloping sheet of lawn and a dwarf hedge, except for the routine gleam of lights in various rooms.

And except for one room, on the ground floor, perhaps a study, overlooking the wide, treelined street, a room into which people went but never switched on the light. He could see the pale flicker of light, as from a door opening, and an occasional shadow moving in the room.

It had to be a watcher or a guard.

There was a thrill of excitement, almost corrupt, at each confirmation—two watchers in the street and at least one man in the house. In some way Perrier was forewarned. It did not matter.

He took the field glasses from his eyes. There was no light left, no need for more confirmation. The eyepieces were rimed with sweat, and his eyes ached with their pressure. He rubbed his neck where it ached.

It had been fortunate that the neighbors who lived directly opposite the Perriers had taken their summer vacation rather late in August. Apparently M. Armand Selincourt was a barrister.

Gardiner was seated in an armchair dragged to the window of the first-floor room which he took to be their son's bedroom. The boy had to be in his teens; there were large posters of the Beatles and rugby players cut from the pages of *Miroir du rugby,* most of them French, one or two in scarlet. There was a daughter. French pop stars and Paul Newman had looked down at him from the walls of her room. The Selincourt family, according to a diary he had found in a locked desk, would not be returning from their touring holiday of Austria and Switzerland for another week. It was ideal for Gardiner. He had eaten from the fridge, consumed orange juice, and stolen a bottle of milk from another doorstep to make himself coffee.

He was grateful, having discovered the other watchers, for the audacity that had made him choose the house rather than a parked car as his base.

He freshened his mouth with orange juice from the fridge, then stood in the darkened kitchen, swigging at the wide-necked bottle. Then he went back upstairs. Though he had smoked during the day, he did not light a cigarette in the now dark room. Instead, he settled his cramped limbs back into the chair, eyes remote.

He could not now afford to warn Perrier; he felt the irritation intensely. Someone had spoiled the corrupt, pleasurable game of terror he had intended playing. Yet he had to take Perrier away from the house and from his new protectors without arousing their suspicions. He had to talk to Perrier, to know who had given the order for his death, the man who had assumed the mythic proportions now invested in him during the last days, the days of silence, and hiding, and preparation. Judas. The man who had betrayed him twice. Perrier knew the name.

He existed now in an intellectual and emotional limbo. He related to no one; his horizons had shrunk until there was nothing outside himself against which to measure what he had become. The skeletal landscape contained only himself, and Perrier, and, like a distant mountain or safe place, the unknown man who had given the orders.

It was a self-induced vision, a shallow imitation of life. He clung to it as reality, seduced by its obscene glamour—the charm of the power of life and death. He felt that he was fulfilling something from his past, his real self.

The talking and the killing must have but the one location—he would take Perrier at his work. Minutes only—that would be all he would need. Unpoetic, it would have to be violent in the extreme to satisfy the state of feeling that had been generated toward Perrier in the past few days.

It was almost midnight when the police car stopped outside the Perrier house. Gardiner put the glasses to his eyes without excitement. He watched the downstairs light come on and saw the rumpled, pajama-clad figure of Perrier open the door. He swung the door wide after an indecisive moment, and the two detectives went inside. A light flickered on in the lounge, and shapes moved behind the curtains.

Gardiner got up from the chair. His car was two streets away, parked in the drive of another empty house and hidden from the road by a tall hedge. If Perrier were taken away by the police, into protective custody—his throat was suddenly hot and full with rage, so that he wanted to scream to clear it.

He did not stop to remove the evidence of his occupation of the Selincourt house but let himself into the rear garden by the kitchen door. There he paused by the double garage, then walked nonchalantly down the path to the street. He knew where the surveillance car was parked and turned in the opposite direction, his gait suggestive of a late-evening stroller, slightly intoxicated.

The hire car was still where he had left it. He got in, started the engine, then turned out of the concealed drive. He drove slowly and quietly across the intersection of the Avenue Charles de Gaulle, on which stood the Perrier house. He saw the police car still parked outside.

He got out of the car and walked back to the corner. Then he waited. Ten minutes later Perrier, accompanied by the two detectives, came down the path and got into the car. Gardiner waited beyond the pool of light from a streetlamp until the car turned the corner of the avenue and headed east. The surveillance car remained stationary.

He ran back to his car and turned it full circle in the road. The taillights of the police Citroën were specks in the distance; then they turned a corner and were gone. He moved smoothly past the intersection and then accelerated.

The Citroën remained apparently unaware of its tail throughout the journey to the center of Paris. Gardiner, content to remain well behind it, as if already sensing its destination, considered dispassionately the reasons why Perrier was being taken into custody. The surveillance team did not belong to the police; that mystified him. Their identity confused things. . . .

He clenched his mind against the vague doubts, pushing like tired fingers against his determination. It would do no good to consider them. He had to keep his attention and concern rigidly focused on Perrier. A growing sense of being cheated possessed him; he was being robbed of the revenge and the information he wanted from Perrier.

The police car turned into the courtyard of the Préfecture de Police in the Quai des Orfèvres at twelve-forty. Gardiner parked his car almost challengingly in the Place du Parvis Notre Dame, near the hospital and the prefecture, and settled to wait.

"For God's sake, Hilary! Don't adopt that hangdog look of spaniel sympathy with me!"

Aubrey was angry, with himself primarily but also with London and even, obscurely, with Lidbrooke. Perhaps most powerfully with him.

Catherine Rollin had been incarcerated in the Czech embassy all that day. Evidently she was not an unwelcome guest. Aubrey instructed the beaters to stay on watch and to miss no movement on her part, though he did not know why he had iterated and reiterated that order. She had given them all the necessary proof. It was speculation of the most unproductive kind to hope that Rollin would walk back out and explain everything away.

Aubrey wondered why she had fled—that was the word that came to mind. Had it been simple fright at his appearance in the rue Soufflot? Did she understand, however dimly, that shades of night were falling about her protested lover? The game, as far as she saw it, was evidently up. Yet—and this was the strangest aspect of the affair for Aubrey—her supposed paramour and an agent of irreplaceable status had not been warned. Lidbrooke had attended that day's session of a senior subcommittee and was now in his hotel room. The courier had sniffed a nasty smell, but the agent had not been warned.

Latymer grinned at Aubrey's sudden outburst and angered the little man even more.

"Don't lose the poor remainder of your hair, Aubrey," he observed good-naturedly. He had himself just received Haussman's call to tell him that Perrier was in the prefecture and that Gardiner had followed him there. Though nervous, even afraid, of his forthcoming encounter with Gardiner, he was pleased with the efficacy of his scheme to flush Gardiner.

"Thank you!" Aubrey snapped. He walked once more the line he had trodden across the fitted carpet, from bedroom to kitchen door, for the best part of the evening. "I did wonderfully well on this operation without your assistance, and I certainly don't require your gratuitous advice at this stage!"

"Calm down, Aubrey!"

The little man turned on Latymer, waving a sheet of yellow flimsy in his direction. "You know what this is, don't you—yellow sheet. Message from Deputy 'C.' We're going to dispatch poor bloody Lidbrooke tomorrow! The executioner's arriving on the morning flight from Heathrow. Can we please meet him! God, do they want us to carry his gun or something?"

"Why is it annoying you so much?"

"Because it's so bloody precipitate, that's why! An unseemly rush into the house of death, and no mistake. It's very, very distasteful, this whole idea of not arresting him, not even talking to him, draining him, even turning him again. . . ." Aubrey paused opposite Latymer. He looked down at the younger man's face, at the clear eyes, the smooth skin. Latymer, he saw, had forgotten Victoria in the imbroglio of the Gardiner affair. One good thing at least.

"No," he continued. "I am not at all happy at this new policy, which seems to be of Constant's devising. I can't forgive 'C' for agreeing to it. If Lidbrooke is our 'mole,' then we know nothing about him, nothing at all. And we're not going to find out!"

He flopped down on the sofa, into the impression he had earlier left, before he had begun his prowling. His face was irritable, one of those faces, Latymer observed, whose most violent expression is a petulant crossness. It was hard to take his anger seriously; everything else about the man, but not that. Yet he was deeply angry.

"But they've had enough, Aubrey—Blake and Philby and before them Burgess and MacLean. And every spy the DS catches gets exchanged for a businessman being used by SO-One. It's Voltairean espionage —*pour encourager les autres,* as it were."

"It's all very well you taking that detached urbane view, Hilary, but Lidbrooke is going to be executed on my sayso—and I don't know whether I'm right!"

"What about Rollin?"

"Why not ask Lidbrooke? But oh no—we've to meet dear, sweet Mr. Napier at the airport tomorrow morning. That nasty little psychopath they kicked out of the SAS! God! It's more than flesh and blood can stand—death at the hands of Napier! I preferred the old method—give a chap a service revolver and tell him to blow his own brains out!"

"Mm. Perhaps—I hold no brief for Napier and his kind myself. And they are a little more prominent at our place of work than formerly. It must be a sign of the times." He rubbed his chin. "Haussman may want something in exchange for all this help he's been giving me. What can I tell him about Lidbrooke?"

"What? You're cleaning up a mess on his doorstep, aren't you?" Aubrey was evidently sulking. "Oh," he added, "tell him we have a suspect and are awaiting confirmation." He raised his hands in the air, then slapped them down at his sides; two puffs of dust rose from the sofa, curling in the light of the lamp. "The bloody impossible French! Them and their defector they bought who came bearing news of a top-level source inside NATO working for Moscow Center. Damn them! Until it was confirmed by 'Franklin,' I was prepared to discount the whole thing. The usual Gallic delight in troublemaking!"

"I'll be on my way, then."

"What? Oh, yes."

Aubrey sat alone for a long time after Latymer had left. He seemed not to notice the passage of time or the discomfort of not moving his position. A frown of thought creased his bland features, and his expression did not alter except to deepen in concentration. From time to time he would shake his head slowly, as if discarding an idea.

It was almost three-thirty when the telephone rang again.

"Rushton, Mr. Aubrey. She's on the move."

"What?"

"Rollin has just left the embassy, in an official car. Three men accompanying and a tail car. Wilde is after them with Evans. He's got a radio. What do you want us to do?"

"Collect me here. What cover have you got?"

"The same range as before, sir."

"SDECE?"

"Yes."

"Good. You'll need those. The others have the same?"

"Yes."

"Then get moving. Pick me up—but don't lose that Czech car!"

It was Orly, of course. Aeroflot to Warsaw, leaving at seven. Aubrey got hurriedly out of the car, brisk, plump in the morning wind that had sprung up and that plucked at his coat and flurried dust from the concrete outside the main terminal building. The sky was already light, grayish and dull but with the promise of another hot, cloudless day.

Evans was waiting for them in front of the glass doors into the terminal.

"They're in the diplomatic lounge, Mr. Aubrey. All nice and cozy with the early edition of the papers and fresh coffee." Evans, a short, stocky individual running to fat, smiled encouragingly, as if to indicate his readiness for anything, especially something with the glamour of risk and a slender chance of success; he seemed to look upon this excursion, Aubrey thought, as a possible reward for two days of surveillance.

"Where's Wilde?"

"Keeping an eye on the door of the lounge from a convenient seat. He's hiding behind the *Paris-Soir. . . .*" Evans's cheerfulness was infectious, and Aubrey permitted himself a small smile. Swiftly he told Evans what he had told Horton and Rushton in the car. The small man nodded sagely and tried not to smile as the scheme was unfolded to him. When Aubrey had finished, he said, "You're the only one whose Frog is good enough for this, sir. We'll have to stand around and mutter throaty noises like they do in the films."

"Very well. But, for heaven's sake, don't keep smiling while I'm trying to extract Madame Rollin from the Czechs!"

"Sir," Evans snapped, keeping his features under control.

"Good. Now, Horton, you go and join Wilde, and we'll be along in a couple of minutes. I'll barge straight in and take it from there." Horton nodded and wandered into the terminal. A gust of warm air sighed from the glass doors as they closed behind him.

"Now, you two. Just play the heavies, will you? You know what these Czech boys will expect to see . . . smoke French cigarettes, there's a cover story in every one!" He looked at his watch, avoiding Evans's grin. "No one leaves that room to get to a telephone before I've finished—understand?" They nodded. "I'll bluff us past the policeman on the door. Right. Let us begin."

The diplomatic lounge was on the first floor of the building, a spacious room set aside for the comfort and convenience of diplomatic passengers passing through Orly. It was a small neighbor to the VIP lounge used for more public arrivals and departures.

The lounge was walled with glass, slightly tinted. There was a wooden door and a French policeman standing guard with a Sten gun. Aubrey passed the black PVC bench on which Wilde and Horton were seated and nodded to them. Then they began a small pantomime for the policeman's benefit; Evans was stationed on the bench, and Rushton and Horton were instructed to accompany Aubrey. They saluted ostentatiously. Wilde was ignored completely, as Aubrey's undeclared cover. Both Horton and Rushton lit cigarettes, and Aubrey bustled up to the policeman, a small, round little man with a fierce downturn of the mouth and narrowed brows.

He flashed his ID card at the policeman and was immediately confiding as far as the occupants of the lounge were concerned, requesting details of their arrival and making pointed references to the woman. The policeman was impressed. Obviously the SDECE man in front of him carried a lot of weight. He held open the door, then adopted a fierce pose before it, the safety catch on the gun thrown to "Off." Evans nodded to him, the nod of a superior being to an ordinary policeman.

The crew of the tail car had returned to the embassy. There were just two men with Catherine Rollin, Czech or Russian, it did not matter—both of them were operatives of Moscow Center. They stood up when Aubrey entered the room, and he saw the surprise on the woman's face as she recognized him. He bowed to her, then to the two men. In his hand he held out for inspection the ID card in its plastic wallet, putting it away as one of the two men tried to take hold of it.

"May I have your names? Madame Rollin I already know." He smiled briefly. She was confused and perhaps afraid.

One of the two said, in atrocious French, "We are members of the embassy staff of the Czechoslovakian Socialist Republic." It was a threat. "What do you want?"

"You have a French citizen in your company—I wish to speak to her."

"This room has diplomatic immunity from French authorities," the taller of the two men grunted. He was stolid, unimaginative, hedged around with the protection his police office gave him in his own society.

"Immunity for you perhaps. However, Madame Rollin has no diplomatic status, as you must realize. She is a French citizen on French soil." He was silent for a moment while he let the significance of his words sink in. "If you will excuse us, I wish to talk to Madame Rollin."

He bowed again. The two Czechs looked at each other, clearly at a loss. They were evidently impressed by the scant regard paid to their official status, perhaps more than by the ID card. One of them said, "I must telephone, please."

"Why?" Aubrey asked. "I do not know why Madame Rollin wishes to leave France in your company —that is her business. But you have no need to telephone. I wish to question her on a French matter." He looked at Catherine Rollin closely for the first time. She was perturbed by the turn of events, but he considered her convinced by his act. She had solved his former mysteriousness.

"I must protest!" the taller Czech said, his shoulders moving in a threatening manner. Behind Aubrey, and on cue, Rushton took a step forward. Aubrey waved him back.

"You may, of course, protest later. Now, Madame Rollin, would you accompany me, please?"

"Where?" She looked like a woken sleeper. The eyes were sharp but shallow with forced attention.

"Hopefully, just a little way out of this room." He indicated with a gesture that the two Czechs had no business to be present. "Do not worry, madame, we will not be leaving Orly at the moment." It was evident that she did not believe him. He saw the two men look at her and realized that her authority was greater than theirs, an acceptance like deference in their faces.

Outside the door he took her to the bench and gestured to her to sit. Wilde looked up and moved

away, while Evans remained. Catherine Rollin looked
around her, as if for a means of escape, then settled
back, the black plastic of the bench squeaking like
leather. She lit a cigarette. When she exhaled, she had
recaptured her usual pugnacious self-control.

"Well, m'sieur. What can I do for you?"

"Why are you going to Warsaw—and in that
company?"

"Is that any of your business—SDECE?" She
asked the question with a sneer. "The pigs?"

He smiled humorlessly.

"We know your opinion of Western security services, madame. Your uncovering of CIA plots in Vietnam does you great credit." He removed the false
smile. "However, what I have to say concerns France,
and it also concerns my colleagues in British Intelligence. . . ." He paused, then snapped, "What is your
relationship with Derek Lidbrooke?"

Her hand covered her mouth, and she appeared
shocked.

"How did you find out?"

Aubrey shrugged in what he considered a Gallic
manner.

"Madame, we have known about you and him for
a long time. What you do in that sordid little flat does
not concern us—except that you are a suspected person and you are now with two men who are evidently
policemen!"

She ran a hand through her hair, pulling it back
from her forehead. Aubrey sensed the sexual appeal
the woman might have to someone like Lidbrooke and
winced inwardly at the obviousness of the manner in
which Lidbrooke might have been trapped. No, he
thought, the erotic element of their relationship would
have to be subordinate and successive. He glanced at
the two Czechs through the glass. Their mood was now
anxious. Soon they would demand to contact their embassy, and Aubrey could not afford to provoke an
incident.

Then Catherine Rollin said, "This is nonsense!
What do you accuse me of—spying? I am a journalist

with left-wing views. Are you pigs interrogating me for that?"

"Madame! I could arrest you now—at this moment!"

"Why don't you?" There seemed a secret source of amusement in the question, certainly a challenge.

"I wish to avoid scandal. I am pursuing the matter in my own way, and you are perhaps an unimportant part. But your relationship with the man Lidbrooke places him under suspicion. I want that suspicion confirmed or removed. Well?"

She was silent for a moment; then she shrugged.

"We are lovers—*were*. There is nothing more to tell. I shall not be seeing him again. I did not know he was a *pig*, like you. Now that I know, I shall not see him again. Anyway, the day you called, we had quarreled."

It was too easy, too simply stated. *A pig, like you.* Aubrey assumed that any innocent affair between them would not have led to any revelation of Lidbrooke's status as a member of the SIS. He would have been a minor diplomat if he had revealed that much. Yet the emphasis had been clear, the indiscretion of anger. He watched her face.

"And is that all? How did you know that Lidbrooke was a member of a foreign security service? Did he tell you?"

She appeared shocked. Right hand over her mouth again, as if to summon back the words.

"No, I didn't know. You made me angry, that's why I said that. Is he such a man?"

Sense of betrayal perhaps? Aubrey could not be certain.

"How long will you be away from France, madame? You do intend to return?"

She smiled.

"Those men are not policemen. I am being escorted by two cultural officials from Czechoslovakia. I shall be in Warsaw for three days, then Prague for perhaps a week. Why? Am I not to be allowed to go?"

"Madame, I have no reason to detain you. I am

not prepared to do so on behalf of another country's security service. You may go."

He stood up and bowed stiffly. She smirked contemptuously and turned away. Horton and Rushton came through the door, and Evans and Wilde joined him. They watched him in anticipation. Aubrey stared into each face and then through the glass at the relieved Czechs and the woman now at her ease.

"Damn that woman! She's just killed Lidbrooke. Handed him over to that little psychopath Napier—damn it to hell!"

Latymer put his hand on the door handle of the car, and said, "Hello, Richard—I've come for a little chat."

He found himself looking into the neat round hole of the barrel of a Browning 9mm. Gardiner had found himself a gun.

It was seven-thirty. Latymer had left Gardiner alone in the car parked under the trees near the hospital until the man was tired, perhaps off his guard, perhaps at his most isolated and vulnerable.

They had kept Perrier in a small first-floor room of the Préfecture de Police, with a single narrow window looking out over the river to the Left Bank and the Quai St. Michel. The remaining hours of the night had been spent in questioning him. Latymer undertook the task himself, while Haussman, only peripherally interested in the matter, it seemed, thrust his head occasionally around the door.

During the hours of their enforced companionship it was as if the Frenchman had visibly diminished. A result, it almost appeared, of the sweat that seeped through the blue shirt, staining the armpits in two widening circles that threatened to meet across his chest. The man smelled, too—a sharp, rank, foxlike smell of fear and captivity.

He had told Latymer nothing, except to confirm, after being bullied, that he and Dupuy had driven the car which had knocked down Gardiner in Rouen. He would give no motive for the act and would not name the man who had given the order. His balding head shone in the light, less greasily than his forehead, thickly bright with sweat. He kept wiping at it with a handkerchief that became a wrinkled gray ball in his fist. He was afraid, righteously indignant, and fawning in turn—but silent a great deal of the time and never to the purpose in his words.

Eventually Latymer left a policeman guarding Perrier and told Haussman what he intended. The Frenchman was gruffly solicitous.

"Watch yourself. You have no idea of the mood your friend might be in. He may not be the civilized Englishman you remember." There was a curious, ironical light in his eyes. "What about Perrier?"

"What do you suggest? Keep him out of Gardiner's way?"

"Hopefully. But I can't hold him here if he wishes to leave. Soon he will have to see his lawyer if he asks."

Latymer went out, and the sky seemed cold. He moved to turn up the collar of his coat and then dismissed the gesture. A detective pointed out the location of the car from the archway of the prefecture, and he moved toward it.

His hand was still on the door handle. His smile was frozen on his face. There was a long silence, and then Gardiner said, "What in hell are you doing here?" He grimaced, as if he perceived some weakness in himself, perhaps observed the true inadequacy of what he had said.

"As I said, Richard—I've come to talk." As if awakening from a trance, Gardiner swung his body in the seat and craned his head to see in a full circle around the car. "It's all right," Latymer added solicitously. "The police know where you are. I'm alone, and unarmed."

He held open his coat to demonstrate the fact, and Gardiner nodded and unlocked the passenger door. Latymer walked around the car and climbed in, his tall frame suddenly bunched in the narrow seat.

"You never were a gunman anyway," Gardiner observed with a brief smile. "You had too much gray matter for that."

"Many thanks."

"What do you want, Hilary?"

"A talk."

"What about?"

"Cabbages and kings, and bodies in La Baule, and *self-defense*," Latymer replied, lightly and carefully. The gun was still pointed at him, close to him now so there was no conceivable chance of his not being hit if it were fired. It was inches from his rib cage.

"What about all that?" Gardiner seemed to resent the words, as if they detracted from him. "I suppose he's still in there, is he?"

"Who—Perrier?" Gardiner nodded, staring straight ahead of him. The traffic was beginning to build up, and he appeared worried by it.

"Are you keeping me here while he makes an exit via the back door?"

"No. He's in protective custody at the moment."

"What has he told you?" There was a barely hidden hunger in the voice.

"Nothing of any interest or value. I think he knows—but he's not telling."

There was contempt in Gardiner's comment as he said, "What did you do to him, Hilary? Ask searching questions—*shout* at him? You don't know the first thing . . . !"

"Was it bad in the Avenue Foch?" Latymer asked insinuatingly. The gun dug him viciously in the ribs, and he winced.

"To hell with you, Hilary! Forget that!"

"Why? You evidently haven't. Look, Richard—I understand, but it's no good going on with this crazy scheme. I think I can persuade the authorities to allow a plea of self-defense in Dupuy's case. . . ."

Gardiner turned to stare at him. Latymer saw, with misgiving, that a younger man stared out at him. Gardiner *was* younger; Latymer had a presentiment that he had lost him, that his words already had a hollow ring. They were the arguments of a civilized man speaking to something alien.

"You don't understand ... ! You don't understand any of it!" Gardiner cried. "That's why you can't make me change my mind." The gun jabbed again painfully in Latymer's ribs. "That's why I'll kill you if you try to stop me, Hilary."

Latymer saw him as a man trying to sever bonds and codes he no longer believed or recognized. *To kill Latymer....* The break would be sudden and complete. Latymer was afraid.

"I—I do. I know what you went through. It happened to a lot of other people too. And you did nothing about it, for so long. . . ." The unvoiced camaraderie of suffering groped for Gardiner, trying to diminish him in his own eyes, like the nineteen fat, useless years of being smaller, *less* than he was now.

"No. Not like me, Hilary. I want Perrier, but more, I want the man who gave the order. I'll go to the end of the world for him." He smiled as if in mockery of his sudden rhetoric. "I don't want anything else. You see, it is as if it was only yesterday, and I've been asleep since. It's because I tried to forget. . . ." His eyes closed for a moment. "But they made me remember it. Dupuy tried to kill me as soon as he recognized me. *I* tried to forget—but no one else had done, not for a bloody minute!"

"It's not like that, Richard! Dupuy was just a fool, and gutless. You frightened him, being there. That was *guilt*. Everyone else has forgotten. . . ."

"But I've remembered."

Latymer knew it was no good. Gardiner had caught sight of himself in a strange mirror which reflected a younger self. Perhaps he was the kind of man he seemed to have become. He had never really known him, he decided.

He could not hand him over to the police. That would be another betrayal.

And he could not take him—he was certain of that.

"What will you do?" he asked. "They won't let you get close to Perrier now."

"I'll find a way, don't worry."

"You may get away from here, but they'll hunt you down."

"You don't have the first idea, Hilary." Latymer saw, oblivious of the gun, the power of the man, the unbelievable power within the skeletal limits of life and death, hunt and be hunted. He saw "Achilles," and perhaps fully for the first time.

It was ludicrous and pathetic, the attempt he had made. Whispering across a chasm of civilization and decency and morality—when he should have yelled.

"I'm very sorry, Richard, very sorry indeed."

"Mm. Are you? Perhaps I am, too. But it's my malaria, the thing that hangs on from the war's jungle. I don't think I ever got rid of it. It just was waiting there for a reinfection. . . ."

Suddenly Latymer said, employing a new perspective, "But you might have lost him even here. Four archways out of the courtyard. You can only possibly see two of them. He might have left, and you couldn't have known! Doesn't that make it all rather hopeless?"

"No. It wouldn't have mattered. I would have found the trail again." There was a resignation and a certainty about him that were more chilling than any other aspects of Gardiner's changed self.

"Why—why did you stay here then?"

"Stupid, wasn't it?" Gardiner smiled. In it there was the glamour that the young men had always possessed—and something else, something only glimpsed in Baker Street or when they dined together and buried since the war. Menace.

"Yes."

"Perhaps I guessed you would come, or someone like you." His face was grave, as if thought were pressing him urgently. "No, not that. Perhaps just the satisfaction of having run the quarry to earth. Or testing the nerve—sitting between the cathedral and the prefecture. The moral absolutes and the danger of arrest." He smiled, enjoying the sudden rhetoric of associations.

He turned his gaze ahead. There was more traffic passing the entrance to the prefecture. Morning and the crowd. He had begun to consider how to rid himself of Latymer when he felt the man stiffen in his seat, and then his attention was caught by movement beneath the archway. He realized that Latymer's eye and brain had been quicker than his own. A sandy-colored suit, the slope of the shoulders, balding head —Perrier was standing next to a bored-looking detective and a taxi was sliding from its parking rank toward them.

"God," Latymer breathed, unable to stifle his reaction.

"Not God, just Perrier!" Gardiner snapped, and the gun came up and pressed against Latymer's jugular. "Out!" The voice was harsh.

Latymer stared ahead and wondered why, if Haussman had been forced to let Perrier go, he had not concealed his departure. It was criminal folly. He did not move from the seat.

"You—what do you intend?"

Perrier climbed into the taxi, and it moved away from the curb, turning into the rue de Lutèce. The gun quivered in Gardiner's hand, then pressed even more firmly against Latymer's neck.

"Get out, Hilary—or I'll blow your head away!"

Latymer opened the door. It was an instinctive reaction, something he had decided against but which he could not help. He knew that Gardiner would kill him, just as he intended to kill Perrier. He had looked in vain for a tailing police car, but there hadn't been one. Perhaps in the rue de Lutèce, coming out of another archway . . . ?"

Then Gardiner hit him across the shoulder with the barrel of the gun and heaved against his body. The pain ran through him, making him sick; then he tumbled into the gutter. The door slammed shut, and the engine fired. He rolled away and had a crazy, inverted view of the facade of Notre Dame, gray and looming. Then he pushed himself to his feet, the effort making him grab at his damaged shoulder. He hobbled after the car as it turned into the rue de la Cité and then the rue de Lutèce.

It passed out of his sight. He ran past the surprised guard, into the courtyard, looking for Haussman.

The taxi was six cars ahead of Gardiner as he turned out of the rue de Lutèce into the Boulevard du Palais, opposite the Palais de Justice. A flash of gold on high black gates, then the stream of traffic over the Pont du Change. It was eight-ten, and he was in the surge of the rush hour. The traffic streamed over the bridge in both directions, and there was no way in which he could get closer to the taxi. He caught only occasional glimpses of it and of the shadowy head of its passenger through the rear window.

He rounded the Napoleon monument in the Place du Châtelet and saw the taxi clearly as it swung broadside to him into the rue de Rivoli. He was still six vehicles behind and locked into the traffic flow. Perrier was an impossible distance from him.

He saw Perrier's face for a moment, looking around him as if blinking in unfamiliar sunlight or afraid of pursuit. He could not know that Gardiner was behind him. The thought of his lack of suspicion, of any focus for his fear, held a grim satisfaction for Gardiner. He thought, momentarily, of Latymer's rigid surprise that Perrier had been released and considered the possibility of some kind of trap. But the release *had* surprised Latymer—either the man had been double-crossed by the French, or there was no trap.

He sensed a seed of disappointment, but the ego swelled around it, and he lost sense of anything beyond the pursuit, willing some of it from his mind, the rest dropping away into darkness.

The brakes screeched as he stamped on them, and the car lurched sideways as the wheels locked. The face of the young woman with the pram—why was she out so early with a baby? he thought—was ashen and then hateful as she glared from windshield to pram and back, her head beginning to wobble like a puppet. There was a pedestrian crossing, and a red light against him, and other people, some of them glancing at him; others, angry with the woman for blocking their path, were passing across his gaze.

He realized his hands were shaking—with reaction, he thought, until he sensed the mounting anger at the young woman as the light changed to green and she was still blocking him, and someone hooted. He spun the car around her, and she had the baby in her arms as if to demonstrate to him the possibilities of collision or wave a banner of normality. But he was around her now and into the rue de Rivoli proper, the great morning artery from the Place de la Bastille to the Place de la Concorde, one-way, thick with traffic that congealed at each set of lights.

Perrier was safe, he realized. A microbe flowing down this sluice of the city's body. There was insufficient time for him to get out of the car and get to the taxi at each of the sets of lights.

Traffic lights at the corner of the Louvre. Sandy stone, and the bare lawn and gravel that fronted the building. The traffic lurched forward again, and he could see the taxi ahead of him; Perrier was still aboard, unaware.

The stream flowed turgidly past the Economic Ministry and the Place du Palais Royal; then they stopped again at the Place des Pyramides, and traffic flowed across in front of them. He became increasingly aware of the danger of the traffic lights. He was still six cars behind the taxi, and at any intersection he could be left stranded by a change of lights. He kept glancing around at the traffic on either side. Four lanes, all closely bunched, yet moving between the sets of lights in a rapid surge, a lavalike suddenness.

There were lights for pedestrian crossings at the Place des Pyramides and the rue de Castiglione which led to the Place Vendôme. Between those two points he had to improve his position relative to the taxi.

Yellow; green. He let out the clutch, twisted the wheel so that the car crossed the next lane of traffic, the howl of three separate car horns behind him. Five cars, and his lane moving with perhaps more speed. Four cars. Yes, it was. An elderly man in the line he had been following, one ahead of the taxi and moving at a sedate pace.

Past, on his left, the Jardin de Carrousel and then the high railings through which he darkly glimpsed the dusty trees and flower beds of the Tuileries. He marked off the narrower streets to his right—rue de St. Roch, rue 29 Juillet, rue d'Alger. . . .

An impatient driver tried to pull out from the rue d'Alger into the stream. An eddy of suddenly halted traffic blared at him and settled on springs, the image of a Citroën settling back like a matron, and then his line of traffic continuing; three cars, two. . . .

The taxi began to pick up speed again and then slowed almost immediately as the lights at the rue de Castiglione halted the traffic, glaring red. Gardiner realized that he was sweating, that his hands gripped the wheel fiercely. He did not allow himself to relax. He was one car behind. Only one now.

Perrier's head, frizzed hair, balding, and the collar of the sandy-colored suit, and the thick shoulders. It was close, pleasingly so; no fierce urge to hurt or kill, but a subtler, more corrupt sense of terror unguessed, the infinite superiority of waiting in a darkened room for an unsuspecting victim. Close, the still air, the oppressive, choking sense of omnipotence.

Perrier turned in his seat. Perhaps he wondered about a police car following him; perhaps his neck was stiff. He saw Gardiner, and then after a long moment he recognized him. The recognition invaded the face, pulling at the mouth until it fell open. "Achilles."

The lights changed, and the traffic surged forward. Gardiner could see, almost level with the taxi, Perrier lean forward and speak to the driver. He was terrified. The gratification was an almost sexual release. Rue Rouget de L'Isle and the English bookshop under the arches, and the taxi was speeding up with three or four other cars ahead of it before the lights at the Place de la Concorde.

Gardiner kept the car almost level with the taxi, judging the lights ahead. Yellow. Perrier was shouting at the driver. Red. The taxi was across the lights, but the driver refused to counter the currents of the square and screeched to a halt. Gardiner was one car back, in the next lane. He moved swiftly.

He almost vaulted the hood of the hire car and closed on the terrified face of Perrier as it stared from the taxi. He pulled open the door, and the atmosphere was heavy with body odor and rank fear. Perrier's mouth opened to say something, but nothing but air was expelled. It was as if his tongue had stuck to the roof of his mouth. Gardiner pulled at the lapels of the suit, dragging the man backward, and the Frenchman's legs scuffed at the road. His body had collapsed in terror. His face, close to Gardiner's, was maplike in the detail of impression and emotions.

"Tell me!" Gardiner ordered, his face pressed against that of Perrier in some kind of parody of love and loving. He straightened the limp form, pressing it against the solidity of the taxi as if trying to make a doll assume a human posture. Perrier shook his head, and Gardiner hit him once so that blood spilled immediately from his nose and split lip. He wanted to hit him again, all reason, all coldness gone—but more he wanted the name, the cryptogram.

"Tell me! Who gave the order? Who?"

A hand fell on his shoulder, and he drove back against the man who must be there—the taxi driver, a pedestrian, elbow driving into something soft. Concussion of breath, but Perrier was pulling suddenly away from his grip; a feeble fist waved close to his face; then Perrier was doubling around the bulk of the taxi. Gardiner heard, distinctly, as if in prelude to the concert of horns as the lights changed, someone laugh. He was involved in some sordid, comic little domestic quarrel. He ran after Perrier, taking the wrong direction because he expected Perrier to head for the rue St. Florentin.

He was heading for the Place de la Concorde.

Perrier was going to get himself killed. Perrier ran, head down, dodging the amused pedestrians, hearing the first scream of brakes as the six lanes of traffic coming from the left around the outer circle of the Place moved in the direction of the rue Royale, encountering Perrier.

Gardiner felt sick.

Perrier handed off a car that slid to a halt, the movement of a rugby player in grotesque. The impact made him wring his hands and overbalance. Other cars swerved to avoid him, and Gardiner began to gain on him because the traffic was already still.

It was the experience of watching the world changed—the noise of brakes, tires, horns, the certainty that he could smell the rubber, the swift-moving lines of jockeying cars and lorries suddenly bunched, distorted, broken.

And the man still moving across the face of the traffic, a desperate, shuffling figure, fleeing for its life.

A car struck him a glancing blow, then careered into a truck that had stamped on its air brakes. Another car ran into the back of it. Other figures now, climbing like dreamers or submariners from their cars, mouths opening slowly like snails to shout words that could not be heard. There was an element of farce in the thing.

Perrier staggered, his trouser leg ripped and the flesh red beneath it. He was twenty-five yards from the lights at the top of the rue Rivoli and dying like a hunted animal. It was as if the cars were dogs and they had been afraid, yapping and nipping around their quarry. Now they saw blood and closed in.

Perrier was blind to each succeeding line of traffic, as they were to him.

Suddenly, with Gardiner still ten yards from him, his body was flung into the air like something worried by a dog, flipped so that its neck broke. The sandy-colored suit, the inverted, twisted face, the clumsy, ugly loop of the body over the hood of a black car. Then he went down, and Gardiner could not see him. But he saw another car rise slowly, then settle, having run over the inert body.

Gardiner felt the nausea in his throat. Perrier was dead. He began to run, blindly himself now, toward the rue Royale, away from Concorde.

8. Professional Expertise

Napier arrived on the morning flight from Heathrow. Aubrey, tired and unshaved as if in calculated insult, had not left Orly since his interview with Catherine Rollin. He had watched the Aeroflot Tupolev take off for Warsaw, climbing into what was already a dazzling, clean sky. Then he had drunk coffee with Evans and Rushton in the main lounge while Horton and Wilde returned to tailing Lidbrooke, who would spend most of the morning and the early part of the afternoon in sessions of a subcommittee.

Aubrey felt wretched. The imminence of Lidbrooke's death was like a heavy stone on his chest making the act of breathing painful. There was a kind of moral nausea attached to it, of course, but more insistently, the depression of a dedicated but civilized man forced once more to confront the stark, final, unambiguous realities of his strange profession. It unnerved him, as if the firm ground had unaccountably shifted or become sandy beneath his feet. He liked to think well of the work in which he engaged, and the execution of Lidbrooke was not a good thought.

Napier looked very young, his hair cropped as if he had just left the army, his skin unlined and boyish. He was wearing a gray suit with narrow lapels and manufactured in some shiny mohair material. It looked cheap, like the pointed shoes that curled at the toes. He carried a single bag as luggage, though

Aubrey knew it contained very little. Napier would be back in London that evening. His eyes were gray and sullen. There was something slightly unfinished, certainly unpolished, about Napier.

When he spoke to Aubrey, his tone was intended to be respectful, though he was at no great pains to disguise the aristocracy of his function. He held out his hand, and the grip was soft, girlish.

"Good morning, Mr. Aubrey."

"Morning," Aubrey replied abruptly.

"Deputy asked me to convey his congratulations, Mr. Aubrey. He's very pleased." There was a slightly mocking light in his eyes. It was apparent to Aubrey that Napier was totally unconcerned at the prospect of executing his own assistant head of section, and there was something hideous in that lack of concern.

"You have your orders from Deputy, I presume?" Aubrey said.

Napier nodded, and Aubrey confirmed, in his own mind, the growing influence of Constant within the SIS, an influence which far outweighed that of Lavender, the other Deputy "C." The control of SIS was slipping into the hands of a career professional, away from the kind of watchdog HM Opposition desired.

Aubrey understood the power of Constant, the decisiveness that had led from his own report directly to the arrival of Napier. Napier had not taken his orders from the head of SO-1, who might have protested, but from the overall operations director, Constant, who was establishing a precedent, a mode of internal operation which Aubrey detested and against which he was impotent.

They took Napier to the car and drove back to the city. The traffic was thinner now that the rush hour was over. Aubrey's hair prickled at the back of his neck as he remained continually aware of the occupant of the back seat. He felt actual physical discomfort throughout the journey.

"What is his program for today?" Napier asked as they crossed the motorway ring. It seemed an age since their pursuit of Rollin. *An age has passed,* Aubrey thought. Napier spoke with complete detachment.

"NATO HQ this A.M.," Aubrey replied, the tone of his voice turning Evans's head quizzically toward him. "Then, after lunch, he has a plenary session of the subcommittee, then home. . . ." He let the words fall away, sensing the thin smile on Napier's lips.

"He'll have to leave the building, Mr. Aubrey." It was not a request.

"And how do you intend to dispose of the body?" Aubrey's lips were compressed, his voice impotently angry.

"A hit-and-run." Aubrey wondered again about Napier's origins. There was a northern flatness in the voice, overlaid with the nasal whine of an urban area. Liverpool, perhaps.

"Constant's idea, I presume?"

"Yes, sir. It's the least fussy way. I'll use one of the pool cars from the embassy, with changed plates." Again it was an order, Constant using Napier as a ventriloquist's dummy. "You'll arrange for him to leave the building, Mr. Aubrey." Aubrey thought of Constant again, hearing him in the voice. He shook his head to clear it of the hateful, clogging images.

The car rolled into the courtyard in the rue de Castellane, and Aubrey climbed wearily out. He was tired now, and he had begun to anticipate returning to London. Evans and Rushton took the car away, and Aubrey preceded Napier to the first-floor apartment.

Latymer was unsurprised by the appearance of Napier behind Aubrey. He, too, appeared tired, and he was nursing his shoulder and a large scotch, despite the early hour. There were heavy shadows beneath his fine eyes, and his skin was pale and drawn. For a moment Aubrey wondered whether Victoria had died and he had just received news; then he saw irritation on his lips and knew that Latymer had in some way lost Gardiner.

"What happened?" he said, indicating a chair to Napier, who nodded to Latymer and sat down. Immediately he appeared to retreat into some comfortable, abstracted state; a piece of machinery switched off.

"I spoke to him. Then Haussman released Perrier right in front of Richard's eyes, and he went after him like a dog after a hare." The image was light, but the voice somber. "Perrier tried to escape—some lunatic dash across the Place de la Concorde. He was knocked down!"

Aubrey's eyes flashed involuntarily to Napier's face. It was impassive. Then he said, "What about Gardiner?"

"Vanished from the face of the earth." Latymer shrugged, and scotch slopped from the glass onto his trousers. With an almost fierce concentration, he rubbed at the wet stain. Then he looked up. "Richard still doesn't know the name he wants. . . . God, it's a bloody mess, Aubrey!"

"I agree," Aubrey replied softly. "What did Richard have to say?"

"Very little. He's changed, Aubrey." Latymer looked up again, and there was a strange and desperate expression on his face. Aubrey was reminded of the occasion on which he had informed him of Victoria's illness. Latymer had perceived some terminal disease in Richard Gardiner. "I don't understand it. Perhaps it needs a psychiatrist to unravel it. I think he will go on now until the end of the world, until he finds his betrayer and kills him. Something—*legendary*, I suppose is the only word. Something out of a myth."

"Don't grant him that kind of status. He's just a little more mad than the rest of us. Life is simple for him as it is." He glanced at Napier and added, "Catherine Rollin nailed down the coffin when I spoke to her this morning!"

Latymer appeared barely interested. Instead of replying, he swallowed at his scotch, choking on the liquor.

"Derek, may I wish you a fond farewell, my boy!" Eugene Van Lederer held out his huge hand to grip

Lidbrooke's long, delicate fingers. Gray hairs sprouted from the knuckles.

Lidbrooke looked into the eyes and smiled.

"Thank you, General—and may I wish you the same, and good hunting, wherever the hunting is to be."

Van Lederer smiled. He was in full uniform and had just attended to last pieces of unimportant business before flying back to Washington. He anticipated a couple more days in Paris, but on a strictly unofficial basis and devoted to pleasure.

His business as chairman was over, but he was a man who appreciated those who contributed positively to the work of the senior committee, and meeting Lidbrooke by chance in the corridor, he had spontaneously greeted him, taken his hand.

Lidbrooke had never been anti-American in his spoken or unspoken attitudes, unlike so many of his colleagues in the SIS. He had always admired their budget for Intelligence, their thoroughness, their gadgetry, and their temperament. He was a man who wore his own emotions and opinions openly, and this made him warm to a man like Van Lederer. A professional, yet with his humanity close to the surface.

"Take care, Derek, always take care!" Van Lederer said with a smile. "Be seeing you."

"Thank you, sir. And you—stay around for the pension from the Pentagon!"

Van Lederer laughed aloud and waved his hand as he moved off down the corridor. Watching him go, Lidbrooke shook his head affectionately. Then the loudspeaker spoke over his head.

"Telephone call for Derek Lidbrooke."

"Damn!" He was irritated suddenly. He wanted his lunch. He made his way to the nearest telephone and requested the call to be put through. It was Kenneth Aubrey.

"Derek, glad to have caught you before you left. Can we have a spot of lunch together? One or two things I'd like to discuss with you, away from the hubbub of the office."

"You're in Paris, Kenneth?" And Lidbrooke was suddenly aware that Aubrey was head of the new section, SO-4, the watchdog on internal security in the service. And he felt afraid. "What—what is it?" he asked, silently damning the throat that was suddenly clogged with phlegm. "I—I haven't a lot of time, you know."

"It'll take no more than half an hour, I promise. Can that much time be spared from your busy schedule?" The voice was sudden with asperity, and Lidbrooke felt prepared for some unpleasantness.

"Oh, very well," he said as offhandedly as he could. "Where shall we meet?"

"Pick me up at the rue de Castellane apartment. Can do?"

"Yes. I'll get a taxi."

The dial tone purred irritatingly in Lidbrooke's ear. As he replaced the receiver, he saw that it was damp and rubbed at his ear, which seemed hot and burning. He was suspicious now because there was a cause for suspicion.

Aubrey, the watchdog.

What the devil did he want?

He walked out of the foyer of the NATO building, past the bright-buttoned marines on guard, white puttees and slim rifles, eyes expressionless, but less significant than the men behind the armored glass of the reception booth who had recognized him and not impeded his exit.

He was worried, and the thoughts tumbled in his head like childish fears. As if he had stolen from his mother's purse or cheated in an exam and been discovered—lurid images of disgrace, embarrassment, failure flickered in his head.

Catherine Rollin. Of course, he had known of the suspicions, had known, too, when she was cleared and downgraded. Not that it had mattered. By then he was involved with her. It hadn't mattered. She was his mistress, and the suspicions, even the possible dangers to his career, all had seemed to add some piquant *necessity* to his relationship with her.

Now what could he say? *I am libidinous, forgive me. Culpa me—mea culpa. The sins of the flesh, and she is very good in bed and I could not resist the sense of danger accompanying every bout beneath the sheets.* . . . *Surely I received your permission when she was downgraded?*

Aubrey would not believe or pity any of it. His blue eyes would glitter, and he would go for the throat.

He walked past a fountain, feathers of spray from the peacock tail of water light on his face, as if trying to cool what he knew must be a burning blush. He would have to explain. Aubrey, his subtle and complex mind—he could never bluff it out as a weakness of the flesh.

He looked swiftly in each direction as he crossed the boulevard toward the taxi rank on the other side. But distracted in thought, he did not hear the anonymous black saloon with the reinforced fenders, the damageproof headlights, and the scratchproof bumper as it pulled out from the curb. It was a classic kill.

Napier's view was of the white face, the slow stain of fear spreading on it lividly, like fungus, then the arched leap of the body as it was flung onto the hood, then the slide of the distorted cheek down the windshield—usually they did not obscure the windshield, except for a moment—the mouth plucked open absurdly by the wiper so that the lip pulled like the mouth of a fish on a hook. . . .

Then the body was behind the car, and Napier knew that Lidbrooke was dead. He glanced in the mirror to satisfy himself finally and then accelerated away from the activity that was beginning to cluster around the body—a marine running as if through thick amber, a taxi driver crossing the road through the same glutinous reality. . . .

Henri Janvier knew of his cousin's death. He knew that Perrier had been taken to the Judiciaire, later released, and then got himself killed in the Place de la Concorde, with the man Gardiner in pursuit. Gardiner had since disappeared.

He sat outside a café, apparently idling away time watching the passersby in the rue de Médicis near the Luxembourg; in fact, he was watching the entrance to

Gardiner's hotel, two doors away. At that moment Gardiner was in his room.

To Janvier, who had found Gardiner's hiding place the previous day, his cousin's death meant nothing, nothing emotional. Naturally he had been in touch with Etienne de Vaugrigard, and the man had, with an air of reluctance now that Perrier's death seemed to make him safe, renewed the offer. Because Janvier reminded him that he, too, now possessed the information Gardiner sought.

Janvier's slow mind was marked by its avarice. He did nothing except for money, a lot of money. His prices were high, and he was especially deaf to the appeals the OAS made to his patriotism when it was bereft of funds.

He poured himself another glass of rough red wine and swallowed a mouthful. It bit the back of his throat, and he could almost feel it coating his teeth. He drew on his cigarette. As he sat at the table, he was anonymously French, attracting no attention, a checkered shirt and loose, old trousers. His jacket, in which he carried the gun, was over the back of a chair, close to his hand.

He was not a stupid man, though slow. His sense of self-preservation was enormous. At thirty, at forty, even at forty-five, he had enjoyed the handwriting of his own violence, the signature of "Plastique" on everything he successfully attempted. The notoriety pleased him, easing by its assertion of identity a loneliness that he was hardly aware of most of his conscious life. Now, over fifty, that flirtation had died, and the narrower, more insistent grabbing of an aging man had overtaken him. Now imitations of his handiwork irritated, even frightened, him.

He had not worked for some months. His prices were unrealistic. It was obvious that he was asking higher prices because he wanted to retire—caring a little too much about the security of his future.

Whatever de Vaugrigard said, it would stretch credibility to assume that Gardiner's death would be construed as that of an innocent victim of the OAS.

So Henri Julien Janvier had got himself a gun.

An old service revolver, heavy caliber, something he had stashed behind the skirting in the damp, cheap apartment he rented under another name in the rue de Bièvre, a narrow, twisting alley that ran down to the Seine from the Boulevard St. Germain. It was something he had intended, in brave, forgotten days, for that final shoot-out when the police came for him. The early days of big money and the newspapers clamoring for his arrest and the secrecy of the rue de Bièvre. Now the street was designated for rebuilding, and the apartment would be swept away, together with the smell of damp that never left it and the narrow courtyard full of rubbish and dogs that relieved themselves against the doorposts.

It would be a simple robbery with violence. A burglar who, disturbed during his work by the occupant of the hotel room, would have killed in blind panic.

Janvier was nervous; he could not disguise that with tobacco and wine and memories. He was a good shot, but he was out of practice. And Gardiner had killed Dupuy, and Dupuy had had the gun. It was why he had drunk most of the wine, though it was barely midday. The only solution was to give himself the advantage of complete surprise. When Gardiner was out, he had to occupy the room in the Hôtel Fleur de Lys, a tourist trap of ordinary rooms and high summer prices, and wait for him to return. He would suitably arrange the corpse later.

His hand jumped on the table, and the dregs in his glass stained the checkered cloth. Gardiner had walked out of the hotel entrance and past him to the Place Edmond Rostand. Janvier did not look at him, hid his face as the man passed, dressed in a summer-weight suit of French cut, sandals, open-neck yellow shirt, and cravat. He was wearing dark glasses and carried a camera. Tourist.

When he had gone, Janvier turned to follow him. He saw him go into the Luxembourg and changed his mind. He was in some danger of being picked out as a tail, and that he did not want. He turned back in his seat and attended with a fierce concentration to the wet rings of dull red wine on the tablecloth. In a moment he would enter the hotel and force his way into Gardiner's room. It would be simple.

He found, not really to his surprise, that his hand was sweating. The knowledge disturbed him. He wiped his hand angrily on his trouser leg.

The sunlight in the Luxembourg was blinding, splintering off the huge ornamental pool in front of the palace and whitening the strips of dusty, graveled path. The grass caused the eyes to ache: a painted color, unnatural.

Gardiner had stilled the shaking of his body by an effort of will. For perhaps an hour after he had returned to the hotel, from the Place de la Concorde, he had not been able to still the racing images, like those of a drunken half sleep, as they flashed upon the mind. He squinted behind his Polaroid sunglasses against the light and against his own disappointment. He felt cast adrift, having exchanged the tiller of morality and custom for one of will or desire. The death of Perrier had snapped cables, torn off a rudder he thought was there.

He began once more to perceive the changes that the death of Dupuy had worked in his personality—changes or reaffirmations, he could not be certain and would not inquire closely. Now cold moral sense vied with hot anger and frustration for possession of him.

He sat down on a bench and watched children playing—bright blobs of color, focused spots of bright sound. He tried to think of his own sons, the somber old children now probably returning to their boarding school. There was no call to him from their direction; they were faces held up, like the white bundle in the woman's hands on the pedestrian crossing, which he did not acknowledge.

A checkered plastic ball rolled to his feet. He watched the dark-faced child approach, picked up the ball in one hand, and threw it to her. It was as if he, the carrier of some virulent disease, did not wish her to come any closer.

He began to think in some sort of sequence.

There were others, perhaps, members of the old group, still alive. Perhaps Vivienne Grodin had not told him everything? He began to imagine the conspiracy against him, exorcising lingering traces of loyalty, evidences of admiration and respect. The faces flickered, and each one of them acquired a patina of guilt. His anger against them grew out of a need to avoid the recent past, which had threatened to come back, and to reforge links with the age of monoliths—1944. He had to go back to work, to seek out, discover.

It did not occur to him to question what was happening. He merely wanted to go on because anything else seemed more painful or empty or complex. If he had to kill them all, he would find out. There was the refreshment of a close shave or a long drink, in that blinding sunlight, to be drawn from such a simplification of reality. He was able soon to get up, to walk back to the hotel with purpose. His steps were swifter, positive.

There was a letter waiting for him at the desk. Gardiner took it from the clerk and glanced at it on his way up in the lift, a gilded cage from a film set or a more grandiose establishment.

The letter bore a Paris postmark, dated that morning. He wondered at it, staring at the anonymous type. Then he ripped open the envelope, pulling out the single sheet, his fingers nerveless with the shock that someone knew his pseudonym. The loose bars of the cage rattled as the lift jerked away from the second floor, where it had stopped. There was no one waiting for it.

It was a confession, in handwriting; he did not believe it, but his blood pumped in confirmation. The flimsy sheet of cheap paper quivered in his grip.

The lift stopped. He moved jerkily out into the corridor, robotic and stiff. It was signed by Perrier—a handwriting and signature he could not certify. It was brief and complete. It was what he would have beaten from Perrier, blown off the kneecaps or electrocuted the testicles to find out. The name of the man. Perrier had known, even before the police had come for him, known he would give in. The will had collapsed. He had written the letter to save himself.

Etienne de Vaugrigard.

He felt nauseated. It was a tangible blow to the stomach.

Etienne de Vaugrigard.

He paused at the door of his room, pushed it open, and found himself looking into the face of a stranger and down the barrel of an old service revolver. It was pointed at Gardiner's stomach.

After a long moment of silence in which Gardiner kept glancing from the letter to the gun, the man said, "What does your letter contain, m'sieur? It seems to distract you even from the gun. That is very strange."

Gardiner looked up from the letter, irritated by the intrusion of the man's voice. He had almost forgotten about him as his attention was drawn insistently back to the name at the bottom of the letter. *Etienne.* . . . He did not know this man. The gun moved a little in dramatic emphasis of the voice.

"Who are you? What do you want?"

"I am here to take care of you, m'sieur. My name does not matter."

The big man smiled. The body was awkward, Gardiner thought, but the eyes were coldly professional. Someone else who had learned his trade by practicing on the Nazis in occuped France. And perhaps Foreign Legion, even OAS.

He was sitting with his back to the window so that the light was not in his eyes.

"Are you anything to do with Perrier?" The man's eyes did not flicker. "What about Etienne de Vaugrigard?" The flicker then. Gardiner held out the flimsy sheet of paper. "It's in here, you know. Your man Perrier—he wrote a full confession. . . ."

"I do not know of Perrier or this other man."

"Why deny it? It doesn't matter since you're going to kill me anyway."

"The latter is most certainly true, m'sieur." The gun steadied again on his stomach.

"Then tell me."

"Knowledge might make you desperate. I don't

want a struggle." The man shrugged, as if in sympathetic understanding.

The conversation had awoken Gardiner. Now his brain raced to solve the simple problem of survival. Knowledge defined itself as distances, reaction times, the quality of the light, the accuracy of the French-made service revolver. It was an amusing irony, he was capable of thinking, to be killed by one of the guns made in the factories of Etienne's grandfather for the Great War. Ridiculous.

"I understand," he said. "I simply hope that you were well paid for this job. Better paid than the bastards who ran me over in Rouen!" He was sweating now, a forced raising of the emotional temperature. He had to look frightened, even cowed. Janvier nodded and smiled. Gardiner saw the assumption of superiority given him by the gun now increased by the fear in the victim's eyes. That sense of comforting superiority would delay the execution, perhaps for minutes.

"A shame, m'sieur. I am sorry for you." Expansive talk, the adoption of mannerisms from the cinema. It was the first time, or nearly so. He should have understood that from the old revolver. This man killed at a distance or had done so for many years; explosives probably. He was unused to this kind of confrontation and was unable to control the mounting satisfaction that the guy gave him. Gardiner had to wait, to prolong the moments.

"For God's sake, I'll give you more than he did, whoever he is!"

"I am sorry, m'sieur, but it cannot be done. I have accepted the contract, and I cannot go back on it." The luxurious delight was still there.

Gardiner said, "Think about it. For God's sake, think about it!"

Again the big man shook his head.

"I was told you would not beg, m'sieur. That you would be a difficult man to kill. You do not impress me, however."

Gardiner was winning. He realized that this man was afraid, that he had been anxious of using the gun, of facing his victim. There had been one like him in the old group. Death at second hand, and they could stomach the slaughter, even delight in it. But they did not like blood on things or the twitch of the body, the wild faces of death. He said, "For God's sake, don't you have any human feelings? I don't want to end here, blown to pieces by that cannon in your hand. I'll *pay* you!"

Gardiner saw the avarice for a moment in the narrowed eyes, the smell of temptation. And he saw the sense of the binding contract and the satisfaction at his present helplessness. The big man could not be bought; he would have to kill him.

They were three yards apart. He had managed that much from pure instinct, the prompting of old reflexes. He was sitting on the newly made bed, and the big man was in the chair. There was little purchase in the soft springs of the bed. He could feel them yielding under his hands now. He had one chance, and only one. One shot from the old revolver, at that range, would be accurate. It was hopeless.

"M'sieur, why not accept things as they are? You are going to die."

"Oh, Christ . . . !" Gardiner's mouth trembled. He concentrated fear and pleading into his facial muscles, and the rest of his body learned the necessary tension. He would have to close his eyes and his ears. Noise and the flash of the gun, close enough to stun him.

The big man in his confidence brought out a packet of cigarettes. He had reached a state of incaution toward the sniveling wretch at the other end of the gun. He could afford this last gesture. He tossed the packet and a box of matches into Gardiner's lap.

"Smoke, m'sieur. It might help you." His big face twisted into a sardonic grin. Gardiner lit the cigarette and held the packet in his hand. He offered to throw it back, then did so. Just a foot or so wide of the big man's lap, low down.

The smoke was still in Gardiner's mouth, expelled with the same kind of force that explodes a ski jumper out into space; his hands dug into the bed, finding the limits of the springs's resistance, and then his body uncoiled. Janvier moved instinctively to catch the cigarette packet. The gun moved aside momentarily.

Then Gardiner was on top of him, the chair forced backward, overturning, the big man's body stretched under Gardiner. The gun exploded, and its smoke was in Gardiner's nostrils. He opened his eyes and saw the big man's face beneath his own, then grabbed the wrist of the right hand, forcing the barrel of the gun up and away from him.

He worked in a deaf universe, grappling with the big man. The gun had done that. He felt the fat hand reaching up for his chin, to force it back, and he went for the eyes—the soft squelch of the jelly, the shudder that he felt and the scream that he could not hear. Then he leaned back, still holding the right wrist, and chopped across the white throat, exposed to him with its stubble from poor shaving. The wrist in his grip went slack, began to fall. The big gun hit the floor, and he heard the distant sound.

He stood up, shaking with relief and the excitement of the kill. He did not look into the big man's eyes or at the head hanging slackly to one side, a dribble of blood combining with the spittle around the full lips. He kicked the gun savagely under the bed, as if in an expression of anger.

It took him only a few minutes to clean the cupboards and the drawers of everything he required. He abandoned most of the clothing but took the money and the *cartes des identités* he might require. Then he straightened his clothing, washed his face in cold water, and left the room. He had the letter from Perrier folded inside his wallet.

"Gardiner has left the hotel, but Janvier hasn't come out." The voice from the telephone was cool, matter-of-fact. *L'Etranger*, who had sent the letter purporting to be from Perrier, was angry, yet relieved.

"Use your official identity, and go in and find out what has happened. If 'Plastique' is dead, then do what you have to. But give Gardiner time to act against de Vaugrigard."

"Very well. You think he's dead then?"

"Of course. He was a fool, trying to take Gardiner with a gun. He should have stuck to his specialty." The tone was gruff, businesslike. There was no place for pity; only a certain satisfaction that he had chosen well, that Gardiner was living up to a forgotten reputation. "Get on with it."

"Shall I report back to you straightaway?"

"Naturally. I'll wait for your call. There is someone on Gardiner, I presume?"

"Fouquier and Matisse. They won't lose him."

"Good. It will take Gardiner approximately ten minutes to discover where de Vaugrigard lives. I want to make sure he talks to him first, not kills him straight away. That's why the confession from Perrier had to contain a reference to someone else's giving the order."

"Clever," was the dry comment from the receiver.

"Find out what has happened."

He sat at his desk for a few moments, his strong fingers drumming on the surface, next to the square blotter. Then he picked up the telephone again and dialed. When a woman answered, he asked for Etienne de Vaugrigard.

"Etienne," he said when he heard the quick breathing at the other end, "you have been a very naughty child! You have tried to protect yourself, not believing that I would do that for you." There was a mocking remonstrance and a world-weariness in the tone.

"What do you mean?"

"To think that you believed I would not know that 'Plastique' is Perrier's cousin. And that you employed them both. And now they are both dead."

"What?" A small choking sound at the end of the line.

"Gardiner has just left his hotel. He won't be back. Henri Julien Janvier was waiting for him inside. He has not appeared. I'm afraid he is dead. In the newspaper tonight you will no doubt read the popular headline *'Plastique est mort!'* " He laughed without humor.

"Oh, my God. . . ."

"Don't worry. He's on his way to see you now, I shouldn't wonder."

"Don't worry . . . ?"

"We will keep an eye on him. He knows who he's looking for, and he will want to talk to you, if not kill you. . . . However, he has been informed that you possess valuable information about the real betrayer. He *will* want to talk first. I'll arrange for you to be protected. You won't be in any real danger."

"Told him? How?" De Vaugrigard was dangerously near the death of all courage.

L'Etranger said, "No worry of yours. Just expect a visit, that's all."

He replaced the receiver delicately and sat back in his chair. It was proceeding according to plan. Gardiner, fresh from another death, was eager for knowledge. When he gained it, he would be unstoppable. The "Wolf" and "Wolverine" were finally in real danger. It had been a wise choice, that of Gardiner. Solution to his problem by a single stroke. Two strokes, he corrected himself.

And the "Wolverine" was in Paris at that moment. Perhaps it might be as well to inform Gardiner, as soon as he had spoken to de Vaugrigard.

A beautiful plan. And the "Wolf" and the "Wolverine" having climbed so high as to be virtually unassailable. No ordinary method of removing them would have sufficed. But a rogue agent, from the war —doors would open because he would not know they were there. And who would ever suspect him?

He laughed aloud, and his secretary looked up in the next room.

He shuffled the papers on his desk, as if mimicking the act of completion, of tidying—and a thought struck him. His mind lurched on its calm pinnacle for a moment, then felt embroiled in another consciousness, as if Gardiner's personality had somehow found entry to his mind.

He dialed the number of the room his phone-tap team was using and waited impatiently for the receiver to be picked up. Strong fingers drumming on the blotter.

"Yes? Challot? Listen. I want to be informed of any telephone calls that de Vaugrigard makes in the next minutes, any meetings he arranges, any name he uses—understand? It's urgent."

He put down the telephone. If Etienne moved, he would be tailed. But he would arrange to meet—whom? *L'Etranger* had an idea, though uncertain. Etienne would run—that had been the purpose of his call.

But what would Gardiner do? The man had just killed again, frenzy of adrenaline, of ego. Boiling in him. Would he stop to ask questions of Etienne?

L'Etranger knew a moment of acute fear, heard at the back of his mind the crumbling of great and solid-seeming edifices. It could, even now, all come to nothing if Gardiner killed before he asked.

"*Merde,*" he muttered, then over and over: "*Merde.*"

Too clever by half, people aren't robots, you can't predict everything—the ideas ran in his head, clichés which assumed a new power.

The telephone rang.

"Yes?" Hand jerking like that of a puppet, snatching the receiver.

"Tap room, Chief."

"Yes?"

"He called the Englishman Latymer, arranged to meet him straightaway."

"Where?"

"The Avenue de Madrid house—suggested an afternoon horseback ride, then asked him to come at once."

"Right."

He put down the telephone, considered for a moment, received an image of a man riding a horse in the field of vision of a telescopic sight, clear as celluloid entertainment, luridly colored, then snapped on the intercom and summoned a senior assistant from the outer room.

9. Movement and Rest

Etienne de Vaugrigard kept a clutch of horses for himself and his family at the stables of the Société d'Equitation de Paris in the Bois de Boulogne. His house on the Avenue de Madrid was almost directly opposite one of the entrances to the *bois*.

Latymer felt oddly defenseless and at the same time ridiculously ill-garbed for his meeting with de Vaugrigard. Bright-yellow sweater, jodhpurs, riding boots that creaked with good leather and desuetude. All the while they changed, walked to the *bois,* watched while the horses were saddled and led out, Etienne said nothing, seeming pleased that Latymer had assented to the change of costume.

Latymer knew that Etienne was frightened, yet he retained his own silence until they had trotted across the tarmac of the rue de la Muette and into one of the *allées des cavaliers* that threaded through the *bois*. Then: "What is it, Etienne? What's troubling you that we need this pretense of normality?" He gestured with riding crop and reins. De Vaugrigard seemed physically struck. Sunlight split down through the heavy trees, and he acted as if it had caught him naked. He urged his horse to a canter, leaving Latymer behind.

Latymer drew alongside after perhaps a hundred yards. Suddenly Etienne de Vaugrigard angered him, and he raised his voice.

"Etienne, I asked you what the matter was? This pretense is getting us nowhere!" The horses gathered speed, Latymer this time anticipating the surge. "What the devil is it? If I can help, I will!"

His voice seemed to calm Etienne for a moment. The man reined in abruptly, so that Latymer was made to turn awkwardly on the docile mare, nudging her close to de Vaugrigard. Looking into the face of the Frenchman, he saw patterns of confusion chase across his features, as if years were passing across the face.

"I have to talk to you about it, Hilary—about Richard Gardiner."

"What about Richard?"

"I lied to you before!"

It was hysterical, almost womanish. They had stopped in a clearing. Sunlight spilled down through the broken roof of branches, sheets of yellow-white. The two horses began to nuzzle each other and the grass. Two middle-aged men, out for an afternoon ride—lucky to have the time and income. Latymer nudged aside the sudden deception of stillness.

"What is it?"

A door had opened; Gardiner's name was talismanic.

"I—I am the one he is looking for, Hilary!" Blurted out, like a child owning up as a circle of parental inquiries closed around him—intense experience, whole years compressed into the tense, clipped words.

"You? What do you mean, you're the one he's looking for?"

"He wants to kill me! Can I make it any clearer than that?" It was one of the most pressingly real encounters Latymer had ever experienced. Some cone of silence enveloped the two of them. Waves of anger, fear, shame emanated from de Vaugrigard.

"Why?"

"I betrayed him—I was the one!"

"You?"

Excuse, justification, imperatives—rushing now after confession. Putting back the torn mask. "I—had to hand Renaud over to the Gestapo, and Gardiner was to be the proof that it wasn't a setup—for *verisimili-tude!*" He spat out the last word.

"Oh, my God . . ."Latymer breathed, then felt the contempt surge through him like an icy wave. "Why did you do it?"

"The group—orders. . . . I was a member of the 'Wolfgroup,' Hilary. Does that mean anything to you? The 'Wolfgroup'—you know what it was for?"

Latymer nodded, his face screwed up like a child remembering some difficult lesson—the algebra of secret betrayals.

"Yes—anti-Communist, wasn't it? Just rumors. . . ." Then, seized by the intimacy of revelation: "You were recruited into it?"

"Yes, yes. I betrayed many Communists to the Gestapo. . . . It was my function. Renaud was supposed to give away the location of 'Duroc' to the Gestapo, prevent the uprising in Paris—that's why I did it. I didn't have any choice!"

Latymer said without trace of sympathy, "Who gave the orders, Etienne? Who?"

De Vaugrigard's face closed with craft. No longer two middle-aged men. One of them had shrunk, an ancient creature in a bag of skin.

"Not until you promise to help me."

"What help?"

"Protection."

"God, Etienne—do you know what happened to Richard in the cellars of the Avenue Foch, what happened to all the others you helped send there?" Latymer felt the moral temperature rising, the condemnation choking him. "You want me to help save your miserable skin?" He paused. "No," he said as if to himself. "Not that. What help can I give you? I don't even know where Richard is."

"You must help me. There's more to it. Something from now, not from the past. . . ." De Vaugrigard was cunning, the horse edged closer, conspiratorial against the flanks of Latymer's mare.

"More?"

And he caught a shadow of movement at the edge of the clearing.

"Yes, more. But promise me. . . ."

"I—"

A shirt or sweater, caught by a sheet of sunlight. The slight movement of a bush. Suddenly another image, the one that had to do with nakedness, of the target he made in the bright color; he wondered, for an instant, whether de Vaugrigard had made him the better target, his own sweater an olive drab.

He had to come out of the bushes—that was part of it, the bravado of execution, not the slinking murder. Richard. Latymer gasped, and there was a pain at the side of his head, as if he had been struck by the gun Gardiner held stiffly out from his body. Execution.

De Vaugrigard, seeing something in his face, turned to follow his gaze. Saw Gardiner.

"You . . ." he whispered, and seemed to accuse Latymer.

"Richard! Listen now—listen to me!"

There was all the time in the world. Latymer could see the thought in Gardiner's smile from thirty yards away. He could see the words forming as the man decided that talk was profitable postponement.

"Hilary, stop shuffling your horse to shield him. I'll kill you both, if necessary." The words were spoken almost softly. Authority, certitude carried them across the still clearing. Loudly, around the mare's head, a fly buzzed. Latymer, watching the steady aim, was careful not to brush it away as it spun around his ears. A bead of sweat ran down the side of de Vaugrigard's smooth face to the heavy jowl. He, too, seemed incapable of movement or careful of it.

"Richard, we must talk. You have to understand this—"

"Understand? I understand. You want to keep it nice and civilized. Don't worry. The equivalent of the parks department won't let him lie here for long. Bad for tourists!"

"Wait!" De Vaugrigard, a strangled cry.

"Ah. I think he wishes to add something to the conversation. Yes, Etienne?"

"I—had orders—orders, from above, do you understand? I can give you names!"

"Names? Did your orders include trying to kill me in Rouen, on top of everything else?"

Latymer listened to the boom of the voice, heard the words bounce off some wall in his mind, rise in volume and import. Gardiner was moving closer to the kill with every moment.

The horse snickered, stamped beneath him, releasing the tension it felt through his thighs.

"No, Richard, you have to listen to him—you have to."

The impotence he had felt in the Place du Parvis, staring at Notre Dame, assailed him again. He would be nothing more than a spectator at this ritual.

Then de Vaugrigard moved, something snapping inside him so that all that was left was panic flight. The horse bucked, surged away, flowing into a gallop. The first bullet whined audibly past Latymer as he spurred toward Gardiner, throwing his shadow between gunman and target. The second and third, loosed off, seemed to miss de Vaugrigard as he gained the trees away to Latymer's right. Then Gardiner was twenty feet or so ahead of him, and he spurred the horse forward, possessed by some madness of relief. He watched the gun come up, level with the gaudy yellow sweater, then suddenly drop and spurt flame, twice.

The horse reeled under him, let out a whinnied scream. Flailing legs and hooves, as he spilled out of the saddle, forward and away from the thrashing horse. His shoulder and head struck the ground. Winded, blinded by sudden darkness. The cries of the horse becoming suddenly fainter, yet more insistent even as the pain in his head increased, the struggle to regain his lost breath.

A shot, and silence from the horse. A shadow between his closed lids and the fierce light. Then he expelled the fought-for breath and dropped into the dark that was waiting for him.

Richard Gardiner shuddered still with the cries of the horse. He had had to silence it, that inhuman screaming, stop the great arch of blood coming from the chest, splashing Latymer's riding boots and sweater. He looked down briefly at Latymer, felt a momentary hatred of frustration, then turned on his heel. In the silence after the shots he could faintly hear the retreating hoofbeats of de Vaugrigard's horse.

He began to run, breath or emotion sobbing in his throat, ramming shells into the Browning as he went. He was angry with himself now, as some kind of rationality returned—angry that he had been going to kill de Vaugrigard, in that beautifully arranged innocence of the sunlit clearing, prompted by the sight of the man's face, the prosperous body, richness of clothes, the palpable fear.

Without asking him a single question—even when he knew that Etienne knew of others, always others, behind and behind, retreating like shadows or ghosts. . . .

He shook his head to clear it and stopped to listen. Nothing. No hoofbeats. He glanced wildly around him, as if he were sensing hostile bodies closing in. Which direction? What would he do now?

Stables, house, car—run, run, run. . . .

Logic of survival. Had to be.

Gardiner began to run, back the way he had come, toward the exit from the *bois* into the Avenue de Madrid.

"What's happening?"

Challot's voice crackled over the car radio.

"We were just about to move in—he had de Vaugrigard and the Englishman cold. But Etienne bolted, and Gardiner missed with his only good shot."

"Where are you now?" *L'Etranger* looked through his own windshield at the cars passing across the Carrefour des Sablons, perhaps half a mile from where Gardiner had tried to kill his target. His own tension was like steam in the car. The driver leaned unconcerned against the hood, smoking, watching pedestrians as if practicing the arts of surveillance or lechery.

"Avenue de Madrid house in sight, Chief. He went in about ten minutes ago."

"Have you located Gardiner's car?"

"No."

"Where is he?"

"On his way here—spotter three called in a minute ago. He's worked it out."

"If you have to, stop him. He mustn't get to de Vaugrigard until he's more rational. What about the Englishman?"

"Still lying where he fell. But he's all right. One of the spotters checked him over. Just concussed, no bones broken."

"OK, he's out of it. Let me know when Etienne leaves. If Gardiner doesn't interfere, tail them, but let it run."

"Understand."

"Channel left open."

L'Etranger felt calmer. He had managed to avoid the consequences of the confrontation. Gardiner had not killed Etienne, and now Etienne would run either to his mistress or to his château. Either way Gardiner would follow him. He did not now believe that Gardiner would kill Etienne out of hand, but every minute that ticked away calmed the Englishman, made him more rational. He waited. The open channel made a buzz of static, flylike, in the car. He found himself looking repeatedly at the microphone lying on the transmission tunnel.

His own confidence, massive as it was—he admitted it now—had been shaken by Gardiner. Yes, shaken. . . .

The amount of blood from the dead horse had made one of the spotters sick, according to Challot. Somehow the image of the breached animal adequately expressed Gardiner. A tremor passed through *l'Etranger*'s hand.

"Chief? He's on the move—daughter's sports car, by the look of it—taking the Boulevard Maurice Barrès toward the city. Running for cover."

"Tail him. Where's Gardiner?"

"No sign of him."

"All units—I want a report immediately, whereabouts of Gardiner. . . ."

"Wait, Chief!" Challot. "That's him, just turning out in front of us. He must have been parked near the house, in the rue du Bois."

"Are you certain, Challot?"

"Yes, Chief. It's him."

"All units—two cars, description to follow, on Boulevard Maurice Barrés, do not intercept, but do not lose. Challot, give them the descriptions."

He put down the microphone as Challot described the two cars—gray Simca, blue Ferrari, *can't miss that one*—and knocked impatiently on the windshield. His driver flicked away a cigarette and heaved himself into the car.

Hilary Latymer painfully dragged himself across the clearing, after he had vomited, and hauled himself to his feet with the aid of the cool, rough bark of a tree trunk. He pressed his quivering cheek against the bark, almost rubbing the skin as if to rid himself of it. The regularity of the movement, its insistence, cleansed him of the image of the horse's carcass and the hideous, magnified clamor of the cloud of flies feasting on the blood. It cleared his head, also, of something of the hammering pain of the concussion.

He wanted to do nothing. There was an element of fear in his resignation. Gardiner, gun aimed, squeezing off those shots, had frightened him. The impact with the dry, hard earth had knocked something out of him, expelled resolution with breath. He didn't want to get in the way.

He stared at the bloodied sweater and the soiled boots and jodhpurs, and knew that he remained involved. Blood had been spilled *on* him, making him a member of the unholy fraternity that embraced Etienne and Richard Gardiner. He had no easy way out.

People he passed as he made his way toward the Avenue de Madrid exit stared at him but made no effort to stop him. The blood might have been his own, and they sensed the urgency with which he weaved and stumbled.

A car hooted, then another, and he almost giggled at the spectacle he must present, at the drunkenness of his passage across the Avenue de Madrid. Then, somehow, ages later or only moments since he had woken on the ground, he was banging on the front door of the imposing white house, and though he seemed to hear his unfamiliar voice through a roaring sea, he was yelling at the top of his voice, "Etienne! Geneviéve! For God's sake, let me in! Etienne! Geneviève!"

He was leaning so hard, banging so furiously, that he almost fell into the hall when a frightened maid opened the door. He stumbled, capered to retain balance, and brought down a vase of flowers on a delicate table. A rug slid from beneath his boots, and he sprawled. He almost giggled again, as if experiencing the drunken analogy that came to mind. He looked up to see Geneviève standing halfway down the main staircase, her face a tight, disapproving mask. He blinked, stared, and the mask became entrenched lines of fear, panic, ignorance, shock. She came down the rest of the steps, knelt by him.

"You're hurt!"

"No, no—your horse, I'm afraid. Dead."

She blurted, "He wouldn't tell me what had happened—to you." It was as if they had acquired an intimacy that excluded her husband.

"He did come back here?"

"Yes, yes. Panicked by something—what happened, Hilary? He wouldn't tell me!"

"Someone tried to kill him. Help me up, I seem to have gone light-headed. . . ."

The two women bent to him, raised him so that he leaned against the wallpaper, probably soiling it. He was aware of that, confronted by Geneviève. He shook his head, which threatened to inflate, or explode, or dissipate—he could not decide which.

"Thanks. Where has he gone?"

He wasn't sure she knew for a moment. Struggle in her, freezing hauteur overcome by sudden panic, by perhaps the sight of the dried blood—perhaps the memory of her husband's face when he returned. She was making herself admit to something she normally chose to ignore, buried from herself—now admitted, even in front of the maid.

"Perhaps I can save him," Latymer urged. "Tell me where he might be."

"The—Faubourg St. Honoré. An apartment there. He will have gone there. It is his—*secret address!*" The hauteur, the inability to admit returned suddenly and closed her mouth, dried the face of feeling.

"The number?" he said, breathless with urgency. She gave it to him. He turned to the door.

"I may be in time—if I hurry. Don't—don't tell the police for the moment. Understand. It's *not* a police matter."

She nodded. She was frozen again, forgetting the admission. The mistress was unimportant, did not exist. Latymer, for a moment, felt sorry for her. Then he opened the door and let himself out.

The afternoon traffic was heavy, and it was more than thirty minutes before he reached the Faubourg St. Honoré, another ten before he turned into the courtyard of the apartment building behind a couturier's. Something seemed to slide inside him, as if it had been balanced on his chest, and now tumbled to the pit of his stomach—a block of ice—as he saw that there were no cars, other than one Citroën, parked in the courtyard.

The wooden door he had to take was open, showing the foot of the staircase to Etienne's mistress's apartment. He unlocked the glove compartment, felt for the gun, found nothing, remembered, with thick-headed difficulty, that he had drawn no gun from the embassy. Cursing, he got out of the car, steadied himself, and crossed the courtyard.

He paused at the bottom of the wooden stairs. Clumsily, with ridiculous effort, he removed the riding boots. Then he began to climb the steps, pausing after each movement. The apartment house seemed still, unnaturally silent, and he was seized by a momentary physical nausea that only gradually became related to anticipatory fears.

The door to the apartment was open. He squinted through the gap, shadowy as if the doors were closed within or curtains drawn; then he pushed the door wide, very slowly. A short carpeted corridor, solid varnished doors, all closed except one—a room in which curtains were drawn. He moved very slowly, stockinged feet soundless on the thick carpet.

It was the bedroom. He waited for what seemed an interminable time, then pushed back the door.

Fortunately the girl seemed more frightened than hurt. He took five minutes to find her, having looked in the other rooms before returning to the bedroom. She was in a fitted wardrobe with louvered doors, and she rolled out at his feet, tied hand and foot as she was, and her wide eyes stared up at him in terror as he loomed over her. He bent down; her skin seemed to retreat in revulsion from his gentle touch; then he undid the knots and took off the gag, smiling.

"There, there," he said, over and over as if to a small dog or baby. "It's all right now, it's all right." An imperative slammed him in the back, palpable as an assailant, but he knew he could not panic or bully the girl. Gardiner had evidently done that already, to find out what he wanted to know.

He went to fetch her a cognac and found himself looking for blood spots as he moved through the apartment, while something else in him measured the money that had been spent to furnish the place.

The girl gagged on the cognac but hugged the glass to her breast. There was some bruising on the high cheekbones and on her bare arms. She was wearing only a thin, sleeveless dress. Shock was beginning to make her shiver in the hot, airless, darkened bedroom. Latymer sat in impatient silence until he said, "Don't tell me what happened, mad'moiselle. Tell me where Etienne went—just tell me that." Somehow he could not ease the urgency entirely from his voice, and she looked frightened. Gardiner had asked much the same question, and his hand had struck her. The girl seemed to be watching his hands, clasped on his lap as he sat on the bed. He kept them very still.

"He was followed here, but where did he go? Where did the other man make you tell—where was it?"

He saw the guilt and the pressing fear. As if someone had pulled down the walls, vandalized the apartment. She was defenseless.

"No," was all she said.

"Yes," he insisted. "Tell me where Etienne went."

He knew he might have to hit her and was appalled at the idea. Repetition of what Gardiner had done, and she would tell again. He began to steel himself, as the urgency came back to him, reducing her helplessness to stubborn refusal.

Then she said, "His château—he went there."

"Where is that?" he asked as her eyes cast about for some tangible sign of security, safety.

She got up jerkily, surprising him, spilling the cognac on the fawn carpet, and rummaged in a drawer. She silently held out a photograph to him. He looked at the snapshot, turned it in his hand. Azay-le-Rideau. He looked up at her, but she offered no information, sensing that only silence was safe for her. Even the date of purchase was emblazoned on the back of the snapshot. Probably the girl had never been there, but Etienne had boasted to her, as perhaps to everyone else.

He left the room quickly and picked up the telephone in the lounge. He dialed the embassy, staring at the print as he waited for the reply.

"Hawthorne? Put McNeil on." He waited again. "McNeil, I want a trace put on a small château belonging to Etienne de Vaugrigard—probably in the Loire Valley. Yes, at once. Where? I see. And, McNeil, I shall want a gun. Revolver, not automatic. Sign the forms and bring it to the apartment in the rue de Castellane as quick as you can."

He put down the telephone. Twenty-five kilometers from Tours, on the Indre, McNeil had supplied at once. The rest would be ready for him by the time he changed his clothes. Together with the gun.

He went back to look at the girl. She was seated, crouched, on the bed, clutching what he finally realized was an evening dress. Pink, elegant, crumpled now but a couturier's model. He wondered how many occasions she had had to wear her comforter. She did not look up at him, and he left her, closing the door behind him.

Richard Gardiner had parked his car some distance from the château. It had been easy to find, the information ridiculously easy to obtain from the girl with a few casual blows. Even though she had never been there, she swore, she knew its location, could have described it in even more detail had he required.

He had watched the apartment until Etienne de Vaugrigard left it, driving hurriedly off down the Faubourg St. Honoré. Only then had he gone in, confident again, convinced that he had not lost the man, wanting the man to believe he was making an escape, was ahead in the game. The young mistress was as he had predicted and was able to supply the information he required. He had hit her because he was in a hurry and because suddenly there flared up in him something of the madness of the Bois de Boulogne. He was damaging something that belonged to his betrayer. That the girl had passed out had probably saved her a worse beating.

Now he was a man holding himself in harsh ropes. He desired, more than anything, to go down from his outlook on a tree-tufted outcrop overlooking the château and confront the man. Kill him, perhaps make him beg; humiliate, hurt, terrify. . . . The words of power circled in his mind, hypnotic pendulums, which his inward gaze followed until their outlines blurred, until the words drummed like blood in the darkness behind his squeezed eyelids.

Yet one thing kept him where he was, looking down on the toy house and the tiny toy car parked in front of it—the thought that inside the house there was a frightened man.

He fed on de Vaugrigard's imagined fear. He was alone, except perhaps for a housekeeper. And the afternoon was waning, the shadow of the outcrop creeping across the lawns in front of the house as if to swallow it. The perch he had obtained, its detachment and sense of power, was what he enjoyed.

He did not think of anything except his destruction of de Vaugrigard. His vision had tunneled so that he could see no moral perspective, until there was no ques-

tions that he asked himself and no sense of what de
Vaugrigard's motive might have been. There had been
times in the past days when he had tossed on his bed,
unable to sleep because images of his past, and the
stench of the present, came at him out of the dark
like intruders or succubi. But not at that moment. There
was nothing to think of except the death of the man
in the toy house below him—once darkness had come.

And from his perch up there, up above the toy
house, it would be an easy thing to squash the toy
man under his foot, like an insect.

Latymer crossed the motorway ring around the
city and picked up the stretch of wide road toward
Orly, before he needed to branch southwest toward
Chartres and the A 10. Already there was the sense
of driving through a dream landscape. There was an
insufficient reality to the road, even when he passed
two cars piled into a ditch and the anonymous gray
blankets that covered shapeless forms at the side of the
road. There was no *color,* he decided, about the scenes
through which he moved, as if all that mattered to him
were the collision of past and present that he feared
would occur at Azay before he could get there. His
headache was receding, as if he had willed it to dis-
perse, or become distracted from it.

And Richard would lose something more of himself if he killed Etienne.

An aircraft lifted into the pale sky to his left,
from Orly. A silver cigar, a further silver wink like
an early star. He sensed that they were moving toward
places he might have known or might have inhabited
with comfort. Not this lunatic chase, the Smith & Wesson heavy and refusing to warm against his thigh.

He passed along the gray outskirts of Palaiseau,
and then he was out of the Paris conurbation, or so
it seemed to him. It was as if the center of Paris
were some kind of cleansed, spacious, distilled crystal-
lization, and the deposits and impurities were clus-
tered around the center in a thick, somber, smoke-
belching ring. Then pastureland, suddenly.

And the villages. Detached from him as he sped

down a narrow strip of the world, as if the road had been ripped up and accelerated into another dimension.

The Forêt de Dourdan, with more than half the journey to Chartres done; the dappling of sunlight through low branches or sliced into glowing bands as he passed in the Peugeot. He stopped at none of the frequent lay-bys but pressed on as the evening began to gather, south toward Châteaudun and Tours. His bruised shoulder ached as he sat rigid in the seat. His head thumped. The traffic thinned as the holidaymakers or the French villagers deserted the roads in favor of hotels and inns or their homes.

He turned the lights on while he was still north of Tours, sudden beams springing out from the car, making the road a glinting ribbon of tar and the trees, tall and slim, sentries of his passage.

He passed the airport at Tours, and a shape he could distinguish as that of an old Dakota lumbered skyward, lights winking. There was something poignant about the slightly swept-back wings and the stubby fuselage, as if he were watching some other aircraft from a previous time climb toward the night sky, carrying agents he had briefed from airfields in the south of England. He turned to watch it, slowing the car, until it was only a black shape, lights under its belly, against the stars.

The aircraft betrayed him to the past, which rushed at him like the beams of cars traveling north. The plane had been a clean image for a moment, something that survived intact and unchanged from the war, unlike, and like, Richard. Then the past came back, and the filthiness of it, and the squalid, violent present.

Richard was a killer; Etienne was a traitor— men were dead because of them.

The center of Tours was busy, and he concentrated grimly, thankful to escape his own oppressive thoughts. He crossed the dark, sliding river by the pont Wilson and then headed down the rue Nationale until he picked up the D 7, which would take him to Villandry and Azay.

Soon the town was behind him, and he drove fast-

er now, as if something were pressing at his spine,
urging him on. He swept in the comet's tail of the
headlights through the dark countryside. Hedges disguised the land. Villandry was quiet, and the empty
streets seemed ominous, as if reverberations of an
event ahead of him had driven the people to shelter.
He was certain that Richard Gardiner would have got
to Azay by now. He began to study every car, and road.

A dog squeezed past the wing of the car on the
outskirts of the village, sudden and large and terrified
in the headlights, eyes glowing in an unearthly way.

Azay was funereally quiet. He turned off the road
and began to climb a tree-covered rise, some sterner
outcrop of rock above the river. Trees closed around
the road, and then the Peugeot passed through open
gates bearing some unidentifiable heraldry in stained
design. He suddenly became cautious, and the car
slowed as his senses braked. He pulled into the trees
and switched off the engine. He wound down the window, and it was suddenly quiet, his ears ringing with
the unaccustomed silence.

He checked the revolver, rolling the chamber in
a series of loud clicks. Five bullets. He had a sense
that he might need them, and he shivered, though it
was a mild night. He got out of the car and walked
through the trees silently. On the ground floor of the
house, as he came out of the trees, he saw a light but
no shadows thrown on the lawn. He skirted the ornamental lake, footsteps careful on the gravel, and approached the facade so that it loomed over him, washed
lighter by the moon. He watched the square of muted
gold quartered by the window frames. Suddenly he
ducked along the wall of the house, moving as silently as he could, until he could raise his head to look
into the lighted room.

The library. And he was too late. The posture
of Gardiner's slumped body relaxed in the armchair,
the glass of whisky raised to his lips, told him that.
Only after he had registered the look of dumb aftermath on the face did he see the body of de Vaugrigard, arranged on a chaise longue, arms folded across

the breast, some kind of ritual that Gardiner had performed upon it. He could not see the bullet hole. There appeared to be no blood on the body. Etienne de Vaugrigard's face, in profile, had set in the death mask. The long, curved nose raised to the ceiling, the lips pressed tightly together, the eyes closed. And the folded arms, the illusion of an untroubled end. It caused Latymer's stomach to heave.

He looked again at Gardiner. The man was ignoring the body and seemed to be deep in thought. There was a frown on the face now, as if the features were moving only slowly, subject to some great aquatic pressure distorting the features. There were no emotions, only the effects of gravity on the facial muscles. Latymer saw the Browning on a table, feet from Gardiner's hand.

He ducked down and crept back along the wall, conscious of every minute disturbance of the gravel and his own hoarse breathing. He reached the front door.

It was open. He pushed at it gently, and it opened silently. He stepped into the huge, dark hall.

He made out, in the moonlight filtering through undraped windows, the huge central staircase and the gallery beyond it. There were rooms and corridors leading off the hall, and he took the one that would bring him to the library. It was carpeted, a thin, faded strip of carpet down the center, the wooden floor gleaming darkly in the pale light from the tall windows at the end of the corridor. A thin line of light, barely escaping, indicated the door of the library.

He paused outside it. There was the chance that the door was locked and that his hand on the knob would betray him to Gardiner. He held the doorknob, having wiped his palm on the seat of his trousers. Then he turned it, with delicate patience, very slowly. The door opened a crack and squeaked. He thrust it open, took in the figure of Gardiner already bending to the low table and the gun, and said, "Leave it!"

Gardiner looked up, into the barrel of Latymer's revolver, stiffened as if weighing his chances, then smiled, waving his hands in innocent retreat. "Come in, Hilary. I'm sure our host won't mind another guest. . . ."

Latymer did not glance toward the chaise longue Gardiner had indicated with his eyes.

"I've already seen the body, Richard, through the window—thank you all the same." Gardiner merely smiled.

Latymer crossed the room, took the heavy Browning, and threw it into a corner. Then he sat down in another armchair, well away from the table and any leap from Gardiner, and then looked at the body.

"The arrangement is rather—*obscene,* wouldn't you say?"

"Sorry it offends you." Gardiner looked at the body swiftly, as if he were the one with the gun and dare not miss any sudden move by a treacherous Latymer. "Yes. Beginning to seem that way to me, too. I thought it a good idea at the time." He rubbed at his forehead, as if soothing away a pain. "I don't know why I did it now." He looked at Latymer and pointed to his whisky. Latymer nodded. Gardiner swallowed at the drink, then sat back in his chair. He said, "It's all right. I shan't throw the drink in your face and hope to leap on you while you're blinded. That sort of thing got a great many of our more amateur colleagues killed during the war." Again Latymer nodded.

"It's over then," he said.

Gardiner shook his head as if maddened by insects.

"No, it's not over!" There was a deep, flaring bitterness, almost a wail of anguish, and his whole being seemed to take its color. Latymer was shocked. He had expected the beginnings of a new purposelessness in his quarry, the dejection in the aftermath of revenge. Even a new sense of self-preservation.

"What do you mean? He's dead now, isn't he? Or do you want to kill all the others?"

"It isn't him—wasn't, should I say?" There seemed an inward collapse of the structure of the face until it registered nothing more notable than sulkiness.

"Then why, for God's sake?" Latymer indicated the recumbent corpse.

"Oh, yes—he betrayed me. He told me that. But he wasn't the only one!" He laughed suddenly, a harsh, braying sound. His eyes were fierce.

"Who else?" Latymer was resigned, suddenly, to an endless debate, a psychopathic condition. Gardiner had rendered himself beyond help, beyond persuasion. "What kind of thing have you become, Richard? What? You can't take your revenge on the whole world."

Latymer realized he was learning forward in his seat, his hands clenched together around the gun butt, the gun angled to the floor. He was overtaken by wariness once more. The old moral considerations, which no longer applied but which he couldn't rid himself of, had tricked him. He still wanted to help Gardiner. He had wanted to regenerate Gardiner, appalled by the fever of madness that had possessed him, not this unrepentant, malevolent presence with burning eyes.

"No, not the whole world, Hilary—just two men." Latymer was chilled by the confidence, the authority of the voice. It was as if there were no gun or Gardiner were holding it. He seemed still unbeaten, uncaptured. Latymer looked at the gun, as if reassuring himself, at the five copper studs of the cartridges in the chamber.

"Just two *more,* is that what you're saying? Just another two, and then you'll stop?" His voice sounded thin and unconvincing.

"Yes." Again the arrogance, the assurance.

"Christ, Richard! It's all dead and buried! Can't you see that, man?"

"No. Because it's not, Hilary. For you, yes—and for him." His head nodded toward the body. "But not for me. I was—*delayed,* by various things, which amounted to nineteen years of my life. But I have arrived, to find the party not quite over."

Latymer shook his head.

"My God, Richard, but something's happened to you. . . ." It was ineffectual, like his sense of being able to help. He admitted, now, that he might even have let Gardiner go—had he fulfilled certain moral requirements. It was ludicrous, pathetic—arrogant and blind, too.

Gardiner smiled. Latymer felt suddenly weary, weary of Gardiner, the pursuit that had accomplished nothing, and weary of the alienness of the life he felt going on in the man opposite.

Who were they? he thought. Some pathetic little men who had rebuilt their lives, now to have them pulled down? Growing protective scabs over the memory of what they had done to Gardiner?

"Don't you want to know, Hilary?" Gardiner asked quietly. He was leaning forward in his chair, his eyes bright with longing. Latymer shook his head.

"Not particularly."

"The names are known to you—," was the reply. The voice was seductive with knowledge.

"Indeed?"

"Indeed. Perhaps you might like to try them on, to see if they fit the mind? What about Constant, for example, and Van Lederer? Don't those names mean anything to you?"

Latymer was seized by the ridiculousness of it.

"Nonsense!"

"To hell with you! That's what he told me. I wasn't betrayed by a damn Frog, but by my own people! By that smooth individual from MI Six who came to see us the day I left for France and gave me all that crap about the importance of the mission—who *set me up!*"

He saw the disbelief on Latymer's face, the stubborn refusal to believe. Suddenly he wanted to convince the man with the gun, to make him understand. The desire unnerved him like a dim memory. He said, "You must have heard of the 'Wolfgroup,' operating behind the scenes in France and other occupied countries, throughout the war?"

Latymer's face creased in thought; then he said in a quiet voice, "Rumors, and rumors of rumors. Nothing tangible."

"Etienne was a *member* of it. It was set up to affect the postwar governments of occupied countries. Wipe out as many prominent Communists in the Resistance movements as they possibly could. They

wanted Renaud all the time, not me. Crazy, isn't it?
I had to go to the wall, just to make it look good.
And Constant and Van Lederer *were* the group! He
told me everything, to keep himself alive. It didn't help,
of course. . . ."

He sat back in his chair and allowed Latymer
time in which to absorb the information, just as he had
required time. He recalled de Vaugrigard's frightened,
mobile face, the collapse of the will behind it, the
pleading—then the sudden and desperate revelations.
At first they had driven everything else from Gardiner's
mind, but when he had finished and confessed that
he had finished, Gardiner shot him.

He glanced at the body once again. He felt no
remorse. Instead, creeping back into him was the sense
of the futility of what he had set out to do. There
was always someone else. And to take on Van Lederer,
who was now, according to de Vaugrigard, a senior
NATO Intelligence officer, was a prospect which
daunted him. Robbed of immediate freedom of
thought and action by the inhibition of Latymer's gun,
he did not feel equal to his task. He looked at the
drapes, the lines of leather-bound volumes, and they,
too, seemed to press on him with a weight of civilization. He had killed a man in this room; now he could
not think of killing other men, not with the evident
comfort, the evident *reasonableness* of Latymer and the
room. Violent death had no place here. He shivered
slightly.

"Verisimilitude," Latymer said quietly without
looking up.

"What?"

Latymer seemed to awaken from some mild
trance. As he looked up, Gardiner was surprised to see
the oppression that registered in his face.

"Just something someone said to me—a very
frightened man." He cleared his throat, which seemed
clogged. "You realize who these two men are? Van
Lederer is retiring chairman of the NATO Senior Joint
Intelligence Committee, and Constant is one of the
two deputies in the SIS. To contemplate killing
them . . . ? You'd do too much *damage,* Richard!

Can't you understand that? It isn't 1944 or '45. It's 1963. The world has changed around you!"

"You advise me to desist in my efforts then?" Gardiner asked with a smile. "You think the task beyond my puny resources?" He was willing a sense of dislike, even hatred, into his voice. He wished to avoid the lethargy that seemed creeping over him, the futility knocking at the front of his mind.

"No. I don't underestimate anything, Richard. I'm just telling you that the thing can't be done. Not by you. I won't let you."

"You'll turn me in then?"

"I have to," Latymer replied, trying to quell the flush of guilt he irrationally felt. In a moment of great intellectual clarity he saw that he had intended that in some way Gardiner should escape the consequences of his actions.

"Yes. I understand that, especially now. Since Constant is your boss, itself a neat irony, you have to protect him from someone like me."

"Look, I don't like the idea of what he did any more than you do!"

"Of course not," Gardiner said mockingly. "You're just doing your duty. What every stupid man claims when the situation turns out not to be precisely what he hoped!"

"You don't even know whether any of this nonsense is true!"

"Men in his position don't tell lies—at least, not well-documented ones."

There was a silence. Latymer appeared on the point of pursuing the argument, then gave it up and slumped back in his chair, reasserting the aim of the Smith & Wesson as he did so. Gardiner nodded at the adjustment and smiled.

It was horrible, Latymer thought. So clinical for Richard, so lacking in any sense of the healing time was supposed to provide, its necessary compromises, its changes of loyalty. It was true, of course. He believed the dead man on the sofa, as much as if he had been given incontrovertible proof. It was a Constant style of operation from beginning to end.

Gardiner was the man he had been in 1944—Latymer could no longer disguise that truth from himself or see the younger Gardiner in the same diffused light of memory. A hard, sharp whiteness showed him the real being. Gardiner had been really born sometime in 1941 or 1942, in the war. Here he was now, unchanged.

It was Gardiner who heard the approaching helicopter first. Latymer saw him sit upright, alert like a hound.

"What is it, Richard?" It was as if the movement had surprised some part of the shared past. Then he heard the steady beat of rotors nearing, lowering from the brilliant night sky.

Gardiner said, "The Seventh Cavalry, unless I'm very much mistaken." He sat back in his chair, a stony expression on his face, his eyes riveted on the gun. He checked Latymer's eyes once, and despite the conflict of emotions he saw, he knew there was no chance of escape. The man would shoot him if he moved.

"You?" he asked.

Latymer nodded. "Yes. I telephoned earlier, before setting out. Someone I know in SDECE. His housekeeper took the message. Evidently he received it."

"You knew I'd be here then?"

"You had to be."

Outside, the helicopter dropped onto the lawn, and the heady beat of the rotors died down through the scale. Latymer could see the red light at the tail winking, see the men in the cabin of the helicopter. He avoided thinking about Gardiner. He emptied his mind of past and present and made of him an object of flesh and bone and blood that he was quite prepared to kill. He almost succeeded and would have done but for the intrusive sense of something that had been lost, somewhere in the mutual past. It continued to make the situation a human one which he could not quite render into two simple dimensions.

The footsteps of men, now that the rotor had died, could be heard on the gravel outside. He saw Gardiner's face flicker, registering the approach of other captors. He saw the face momentarily livid in defeat and frustrated rage, then the stony indifference again.

The door of the library opened cautiously, and then Haussman, in a light overcoat, stepped into the room. His mane of gray hair was awry from the downdraft of the rotors; his face was red, and his sharp eyes flickered from Gardiner to the corpse and back again. He nodded to Latymer and went outside. Latymer could hear him talking to someone in the corridor. Then he reentered.

He looked at Gardiner, nodded again as if in acknowledgement or recognition, and then recited, in a flat, official voice, "Richard Gardiner, you are under arrest. You will be charged with the murder of Etienne de Vaugrigard and also with the murders of Henri Janvier and the man Dupuy. You do not need to say anything to me. However, is there anything you do wish to say before you are taken to Tours police prefecture and then to Paris?"

Gardiner shook his head and stood up, ready to leave. He looked at Latymer and deliberately smiled in a confidential way. He intentionally brought their mutual past to mind. Latymer nodded and then looked at the body, as if admitting other imperatives.

A moment later Gardiner had gone with Haussmann. Latymer got up and poured himself a large brandy. He swallowed at it, shuddered slightly, and returned to his chair. He did not want to think. Haussmann would watch Gardiner being taken away, and then he would return and they would have to talk. But not for the moment.

It was over, he admitted cautiously. Gardiner had destroyed himself. And he was wretched about it, so that the paucity of his own circumstances struck him with new force. *Victoria, dying.*

And he worked for a man who had betrayed Richard Gardiner.

The thoughts revolved with a slow frenzy as he sat sipping his drink. He lit a cigarette and then let it burn unnoticed between his fingers. The thoughts continued, depressing him further.

In France they still employed the guillotine. Gardiner, with his head struck off. . . .

3

THE NATURE
OF THE BEASTS

We had the experience but missed the meaning,
And approach to the meaning restores the experience
In a different form, beyond any meaning
We can assign to happiness.

—T. S. ELIOT, "The Dry Salvages," II

10. Contact with "Franklin"

The Hôtel Belvedere was situated on the rue St. Antoine, near the Place de la Bastille. General Eugene Van Lederer had booked a room on his arrival in Paris for the meeting of the Senior Intelligence Committee; he had lodged at the American embassy until this particular night—particular because he had brought his mistress to the hotel.

Mme. Catherine Vigny was married to a senior official of the Quai d'Orsay, the French Foreign Ministry. They had met, and commenced their affair, when M. Vigny was an attaché at the French embassy in Washington, a tour of duty which had ended twelve months earlier. Since then Van Lederer and his mistress had met only when he was in Paris. Always they took the same room at the Belvedere, perhaps because it provided a degree of familiarity in their locationless relationship.

The pattern was simple—dinner, then lovemaking. Which was passionate, untender, and assertive on his part, submissive on hers. It was, Van Lederer had admitted to himself on more than one occasion, the youthfulness of his mistress, only a little over thirty, that attracted him and kept him attracted. And the convenience of not seeing her too frequently.

They had finished making love when the telephone rang. Van Lederer was idling into sleep, his mistress satisfied for the moment, her demands having been such as he could amply fulfill on this occasion, inflating his sexual vanity and increasing his sense of well-being in the aftermath of the climaxes they both had reached. Then the unfamiliar foreign telephone, cutting into drowsiness, rousing the mind.

"Van Lederer," he grunted into the telephone. The woman at his side, one breast free of the sheets as she turned in her half sleep, moaned softly. He had, as he always did, left the number with the embassy's security staff. But it had to be something of an emergency before they would presume to intrude upon the open secret of his nights with Mme. Vigny.

"Sorry, General. . . ." There was a faint hint of amusement from the other end. "We have a slight emergency on our hands. Source 'Franklin' is arriving in Paris tomorrow—you're delegated to meet him. There are some broad hints that he's loaded for bear, and Langley won't trust my staff to handle it. They're afraid he wants out. . . ."

Van Lederer sat straight up in the bed. The bedclothes slid from his mistress's back, baring the arch of the spine.

"You have to call me at *this* time, when we're worrying about tomorrow?" There was a rough humor in the voice and a sense of shared secrets and actions more arcane, and more satisfying, than those he indulged in with the woman.

"Sorry, General. Langley sent us the message 'Priority Blue,' and that meant waking you up. Sorry." There was a shared intimacy, a joke ebbing between the two men.

"OK, Buckholz. I accept your apologies. But why me? They've got time to fly someone over here by tomorrow." There was no irritation in the voice.

"You're the man, sir. You set up 'Franklin,' and you're still here in Paris."

"And you can bet Langley knows *why* I'm still in Paris!" Van Lederer looked at the woman beside him, who had moved again in the bed so that the breasts, slightly flattened as she lay on her back, were exposed. There was a renewed lust at the sight of the helpless, unconscious nakedness. Increased, perhaps, by the anticipation of the meeting with "Franklin."

"See you then, General."

"What's his cover—how did he contact? I don't want to walk into some KGB outfit trying to lift me or someone like me."

"Normal channel. He's inspecting the resident and his personnel at the embassy in Paris. Slacking on the job or something. Or maybe they suddenly don't like the idea that their boy Lidbrooke is dead. . . . No sweat, General. It's all aboveboard. Just watch the contact. He's too valuable to bring over unless it's necessary, and he's got good stuff—the best. He may just be a little windy. Oh—and there's confirmation from London about Lidbrooke's accident. Langley is sending flowers and a cable of congratulations."

"Yeah, sure. Now will you let me get some sleep?" Again the amused tone.

"Sleep, General? G'night." The receiver purred in Van Lederer's ear.

"Sure," he murmured. "Why not sleep?" He put down the receiver and lay back in the bed, his head against the quilted headboard, hands knotted behind his head.

"Franklin" was his baby, that much was true. Three years ago, in Washington, he had helped turn him into a double, working for the CIA. And "Franklin" had the best motives, it appeared—fear and disillusionment. He went back to Moscow, promoted, known only to a handful of top advisers around the director at Langley and in contact with only one of the security staff at the U.S. embassy in Moscow. Van Lederer, almost as a reward, had got the chairmanship of the NATO Senior Intelligence Committee soon after "Franklin" returned to a top job in the First Chief Directorate. "Franklin" was a winner from the beginning —a beautiful, beautiful winner.

Van Lederer had had one other telephone call that day, to remind him of the existence of someone called Richard Gardiner. He had had to be reminded who the hell the man was. It had been 1944. A hell

of a long time ago, more than a world away. This
guy coming back for revenge, like some ghost in a
play. Looking not for him and Constant, not then, but
for Etienne de Vaugrigard. Etienne, chicken Etienne,
running for his life. . . .

Van Lederer enjoyed his superiority over other
men, as over women. He was not frightened by the
idea of Gardiner, the man who had gone down to the
cellars of the Avenue Foch with Renaud. It was crazy
to be scared. Constant, in his infuriating cold voice,
had supplied him with a timely reminder.

He shook his head and looked around the darkened bedroom. The illuminated face of his watch told
him the time was three-thirty. Ridiculous. There was
no idea in the reality of Gardiner, none at all. He proposed to take no action about it.

He stirred in the bed and touched the woman on
the breast. She muttered in her sleep. Suddenly aroused
by the unconscious display of nakedness, he pulled
back the sheets and browsed his lips against her skin,
against the flat stomach, the pubic hair below it. He
felt himself harden, and the woman's legs move. He
moved his tongue against her skin, pushing it deeper
until the thighs parted. It was piquant, irresistible, the
fact that she was still asleep. Helpless nakedness. He
thrust his tongue against the softness, felt the body tremble against him. He would not wake her, not yet. . . .

Latymer picked up the telephone. Its noise had
insisted until his dreams could no longer contain it,
and he had woken. He pulled the instrument onto the
pillow beside him, then clumsily fitted the receiver to
his cheek, the action of a man relearning some part
of his life. His watch face informed him it was six.
Faint outline of the window, curtains lightening.

"Yes?"

It was Haussman. Latymer came bolt awake as
the voice's first words chilled him.

"Hilary, I am as angry at this as you will be.
Richard Gardiner escaped from police custody two
hours ago!"

"What?"

"I am afraid it is true. He got out through a toilet window in the Tours police headquarters—how he managed it . . . ? Of course, the police have been incredibly stupid. They did not realize quite what kind of man he was. . . ."

Latymer felt a strange thrill run through him. He said, "Are they searching now?"

"Naturally. And I am drafting some of my men into the area. . . ."

"Good. But they won't catch him, you know. Why weren't you there?"

"I was. I did not offer to accompany him to the lavatory, however." There was a sense of irony not entirely divorced from humor in the voice.

"It means he'll be after Van Lederer, doesn't it?"

"Yes. I shall warn the general and offer him protection—if that will be of any use."

"Perhaps. Very well, Jean-Jacques. I'll call on Van Lederer myself and put him in the picture with regard to Gardiner."

"Thank you, Hilary. It would not be politic for someone like General Van Lederer to be killed on French soil, especially by an Englishman."

"I understand,'" Latymer replied, suddenly frosty. "It would not be *politic* in any way for another death to occur in this matter. I'll speak to him. Tell him I'm on my way when you call him. And will you screen him as from now?"

"Of course. I have given orders, though I do not expect Gardiner to have been able to make his way to Paris in so short a time. . . . The general is staying at the Hôtel Belvedere in the rue St. Antoine. He is with a married lady, and I do not expect him to leave the hotel with any great speed." There was a dry chuckle at the other end, then, "*Au 'voir,* Hilary."

"Good-bye."

Latymer put down the receiver, and the impressions and reactions tumbled through his mind, transmitted, it appeared, to his hand, which began to tremble as soon as he released the receiver. He stirred himself and sat up in bed.

His reactions were complex, diffuse, and difficult to

comprehend clearly. He had grown accustomed to not examining his thoughts in the past months. Now the only simplicity of the matter lay in the enormity that Gardiner, free, was a danger to U.S. Army Intelligence, the NATO Intelligence hierarchy, and the SIS: a rogue element in their complex infrastructures, a loose piece rattling in their works.

To kill Van Lederer, then Constant.

Unthinkable. They were far too valuable to their respective, and common, agencies to be sacrificed to any wild impulse toward a larger justice. Expediency demanded that Gardiner be stopped; at the same time a vague, infinite pity settled on Latymer, though he could not precisely define its object.

Gardiner would be killed, he acknowledged, as soon as Constant realized his danger. Because Gardiner had been good—was still good; amoral, clever, lethal. The morning seemed cold, though he knew quite certainly that it was close and hot, as the night had been. He admitted, as the tremor passed through his body, that there was no control he could exercise over Gardiner.

The telephone rang, startling him, even as he considered what calls he should make himself.

It was six-thirty.

"Yes. . . Oh, what do you want, McNeil?"

"Sir, I have a message for you, priority, and direct from Deputy, timed at six-seventeen. Shall I read it out?"

"Yes." There was a hollow feeling, like foreboding.

"It reads: 'Imperative you return London immediate. No discussion possible on this.' That's it, sir. Nothing else."

"Damn!"

"What was that, sir?"

"Nothing, McNeil. Thank you. When is the first London flight out of Orly?"

"Nine-thirty, sir."

"Get me on it."

"I already have, sir."

"Thank you, McNeil."

He put down the receiver absently, as if he had

already forgotten its existence. *Why?* The question was absolute. Constant had ordered him back to London. What in the devil's name did he intend to *do* about Gardiner?

As he got out of bed, the thought was like a heavy weight of undigested matter in his stomach. Constant was consigning Gardiner to Van Lederer. And the CIA. There could be little doubt of it. It was typical of Constant—have Gardiner finished off by someone like Napier, only with an American suit. There need be no unnecessary fuss in Whitehall. Latymer cursed as he began to shave. He felt separated by a strange, haunting gulf from Richard Gardiner.

It was ten before Van Lederer arrived at the U.S. embassy. He went directly to the third-floor office, overlooking the avenues of trees bordering the Champs Elysées, which was normally set aside for him during his visits to Paris. Then he summoned Buckholz, the embassy CIA resident. As soon as the bullet-headed, square features appeared around his door, he threw up his hands and said, "Hell, Charley, what do we do?" There was no trace of nerves in his voice or behavior, only an impatience as at some small part of a jigsaw working loose—threatening the whole design.

"What with 'Franklin,' you mean?"

"Yes, with 'Franklin.' I've got to talk to him, and I've got to be free to do it. We can't have saturation surveillance and a screen when I meet with him. Moscow Center is bound to be taking precautions, and they'll spot one of your guys if there're too many." He rubbed his cheeks with his big, hairy hands. "This guy could wreck it—understand?"

He looked into Buckholz's eyes, knowing his competence, knowing him destined for high rank at Langley, given time and a clean record. If he believed. . . .

Van Lederer smeared the thought like wiping away a drop of spilled liquid. He would not admit that he was afraid, fearful because of the weight of the past, the sense of what must have been done to the Englishman who now threatened him. He was relieved when he saw Buckholz nod.

"I agree, General. We've got to look out for 'Franklin.' The whole operation could come unglued if this guy Gardiner gets onto you." His pale eyes widened. "Hell. Imagine if he got 'Franklin' while trying to get you! The whole contract has just the sort of opportunity he would be looking for."

"Right. So I want action on this, Charley—real action. I want this guy wiped, and quick!"

"OK, General, it's your show. What about the French? They're covering you at the moment."

"Yeah. I'll get that cleared, and your boys can take over. If 'Franklin' comes in today and wants to meet, he'll have to wait until tomorrow. That gives you twenty-four hours. This guy doesn't know me, but he'll know who and what I am. So he may come here looking." Van Lederer turned in his chair and waved his arm at the window, through which sunlight filtered, slatted by the blinds. "He'll be out there, somewhere, waiting to pick me up. He'll have at least some description from de Vaugrigard, the guy he knocked off." His voice suddenly became harsh, more violent, as if he were attempting to diminish the threat that Gardiner posed. "He wants me, and he wants me bad. But he's alone, got no help from anyone. You can get him for me, Charley—get him."

"Sure, General." Buckholz saw the general's body stiffen against the implicit comfort of his tone. "We'll get him. Don't worry about it."

"I only worry about 'Franklin,' Charley—remember that." His eyes were hard, shallow gray surfaces in his expressionless face.

"Sure, General. But we could do with some shots of this guy. It would help. And we got to make sure the French keep their noses out. If you want this to be a kill, then we got to have a clear field of fire—real and diplomatic."

"OK, I'll get onto that. I'll talk to Constant in London and then to the SDECE. Who's the man?"

"Haussman—you know him?"

"Yeah. He'll swallow an operation from us—until someone gets hurt; then he'll have his mob and the Sûreté crawling all over us. He's typical French Intelligence. Wouldn't stop us but couldn't pass up an opportunity to kick us in the balls either."

Buckholz smiled.

"OK, General. I'll get the team together and bring them back to you."

When Buckholz left, Van Lederer wasted no time, instructing the secure switchboard to put through a call to Queen Anne's Gate and Constant. The connection took seven minutes, and a number of code names, to establish; then the American heard the familiar drawling of Constant's voice. He received, suddenly, an image of the Bloomsbury house, and he could see the back of Etienne de Vaugrigard's head and Constant's thin, ascetic face with its humorless smile and infinite superiority.

The two men spoke as if they were still working in the closest cooperation.

"So you want me to sweep the shit up from your doorstep, Michael?"

"Ah, Eugene, good morning. How are you, and how is the weather there? It's a cool but sunny day here."

"Cut it, Michael!" Van Lederer snapped with a fierce amusement. "You know why I want to talk."

"Ah, yes. Our common ghost."

"Yes, that's him. Jesus, I never even met this guy—I don't know what he looks like, and I hardly remembered his name. Now he comes out from under some stone. Where's he been for the last nineteen years, for Christ's sake?" Van Lederer paused, then snapped, "I'm meeting 'Franklin' today or tomorrow —you know what that means. This guy could blow the whole damn thing sky-high—that's all that's wrong at this end! How are *you* feeling?"

After a silence Constant said, "Of course, you'll have to silence him. He must be got out of the way, as soon as possible. How will you do it?"

"Jesus, you're a bastard! You pulled your guy out because you knew it forced me to take care of this nut! And you wouldn't have to get your lily-white hands dirty! You're a bastard, man!"

"Sorry, Eugene. I didn't realize about 'Franklin,'

which does rather complicate things. However, if that is the case, it's all to the good my man is out of the way, wouldn't you say? What can I do to help?"

"Photographs. And as much information as your man has, the one you upped and outed this morning."

"Very well, I'll do that. By the way, did you have a word with Lidbrooke before his—demise?"

"Yeah. I wished him all the best. Nice touch, huh?"

"Quite. I'll get those things wireprinted to you as soon as possible. You might get the same sort of thing from the French. . . ."

"I'll try. Don't take any wooden nickels, Michael." He put the receiver down.

Now that he had spoken to Constant he minimized the problem. The discussion with Buckholz and the confidence of the Englishman conspired to make Gardiner a puny enemy, impotent and incapable. The sexual imagery satisfied him. Like his control of women, he sensed he controlled this situation. He plucked at his nose with thumb and forefinger, his forehead creased with thought. Now that he considered it he felt a certain satisfaction in having to confront a palpable enemy.

If that was the way Constant wanted it, then he would get Gardiner's head on a plate. He no longer resented Constant's implied challenge to his ability to survive. Now he welcomed it.

"This situation has got entirely out of hand," Constant remarked to Aubrey and Latymer before motioning them to be seated. There was a long moment when they were made to feel like miscreant juniors brought to the housemaster's study; then he had snapped out the single sentence.

"I understand your irritation, Deputy. But this was in no way an official inquiry by the department—or any department, come to that." Aubrey was at his most bland and comfortable. The blue eyes were ingenuously wide, the features round in babylike innocence. Constant refused to be humored by the performance.

"I should have been informed what Latymer was doing in France—I don't like these *private* inquiries. They usually have the messy incompetence of the Irishmen who offer to tarmac one's drive—they are as likely to tarmac the lawn!" He glared frostily at each of them in turn. "Even if you began in this cavalier manner, it should never have been allowed to reach this stage! This man has been wandering freely around France, doing what damage he will. You, Latymer, should have informed the French of everything you knew—*everything!* And you should have let them take care of him."

Aubrey glanced at Latymer and saw the cold blaze in his eyes, the pinching together of the nostrils; he shook his head in warning, but Latymer took no notice.

"Take care of him, Deputy?" The voice was superbly modulated, despite the anger which rubbed at its veneer like sandpaper. "You had two attempts yourself once upon a time. Gardiner appears to have survived those without too much trouble!"

Constant's eyes blazed. He had expected to chafe both men, but he had not expected either of them to strike at him.

"What do you mean by that remark, Latymer?"

"Simply this, Deputy. The 'Wolfgroup' left Richard Gardiner for dead. It cannot be surprised that an agent of his dedication and caliber should come back from wherever he went and seek them out." Latymer sat back in his chair and studied the wall to the left of Constant's head. Behind Constant, the bright morning filtered through the curtains, and the sounds of the minimal traffic through Queen Anne's Gate were excluded by the soundproofing of the first-floor office. Constant had this office at the headquarters of the SIS and another, more official habitation at the Foreign Office.

"I see. And no doubt your misguided sense of fair play would like to give him a sporting chance, mm?" Constant was gratified by the sense of complex and contradictory feelings that he saw mirrored in Latymer's eyes.

Aubrey said, to mollify, "What do we do, Deputy?

Now that the situation is here, I think recriminations are futile. What is to be done about 'Achilles'?"

Constant glared at Aubrey, suspecting some hidden significance in the use of the old code name.

"Quite. There is no point whatsoever. I will explain my feelings on the matter. Simply put, they are these. I think that Gardiner is being operated by someone else. Whether he knows it or not. No private revenge takes this long to work itself out. And besides, he's been far too successful to be working alone."

He allowed them time to digest the opinion.

"On what do you base your assumption, Deputy?" Aubrey asked.

"Suspicion, mostly. But other things. Such as the news blackout on the murder of Dupuy—we didn't request it. And his escape from the French police. Both points are most questionable."

Latymer said, "There's one other thing—the death of Perrier. He was released very conveniently for Gardiner. Though, as it turned out, he could have learned nothing from him." Constant looked at Latymer and accepted that the man's anger was past. He had given both Latymer and Aubrey a sufficient bone to occupy them.

"Then it has to be the French," Aubrey said, unconvinced.

"Not necessarily. What motive would they have? Frenchmen may be involved, but that's something else. SDECE, that most nymphomaniac of intelligence services, may have been penetrated yet again." He permitted himself a wintry smile for a moment. Aubrey chuckled, genuinely amused.

"I agree," Latymer added. "The release of Perrier worried me. But if Gardiner didn't learn anything from him, which he could hardly have done in the circumstances, then who told him about Etienne?" He stared at them both for a moment, then realized that he had admitted to himself, for perhaps the first time, the ramifications Constant had erected around his Samaritan task. The recognition silenced him.

"Well?" Constant said with a grimace of satisfaction. "What are the results of your new deliberations? Enlighten us, Latymer, if you please."

"There are—things that might support your contention, Deputy. Things I hadn't considered. . . ." It was appalling, as if Gardiner were being betrayed all over again. "But they don't make sense," he added feebly.

Constant steepled his long fingers and looked at them over the spire. He said, "Let us use what minds we have merely to posit a likelihood. Revenge, if you like. Simple revenge. For Blake and Philby perhaps. Or merely to—weaken the succession?" There was a slight pause. "I do make a rather important, if not expansive, target, gentlemen. And Eugene Van Lederer thrown in as a bonus when Lidbrooke or someone else finds out about the old 'Wolfgroup.' "

"You make it sound like a former pupils' organization," Latymer observed acidly. "Was it? And how did the secret leak out?"

"I have no idea. But it could have. You must have known in SOE about the rumors—and there must have been people in the Abwehr and the Gestapo, as well as the SS, who understood what was going on. I don't know how your man got the names, but apparently he did. Then Gardiner is primed, by this unknown or by Moscow Center, and away the thing goes. Running on castors." He raised his hands in the air to signify an explosion.

Latymer, watching the imaginary cloud rise above the desk, said, "Ingenious, Deputy. But why not the simple revenge of Gardiner for what you did to him? It makes a weird kind of sense. At least, it would to Gardiner—the Dupuy thing having triggered it all. Besides, how could anyone keep such close observation, predict his behavior?"

"You're not surprised at it. Why should anyone be who had studied the subject?"

Aubrey said softly, "Then we ought to take him alive, if possible."

"Not necessarily. I don't think he knows anything."

"Do we have to kill *everyone,* Deputy?" Aubrey asked in exasperation. He stared at Constant for a long time, then subsided into his seat again.

"It is, in this case, not up to me. I'm afraid that the CIA insist on taking the greatest care of General Van Lederer, and I have no power to prevent any steps they may take to do so. They would hardly be likely to accept our unproven word for what is happening." He smiled.

"But if what you suppose turned out to be true, shouldn't you at least inform the French?"

"The SDECE can clean out its own place."

Latymer, watching carefully, considered that Constant was masking a distinct self-preservation beneath his elaborate theory. It was all possible, he admitted—but less likely than the fact that Gardiner wanted revenge, even after all this time. After all, neither of the two men with him had actually *talked* to Gardiner, as he had done. Gardiner was certainly in no doubt about why he was doing things.

The telephone rang as Aubrey was about to speak. Constant picked up the receiver with irritation, listened, frowned, and then put it down. He said, to Latymer, "I'm afraid that was the hospital—your wife. They think you ought to be there as soon as possible. Naturally, you may leave at once." He tried to appear concerned but failed. Latymer felt the news like a blow to the stomach that he had prepared for, but that still surprised him. He muttered something to both of them and excused himself. Aubrey signally avoided looking at Constant for a long time after Latymer had closed the door behind him.

He could not say, precisely, when she died. It was the final betrayal, the last moment of inattention in the sequence of indifferent moments that seemed to make up love. He noticed, though that seemed a work of protraction rather than a moment, that she had stopped breathing, that the white sheet, which canceled her body, had stopped rising and falling. He had not been able to hear her quiet breathing. He felt obscurely cheated, as if she should have breathed raggedly loud, or death should have shaken her throat like a rattle. It was meaningless, the manner of her going. No climax at all, to anything.

They had made sure she would die in her drugged sleep. It was a mockery, ghastly.

In final mockery—after he had bent to her nostrils, wanting to feel the breath caress his cheek, and then had reseated himself—there appeared no change in her. Even the pallor of her skin retained the gray tinge he had come to associate with those last weeks. He could not bear, suddenly, to be in the room with the body. The woman, in company with all the dead, had wrested herself from him, given the lie to the life they had had together.

And there was nothing in him. He was bereft of emotion. The tearing pain had gone, as if she had released her grip. There was no flicker of light through leaves such as her pain, her dying, her aging might have induced. Nothing.

He made the arrangements for the removal of the body and resisted the specious comfort that was offered him. The day was still bright when he went outside, the early evening providing a sunset glow ridiculous and inappropriate.

It was fifteen minutes, and ten miles, from the hospital before he had to stop the car and vomit into the thick, tufted grass beneath a dark hedge. It was not for a long time after that his body stopped shaking from the spasms and he was able to drive on, in the direction of the empty Chelsea house. By that time his numb mind had returned to life, and he could recall her clearly—so many painful images.

Gardiner knew, at the point when the traffic began to thin as the last of the rush-hour travelers deserted the center of the city, that however clever he had been, or however lucky, there was now no other step he could take. In the Champs Elysées he hated the sense of being alone, as before he had cherished it, because isolation now meant powerlessness. In trying to locate Van Lederer, he dare not reveal his interest to anyone. The stakeout of the U.S. embassy was necessary but grew more futile as the hours dragged by.

He had reached Paris halfway through the morning, thumbing a lift for most of the way in a truck, once he had got clear of the immediate area of Tours in a stolen car. He had crashed the car into the Loire.

He had hired another car in Paris, and it was parked at the Rond Point, a distance away, but safe. To hire it, he had used the last of the identities with which he had been furnished by stolen *cartes*. He was Armand Skrela, from Toulouse. On holiday, without his family, in the wicked city. To accompany the *carte,* he wore a bright striped shirt, light slacks, and sunglasses. Suspended from his neck by a leather strap was a camera to complete the disguise.

He began to pick out the surveillance activity as the hours passed. It informed him that Van Lederer was in the embassy and that he was expected. He wore the sunglasses, then discarded them, left the camera in the car, wore a light jacket, then discarded it again. He used the other side of the Champs Elysées and the metro tunnel to cross the Place de la Concorde. He identified the pattern and saw that as yet they had no photographs of him and were hunting blind. He kept moving, always with apparent purposelessness, and tried never to reappear in the same place in exactly the same disguise. It was difficult; it stretched the nerves. But it obviated the need to ponder his situation. Only the successive moments were real.

He made one telephone call, posing as a British journalist, to NATO headquarters and was informed that General Van Lederer was not in residence but that he might like to try the U.S. embassy. And he had searched in the photo-library of *Paris-Soir* until he found an old photograph of the man. And that was all the pressure he could apply.

When he returned to the sandy-colored Simca he had hired, to collect the camera again, he found a large buff envelope on the driver's seat and no evidence that the car had been forced.

He sat in the seat, shaking. Clumsily he tore open the flap of the envelope and fished out a clutch of glossy prints. They were all of Van Lederer, neatly labeled on the back in ink. He was shocked into stiffness, a paralysis of the will and muscles. Had the surveillance team found him then, they could have taken him. He could not even control the sweat breaking out on his forehead or the trickle of coldness on his sides. The car was stifling, and he wound down the window.

And the release of Perrier, and Latymer's evident shock, as at some betrayal, and his escape from the police—so easy, with security so unexpectedly slack.

It was someone helping him—someone with influence. As he opened the parcel of his fears, clumsily and greedily, this was his conclusion. Not that the photographs were a trick. He was a cog, part of a larger design or pattern. It appalled him. Angered him, too, in an extreme reaction to the loss of solitariness.

Why?

He was being given Van Lederer—he remembered, with an effort, that the man was high in NATO Intelligence, a fact Latymer had confirmed—on a platter. Free, gratis, for nothing. Someone was concerned to make Van Lederer his creature, his for the taking. Someone wanted Van Lederer dead.

"Why?" This time the thought reached his voice, and he startled himself.

As if with the shock of cold water, the face of a passerby, glancing at him momentarily because of his stifled cry, woke his will.

He had to think. . . .

Someone wanted Van Lederer, perhaps Constant as well, out of the way. It had to be an intelligence operation. KGB or some satellite service taking its orders from Moscow Center. *Did he balk at it on the grounds of patriotism?*

No.

Decisive. It *was* simple. Even as the implement of an enemy, he still *wanted* the thing that others seemed to want. *Yes, he wanted it.*

He saw, as if through a tiny gap in a door, the blank future that lay in front of him—and it turned the scales. He was committed, whether he wished it or no. Dupuy and Perrier and de Vaugrigard were dead, and he was now pursued for those murders. It did not mat-

ter who was operating him, even controlling him. Or
why.

It was a bleak moment, so bleak that he thrust his
head out of the window to suck in the dry air outside,
redolent of petrol fumes and the dusty scent of trees
and flowers in the middle of a city. It did not clear his
head or drive away the tunnellike straightness of the
path he found before him. There was no driving that
away.

In the end it was his stubborn narrowness of mind
that rescued him. He would not open up the past or the
present but would move across them as across treacherous, rotten ice.

He closed down the vision of the future, which
winked out like a screen switched off. There was a
very limited time scale and a double object. Two
deaths, and completion of everything when the second
man died. *Just think of that. Just that.*

His head was dizzy with effort when he got out of
the car. All the time his mind had been in turmoil, he
realized, he had been studying with some other part of
his awareness the photographs of Van Lederer. That
pleased him, the functioning of the personality he most
admired, the complete and utter man of action. He
had begun to live in his own dream of himself. To be
that was like living with an unsuspected amnesia. A
surface, without depth.

It was a kind of freedom, that. At least he clung
to the idea that it was.

He knew they must have picked him up—at least
they were suspicious that he was out there, somewhere
on the Champs Elysées—when he saw Van Lederer
leave in the open sports car. It was the evidently un-
suitable car that gave him the answer. It was a dummy
run, to draw him out. He stayed where he was, the
single still point, it seemed, in the moving scene, until
the second car left the gates. . . .

He picked out two other cars, parked, their
drivers' faces oblique and anonymous inside them.
They were waiting for him. He remained still, until
the desire in him to move, to pursue, was as tangible
as an itch. Van Lederer crossed the Place de la Con-

corde in the sports car; he saw the mane of gray hair above the civilian clothes as they blended with the thicker traffic, heading down toward the last set of lights in front of Les Invalides. Then he lost sight of him and walked slowly back toward the Rond Point, watching two well-dressed children strolling with a nanny.

He walked on beyond the hire car and did not return from his window-shopping until he had reasserted his tourist mask. He waited across the street until he was sure there was no one watching the car, then crossed to it, climbed in, and drove out into the Champs Elysées, heading up the avenue toward the Arc de Triomphe. It was time for him to find somewhere to stay, just for that night. Then he would come back.

As he drove, the envelope lay on the passenger seat, at the edge of eyesight. He began to wonder about it, but without any questioning of his own direction.

L'Etranger lay on a comfortable sofa in the lounge of an apartment on the Avenue de Wagram, one of the thoroughfares running away from the whirlpool of the Arc de Triomphe, as Gardiner's car passed beneath his third-floor window, unobserved.

One of his men had placed the buff envelope in the Simca, just as another of his men had facilitated Gardiner's escape the previous night.

That had been a desperate, hurried action. To learn that the Englishman, Latymer, had cornered Gardiner in Etienne's château at Azay was an unexpected shock, however close Latymer had always appeared to his quarry. Latymer had always, he admitted, been a rogue element in his calculations concerning Gardiner.

The man drew on his cigarette and puffed the smoke toward the high, ornate ceiling of the lounge. His stern face was relaxed, but the muscles seemed habitually tight, the expression of his determined will, whatever his superficial mood. At present he possessed a certain sense of wellbeing, but without absolute confidence. He had spent twenty-four hours with the nuts and bolts of his complex operation and had almost lost sight of its larger design.

He had shown his hand in the photographs of Van Lederer. And he wondered whether Gardiner had opened the case of his camera and found the pictures of Catherine Vigny, the woman who might flush Van Lederer out into Gardiner's fire. Van Lederer was in her company in two of the shots, and her address had been penciled on the back of one of them.

He was almost certain that he could predict Gardiner's reaction. His whole operation had been based on a correct reading of the man, and thus far events had robed themselves as he wished and predicted. But with his primary targets altered as they now were, he had had to declare his hand. Gardiner worked best against the odds. In this case . . . ?

He got up and crossed the carpet with a heavy tread. He opened a delicate cabinet that seemed threatened by his bulk as he stood before it and took out a bottle and a glass. Pernod. He poured himself a large measure, added water, and then returned to the sofa, sipping thoughtfully. The sharp aniseed taste on his tongue pleased him, and he raised his glass silently in salute to someone not in the room—perhaps only to himself.

Naturally, when the operation was over, he would meet Gardiner. He relished the thought. He had wished it to come as a complete surprise, but perhaps it did not matter.

He sighed, a sound strangely loud in the empty room. The CIA might use the woman to bring Gardiner out. He would have to anticipate that. That might prove unfortunate.

Of course, he had proof, and he might have done it another way. But proof could always be labeled forgery or fake, and he might have come under suspicion as its author. Gardiner was an opportunity heaven-sent. A human bomb, planted at the door of the two men he had to destroy.

At eight, Paris local time, KGB Colonel Innokenti Vassilyich Petrovich, source "Franklin," stepped off the Aeroflot flight to Orly, dressed in civilian clothes but making no other concessions to secrecy or a low profile by his manner or bearing. It would have been evident to anyone watching with a trained eye that a high-ranking officer of the Committee for State Security had arrived. A note, together with a photographic record, was made by the SDECE team, and a CIA officer also recorded the arrival with a certain satisfaction and excitement.

Petrovich was greeted by two men from the Soviet embassy, with whom he shook hands rather reluctantly and on whose part there was a marked deference toward him. They walked quickly through the diplomatic lounge, where his official accreditation was accepted by the passport official. His single suitcase joined him there, and neither it nor his briefcase was subjected to inspection.

A black saloon, a Mercedes rather than a Zil, was waiting for him. Petrovich was installed in the rear seat, and the two men with a coarser-grained sense of self-importance slid into the front of the car, separated from Petrovich by thick glass.

While the car purred toward the city, Petrovich smoked the American cigarettes which he obtained cheaply at the official KGB shop across Dzerzhinsky Square from the Center, and perused some papers. The papers referred to his supposed inspection of the resident and his staff and to a new initiative to penetrate the SDECE which he was intended to implement.

There was no nervousness in anticipation of the meeting with Van Lederer; instead, a cautious self-congratulation, a pervasive, though subtle, sense of well-being.

11. Venery

Having slept well and shaved and bathed in a leisurely fashion, Petrovich visited the KGB resident. He was dressed in a dark-gray suit with white chalk stripe and wore a striped shirt and bright tie. It was a conscious effort to rid himself of his Soviet trappings. Bukhov, the resident, was dressed in his normal attire, the uniform of an embassy chauffeur. He shared the same rank as Petrovich in the KGB, in common with most of the senior residents, but in Paris a lieutenant colonel fronted for him; it was he who strutted, ordered, was photographed and filed as the resident, while Bukhov went about his real business.

Petrovich had let his hair grow longer, in a more Western and less military fashion. Bukhov's dark hair was clipped short and shaved over his ears, so that the skull there shone in gray, oiled bristles. His thick neck threatened the tight uniform collar. When Petrovich found him, he was seated in the small rest room allocated to the chauffeurs, which also served as his office. It was in the underground garage and was soundproofed.

"Well, Innokenti Vassilyich, you slept well, I hope?"

"Indeed, Sergei Kuzmich. I thank you. A very comfortable room." There was the sense of the two men sparring, but only as a preliminary and superficial exercise, as if they were enjoying some course of fitness exercises for the intelligence.

"It is arranged—the contact with 'Wolverine,'" Bukhov said. "The fourteenth choice of location, at lunchtime. The Luxembourg will be crowded at that time. I have had prepared a selection of sandwiches which will assist your cover." Bukhov smiled. "Your Western persona is most impressive!"

"Too obvious, you mean?"

"No, not at all. Very French businessman, I should say. A good choice, though perhaps the suit is a little dark for the summer—carry the jacket, perhaps?"

Petrovich nodded.

"What of the Lidbrooke business? It *is* over, is it not?"

"I am fairly certain that it is. It was handled most carefully, and there were no mistakes. Lidbrooke is, I am certain, accepted as our 'mole.' Swift action has a conviction of its own, an inertia which persuades ... ?" Bukhov smiled, showing strong teeth. He was a man still in the prime of years, though the short haircut and the thick nose gave him an older, more peasantlike appearance than was the truth. Like all the younger generation of foreign residents, he was a graduate of the KGB training school and of the Lenin University.

Petrovich nodded, apparently satisfied. He had met Bukhov on each of his visits to Paris as source "Franklin," and he liked and trusted the man. He was calm, efficient, and not hidebound like many of the older, more senior men at the Center, Beria's survivors and those who had been trained in the NKVD and the MGB.

"I agree. It was a good choice of subject and a better removal than might have been expected in such a hurry. You are to be congratulated on picking Lidbrooke as a possible scapegoat. When I supplied Rollin, who is *very* persuasive in bed, I gather, Lidbrooke jumped into the trap. He was a sexual fool, as his dossier always suggested." He paused, then, changing the subject, said, "I have to provide the 'Wolverine' with information that satisfies the suddenness of this meeting. I have prepared documents that suggest I may be under suspicion by the SID and another set from the last three meetings of the Politburo Security subcommittee which suggest the introduction of sweeping changes in the structure and manning of our organization. Though I will plead with the Americans to be got out, Langley will be tempted by this great prize and order me back. No doubt they will promise me the earth. Jam tomorrow is, I believe, the expression."

Bukhov laughed.

"Will you ever go over, Innokenti Vassilyich?"

"It is not beyond the bounds of possibility." He smiled sardonically. "But only when the Center can be certain that I have done enough to merit reemployment within the CIA. When that position is achieved, I shall scream to be got out!"

"Very loudly, I have no doubt."

"What are the arrangements for this lunchtime contact?"

"The usual—very sparse. You will follow the prescribed pattern of movements from here, and the tail car will break down at a predetermined point. You will not, of course, realize this, and the relief car we send out will not find you until after your meeting. I suggest you be especially careful in trying to lose the tail car *after* the breakdown, to convince the Americans of your fear of our people." Petrovich nodded. "There will be at least one man in the gardens. He will be your emergency bell, should you need one. . . ."

Petrovich was already shaking his head, but he said, "Of course. But the 'Franklin' cover is intact, Sergei. It was not my danger that worried the Center, but the establishment of the SO-Four department specifically to find our 'mole.'"

"Which reminds me—two of their men were in on the Lidbrooke thing: Aubrey, the small, fat one, and Latymer, his senior assistant. Both of them have now returned to London, I believe."

"Good. All is arranged then. All we need now from

my meeting with the 'Wolverine' is a full report on the sessions of the NATO Senior Intelligence Committee, together with CIA reaction to the death of Lidbrooke." He looked at his watch. "Send for some coffee, Sergei—we have time for a cup."

Van Lederer listened to the voice of Catherine Vigny and sensed how well she had been coached and controlled by Gardiner before he allowed her to make the call. Obviously she was fully aware of what she was doing and by now she was convinced that her own survival depended on the quality of her performance. Had he not been warned about Gardiner, he might have believed her.

The story she told concerned her husband, who had written from Bonn in reference to certain rumors which had reached him. He was threatening to expose Van Lederer to scandal. It was a very good performance, he admitted. The girl was an accomplished actress. He looked across at Buckholz, on the extension, and saw the frown of concentration he was employing to hide his sense of success. Van Lederer himself felt a keen anticipation, a sense of the power of the assassin in the dark room.

He let the woman continue and was duly frightened and solicitous. He remarked at length that he was too busy to come, and then, a further chord on the instrument of Gardiner's belief, he argued that they had agreed he should not be bothered by her in this way—he almost began to quarrel with her. Finally, he said, "Catherine, it's damned inconvenient, and probably damned stupid, too, for me to come out there to you. But all right—give me half an hour, maybe an hour...." He glanced at Buckholz, who nodded. "I'll come, so for God's sake, get a grip on yourself!" He sounded impatient, weary of her suddenly. "Don't go to pieces. I'll see you."

He put down the telephone and exhaled loudly in unison with Buckholz. It was as if neither man had breathed since the call had been put through. Then, staring at Buckholz, he said simply, "Get him."

Gardiner was suspicious simply because the task he had set the girl was an impossible one. She had been good, and as he listened on the bedroom extension, watching her as he did so in the long mirror on one wall as she sat in the spacious lounge and made the call, he had to admit that Van Lederer sounded convinced. Yet. . . .

It was the fact that Van Lederer had to know about him, that he would be cautious to a final, unguessable degree, especially after the decoy run in the sports car had failed to draw him out. He had not asked the girl to meet him on some neutral ground; that had to indicate he knew Gardiner was there.

He put down his receiver and walked into the first-floor lounge, its tall windows overlooking the Avenue Gabriel, the heavy curtains pulled back and the sunlight pouring into the room. He felt clean in that room. He went to the window and looked out at the Avenue Gabriel and its urbane affluence. He had spent the night in a sordid, nameless hotel out among the dirty sediment of workers' suburbs beyond the motorway ring. He had found the snapshots of Catherine Vigny and her address scrawled on the back. He had felt the sense of being the creature of another. But he had come there and forced the woman to make her telephone call to the "Wolverine." He turned to the woman then and saw that she was exhausted and suffering acute, if temporary, remorse. He knew that mood would pass, that before long she would wish only to be absent when the act was performed. She would feel nauseated at the prospect of blood and violence, at the smell of fear, but not at her betrayal of her lover. She might even worry about damage to the carpet.

A little guilt might return later, before use and custom and marital ordinariness made her secure. It was easy to despise her, and perhaps he did so as an antidote to her undoubted attractiveness. He felt, perhaps for the first time since the end of his affair with the girl in Dorset, a sexual urge which he disliked but could not ignore. She was still dressed in the flimsy, clinging silk nightgown, with its narrow shoulder straps

and low bodice. White, against the suntanned skin. The
shoulders were flawless, and he was reminded of his
wife. He decided to hate her as another cuckolder.
Yet she was immediately desirable. He did not know
the other men her body had been given to—except
the "Wolverine."

"Well," she said, and he could have sworn that
she was aware of the half-formed desires, "I've done
what you asked. Now you can kill him—bastard!" The
defiance was brittle, temporary, and masked her own
guilt.

"You have indeed, madame—and very nicely, too,
if I may say so." He stood in front of her and bowed
ironically. She curled her lip in contempt and fear,
rubbing her arms suddenly as if he had hurt her. In
fact, he had not touched her.

"What do we do now, eh?" she asked, seeming
to taunt him. "Do we just sit here and wait for him
to come?"

He sat down next to her on the low sofa, the cush-
ions seeming to climb around his limbs as if to hold
and detain.

"I think we will," he said. He had placed the gun
in the pocket of his jacket, as if to increase the ordinariness of the morning now that the call had been
made.

She said, "Who are you? What is he to you?"

He shook his head and was silent. She plucked at
the stuff of her nightgown absently but intently. She
had aroused her own curiosity and wished it satisfied.
And she seemed conscious of his proximity in a more
evidently sexual manner. It was an awareness she did
not enjoy, he could see. Yet it pressed her, perhaps
because her sexuality seemed a way of ensuring her
safety. He saw the pout of the full lower lip, the
slightest closing of the eyes. He said, "What about
some coffee, madame—would you make me some?"

Catherine Vigny shrugged, stood up, and moved
out of the room. She crossed a bar of sunlight, the
motes leaping around her like stars, the silk nightgown
rustling. He followed her to the kitchen, where she
seemed relieved to see the old housekeeper he had sur-

prised when he made his entry via the courtyard door, tied to a chair, wide-eyed but unharmed. Then she took little more notice of her. She filled a percolator and carried it back upstairs.

The percolator plopped rapidly in the silence of the room, and the red light went on with a sigh. She poured coffee into a delicate cup and handed it to him. Her hand trembled very slightly.

She lit a cigarette. He sensed the suspension of thought or perhaps the decision she had made. She was frightened because she knew nothing about him, therefore could not be certain of her own fate. She had decided to use her sexuality. She was displaying like some exotic bird. And he was, despite himself, increasingly sexually aware of her. His mood of anticipation at the possible meeting with Van Lederer had become a desire to touch her.

He put down the empty, toylike cup and reached across to her and cupped her breast in his hand. He felt the nipple harden involuntarily, and he squeezed the breast, flattened and pushed upward gently. He watched her eyes—satisfaction and perhaps pleasure. There was something of appetite in her, some ability to suspend awareness of her situation in favor of immediate desire. Her eyes were suddenly wide with challenge; she seemed to welcome his admission of desire, as if it contained him at her level, removed any lingering sense of his superiority or danger.

He said, "Madame, I only wish I had the time—truly, I do." Then he stood up, and smiled at her. He had decided the moment before that he would hurt her, insult her in order to reassert his superiority. He had not done so. It would have cheapened what he intended, the ritual of the slaughter, even further. The hand which had clasped her breast was hot, somehow soiled. He added, "I shall have to tie you up, madame." Her eyes were wide with a new fear. "No, I shan't hurt you. But I think the general, your lover, suspects something. . . . No, I'm not blaming you, madame. It is merely the nature of the beast. Now, if you would like to put on some sort of wrap, in case of feeling cold. . . ." She had become indifferent again, sensing she was in no danger.

He tied her with cord from the curtains. There was no need to hurt her, and he tied the knots expertly so that she was incapable of freeing herself.

"It doesn't hurt?" he asked solicitously, and she shook her head vaguely. "Very good. Now I'll have to gag you, but I shan't bruise your mouth. It won't be too uncomfortable. . . ." He used a silk scarf from a bedroom drawer. Her eyes watched him with a resignation which he was forced to admire, but which he could not be certain was not stupidity or a total absence of imagination.

He crossed to the door, turned and nodded to her as she sat trussed on the sofa, and then closed the door behind him. He went downstairs and checked the old woman's bonds. She still seemed to resent him for the indignity she had undergone when he had removed her dentures before gagging her. He let himself out and walked through the courtyard to the front of the house. Only ten minutes since the call—hardly time for them to stage anything.

The Simca was parked in the Avenue Matignon, around the corner and two hundred yards away. Unsuspicious outside a restaurant. He walked to it; then he began studying the Avenue Matignon, assessing it for his purposes.

He could not stay in the car. It was the first thing they would be looking for, a man in a parked car—and he knew it would be *they,* the unavoidable plural. He would be taking on the resident CIA staff at the embassy. A small, skilled team—though perhaps not containing any top men who had served tours of duty in East European embassies. They would be young men learning the job or second-rate older men. He would have left then, but for the chance that Van Lederer, with such cover, might come himself, just to observe.

There was nothing that would serve as an unobtrusive vantage point. The avenue contained private apartments, a few couturiers, art galleries, restaurants.

It was busier now, with shoppers and window-
shoppers, delivery vans, and some through traffic between the Faubourg St. Honoré and the Champs Elysées. It would have to be a moving surveillance. He
took the camera from the back seat and hung it around
his neck. Then he walked back to the Avenue Gabriel.

It was ten-fifteen when the first car arrived, parking well down the avenue from the Vigny house. Gardiner had strolled to the corner of the avenue, gazing
into the plate glass of the few shops in the Avenue
Matignon. Casually he came level with the car and
saw that Van Lederer was not one of his three occupants. He knew then, with a sharp sense of disappointment, that he would be unlikely to show. This was the
observation car, and he would have been in it had he
intended a personal appearance.

He watched the two other cars arrive and checked
their occupants, then watched their approach to the
house. He picked out the team's leader and guessed
that Van Lederer had sent the resident himself. He
evaluated correctly the danger to himself.

Gardiner walked slowly back down the street into
the Avenue Matignon until he reached the Simca. When
he opened the door, he saw the buff envelope on the
passenger seat. It shocked him, yet somehow he had
expected it, even relied on it when he knew that Van
Lederer would not show. He turned the key in the
ignition and turned the car out behind a small van,
then into the Avenue Gabriel. He passed the Vigny
house and saw two men in lightweight suits standing
in the courtyard—glimpsed through the archway.
One of them was smoking.

Through his disappointment, relief leaked like an
odorless gas, exciting the nerves, pressing out drops
of sweat on palms and forehead.

The buff envelope burned at the corner of his vision.

Van Lederer was in place in the gardens of the
Luxembourg before eleven-thirty. He received a report
from Buckholz that Catherine Vigny and her housekeeper were unharmed, and both of them had iden-

tified Gardiner as their intruder. The CIA team had scoured the avenue as soon as they discovered he was gone, but they had found no trace of him. Then he had left the embassy for his meeting with "Franklin," a meeting which soon drove all thought of Gardiner from his mind.

"Franklin" was his control and his contact, the KGB agent to whom he made his reports on the workings and decisions of the NATO Intelligence Committee. And this was to be his final report.

He parked his car in the rue Gay Lussac and walked across the busy Place Edmond Rostand to the gardens. A CIA man followed him, and a second member of Buckholz's staff front-tailed him. He could see the man fifty yards ahead of him. It did not matter; they assumed he was going to an appointment with a Russian double. As the piquancy of the double bluff he was operating reached down into him, he knew that Gardiner was a nobody, a loser. It was easier than ever to think that with the bright light, the water of the ornamental pool glinting like steel, the smell of dusty flowers, and the air hot in the nostrils. A loser. He could leave him to Buckholz, after he had made his report to "Franklin." Gardiner was a man he had never met, just a victim of one of dozens of such betrayal operations.

He strolled under the stunted, emaciated trees on the western edge of the gardens, the noises of children and hot, exasperated mothers and nurses accompanying him as he stepped on the earth beneath the regimented trees. A blond girl swung from a climbing frame, giggling shrilly as a boy tried to tug her down; another girl hung by the crooks of her knees, her hands trying to keep her inverted skirt modestly in place. He looked, too, at young women, fashionable bright blobs of color, smooth, willowy movement that further increased his sense of well-being. No thought of his present vulnerability to someone like Gardiner was able to dispel the comfort of the day which extended into the secret areas of his life—his relations with the girl and his treachery, which he had long ago ceased to consider as such.

Power. He had admitted that a long time ago. Years of the postwar period in the emergent CIA and a brilliant career outlined. The reenlistment in U.S. Army Intelligence after Korea and the same kind of success. There was no reason on earth why he should have become a double for the KGB. Except power—the secret kind, the superb and massive joke that accompanied him like a constant companion or a lover, knowing himself to be completely other than he was presumed even by his closest friends and colleagues. Whenever he contemplated himself in this light, he was aware of the most luxurious sense of self-congratulation, something as fierce and present to him as a woman's aroused body.

Philby's removal from trust had been a severe blow to his masters at the Center. He had been designed to be an eventual head of British Intelligence. Philby's downfall had precipitated his own recruitment because Philby had also been close to the NATO Intelligence hierarchy. He recalled the meetings with "Franklin" in Washington and the classic bluff of pretending to recruit Petrovich while being himself recruited. Then the succession of meetings in which he supplied information to the KGB while receiving disguised low-grade intelligence and the occasional top-level stuff from "Franklin" to preserve the fiction.

He had deposited the tapes he had made of the last meetings he had attended in the preselected drop that morning, early; this meeting was to supply a simple verbal summary and an instructional briefing by Petrovich; also, it was precipitated by Lidbrooke. The SIS and the CIA both were satisfied that he was the traitor inside NATO.

Van Lederer anticipated a period of inactivity on his return to Langley and until his transfer to Saigon. There, he knew, in that whole new ballgame, he would be of immeasurable value to the KGB. Not that the degree of his usefulness particularly interested him, only the secret power it evinced.

He replaced his sunglasses and walked out from beneath the ranks of trees into the bright sunlight. He saw "Franklin" carrying the jacket of his suit and a packet of sandwiches. In unconscious imitation, he patted his own pocket, touching the greaseproof wrapping of his own lunch, hearing it crinkle at his touch.

He watched "Franklin" sit down on an already-occupied bench and wandered past him. He patrolled the ornamental pool, looking at the leggy, desirable girls—except that it was too hot, he thought, and he had other business.

At twelve-fifteen he sat on the same bench and opened his lunch, seeming to take no notice of the man who sat near him, steadily munching at his own sandwiches.

It was after three when Van Lederer got back to the embassy. He felt heady and leaden with the sunlight and the talk and with sitting on after "Franklin" had left and then with making some kind of tour out of a stroll around the Sorbonne area before the car picked him up and took him back to the Place de la Concorde. The sports car he had driven to the meeting would be collected later in the day.

He sat in his office and told his temporary secretary that he wanted no interruptions and would take no calls. Then he filled a paper cup with water and took two aspirin. He closed the blinds and sat at his desk in the premature evening of the room, relaxing.

He had anticipated the meeting almost entirely. Except for Petrovich's irritating habit of requiring some kind of ideological commitment from his agents. That had always annoyed Van Lederer. The Center demanded no such commitment; often they were suspicious of it. In Petrovich, it was a cast of mind. Of course, he knew the cause. Petrovich was well aware of the old "Wolfgroup"; it was a thought to make him smile. He had never possessed an intellectual hatred of communism. It had been the secrecy of the group, the enormous power of life and death, that had held him. The old man, Grantham, long dead, who had persuaded Churchill and Roosevelt of the necessity of such a group, had possessed the hatred, but he'd never demanded it from Constant or himself—only efficiency.

He felt himself relax. His neck muscles un-bunched, were less unyielding to the touch of the thick fingers. He put his feet up on the bare desk and clasped his hands behind his head. He stared at the ceiling.

It was without genuine irritation that he picked up the telephone when it rang at three forty-five.

"I thought I said no calls, Miss Belding."

"I'm sorry, General. This is code-identified, and I thought you'd like to take it." She sounded coolly efficient.

"What identification?"

"NATO code name 'Goriot,' General."

"Mm. Put him through." He listened to the clicks, saw in his mind the strong face that belonged to the code name, so inappropriate to the name of the inoffensive, leeched old man in Balzac's book. "Yes?" he said when he heard the voice. "What's up?"

"It is important that I meet with you today. I have some information concerning the man Lidbrooke which I find most suspicious. . . ."

"Lidbrooke? What do you mean—suspicious?"

"I think the SIS may have killed the wrong man —that's how suspicious it is!"

"For the love of Christ, are you sure?"

"No, by no means certain. But definitely suspicious."

"OK, OK—let me think about this." He could feel the muscles tying up once more at the back of his neck, and his head seemed to throb. Sweat broke out across his back, sticking his shirt to the back of his chair when he moved. He concentrated on controlling his voice. "Why come to me, 'Goriot'? You've got your own men, surely? Remember, I'm retired as Chairman. . . ."

"Which makes you an excellent confidant for my purposes. Look, let me show you what I've turned up, and you can judge who to take it to, if anyone. Meet me at the Café Chartres in the Madeleine, say at four-thirty? It's just around the corner from you."

"Why not come here?"

"No! I want *you* to see this first. Then I'll come back with you if that's what you advise. Agreed?"

"OK—yes, I'll be there."

"Good. *Au 'voir.*"

Van Lederer put down the receiver and realized that it was damp with sweat at earpiece and mouthpiece, as if he had been thoroughly soaked in the last few moments. A hot shower. He wiped his hand on his trouser leg, leaving a damp stain on the light cotton. He stood up, flexing and unflexing his hands as if he had been typing or writing without pause for a long time. Then he rubbed them on the buttocks of his trousers, so that he could not see the stains he made.

"Oh, Christ!" he breathed aloud and looked at his watch. Three-fifty. Time stretched out before him, forty minutes becoming an endless age, tormenting in prospect.

It couldn't be—couldn't be! There was no way anyone could know. But the timing of the call from "Goriot" terrified him, making him incapable of remaining still. The time passed with terrifying slowness. Even his bladder felt overloaded, and his heavy body wholly uncomfortable and no longer under his control. He was a man normally incapable of fear. Now some facade that hid the worm had collapsed.

He left the embassy at four-twenty and strolled, in changed casual shirt and clean slacks, up the rue Royale toward the soft-edged bulk of the Madeleine, its massiveness made lighter, more airy and Grecian than usual by the heat haze.

The fashionable rue Royale was crowded with tourists and Parisians returning from work, heading for the cafés. He brushed uncomfortably against bodies, sensing obscurely, as if hearing a distant, shouted warning, the vulnerability of his position in the crowd. He tried to dismiss the idea and to concentrate on the meeting ahead. He tried not to anticipate the worst, but the sense of his discovery was close like the people around him, against whom he seemed to push ineffectually, oppressive like his headache or a nightmare.

He shook his head, as if to clear it.

It was at that moment that the silencer of the Browning pushed against the space between his shoulder blades, and Gardiner shot him. The bullet passed through the heart and emerged through the chest wall. The dying Van Lederer staggered against a passerby, clasping at her dress and tearing it; she was stunned by the grossness of the assault until she felt the warm, sticky blood and saw the dead face sliding over her breast down to the pavement. She began to scream.

Van Lederer had felt the slight pressure of the gun, but little more than that. The gun slid down his frame, tickling him, like a drop of sweat rolling down his back. Then the tearing pain and the blackness so immediate that the pain was only the briefest of moments.

Gardiner slowed, stepped to one side, and looked into a shopwindow. The gun was unobtrusive in his pocket again. Then, as the crowd began to hover, bottleneck the pavement, he crossed the rue Royale and headed for his car. He intended driving out of the city before catching the train to Calais and the channel ferry.

12. Tethered Goat

As Constant looked at him, as if for the solution to something, Aubrey said, shaking his head, "I'm afraid you're right, Deputy—you're next."

Constant stared at the smaller man, as closely shaved as ever, the slight smell of his after-shave seeming to increase Aubrey's self-contained assurance. He was dressed in his habitual dark jacket and striped trousers. He smiled disarmingly, and Constant was once more irritated by his perception of a deeper and sharper mind than his own behind the round, childlike face.

"Your confidence is most comforting, Aubrey. The fact is, however, that General Van Lederer is dead, and I am alive. I intend remaining in that condition. I do *not* intend that Richard Gardiner should do so. Do I make myself clear?"

He ignored Aubrey and looked across his room at Latymer. The man's eyes were dull, almost closed. He had shaved that morning, but carelessly, and his general appearance, usually so groomed, had an unkempt-ness about it. The tie was carelessly knotted, and the jacket sleeves were creased, as if Latymer had been wearing the lovat suit for a long time without removing it. He nodded in answer, but without real understanding. Constant, irritated, checked himself by remembering the death of Latymer's wife. It would not do to challenge the man there and then. Aubrey could talk to him later in his unctuous, Dutch-uncle style.

"We understand you, Deputy," Aubrey said in a tone designed to soothe, take unawares. Constant had heard Aubrey managing committees and interrogating defectors and felt he could not trust any of the man's voices.

"Good. That is most gratifying, Aubrey."

"What do you suggest? The airports and ports are being watched, and every policeman in France and England must have his picture by now. What else do you suggest, Deputy?"

"Mm." Constant steepled his fingers and looked over the thin tower. "I have given this matter the most urgent consideration. It would appear likely that Gardiner will effect an entry into this country extremely soon. Van Lederer was murdered yesterday afternoon. Gardiner could have caught the night ferry, he could already be here."

Aubrey realized that Constant was making a display of his unruffled nerves.

"I agree, Deputy. He could have made slight

changes in his appearance, and if he's traveling on a simple *carte d'identité* as a French citizen, then we might well not pick him up. Assuming that, what is our next move?"

"First, do you agree that Gardiner must be being operated by an enemy of this country?"

"Is that important?"

"I think it is." Constant's white skin took on the faintest pink tinge at the neck. "I think it's important that we not only stop Gardiner, but find out what is happening here." Aubrey, unsure how much of what he heard was disguised self-interest, merely nodded. "Good. That means taking him alive—at least temporarily." There was a sudden light in his eyes, a new urgency in his voice. "We *must* know what is going on here, Aubrey. From what I gather from the resident at the U.S. embassy, there was a telephone call, properly code-identified, that led Van Lederer to make that foolish last walk. One thing, therefore, is clear. Either Gardiner knows current NATO code practice, or he was fed the information."

"You're assuming he made the telephone call?"

"Not necessarily. But it's likely. If so, then he learned that code name from someone. Any name would do, from someone high up."

"French code name—from Balzac?"

"Yes—'Goriot,' in fact."

"That's . . . ?"

"Haussman—SDECE. I've spoken to him, and he made no such call."

"You believe him?" Latymer asked suddenly from his chair in the corner of the office, placed so that he gave the appearance of being half-wedged against a tall gray filing cabinet.

"I have no reason not to," Constant replied coldly. "Have you?"

Latymer looked at him, and there seemed a light of interest for a moment; then the dullness returned to his eyes, and he observed the edge of the patterned Persian carpet intently. Either that or the absent stirrings of his left shoe.

"He's assisting in some kind of trace, I take it?"

Aubrey asked, disturbed by the sight of Latymer and trying to distract Constant's disdainful attention.

"Naturally. He has promised to make as full an investigation as possible. Of course, there won't be time to come up with a satisfactory answer before Gardiner is in a position to make an attempt on my life—to finish this bizarre task." He smiled without humor. "I wish, in a way, it was as simple as Latymer has always tried to suggest—an old wound reopened. God knows, we did some pretty rotten things in the old group, but I can still believe them necessities of war at the same time as I could sympathize with Gardiner. . . ." Aubrey, disbelieving every word, controlled his expression with great care. "But this is nasty. It's Lidbrooke's ghost come back to haunt us. Can you understand that, Aubrey? This is the Center having a last fling to get even with people like us."

Aubrey was silent for a long time; then he said, "I can just about see that, Deputy. In a strange way, it makes sense. But how did they get wind of Gardiner in the first place? The NATO code names I can understand. They're not important. But the whole—*unlikelihood* of this business!" He raised his hands, palms outward, in defeat.

"But having done so, it is just too *arcane* to be ignored—wouldn't you think so, Aubrey?" The voice was almost seductive. Aubrey, looking into Constant's face, nodded.

"I agree. So—what do we do?"

"It is, gentlemen, the time of the tethered goat," Constant said. Once more Aubrey was rubbed uncomfortably by the sense of the man's delight in his own cleverness. Aubrey despised Constant's intellect from his own sense of pride; he was a man of natural humility until forced to deal with intellectual inferiors who paraded their assumed superiority before him.

"Tethered goat?" he said bemusedly, playing his own secret game, amused at the way his pretended ignorance could inflate Constant's ego.

"Yes. A trap for our Mr. Gardiner. I signpost my whereabouts, and we draw him to us. Then we take him and find out what he has to say for himself."

Aubrey leaped on the flaw.

"And frighten away his masters, who remain unknown to him in all probability." He smiled helpfully.

"I had considered that," Constant observed acidly. "Perhaps, if we could persuade him he has succeeded, then he will go away again. Then from the shadows will undoubtedly step the people who have been operating him. Even if only to stop him themselves and remove the evidence."

Aubrey looked at Latymer as he considered the idea. He seemed to have adopted the envious passivity of the man at the roulette table without money, intently watching other people win and lose.

"Mm. It all sounds reasonable, Deputy." He knew Constant didn't give a damn as long as Gardiner didn't kill him. He knew he was being offered a tempting worm on the end of a line, but he swallowed the proffered bait. He *wanted* to know who might be making this strike against the SIS and the NATO Intelligence Committee. Even if only to point out to "C" that the death of Lidbrooke had been premature and ill-advised. He said, "Very well. That means a place where you're safe and where he has a chance of getting to you—not London. It means a device whereby he can be duped and a means of tailing him secretly when he goes away. Either that or we talk to Gardiner and try to get him to help . . . ?"

Constant shook his head slightly.

"I don't foresee that approach being very successful, do you?"

"Perhaps not," Aubrey consented reluctantly. "Where do you suggest we place you as a tempting target, Deputy?"

"I considered my place in the Peak District—what have you to say to that?"

Aubrey nodded his head after a moment. He could visualize the country house, its gray facade somehow without lightness and grace or good humor, like its owner. It was set in its own grounds, which could be successfully patrolled. Yes, it was perhaps a good location.

"Why not one of our own country places?"

"Too specialized. Too safe from intrusion, wouldn't you say? We do want Gardiner to come into the web, after all."

Aubrey, seeing a far glow behind the pupils of Constant's eyes, realized how well the choice had been made of the head of the "Wolfgroup." In Aubrey's experience, only long-dead Grantham had the perception and the cold amorality to admire and promote Constant in that way.

"Agreed," he said. "How do we inveigle him there?"

"Something in the newspapers, I think, referring to me in my civil service capacity. An accident, even the overture of a mild heart attack, which would lead to my having to spend some time recuperating. . . ." He was smiling again, preening himself before Aubrey. Aubrey swallowed a sudden vile taste at the back of his throat.

"That would seem to fit the bill, Deputy. When?"

"No time like the present. I'm due to attend a Foreign Office reception at lunchtime; perhaps I should fall down, gasping for breath, in the middle of it."

"Yes. That would make the evening editions and tomorrow morning's nationals. Do you think he's already in England?"

"Don't you?"

Aubrey nodded.

"What men will you use?"

"I thought the same Beaters, armed, of course, who were drafted into Paris for your Lidbrooke operation. Plus some of the SO-One personnel, under Napier's command. You know, by the way, that he's been appointed temporary second-in-command of that department?"

"Nice for him," Aubrey remarked acidly.

" 'C' confirmed the temporary appointment yesterday. They will, naturally, have orders to take Gardiner alive, if at all possible."

"Quite."

"I'd like you to get up there today and make the dispositions; the men are already on their way."

"Naturally." Aubrey forbore to raise his eyebrows.

"You know the way?"

"I can find it, Deputy."

"Take Latymer with you," Constant added darkly.

Latymer, hearing his name, looked up and said as if to himself, "It's a bloody messy business, Deputy, wouldn't you say?"

"Gardiner's mess, not ours."

Latymer looked away from the man's eyes and stood up. Aubrey went to the door and took Latymer almost unconsciously by the elbow, as if to guide a blind man or some ancient. He said to Constant, "We can expect you this evening then?"

"I shall be there."

Constant watched the door close behind his subordinates and sat back in his chair. His body, though inclined at a new angle, looked no more relaxed than when he had been bolt upright. He placed his fingertips in the same thin tower and regarded the door of his office over them. His face, narrow and bloodless, seemed less formed somehow, the skin less stretched across fine and prominent bones.

He could not guess who was running Gardiner. Naturally, Moscow Center, as he had suggested, was the obvious choice. Except that *he* was Moscow Center's man.

He sighed aloud, but for no specific emotion or precise thought. He looked briefly at the ceiling, then focused again on the door.

He was Moscow Center's man.

Strangely, he had never known the same to be true of Philby, though they must have been working for the same long period, since the old NKVD days. Unlike Philby, he had not been recruited at university. He had dabbled with Marxism, had known one or two of the lesser lights in the circle that gathered about Auden and Isherwood and the others. But little *political* activity. In those days he had still believed in the system he considered would amply reward his brilliance.

With clarity of introspection, he corrected himself. He had begun to believe, even during the war, that the system to which he had given a temporary allegiance was about to fail him in some important way. Even at what he might have considered the height of his secret power, as co-leader of the "Wolfgroup," he sensed that he had been appointed because of some *lack* within himself—it was a *dirty* job, and they had given it to him and Van Lederer because the job suited them.

Constant stared at his fingernails, as if he saw dried mud beneath them. Yes—his head nodded in confirmation—though he had reveled coldly in the power, the laughter behind the mask, he had known that it was their assessment of his nature, and usefulness, that had given him the appointment. They thought him fit for the dirty jobs—for the night-soil work, for the secret murder, the bureaucracy of death.

It had shown in the last months of 1945. Instead of promotion to a senior position in London, he had been posted to the intelligence side of the Control Commission—the interrogation of refugees from the Russian zone, the questioning of suspected Nazis—an office boy, little more, under the ineffectual, alcoholic command of a man called Naismith, whom he despised and who laughed at him, showing him the disrespect and contempt of London over the rim of his glass.

Just months after being "Wolf"—only *months . . . !*

In Berlin, in 1946, had come his recruitment. After six months or more of being disowned by London, being looked down upon by people who wished to believe that the war had been won by methods learned on the playing fields of their schools and not in the cellars of the Avenue Foch. *That sort of thing was done only by the Germans, surely, old man*— Naismith had said that, or something like it, when Constant, for once drunk in Naismith's company, had blurted out a little of the devalued secret currency of the "Wolfgroup." Naismith had called him a liar, laughed at his drunken persistence. . . .

He remembered suddenly, finding his mind jumpy and perhaps as an antidote to Naismith's leering contempt, Plekhanov, a huge, hairy man, bearded and with shovellike hands, their backs covered with black hair. And broken fingernails. He was everything that Constant despised—coarse, vulgar, arrogant, ruthless. He remembered with such vividness that he looked down at his trouser leg, as if he could still feel the weight of Plekhanov's hand on his thigh; he could smell the spicy meal still on his breath and see the red lips moving in the beard, see the hard dark eyes staring into him, seeming to know him utterly.

The operation had gone wrong; his team, sent into the Russian zone to lift two high-ranking SS officers recently captured who were possible leads to the whereabouts of Eichmann, perhaps even Bormann, was captured, after being shot up, and interrogated by the NKVD. He was missing from the Allied sector for two weeks. When he got back, suitably wounded and exhausted, he was Moscow's man.

Why?

The reasons came fresh out of the dark at the back of his head, as if new. There had been no inquiries about his team, or himself, from the Allies. He had been written off; it had been the final contempt. *Expendable.* Men who had flattered, who had congratulated, the secret meetings, the chains of command he ascended with the ease of a counter in a game of snakes and ladders. . . .

He smiled to himself, a bitter opening of his lips like a wound in the face—snakes and ladders. While he was going up the snakes, he was always regarded as one. And when he went into the Russian zone, he was going down their ladder, the one they had prepared for him.

They wanted him dead and buried and forgotten —a reminder to them all of the kind of unspeakableness they had willingly sanctioned in wartime, *the exigencies of war,* Grantham had told him, *desperate remedies.* Unctuous clown, dead by 1944 when a not-so-secret V-bomb fell on his home in Surrey. But Grantham might not have abandoned him to those who inherited the offices in Whitehall and Queen Anne's Gate. . . .

He would have done. Constant nodded his head again.

He had been written off.

He had learned to hate irrevocably the people who had abandoned him in that tiny, damp, icy cell, with the bucket of urine and vomit and feces in one corner stinking like the corruption of the entire planet. His hands had been *dirty,* his body covered with the lice from the previous occupant that had waited in the rotten straw of the mattress for him; he had woken screaming, beating at his cold body, trying to wipe and slap them from him.

A system too vile to reward his brilliance.

He abandoned it; it was washed from him with the lice—disinfectant, carbolic soap, hot water, clean clothes, a cigarette, a meal, vodka.

Was it as easy as that?

Yes, it had been as easy as that. Plekhanov, when he came, had known all about him, even about the "Wolfgroup." He had told them more. It was not held against him; rather, it seemed to guarantee something. And they promised him that he *was* appreciated, always would be. A hero. *Wealthy—he already was. Never mind, more money, paid anywhere, in any currency.* But always the heroism, the respect of a few people, the leaders of the Soviet people, the new Soviet state. They would know of him, respect him.

They had selected him even at Oxford but had bided their time. Didn't he ever suspect?

He had done nothing, declared himself in no way, when he returned. He was designed to penetrate as deep, climb as high, as he could before he was activated.

There had been no material reason for his bartering with the NKVD. He had money from his mother's family. But he had been powerless. The years of the war, his sense always of being a despised *implement* of others, had crystallized in that filthy, stinking, tiny cell in Berlin when he knew his masters had abandoned him. Plekhanov had held up a mirror for him to regard his brilliance, and he had been dazzled.

He had used the slight patina of heroism that

clung to him in the months after his return to assist his
posting back to England and there had set about the
task of climbing the snakes and avoiding the ladders. . . .

And the hugeness, the cosmic size, of the joke.
People began to forget his wartime activities, to re-
spond to his efficiency, his quick mind, his natural aptitude for the clandestine, even the ruthless.

He began to climb—rehabilitated, respected, admired, envied. He watched each stage of his climb
as a sequence of more flattering emotions wrung from
people he despised. And reveled.

Quite, quite ridiculous. There were times when
he had to bite his thumb until it bled to choke back
the laughter that threatened after listening to someone
who now had to bury a contempt he had once felt
secure in showing and come up with a pretense of deference.

And there were other times when he considered
he might be betrayed, exchanged, and exposed—
though he survived the disgrace of Beria, the death of
Stalin, the rise and regime of Khrushchev. From NKVD
to MGB to KGB. Under each regime, he had remained on the most secret files of the chairman and
his deputies. Plekhanov had been swept away, an old
and impotent man, in a show trial staged by Khrushchev
as part of his liberalization of the Russian image
abroad. During those years in the late fifties he had
feared often that he might be traded as some gesture
of goodwill toward the British.

But he had held on, and his name had never
been known, and the files that referred to him remained locked away. "Wolf," the old code name,
meant nothing to most of the Center's people. Only on
a handful of occasions since 1946 had the Russians so
much as contacted him.

He sighed again, and there was a more distinct
pressure on his breathing, around his heart. It was as
if he were on the point of suffering the heart attack
he had discussed with Aubrey. He stretched his arms
above his head and then slipped his fingers into the
pockets of his waistcoat. He tried to be at ease.

Someone knew about him, may have known about him for years. That was frightening, unnerving. Someone was using Gardiner, a concept he was forced to admire, to finish off both the "Wolverine" and the "Wolf." A "Wolfsbane." A poison, to be administered to the "Wolf."

He had never himself leaked stuff from inside the NATO Intelligence network. When the Center had wanted someone to do that, they had come to a meeting place in Helsinki—a KGB deputy chairman, no less—and asked for his help. He had to find an agent. They wanted to know about relations inside NATO, especially about the French. They were determined, since the collapse of their network inside the SDECE, to penetrate the whole Western alliance at its most fecund point—NATO.

Van Lederer had been his choice. The American had tumbled greedily for the prize of secret power offered him. As Constant had known he would.

The pressure to find the source of the leaks inside NATO, especially the setting up of SO-4 under Aubrey, had had to be countered by the dummy use of "Franklin," Van Lederer's Russian control. So the rumors of reports reaching the Center from the senior committee had been confirmed by "Franklin" in his dummy role as a CIA agent; it had had to be done to protect "Franklin" and his credibility as a double. But they had needed a scapegoat quickly, and they had set up Lidbrooke with Catherine Rollin.

Which should have been the closing of the matter and the guarantee of safety for Van Lederer and even for himself.

Who could have known?

He did not, could not, guess. Instead, he wanted to destroy Gardiner; irrationally, he wanted to wipe him from the face of the earth. Even if he never found out who was running him. He had to control that—*wildness*. He was being threatened from some organization—CIA, SDECE, BND, SIS. . . . It might even be Aubrey. *Someone, someone knew about him!*

Danes, Turks, Norwegians, Italians . . . ?

Insoluble, unless he caught Gardiner, persuaded

him to talk or that he had done his job, and then
waited for his puppet master to come out into the light.
Then he might see the hands dangling the strings and
recognize the whorls and circles of the fingerprints.

But he had to risk Aubrey finding out about himself.

There was only one alternative to knowledge—
and that was to run, and run now. *Hero of the Soviet
Union,* bobbing up like a cork in Miscow. He would
not do that. It was not heroism or loyalty to a system
he had never completely embraced in all the postwar
years; rather it was the counsel of inadmissible despair.
There was nowhere to run. He could not entertain the
uselessness of living on a pension in Moscow, in some
unholy alliance with Philby and Burgess and MacLean
and Blake and others whose names had never been
made public. Never that kind of folly—like an old,
old man sitting in a windy park in a raincoat, wearing
a tarnished medal. He had seen that once and never
understood the significance.

Since he could not entertain the concept of despair, he functioned practically. It was practical to
eliminate the opposition, overt or secret, and imprac-
tical to run from it.

He got up and went to the window. From his
window in Whitehall, he had a grander vista than this
quiet pavement, the few parked cars and pedestrians.
No. Overt power was within his grasp, the succession
all but assured. He *would* have his revenge on them,
those who had left him to rot in Berlin, in the hands
of the NKVD. The SIS could, and would, be made to
pay for that, inordinately—with a Russian agent as
"C," head of British Intelligence. He could dupe, finally and absolutely, the system and the class he had
learned to hate and despise.

He shook himself like a wet hound and went
back to his chair. It was time to have his heart murmur
and to set up the medical team which would be needed
for authenticity.

He thought of Rawlings, his house in the Peaks,
just within the Yorkshire county boundary. The killing
ground. For Gardiner.

Gardiner lay on the narrow bed, the bedspread pulled back, exposing the one thin blanket and the white sheet, reading the *Evening Standard*. He was tired, but his mind would not rest; the body, too, a recipient of that nervous disease, was restless, and he moved his legs and feet spasmodically as if to compensate for an absence of more complete physical activity.

He had remained awake throughout the night, spent on the train and the night ferry from Calais to Dover. Then the train journey to Victoria, and the watchful habitation of a compartment of strangers, and a sharp awareness of those figures glimpsed only as they passed the corridor window, categorizing their clothes, their appearance, so that he could check their movements for anything suspicious or threatening.

To emerge from the station concourse and walk to a bus stop had been an effort where relief of the mind came to the assistance of weary limbs. He had spent some hours walking the streets, having left his suitcase at Euston, an unexpected station for anyone looking for him. When he had settled on his obscure and cheap hotel in Bayswater, he collected the suitcase and booked in. The single room allocated to him as a man with an assumed northern accent, down on a minor business trip, was narrow and sparse. He hardly noticed it; it was no more than a staging post.

He discovered the item in the newspaper concerning Constant while his mind was still revolving the difficulties of making the kill. Constant, forewarned and dangerous and heavily protected by people like Latymer and even Aubrey perhaps. He liked that, adopting his former friends as opponents in his new war, a pleasing sense of the complete reversal of the past, one which identified himself to himself more strongly. It gave the hungry ego a loneliness that it craved and a sense of being the underdog.

At first it seemed just the opportunity, but as he sought the mind that had arranged the information rather than simply the facts of the report, he understood that it was a trap. Even the address was given, of the country home. Vaguely, to be sure, but with sufficient clarity to help him find it. With nothing but the aid of an OS map.

His momentary disappointment was fierce and deep. It was a trap, and he was meant to understand it as such. It was a cry from the battlements, even a vulgar gesture in his direction. And he *did* feel challenged.

He wished he had a rifle. Thought came down to that, emotion coalesced around that one object. With a long gun, he could overcome the odds against him.

It was as if he could picture the house. Grounds patrolled, dogs perhaps, certainly marksmen—and Constant at the center of the sudden web, woven in an afternoon.

Hurry. That was the thing. *Pressure.* He saw the house and its grounds not as a landscape, but as a grid, crisscrossed by the burning, wirelike patterns of patrolling men. A time-and-motion study of a trap.

He needed a car then. The train would be slow and inexact. He had to be there as soon as possible. By the following morning. They might guess he was already in England, but they would expect some passage of time, some caution. He had changed his foreign currency on the boat, for sterling.

A hire car. And a rifle?

The imponderable. It required a piece of luck. In the long gun he sensed safety, a potency that gratified his sense of being one against many. He needed it, but he could not obtain one—yet. He swung his feet off the bed. He glanced around the room, as if seeing it for the first time and leavetaking in that same moment.

Papers. The only English ones he had were his own; they left a trail, but not a quick, rank one perhaps. *Money.* He picked up his wallet from the bedside cabinet. *Watch.* Time still for car-hire firms to be doing business. *Clothes.*

Swiftly he changed his crumpled lightweight suit for slacks and a sweater. Then he put on the stoutest pair of shoes he possessed. As he bent to lace them, the sweater was already too warm. But he would need

it; it stayed. He pulled on an anorak finally and transferred his English papers and his wallet to one pocket.
The last *carte d'identité* had already been disposed of,
in a wastebasket fixed to a lamppost with looped wire.

And there was nothing else. The suitcase sat
openmouthed, as if reminding him of something. *Nothing else.*

A faltering moment, a sense of nothingness; the
loss of identity, the certainty of who he was. Then,
moving to the door, he gripped the doorknob, and
there was in the movement the use of limbs suddenly
fresher, the creeping, fidgety tiredness dismissed. He
closed the door behind him to track the line of a
stained strip of carpet down the corridor. The clerk in
the pinched and dim foyer took little notice of him when
he deposited his room key on the desk, the plastic
slapping against the wood veneer.

Inside the house it was growing dark, the sunset
streaming more thinly into the westward-facing library,
the room that Constant had assigned to Latymer and
Aubrey as an operations headquarters. The two men
sat around an old long table, maps and sketches scat-
tered on its polished surface. The light of a single desk
lamp spread a white, arctic sheen on the papers and
the wood. An enlarged photostat of the relevant OS
map was receiving attention from Aubrey, who was
working in his shirt sleeves and attempting the double
task of concentrating on the operation and of drawing
Latymer out of the moody silence in which he had
made the journey to Yorkshire, through the crowded
minor roads of the Peak District and the holiday traffic
and the magnificent scenery.

It was difficult. Latymer was inside his own head,
locked up there with God knew what dark thoughts
and the floating, detached image of his dead wife.
Aubrey considered he was taking Victoria's death
far harder than he had anticipated. He had become
almost impatient with this retreated, sullen display of
grief and loss.

"All the patrols are on now—the relief teams
housed and asleep. To take over at midnight, until six.

Then the present teams back on again. Five acres to cover, and we haven't a man to spare. The two of us will have to take a turn later."

He looked up into Latymer's face, the drawn pallor suddenly sharp to him in the edge of the lamp's whiteness, a shocked awareness of what the man had suffered and was still suffering.

"Yes," Latymer said.

"You have been listening, Hilary?"

"Yes," Latymer replied resentfully. It was as if Aubrey were trying to drag him away from a favorite place or wake him from a dream. Yet the unrelieved misery of the hours—how many had passed?—that had followed her death was something that he wanted to escape. If he could do it without betrayal.

Then Aubrey said, "Do you believe this business of Richard being used by a foreign power?" There was a waspish attempt to denigrate Constant in the tone. "Or do you think Mr. Constant doesn't trust us to do our best without appealing to national security?"

"What do you mean?" Latymer was struggling with a foreign tongue.

"I mean—is it real?"

After a silence Latymer said, "It could be real. Richard has been very lucky and very efficient. And the telephone call. . . ."

"Mm. That is a stumbling block, to be sure. Anyway, it will keep Gardiner alive. Unless Mr. Constant has other plans."

Latymer appeared startled or afraid they had been overheard.

"You think he'll have Richard killed then?"

"I don't know. He may. Do you want that to happen?"

"Why not? He killed Van Lederer. Normal procedure would be to eliminate him as a priority danger. . . ." There was something mechanical about the voice.

Aubrey, exasperated, said, "What the devil's the matter with you?" He stood up, pushed away the heavy chair, and walked across to the drinks tray on the heavy sideboard, near the window that was a dull ocher square in the dark room. The landscape outside was sinking into two dimensions, total shadow. And though he knew that Gardiner was probably not yet out there, he shivered. He did not know for whom.

He poured two scotches and took them back to the table. Latymer, who had heard the gurgle of the bottle and the splash of soda into Aubrey's drink, looked up, took the tumbler, and swallowed at the drink. He coughed, as if unused to it.

"Well?" he said, indicating the drinks with his eyes and knowing that Aubrey intended being confidential—and probably unorthodox. There was not the habitual smile or tense moment of pleasure as he realized the fact.

"Listen to me, Hilary—and if you've ever listened to anything in your life, listen now." He allowed a moment in which to gain Latymer's reluctant attention; then he said, "Constant wanted Van Lederer to kill Richard—wipe him out in some CIA heavy-activity operation. But he said he suspected, even then, that Richard was being operated by some third party. . . ." Aubrey's pale-blue eyes were alight. Latymer knew he was worrying at the problem he had set himself. He tried to attend; it seemed that, reluctantly, thoughts of Victoria crowding his awareness now slipped further into his consciousness, occupying the dark corners where they would eventually take up their habitation. He shook his head, and Aubrey misunderstood the gesture.

"What's wrong with my thesis?" he asked in irritation.

"No, nothing. It was something else," Latymer replied, pressing down the rising idea of betrayal. He refocused his gaze, and Aubrey thankfully saw it sharpen, come to terms with the immediate.

"Right. Constant will kill Gardiner to save his skin —just as he killed Lidbrooke as soon as there was a shred of proof against him!" The fact still rankled. "So —what are we going to do about it?"

"Do?"

"Do you want Richard to die?"

"I suppose not—but. . . ."

"No buts. None at all. I'm not letting the chance

of a sight of Richard's mysterious operator get away from us, just because Mr. Constant can't take the first whiff of grapeshot—that is not how I see my duty." He frowned at the suspicion of pomposity in what he had just said, then went on. "We have to stop Constant, get to Richard before he does, or someone like that little snake Napier. And keep him safe until *we* can find out what's going on!"

"You realize what you're doing, of course?"

"Of course, I damn well do, Hilary! I know what's at stake here!" He bit back his temper and added with a sigh, "Heavens, why can't it remain as simple as it was twenty years ago, eh? Naughty Nazis, and good brave Englishmen and Frenchmen and Poles and even Russians. All sweetness and light, even in our peculiarly dirty game. Betrayals, of course, duff gen, bad ops going sour on those we sent out. . . . But even then there was Constant, spinning a web, a spider pretending to be a wolf!" Aubrey's face was twisted in dislike. "He wasn't fit to tie Richard Gardiner's bootlaces, Hilary—you know that as well as I do!"

Latymer looked around, again as if for some observer, some floating ear that might come out of the dark to eavesdrop. Then he said, "Take it easy, Aubrey. I know exactly how you feel, but it won't do any good to let off so much steam—not here anyway."

"Oh, I feel so damned *old,* that's the trouble!" He swallowed a mouthful of whisky. "So damned old. . . . While that spiderish individual goes on for ever." He laughed suddenly and harshly. "He's the sort of chap one thinks of as belonging to the other side, not at Queen Anne's Gate with the rest of us British!"

"I entirely agree, Aubrey. But there he is, and there he will remain."

Aubrey waved a dismissive hand.

"Permanent, like arctic frost—eternal, like acne."

"What's the matter, Aubrey—*you,* the politico, unable to hide your feelings? What is it?"

"I don't know—something nasty waiting around the corner, I suppose. Caesar's dreams, or was it Calpurnia's—I forget? And the dear, ineffectual prince talking to Horatio—'how ill all's here about my heart,' or something like that. Premonitions. It must be old age!" He tried to shake off the mood by sitting up. Then he fell back in his seat. "No, I can't shake it off, and I can't stand by and let *Napier* or one of Constant's 'Black Hand Gang' finish off 'Achilles.' We have to find him!"

Latymer, at last temporarily released from the spell exercised by his wife's memory, said, "All right. What do we do?"

"Ah!" Aubrey swallowed the last of the whisky and put down the tumbler—a prop he no longer required, having learned to move his intellectual limbs freely again.

"What have you in mind?"

"Tell me—when will he come?"

"Dawn, of course. When the guard is about to change and men are tired and bored and off their guard."

"When else, indeed?" Aubrey was almost jolly. "Now, let's look at the map, my boy. Where?" His finger tapped the photostat which showed the stretch of country around the estate, the reservoir, and Broomhead Moor to the west and south. The narrow Ewden Beck wound from west to east across the map, toward the two reservoirs and the village of Ewden. As for the estate itself, it comprised spacious gardens, open grounds, and a bordering conifer plantation. Only one north-south road, a minor one, passed the edge of the estate, perhaps half a mile from the house.

"Which way will he come?" Latymer asked.

"And how?" Aubrey replied, pursing his lips and gripping them between his fingertips. The two men crouched over the map in the white, dead light.

"Car, that's easy," Latymer replied, as if playing a game. "Ease of movement."

"Right. Up the motorway and then through Sheffield perhaps? Mm. It would seem likely, wouldn't it?" Latymer nodded. "Right. Then he'll have a look at the place before first light. What action will he decide upon?"

"Kill a man and obtain a rifle, if he hasn't already got one."

Aubrey looked at Latymer as if reminded, amid a romantic speculation, of an unpalatable reality.

"You're right, of course. We mustn't pretend we're saving Sir Galahad from the dragon, must we? Where will he hide the car?"

Latymer tapped at the map.

"Here. Wigtwizzle. Deep in the plantation, I should think."

"Mm. What about . . . ? No, you're right. Good, good. . . . Mm. That road there?" He pointed to a minor road running northward into the stretch of woodland on the southern side of Broomhead Reservoir.

"Any one of three roads there."

"But all bring him to the eastern edge of this estate. In which case, we ought perhaps to assume tentatively that he will take a man out down in this corner?" He pointed and glanced into Latymer's face, seeking confirmation.

"Useless to speculate, really, since he knows that *we'll* be the ones waiting for him and that we will be carrying out just this kind of exercise. . . . However, for want of a better suggestion—yes. I agree. There."

Aubrey was silent for a time; then he stared into Latymer's eyes and said without inflection, "Then we'd better be down in that corner ourselves, at first light." He smiled acidly, and for a moment Latymer was forcibly reminded of Constant. "And you know who I'm going to post there? No? Our little friend Napier!"

Jean-Jacques Haussman of the SDECE, NATO code name "Goriot," arrived at Gatwick soon after midnight in a small aircraft leased to his intelligence service. He was alone, except for the pilot. His ostensible mission was to inspect security staff at the French embassy. He did not, however, go to the embassy. Instead, the driver who met him at the airport headed the car across London, and within an hour of landing Haussman was on the M1, heading north.

It was perhaps the first day of autumn, coming early in September; there was a chill, damp, enveloping mist across the folds and open spaces of the estate, and it clung heavily to the dark, sticklike boles of the conifers of the plantation and Wigtwizzle Wood that lay beyond it.

Aubrey and Latymer both were in heavy overcoats, dark, unmoving figures perched on shooting sticks, concealed in a brake of rhododendron bushes whose glossy dark leaves hid them from the fence that bordered Constant's property, and which, since the brake assailed one of the slight rises of the land, allowed them to keep watch on it and the man who patrolled that southeastern corner of the estate.

The visibility was bad, and both men were extremely cold. Each of them sat like a statue, field glasses to eyes, faces compressed into lines of cold and concentration. Latymer could see the road, like the dim stain of a racecourse beyond the white palings. Except for unseen birds, it was totally silent.

He knew that Gardiner would not use the road. He would have to cross it, but he would never use it to make his approach. The car would be hidden deep within Wigtwizzle. He focused on Napier, head down and face tired as the glasses held him; only by watching Napier would he ever catch sight of their real quarry. . . .

His mind played with the word, its implications. In what sense was Richard Gardiner their quarry? Aubrey's decisions had made a certain quarry of Napier, the man who was yawning, face half turned to his glasses at that moment. He was the theatrical tethered goat that Constant had supposedly made of himself. Aubrey, in exposing Napier, was making himself think in channels too much like the oiled grooves of Constant's mind. He still did not know whether Aubrey and he would surpise Gardiner before or after his attack on Napier.

What would they do with Gardiner when they had him? How could they conceal him or use him to flush out the unsuspecting operator? It was ludicrous to imagine spiriting him to some isolated pub in the Peaks, where over a pint of beer they would calmly discuss the next move.

Yet what else was there?

And Gardiner ought to pay. . . .

Etienne, Dupuy, Perrier, even Janvier, the professional assassin—the moral rectitude deep in Latymer's nature felt that the man ought not to be able, by complying with Aubrey's scheme, to avoid retribution.

"There?" Aubrey breathed, a question, not a confirmation. "Over in the trees on the other side of the road. Is that a shadow or a man?"

Latymer swung the glasses up slightly, so that only Napier's head remained in view, and adjusted the focus. Napier's features blurred. Under the conifers, the edge of Wigtwizzle, damply dark and wreathed in the gray mist, he saw something move cautiously. He felt a surging in his empty stomach, as at the infusion of alcohol or fear. He refined the focus still further, even as he heard Aubrey say, "I'm afraid it is. . . ." He did not sound genuinely sorry, but rather pleased that his prognostication had been proved correct.

"Are you sure?" he asked, knowing the answer. A glimpse of a white face, an anorak, the purposeful movement from trunk to trunk. It was a hunting animal. He swung the glasses so that he focused on Napier's features again. By his still posture, the tired slope of the shoulders, it was evident that he was unaware of Gardiner's proximity. Fewer than fifty yards separated them. Only feet of that completely open, the road and the frail white fence that would separate the two men for much too short a time. He had a sudden fear that Aubrey was enjoying the spectacle in a detached, imperial manner. He took the glasses from his eyes for a moment and saw Aubrey's features settled in grim satisfaction; he felt himself a party to what Aubrey intended, an ineffectual spectator of the drama.

He pressed his glasses back to his eyes. Something in him wished for Napier's death as a kind of justice on the crude implement of Constant's will. . . .

He ought to stop it, warn Napier. And he realized that if he did, Gardiner was a dead man. He was now only yards from the road, still moving like a stalking animal through the last outliers before the strip of road and the fence.

"What are you going to do?" he breathed urgently.

"Nothing," was the calm reply.

"What?"

"Be ready to move as soon as. . . ." He left the sentence unfinished.

"You can't do that!"

"I am doing it," Aubrey retorted, his tone warning that discussion was at an end. "Be ready to move when I give the word—it's a hundred yards or more. Let's hope he doesn't shoot the little worm from the other side of the road."

Latymer concentrated on the scene, as if by staring in dawning horror at the unfolding scene he were contributing something, avoiding the uselessness that seemed to invade him. For a moment he despised himself, as he despised Aubrey and Constant.

Richard Gardiner had taken advantage of Napier's lighting a cigarette. The man should not have done so, but he had previously glanced at his watch and decided that he was on the point of being relieved. He had his shoulder half turned toward the road as he bent to his cupped hand and the lighter flame that Latymer could see flickering.

Gardiner was over the road swiftly, soundlessly; then he vaulted the white fence that no longer marked Constant's inviolable territory. And Napier, head coming up, suddenly warned by some professional instinct, the rifle turning in his hands, coming level to a bead. . . . Then the splayed arms like a man drowning, and the head flung almost off its delicate perch on the shoulders, and the slow collapse in which tragedy became farce as the body subsided into the long, wet grass near the fence.

Latymer could not say at what point Aubrey began running or at what point he stopped observing events through the glasses and saw the suddenly removed figures with the naked eye. He only understood that his Wellington boots were slopping through the wet restraints of grass, and Aubrey's dumpy little figure was ahead of him, moving with surprising speed along the fold where the brake had hidden them, which would take them toward Gardiner's right, an accident of the ground which Aubrey had decided to exploit as soon as he had seen it.

Gardiner had only just moved, only just lowered the stiff arms, released the Browning from the two-handed grip so that it hung more innocently in his right hand. He had taken perhaps two, three steps toward the prone Napier, toward the rifle concealed by the long grass.

"Stay where you are, Richard!"

Aubrey's voice was ridiculously high and his articulation damaged by his labored breathing. Yet the gun was extended in the posture of challenge, knees slightly bent; then Latymer, too, was atop the slight remaining rise and looking down at Gardiner, and his own gun was held stiffly and pointed slightly down at the center of the woolen shirt—dark olive-green—and Gardiner's navel.

"Don't make us kill you, Richard!" he shouted, but his voice sounded, even to him, inadequate and quite unthreatening.

13. At the Kill

It was patently ridiculous; he understood that. Ridiculous to move, to exercise even an eyelid. Ridiculous, too, the tableau of three middle-aged men, two of them in dark, formal coats and Wellington boots and himself in slacks and anorak, the slacks stained by his passage through the wet grass and clinging to his legs, some foolish return to the arena by aging boxers with tired legs and fuddled minds.

The image was incredibly clear to him, so that he forgot to move, to make the attempt. Latymer and Aubrey might have hesitated a fraction had he done so, but they would have killed him. He knew that. Something out of the past, the athletes of a former time with thickened waistlines and minds that carried too much fat. . . . Ridiculous.

Aubrey walked slowly and somewhat uncertainly down the slope, gun still held out in stiff arms. Latymer moved to one side and came at him from a different direction. He looked down at the long gun in the grass and then held out the Browning to Aubrey, butt first; Aubrey took it and dropped in into his pocket. Then he said, "How are you, Richard? Welcome back."

"Back? To where, Aubrey?"

"It's been a long journey, Richard."

Gardiner swiveled his gaze to watch Latymer post himself ten yards away, to his left. The Smith & Wesson dropped to waist level and remained pointed at his middle. There was no way, he accepted, that he could turn the situation to his advantage.

Strangely, he did not consider the frustration of his hopes and the closing of the cage upon him; there was something ultimately unthreatening about the guns held by two old acquaintances. As if they were empty or some nonaggression pact had been sealed between them. He said, "Marked by bodies, Aubrey." His face seemed momentarily to crumple. "But—I had to kill them. I was meant to kill them." Aubrey's gaze was unwinking and did not move from his face. The round features, still so schoolboyish, were bereft of emotion. "They tried to kill me, Aubrey. After all this time. All of them. It was—fair . . . ?" The slightest question in the voice.

He seemed to loathe himself suddenly—a spurt of feeling as if an artery had been severed. A spasm of ugliness, directed upon himself, flickered across his face. He wanted to tell them, to find some kind of comprehension in them; in the same moment he despised the weakness that made him want to babble to them. He went on.

"I—I don't want your sympathy—anyone's sympathy! Yet I need you to understand. . . . You do understand that I *had* to kill them?" He waved his arms weakly, as if signaling for help. He felt that they condemned him, and he hated their contempt but was pierced by it. "You see, it's as if all the rest of it—the time between—didn't exist anymore. It was still 1944 —Christ, you'd have given me a bloody medal if it *was* 1944!" The words ejaculated hatred. He felt he had betrayed something, but he could not understand what it was.

"And Constant was behind it all the time, mm?" Aubrey said. Gardiner nodded, and Aubrey almost flinched at the emotion in the blazing eyes. The prone corpse seemed to obtrude on their conversation. "It's over, Richard. I might even say I'm sorry for you. But Constant is too important for you to be allowed to remove him—whatever the. . . ." He left the sentence incomplete. "Too important."

"What do we do?" Latymer asked and then, as if fascinated by some strange illness, asked, "Why did you do it? After all this *time,* Richard?"

Gardiner looked at him sharply and shrugged as if reaching for some answer hard to articulate. Then the shrug was one of incomprehension, sullen silence.

"We're not taking him back to the house, if that's what you mean," Aubrey said. "Not until I've spoken to him, that is. We'll take him to the shooting lodge, up on Broomhead Moor. There's a track from the house, but I don't want to use that. . . . Too many eyes." He saw on Gardiner's features the livid growth of hope, like a hectic breaking under the surface of the skin.

"How then?"

"Where's your car?"

"About a mile and a half into the woods."

"Good. We'll take that. We can reach the lodge by taking another track, south of here. Drive almost up to the lodge on the blind side from the house. There's no watchman placed up there." Aubrey smiled. "I was careful to avoid that."

Gardiner watched the slight smile on Latymer's face and the self-satisfaction of Aubrey. He felt a sudden resentment but let the feeling slide away, unconsidered. He wanted his brain to be empty, to receive impressions as they came, to prepare itself. Yet he also wanted to go on talking to these two men, who belonged to the past that was now his only possession; they made that past less chill and alone than it had been. Despite the guns, they were not his enemies.

"We'd better get on then," Latymer said.

"Quite. Richard, Napier's not a very heavy gentleman, even in death. Put him across one of your broad shoulders, would you? We can deposit him at some distance from here and under cover. Then you can lead the way."

The walk through the empty wood, the thinning mist still obstinately clinging to the dark trees and wet grass, was conducted in silence, like a search or a solemn procession. Latymer and Aubrey kept a respectful distance from Gardiner's back.

Latymer was unable, however, not to concentrate, until the sight caused him an acute physical revulsion, on the bobbing dead head of Napier as Gardiner effortlessly carried him. He noted the neat squaring off of the hair at the nape of the neck, the flopping forelock against Gardiner's anorak, the white cheeks and pinched, sharp nose when the head swung into profile from time to time. There was something nightmarish about the image—Napier was being carried like a sack because of Aubrey's sense of justice, or revenge, or even callousness.

When Aubrey ordered Gardiner to dump the body in some bushes, peremptorily, then ordered him to move ahead again, it was done without pause almost —certainly without feeling or chagrin. Quite horrible.

The car journey, with Latymer driving, was conducted in the same silence in the warmth of the Ford's interior. Aubrey rested the gun on his folded arms but pressed it into Gardiner's side. He seemed pleased with the progress of the car or events, and Gardiner, tired as he suddenly was, slumped against the passenger window, his head pressed against the cold glass.

They left the car half a mile from the shooting lodge, in a dell of brown heather, the mist still thick there, though as they walked out of it, the sun was diffusedly attempting to breach the gray, cold blanket. This edge of the moor, which climbed slowly toward Middle Moss and Howden Moors, was a gradual slope down toward the Ewden—toward the woods they had just left and the house. Rawlings was still lost in the mist, but the lodge itself lay in a slight hollow and was invisible to the house.

Gardiner halted before the closed door, as if reluctant to enter. He turned to Aubrey, who remained where he was. Latymer passed them to open up the squat, solid wooden building, low and flat-roofed, something from a frontier time. Latymer said, "Is it kept locked?" Aubrey was about to reply when Latymer's hand pushed at the door and it swung silently open. Latymer stepped in, and Gardiner was immediately behind him, Aubrey bringing up the rear.

Aubrey had passed through the door behind Gardiner when the occupant of the lodge spoke, *"Bonjour,* gentlemen—welcome to my humble abode. Do please come in. And, M'sieur Aubrey, please do not use your own people as a shield from behind which to shoot me."

Aubrey stood to one side, the gun pointing uselessly at the floor, and said, "Not my sort of game, that, hiding behind somebody else. Though it is yours, I gather, 'Goriot.'" Aubrey made an effort to smile, to keep shock from his voice.

"Ah—the price of fame," Haussman acknowledged, his gun still pointing at Aubrey. He calculated that there was no immediate danger from any of the three, but if there should be, he assumed that Latymer would not move and endanger Aubrey. His big, square face was smiling, but there was no trace of humor in his flinty eyes. The shock of wiry gray hair was smoothed down, and he looked alert and untired. It was as if he were at the end of a long quest or a race in which the prize had proved to his satisfaction.

"You are Gardiner's operator, I take it?" Aubrey said. Haussman nodded theatrically.

"Operator?" Gardiner whispered, as if emerging from a trance. "The photographs—you?" Again Haussman nodded. The gun flickered to cover Gardiner, then back to Aubrey again. Gardiner turned to Aubrey. "What the hell is going on?"

"Shall I explain?"

"As you wish," Haussman said indifferently. His eyes watched Gardiner for movement, even though he knew he was the only one of them unarmed.

"This man is a senior officer in the SDECE, French Intelligence, Richard. He has been using you —as you appear to know—as his field agent. Van Lederer was one of his targets; the other is obviously Constant. Am I correct?"

Haussman nodded again. He watched Gardiner's hands bunch into fists and the face work in hatred. He said quickly, "I think it better, gentlemen, if we all sit down. There will be less encouragement to sudden moves if you are all seated. . . ." He pointed with his free hand at the wooden chairs gathered around the table.

For a moment the three men seemed reluctant, even frozen; then Aubrey sat down, and Latymer followed. Gardiner seemed to hesitate, then took his place at the table. All three of them now faced Haussman, whose chair was pushed back from the table, for safety. The gun remained steady on Aubrey. Gardiner appeared to have slumped in the chair like a runner whose legs have given out. He evinced little interest in the man who had operated him. A creeping sense of being the creature of another will overtook him, a subtle paralysis. Haussman sensed his helplessness, as he saw the growing alertness in Aubrey and Latymer.

"Now we're gathered here," Aubrey said, "what do you have to say to us, housemaster?"

Haussman appeared puzzled, then said, "A

quaint English joke, I presume? There was much the same cryptic nonsense when I worked on de Gaulle's staff in London."

"You don't hear so many now that you work with the staff of Moscow Center, I suppose."

Haussman shook his head.

"I shall explain. But first of all, you must rid yourselves of the misconception that I am Moscow's man."

"Surely not Peking?" Latymer asked. "It must be one of the satellites then. Do you distinguish between Moscow and Prague or Budapest?"

"Please, you will listen. You may come to understand something other than your silly jokes by the time I have finished."

Aubrey raised his hands, palms outward, to signify acceptance.

"Please go ahead," he said, placing his gun on the table, its butt toward Haussman. Then he looked sharply at Latymer, who disgorged his own gun and laid it on the rough surface of the table. Haussman nodded in satisfaction.

"On my part, gentlemen, I shall be similarly frank —and I shall allow whichever of you has M'sieur Gardiner's gun to keep it, for the moment. . . ." He smiled, and Aubrey's face, without betraying any emotion, smiled back. "I have no men here apart from my driver, who is obtaining some coffee and breakfast in Ewden village. He will return soon. I did not expect you, and so there will not be sufficient food—however, there will be coffee."

"Many thanks. It wasn't a pleasant night. Rather damp for yesterday's spies, wouldn't you say, 'Goriot'?"

Haussman seemed to warm to the code name and the good-humored irony of Aubrey's tone.

"We are assuming, I notice, that no one is going to get killed here? There is no place for violent death in this little reunion, mm?"

"Good."

"What's your story?" Gardiner asked abruptly, his voice sunken into sullenness.

" 'Achilles,' I apologize to you. You were being

used by me, and I understand, I think, what that has meant to you. I have robbed you of your pride, is that not so?" Gardiner was silent, and after a moment Haussman looked away from his eyes and said to Aubrey and Latymer, "You are ready to listen?"

"We are at your disposal, Jean-Jacques. Indeed, I might say you have a captive audience. . . . Please do proceed."

"Very well. I will begin by telling you that your Mr. Constant is Moscow's man—not myself. So was General Van Lederer. . . ." He paused, and though Latymer was about to protest, he was silenced by the unchanging stoniness of Aubrey's features. Haussman continued, perhaps disappointed by the lack of reaction. "Very well. There is proof, and in the case of Van Lederer it can be checked with a reasonable degree of certainty. If the CIA can be persuaded to make the checks. . . ."

Again Aubrey was silent, and his silence affected Latymer, whose features were far more mobile.

"But . . ." he began, and fell silent.

"I see. A conspiracy of silence. I obviously do not surprise you. Van Lederer was Moscow's man on the NATO Committee, not Lidbrooke. Constant devised and ordered the framing and death of Lidbrooke to prevent the inquiries proceeding any further. I'm sure that you considered the murder of Lidbrooke ill-advised and hasty?" Aubrey's left eyelid flickered twice, but still, he said nothing. The silence, every time Haussman stopped speaking, was more strained and tense than before. It did not seem to emanate from Gardiner, the rogue piece in the chess game, but from Latymer and the robotically stiff Aubrey.

"Naturally," Haussman continued, "you are too professional for the matter not to have caused you concern, however. Van Lederer was being operated by the man the CIA calls 'Franklin,' their newest and brightest source at Moscow Center. He is, in fact, a bona fide agent of the KGB, and not a double."

"You can prove all this, of course!" Latymer snapped in the moment of silence.

"With difficulty and with cooperation—but yes,

I can. You may discover that my superiors in the Quai d'Orsay, however reluctant, will confirm that I have been engaged in this operation with their knowledge and approval, which would make it more difficult to believe in me as Moscow's man. To discover Van Lederer's culpability, you would need to go back to the very beginning of his supposed persuasion of 'Franklin' to work for the Americans—there were unscheduled meetings, then, and some rather strange contacts. . . ." He paused, then: "But in the matter of Constant—he is a 'mole' and has been for a very long time."

"You realize what you're saying?" Latymer asked again. His mind seemed, to Aubrey, suddenly slow and dull and conventional. He was tracing well-signposted paths, trying to avoid the information that was being supplied. Aubrey glared at him.

"I do. I did not expect to have to inform anyone of this." Haussman shrugged. "But you caught 'Achilles' before he could complete his task and brought him here, to me. Now you have to be told."

"What *task?*" Gardiner asked, his lips twisted lividly into a scowl. "What do you want with me?"

"Ah. You, given the information I possessed, were the answer to my problems, m'sieur. A survivor of the operations of the 'Wolfgroup.' I learned of you from Etienne de Vaugrigard, who betrayed you to the Gestapo." He watched the slight shudder run through Gardiner's frame, then continued. "I was investigating his links with the OAS, and he told me this strange story about the 'Wolfgroup,' to ensure his loyalty. That was before he confessed, when confronted with facts, figures, and photographs. And he mentioned the names of the men who headed the group—Constant and Van Lederer. It was almost too wonderful, too convenient, to believe. I promised to protect him against you, as long as you could be led to him. I must admit that when I checked on you, I assumed you had tried to make yourself forget the war and escaped into the skin of a civilized man. I brought Dupuy to you, a passive trigger for the kind of man you once were—I gambled that you had not changed too much."

In the sudden silence Gardiner's breathing could be heard, mounting to some kind of climax. Haussman steadied the gun on his stomach and glared warningly. Aubrey, sensing desperation, laid his hand firmly on Gardiner's arm, restrainingly. He said, "Richard, it's not worth it. You'll get yourself killed."

Gardiner turned on him as Aubrey had hoped, his rage transmuted into words rather than imminent action.

"Do I give a—*fuck* whether I get killed or not?" he seemed to scream. "This—*shit* knew me inside out. Knew me so well that he could *count* on me doing what he wanted!"

Aubrey's eyes widened.

"It doesn't. . . ."

"Yes, it does. I knew someone was helping me —I didn't care who or why. I still don't. I'd have killed them anyway. It's the being so sure!"

"I apologize, m'sieur. Had I gone to the CIA or the SIS, I and my organization would have been immediately suspect. We are not the golden children of NATO at the moment, you understand. . . ." He smiled ironically. "The general who governs France is a great man, but he does not like the British or the Americans, and they mistrust him. This would have been seen as a ploy of his, to cause trouble, even an excuse to leave NATO. So, when you were introduced to the board, by accident, I had to use you." He stared at Gardiner, his eyes gleaming. "And for all you protest, m'sieur, you have lived as never before during the past weeks. You have *enjoyed* yourself!"

Gardiner winced at the glint of knowledge in Haussman's eye and at the weight of truth the statement carried. He seemed about to speak, then lapsed into silence. Haussman turned his attention to Aubrey and Latymer, as if Gardiner had become relegated in importance.

"I and my masters were working for the future. France has no future outside NATO, whatever may be said to the contrary. And we were increasingly concerned at the leakages from inside the Intelligence Committee. We went to work, and we discovered the

source of the leaks to be Van Lederer. It was a long
and difficult business, the process of elimination. At
almost the same time we received word that Constant
had been turned by the old NKVD, way back in
1946. A man called Plekhanov, long since dead."

"How do you know that?" Latymer asked in the
same waspish, insulted tone. Aubrey sighed with irritation but maintained his concentration on Haussman.

"A long time ago Constant was operations director
of Berlin Station—almost from the day the war ended.
He disappeared for two weeks—missing, presumed
dead or captured. Old cold-war stuff. Then he turned
up, beaten and ill and wounded, but alive and escaped
from custody. Welcome home, hero of the hour!"
Haussman snorted. "We learned about it only when a
low-grade defector, a Pole sold to us by the Italians
after he defected from their Rome embassy staff, came
into our possession. We paid over the odds for him
because he once worked in the French sector of Berlin." Aubrey nodded, doll-like and stiff, so that Haussman was surprised by the movement. "He was on
Plekhanov's staff when Constant was taken—and
turned. When we learned that and saw how high
Constant had climbed, we knew he was more dangerous to you and to us than Philby would ever have
been. But what to do? He was already a deputy in SIS
and above suspicion." He paused, then added finally,
" 'Achilles' fell from heaven into our hands, gentlemen. We used him."

There was a long silence, strained and echoing,
in which the lives of the four men seemed to sound
hollowly, like their breathing. Latymer looked at Aubrey to break the intolerable quiet, but Aubrey seemed
removed from speech by some huge impediment or
paralysis. Gardiner, he saw, had retreated into pro-
found melancholy. He was reviewing his life, and there
was nothing Latymer could find to say to him. He
hated Haussman and his ingenious and violent scheme.

They heard in their separate silences the faint
noise of a car, at some distance, and then an interminable time passed before a big man with a heavy

mustache pushed open the door, paused, then spoke to Haussman in French.

Then the driver made coffee, and the creeping aroma seemed to unfreeze each mind, steam easing a postage stamp from an envelope, encouraging speculation once more. There was also a sense of unity, strange and ephemeral, yet present.

The driver served the coffee and then left without a word from Haussman, presumably to patrol the area around the lodge. Each man, hands cupped around the mugs taken from a cupboard in the tiny, primitive kitchen, drank gratefully. Latymer sensed it was some kind of pledge, as if he and Aubrey had admitted the truth of what they had been told.

Suddenly Gardiner said, "You're all bastards— the lot of you!" There was the same fierce light in his eyes, but as if he were no more than a recalcitrant child, he seemed quelled by Haussman's stare and relapsed into his former mood, so much lumpy baggage thrown on the chair. "Bastards. . . ." As if he wished to share the complicity of the moment, he drank.

"You still say nothing, Aubrey?" Haussman said directly, lighting a cigarette and offering the packet. Aubrey shook his head; Latymer accepted. The acrid tobacco stung his throat, but the rich smell of the French cigarettes filled the lodge's main room.

"Mm," Aubrey murmured. "It does seem incumbent upon me to say a few words—I realized that."

"You disbelieve me?"

"Not absolutely. Disappointed in your methods, that goes without saying. But not entirely disbelieving. I would need proof, of course. Where is this mysterious Pole now?"

"Still in France, Retired to the country. He grows flowers, I believe."

"Then I would wish to start with him."

Latymer sighed and saw Haussman deliberately relax. A moment of supreme importance had passed, although there had seemed an inadequate preparation for it. But Aubrey had accepted the thesis as a thesis and was prepared to test its worth.

"Good. That is very good."

Aubrey turned his attention to Gardiner, and after a long moment he said quietly, "What do you feel now, Richard? You've heard everything."

Gardiner stirred in his hard chair, stared at Aubrey, and seemed about to defy the whole moment, the whole atmosphere, then said, "What is there for me to say? It's all sewn up, isn't it? I don't matter a damn anymore, do I?" He seemed to wish to return to an enforced isolation, as if it comforted him more than conversation. Latymer looked at him, unable to guess what might be going through his mind. Gardiner said, "Of course, Richard Gardiner would be your accredited agent in this—a member of SDECE, for the purposes of crimes that might have been committed by him in France?"

"Naturally."

There was a smile about Gardiner's mouth, as if he were contemptuous of the offer. Aubrey added, "Either that, Richard, or we make it an operation of ours, and you work for us."

"I'm not part of your plans or the world. And I won't be."

Aubrey appeared exasperated by the rejection of his offer.

"You don't want to be arrested by the French for murder—nor do you want to be taken out by the CIA. They're very hot on that, making people disappear."

"Balls."

"Stop behaving like a sulking schoolboy, Richard! Haussman was right when he chose you. You did it because of what *you* are, not because of what he is or did. Try to consider things a little more rationally than of late and come to a sensible decision."

"Sensible—in your world?" There was a coruscating scorn in Gardiner's voice.

"In our world," Aubrey explained patiently, "grotesque and ruthless and nightmarish as it sometimes is, there is all the more need for good sense and rationality. Unfortunately that is what you forgot, M'sieur Haussman, in setting this rogue element loose." Haussman appeared unabashed. "I accept some of your reservations concerning the SIS and CIA, and I understand the acute attractions of de Vaugrigard's story. . . ." He paused; then: "But the affair is now in our hands. If you can convince me, then I am prepared to go into the whole thing thoroughly. If you trust me to do that?"

Haussman nodded. He got up from his chair, laid his own gun on the table, butt toward Aubrey, and held out a huge hand. Aubrey shook it with delicate fingers and smiled briefly.

"I agree. But what is to be done for M'sieur Gardiner?"

Aubrey looked down at the sullen, petulant face, *Yes,* he thought, *it is petulant now. He is merely sulking and no longer dangerous.* He said, "He, too, becomes our concern. I don't think you need worry about him, since he is already beginning to realize that the very things which made him 'Achilles' are the qualities you desired in your hit man. He will feel complimented eventually."

Gardiner looked up at him, his eyes cold. But he said nothing. Perhaps there was the faintest hint of agreement, however grudging, about the mouth.

The door opened suddenly, and the driver came in. Each of them turned to him as to an intruder.

"Men coming," he said, addressing Haussman. Latymer watched the petulance on Gardiner's face slowly drain away and suspicion, cunning, seep back to take its place. He felt incapable of reaction himself, as if the news had robbed him of motive power or as if the power around that table resided only in talk, words. Then Aubrey rose in his chair.

"Tell me," he snapped in French, "how many and from which direction?"

Haussman nodded, and the driver replied.

"Four in the main party—coming from the direction of the house. But I saw others, circling to come from the other way. . . ."

"Then he knows we're here." Haussman seemed, to Latymer, suddenly crumpled. Even words were paltry. Strangely, he felt no sense of immediate danger, imminent discovery. Some placidity had emerged from somewhere, the comfort of watching a performance only as a spectator. He shook his head as if to clear it.

"He knows *we're* here, I suspect," Aubrey observed, indicating himself, Latymer, and Gardiner. "They've probably found Napier's body."

"What will you do?" Haussman asked. He, too, seemed to acquiesce in the situation, resigning all power of decision to Aubrey.

Aubrey's face was compressed with thought for a moment; then he said, "Are they between here and your car?"

The driver shook his head, shrugged.

"Not at the moment. . . ."

"Then it is time for you to go!" He looked directly at Haussman, then at the round-shouldered, slumped form of Gardiner. Gardiner appeared indifferent once more. "This is now a legitimate intelligence operation, Haussman. You will go back to the embassy and wait for me to contact you there. Agreed?"

Haussman stood up slowly and looked at Gardiner as if reluctant to part with some possession of his, prized and effective. Only then did he pick up his gun from the table; he looked at it, then slid it inside his coat.

"Very well, Aubrey. When will you arrive in London?"

"Soon—today, tomorrow. Now—please go!"

Haussman nodded once.

"Very well. I leave matters in your—capable hands then."

He motioned to the driver, who went out, then called back, "All clear."

Then Haussman, too, was gone. Latymer stood up and looked at Aubrey, who gathered up the cups of coffee and carried them into the kitchen. Ignoring Gardiner, Latymer followed him.

"What do you intend?"

Aubrey swilled the mugs under the cold tap, then stacked them in the cupboard below the sink. When he looked around at Latymer, his face was mobile with ideas.

"We have captured a very dangerous man, Hilary. Deputy will be delighted, I'm quite sure. We have to ensure that he has *no* suspicions whatsoever that we have talked to anyone, that we know anything."

He wiped his hands on his coat and went back into the main room of the lodge. Gardiner sat with his hands loosely on his lap, as if they had no power of sensation now that they no longer held the coffee mug.

"Richard—Hilary, watch the window, there's a good chap—Richard, listen to me. Just play dumb. Understand?"

Gardiner looked slowly up at him, resentment blazing in his eyes for a moment.

"Oh, dear, I do hope you're not going to be difficult about this. . . ."

"No. I won't be *difficult!*" he replied contemptuously, mimicking Aubrey.

"Good. We followed you up here and caught you resting. Don't worry. You'll be safe, as long as Constant thinks you're neutralized as a threat. . . ."

"But I am, aren't I?"

"Perhaps."

"It's Deputy," Latymer said from the window.

"Who else?"

"Two of Napier's men—Laker and Monro, on either side of the big white chief."

"Check the other windows."

A pause; then: "Evans is at the rear of the house. Wooller's there, but I can't see any others of our team."

"What?"

"They're not there. What does it mean?"

"Were it not for young Evans, I'd say it was the execution squad. But perhaps not. . . . Constant can't be certain of who is in here or what might have gone on. I just hope Haussman and his driver haven't been spotted. I think it's time for a word with Deputy, don't you?"

Aubrey went to the door, opened it cautiously, and stepped out. The air was less chill now, and only the last fingers of gray mist wreathed the place. Constant smiled sardonically when he saw the short figure in overcoat and Wellingtons. He had dressed himself in a shooting jacket and knee breeches.

"Ah, Aubrey. We were just coming to find you. . . . We found Napier. Have you found Gardiner?"

"Yes, Deputy. He gave us quite a chase, but we followed him here. He's inside, disarmed and harmless."

"Well done."

"Thank you, Deputy."

"Wooler reported a car on the road from Ewden —dark-looking chap driving. Seen anything of it?" Aubrey looked at the shotgun broken across the crook of Constant's arm. He was careful to control his voice.

"No one called. He may be around."

Constant smiled and said, "Quite. Well, should we not have a word with Gardiner? Has he told you anything yet?"

Aubrey looked at Laker and Monro and shook his head. There was only one thing to be done. He said, "I'll get him out." He turned his back on Constant and shouted, waving his arm as he did so, "Hilary, bring out the prisoner, will you?"

The door opened, and Gardiner emerged, followed closely by Latymer, who ostentatiously pointed his gun at Gardiner's back. Gardiner looked suitably truculent and defeated. Latymer closed the door of the lodge behind him.

"Ah," Constant said as Aubrey turned to face him.

"Good morning, Deputy," Latymer said briskly. "We have him, as you see."

"Indeed. How did you manage it, Latymer? Excellent work, and with such a desperate character." Aubrey noticed that after a moment's initial inspection Constant avoided looking into Gardiner's face. Perhaps he was unnerved by the pure and unqualified hate he saw there. Evil eye.

"When we found Napier, the trail led here. Gardiner was sleeping, Deputy. Easy, I'm afraid," Aubrey remarked conversationally.

"Mm. And he didn't take Napier's rifle. I find that very strange, don't you?"

"Perhaps so, Deputy. But you can ask him about that later."

"Quite so. Yes, perhaps we should be getting back—lots to do, eh?"

Aubrey held his breath and avoided looking at Latymer. Then he said, "Will you lead the way, Deputy?"

"Yes." Constant seemed undecided; then he said, "Laker, Monro, we're taking Mr. Gardiner back to the house. You two had better stay up here and scout about for that foreign-looking chap that Wooller says he saw. I don't suppose there's anything to it, but just in case." He turned to Aubrey and smiled. Aubrey, turning his gaze from the expressionless faces of Laker and Monro, detected no sense of irony in Constant's face. Yet he could not rid himself of the feeling that he had failed to convince the man, that Constant knew Haussman had been in the area.

If he knew that, then Aubrey might have consigned Haussman and his driver to death. Constant would not take the slightest chance. Aubrey, suddenly out of his moral depth, choked on the bitter water he swallowed. He could only, faintly, hope that the Frenchmen had already got away.

"Shall we . . . ?" he asked with a forced lightness of tone.

"Of course. You lead the way, Aubrey. I'll bring up the rear. Both of you keep a good watch on our friend." This he addressed to Latymer, who nodded.

They walked down the edge of the moor toward Rawlings, nestling amid trees, the road a thin ribbon bordered by the white fence, in a silent procession. Latymer watched Gardiner carefully—Constant's shotgun was still broken over his arm, but it was loaded and the work of a moment to close it, aim, and blow Gardiner's spine through his rib cage, supposing he made a run for it. Thankfully, Gardiner appeared dulled and spent again, rather than secretive and tense with plans.

Aubrey listened behind him for distant shots or voices as they dropped away from the lodge. He was very afraid, but he heard nothing. Evans and Wooller and others of the original Beaters—two more that Latymer had not seen from the lodge windows—followed at a respectful distance.

The sun climbed in the sky, and the mist dispersed so that the cloudless expanse above them was palely blue, already bright with heat. Aubrey shed his overcoat and began to wipe at his neck and forehead with his silk handkerchief. Insects hummed noisily in the long and drying grass on the lower slope near the road.

All the way to the house Aubrey surreptitiously looked around him, for Laker and Monro. He saw no sign of either of them.

Aubrey sat in the library, watching Latymer over a tumbler, his mind clogging on the directions he might take, the actions he might consider. Gardiner was being questioned in the wine cellar by Constant—Aubrey wondered why people like Constant always chose the cellar—but he had no fears that Gardiner would betray the existence of Haussman or the information he had imparted. He had sent Evans along as an extra guard—the interrogation might be painful, gratuitously violent to satisfy Constant's relieved fear, but it would not be fatal. And nothing like those days in the Avenue Foch must have been. . . .

No, he had no fears on Gardiner's part. Only on his own, and beyond the self, fears for the service itself. He was unable to perceive Constant's next moves, and his blindness disturbed him.

Eventually Latymer spoke, disturbing the silence of the sunlit room.

"What sort of danger are we in, Aubrey? I inquire from mixed motives, naturally."

Aubrey looked at him, and his mind closed on a momentary irritation at Latymer's habitually languid way of speaking.

"I don't know, Hilary. I just don't know, and it *irritates* me that I don't. I want to know where Laker and Monro are. They haven't come back yet, and that worries me. Haussman's car must have left tracks—they may even. . . . No, I don't think I want to say that just at the moment." He shivered theatrically and swallowed some of the whisky.

"You think Constant knows—suspects?"

"Oh, yes. He's suspicious all right. I suspect he's ordered Laker and Monro to kill on sight. There's something about the easy way we took Richard, something about the whole thing that would appear wrong to him—false. His senses are those of a threatened animal. He'll have got wind of something."

"Well, what do we do?"

"About what we know? I'll have to talk to 'C,' naturally. He'll have to talk to Haussman, Haussman's superiors, anyone and everyone."

"The whole thing—it's fantastic, Aubrey!"

"Yes. Very theatrical. Bloody clever. I want desperately to believe it because I can't stand the sight of Constant! I don't like his methods, his men, or his personality. And it all fits! That's the beauty of it, Hilary. Such a pattern to it all, and going on over all those years. God, the man is next in line of succession, until and unless he makes a prize pratfall!" He shuddered, for effect. "Think of it—being run directly by Moscow Center!" He laughed. "As Arthur Bullen might say—enough to put tits on yer!"

"Stop clowning, Aubrey. Can we take Richard back to London with us—without arousing opposition?"

"Mm. I should think so. After all, I'm officer in charge for the moment. Constant can't not show up with Gardiner, after all. No, I see no difficulty there."

He got up and went to the window. By the set of his shoulders, the pugnacious stance, Latymer understood that Aubrey, having talked out his problem, had solved it. The depression was lifting. Aubrey's hand tilted the tumbler to his lips, and he drained the last of the scotch. Then he turned to Latymer.

"Fill them up, Hilary, would you?"

Latymer took Aubrey's tumbler and his own and then joined Aubrey at the window with generous measures in both glasses.

"Everything is going to be all right then?"

"Oh, I should think so, Hilary. Silly to worry,

really. Constant should soon tire of roughing up
Richard, and then we can all get down to pretending
that the operation has drawn to a satisfactory conclusion."

"You believe Haussman then?"

"Oh, yes. I believe him. At least I'm prepared to
believe him, which is the same thing. I just have to
get 'C' to circumvent Constant for a while, until we
have checked the whole thing out. Not that he'll get up
to too much harm with Van Lederer out of the way."

He stopped. Latymer, seeing his intent gaze,
looked out of the window. "Laker—and Monro," he
breathed.

"Quickly—get your field glasses."

Latymer crossed to the table and then returned
to the window, handing Aubrey the glasses, taking
his whisky. Aubrey fiddled the leather strap free, then
raised the glasses to his eyes. Aubrey looked out at
Laker and Monro approaching the house from the direction of the shooting lodge, their shotguns broken
over their arms—no, Laker had a rifle, Monro the
shotgun.

"Well?" he said impatiently. Aubrey handed him
the glasses.

"What do you take that to be that Monro is carrying in his left hand?"

Latymer refocused the glasses. Sky, then down to
Laker's face, set and expressionless as the two men
came across the grounds toward Rawlings. Monro was
partly hidden. Latymer was about to exclaim against
his being obscured, as if he might thereby get Laker
to move, when he saw what Aubrey wished him to see.

"A briefcase?"

"Do you think, in all honesty, Hilary, that Monro
is moonlighting from the service as a part-time execu-
tive or schoolmaster? Would that be a reasonable assumption on our part?"

Latymer concentrated on the idly swinging case
in Monro's hand. Unbelievable. Frightening. He had
noticed the catch in Aubrey's voice which the languid words could not disguise.

"No. They've—found it, somewhere. . . ."

"Exactly my thought. And it doesn't take a seer to tell you where. Or does it?"

"Then they've—?"

"They may indeed have."

"Oh, my God—two SDECE men, just like that!" Latymer couldn't make his fingers click audibly, as if they were cold.

"Just like that—quick and perhaps even silent." There was a wintry smile on Aubrey's face, which appeared drawn and much thinner and older.

Latymer saw Laker and Monro pass out of his field of vision, toward the front of the house.

"I—we have to make sure, Aubrey—have to. . . ."

"Yes, I suppose so." A pause; then: "You'd better be on your way, hadn't you?" Latymer nodded but did not move. "I'll wait for you here. And don't be too long. It might make Deputy suspicious!"

Latymer did not find the bodies. Only the car, obviously and innocently empty. No damage—it appeared. He made it out, hidden as it was by thick bushes, and moved cautiously toward it down the slope of a dell no more than a quarter of a mile from the lodge. He could see tire tracks leading into the bushes —and then a set of tire prints deeper in the soft ground, as if the car had stood there for some time.

It seemed at first as if the sunlight dappling down through the trees was reflecting off dew in the grass. When he got closer, still perhaps thirty yards from the car in the bushes, he saw that the sunlight was re-flecting off shards and splinters of glass. His boots crunched on them—many of them.

Windshield. He knew it, casting about, kicking at the grass, treading on the deep tire impression, look-ing around, so that he saw the way the car had been heading, presumably from the point where it had been parked.

Flattened grass, a swath, as if something had been dragged from this spot. . . .

He hurried to the car then and pulled away the masking twigs and branches, the noise seeming amplified, as if his movements were suddenly those of outrage, frenzy.

The car was empty, as he had known it would be. There was no windshield—shotgun blast at close range? He wrenched open the driver's door. Glass on the seat, in the padding of the roof lining, in the dash. . . .

Flies buzzed—but only a few, because there was no body, and only a little blood, which was quickly drying. The bodies must have been dead almost at once. No blood on the back seat. Perhaps Haussman had—

Had only got out, to be shot or bludgeoned. It didn't matter, and they had not heard the shots, not here down in this dell on the far side of the lodge.

Latymer was sick with understanding. The procession of bodies. Sick, too, because of his own danger, the danger that discovery brought. Sick for Aubrey. . . .

The car had been left for collection. He scouted around hurriedly but saw no sign of the bodies. He reluctantly, yet urgently, climbed the dell again, looking back only once. The events down there were part of the past already. What he had to do now was warn Aubrey.

"Getting rid of a couple of SDECE men is serious, if it ever comes out—but *us?*"

Latymer felt Aubrey watching him closely from the window. As for himself, he sat and stared at a painting above the library fireplace—a landscape that seemed to need a stag or a maiden. Something anyway—even an empty car and a small bloodstain.

To Aubrey, looking from the window, Latymer's fine features were haloed with light, the gray hair made golden again. He looked remarkably young, the features softened by the light behind them. There seemed a confidence about the man that he could not share, a sense of invincibility given him by his club tie and sober suit.

"I don't know—but I shouldn't count to coming out of this unscratched. You've heard of the Bushido-Endgame, after all. . . ."

Latymer looked quizzically at him.

"You mean that he might kill us, and Gardiner, and do whatever damage he can before anyone catches up with him?" His voice was uncertain. "I don't believe it."

"What about Stolze, that East German in the BfV in '57? He was the case who gave rise to the term 'Bushido-Endgame'—maximization of destruction by a double on the point of being exposed. He wiped out two networks singlehandedly, rolled up a ciphers department, and leaked two dozen or more new names to the Abteilung before he got himself shot. And there have been others—our man in Prague, Dempster—killed the head of his section, gelignited the records of Czech Intelligence for Africa and Western Europe, then threw himself under a train as the police were chasing him along the platform of the station. . . ."

"All right—I believe you! He may do that. What do we do, then, to prevent it?"

"I'd call 'C' direct, but I'm certain that would seal our fate, as the romantic writers have it. . . . Of course, it's possible that Constant, having been a 'mole' for so long and, I'm certain, never having been activated as a double, might not feel obliged to blow himself to the heavens to damage us. . . . In which case, he'll simply pack his bags and disappear."

"You think so? I confess I don't understand the man—can't feel the way his mind works." Latymer was languid again, as if the more sordid aspects of his fate had vanished, replaced by something more comfortable and gentlemanly. "How do we stop him?"

There was a long silence, and then Latymer heard Aubrey say, "We have the weapon here to hand. The thing is, ought we to use it?"

"What do you mean?"

"*Who.* His name is Richard Gardiner. We might just complete Haussman's design for him. A fitting epitaph."

"You're serious, Aubrey?"

"Deadly serious." He stood up, crossed the room to the bottle of scotch on top of the cabinet. "Just like Constant to offer a man blended instead of malt. . . .

He probably buys it in a supermarket. I suppose that should have warned me years ago . . . ?" He poured himself a drink, turned to Latymer, who held out his glass to be replenished, and said, "I am serious, Hilary. We must get rid of Constant. We can't afford another scandal, and we can't have him going over, under, or behind the curtain and making us all look fools—imagine the restructuring, the blown networks, the names. . . . No, we can't have that. Philby was bad enough, but Constant is privy to the whole picture! And he won't stay here, not now, unless he can get rid of us, bluff the French, and be certain that no one will ever ask questions. And he can't be certain of that." Aubrey was punctuating his sentences by pointing with the hand that held the glass. The liquid slopped in the tumbler, catching Latymer's attention as he tried to find opposing arguments.

There were none.

"I accept most of what you say. But—how can we?" It was almost a plea, as if he were now being asked to bloody his hands, having retained some moral aloofness up to that point. He seemed to resent his position.

"I know what you feel, Hilary—systems, routines, all tell you not to kill your superior. But you do believe that he has killed Haussman and his driver on *suspicion,* no more than that? Well, do you?"

After a long and strained silence that became artificial and evasive, Latymer said, "Yes, I do believe it. And that makes the rest of it true."

Aubrey touched him on the shoulder.

"Thank you, Hilary. I'm glad you're with me." He moved away, as if embarrassed at the nakedness of Latymer's eyes as they looked at him and the sense of lost innocence they seemed to express. He sat down heavily.

"Right. Where shall we begin?"

"Do you think Constant will run?"

"Yes, I do. On balance, he will come to consider that the wisest course. However much he would like to get back at Gardiner and us. He'll settle for having paid off Haussman and be blowed to the rest. Let us assume that he arrives in this room before very long and tells us that he has to go back to London or some such—then what do we do? And what about Gardiner?"

"Do we have to use Richard?" There was the same plea in the voice, as if Latymer had remained uncommitted.

"Yes, we do." Aubrey's face was grave. "If we kill Constant, then we ourselves may be considered agents of a foreign power. . . ." His lips twisted around the euphemism. "Only a rogue element. That was what Haussman intended when he used Gardiner—and he was right."

"Right? What *right* is there in the matter?"

"Very well. Lie down and let the Constant steamroller drive straight over you! Or let him get away with this and make his peace with his Moscow control!" Aubrey was angry, scything in his sharpest voice at the hedge of moral intractibles that Latymer had erected around himself. "You want to do *nothing*, Hilary? It is not in our power to do nothing, to let things carry on as they are. Can't you see that?"

Latymer's face acquired a sullen scowl; then, after a silence, he nodded his head.

"Yes, I see that. It's just that. . . ."

"I don't want him to be used either. But he has to be. Constant has to die in his identity as the 'Wolf,' not as a Russian 'mole.' He will do that if we release Gardiner."

"*If* Constant decides to leave," Latymer warned.

Constant did not stay for lunch. A little after twelve he entered the library and was at his most affable and untrustworthy. Aubrey, conscious of the game the deputy was playing, acted as if he suspected nothing. Constant stood in front of the fireplace and looked at each of them.

"I'm afraid I've been summoned back to London —immediate from 'C.' " He let the words sink in. "A small aircraft will be at my disposal this afternoon—a field near Sheffield. I'm sorry there won't be room for the two of you and your captive. . . ." He smiled. "However, I would wish you to return to London as quickly as possible. There is sufficient transport here for the purpose."

"What is our destination, Deputy?"

"Ah. I don't think we've finished with Mr. Gardiner yet. It had better be the country house for the moment. Hand him over to the staff there, and we can wrap this thing up with your reports." He added, "It only remains for me to thank you both, sincerely. I am most grateful for your help. . . ." He nodded to each of them, then said, "Well, I must be on my way. Good day, gentlemen."

As soon as the door snapped shut behind him, Aubrey said, "I'll delay him—get Gardiner out of the cellar, and make sure he's armed!" Latymer seemed charmed by Constant's smooth, normal tones. Aubrey barked, "Do it! Gardiner has to be free before Constant leaves. When he's gone is time enough to get through to 'C' and try to explain this thing. Get on with it!"

Then he was through the door and calling after Constant. Latymer did not hear what he was saying as he and Constant went into another room, and he crossed the hall, heading for the cellar door.

He flicked on the light and walked gingerly down the stairs. There had been no one on guard at the door, and he wondered for a moment if Constant had killed Gardiner. There was a strip of light coming from beneath another door, and the coolness of the cellar struck him. The smell of mustiness, but not damp. Something unused, like the house itself. He pushed open the door, and Evans looked up from his chair where he was reading a newspaper and avoiding looking at Gardiner, who was slumped in another chair, his head on his chest.

"Hello, Mr. Latymer, can I help you?" Though he completed the words, he did not complete the sense. Latymer had the revolver in his hand, and it was pointed at Evans.

"Untie him!" he snapped.

"What the hell . . . ?"

"Do it!" It was an echo of Aubrey's bark, and it seemed to retain its force, urging Latymer to action, cleansing the sullen body of lethargy and reluctance.

Evans looked at Latymer and then did as he was told. Latymer looked into Gardiner's face, which revealed the gratuitous bruising of his interrogation. The gray eyes were sharp with concentration and the beginnings of a sense of hope. Latymer recoiled almost physically from the killing thing he saw in the face.

Beyond the single naked bulb and its hard circle of light, the racks of bottles retreated into shadow. Yet the nature of the place as a wine cellar could not mask its naked function at that moment. The eyes focused only on the lit area, the whitewashed bare walls and the chair placed in the middle of the flagged floor, and the form of the man in the chair and the guard.

"Who did this to him?" he snapped at Evans, fumbling with the last knots behind Gardiner's back.

"Simons, mostly."

Gardiner stood up and rubbed his wrists, then chafed the discolored ankles where he rolled down his socks. The cords had been tied very tightly. Then he looked at Latymer.

"Time to go, is it?"

"For you, yes. Constant is leaving." He glanced at Evans. "Tie him up." Evans appeared affronted, and Gardiner surprised. "Don't waste time—just do it!"

Evans sat meekly in the chair, events having outpaced his optimism, his essential lack of gravity with regard to his work. Gardiner tied him swiftly and expertly.

Latymer, realizing that Evans had to overhear, wasted no time.

"Constant is leaving. He has to be stopped. For all sorts of reasons, you're the man to do it. You know why. He's killed the Frenchman, and now he's on his way out."

"You *want* me to kill him?"

"Yes, damn it!" He watched Gardiner pick up Evans's gun from the chair where it had been meekly laid and looked at Evans's wide face, still shocked. "Evans, this is Mr. Aubrey's operation, as from now. Be sensible, and sit where you are. I'll release you before very long—understand?"

"Yes."

"Now, Richard. Upstairs. Constant is heading for Sheffield, and that means the road through Wigtwizzle and then alongside the Broomhead Reservoir to Ewden. It will be one chance, and only one. Understand?"

"Give me a long gun," Gardiner said simply. Latymer watched the face set in a pattern he had only glimpsed before in the car opposite Notre Dame when Perrier had been deliberately released by Haussman and in briefings in Baker Street a world ago. Now it seemed his natural and habitual expression.

"There isn't one—"

"Bloody incompetent!" Gardiner snapped. It was grotesque, the most unexpected of remarks, but in the narrow tunnel of Gardiner's view the only one applicable. He grimaced and turned to the door. "What about him?" he said of Evans.

"Leave him!" Latymer snapped in sudden unease.

Gardiner smiled contemptuously and then went through the door and up the stairs. Latymer saw the situation outpacing him now; Gardiner was in control of his own destiny, crude and violent as it obviously was—and as he wished it.

Wooller was crossing the hall, a rifle slung over his shoulder. It was chance, and Latymer, had he seen him before Gardiner, might have cursed it. Gardiner, seeing only the gun clearly and the bulk of the man out of focus and muzzily dark, fired from the waist twice. The explosions rocked Latymer, echoing off the paneling of the hall, the dark, closed doors. When he saw Wooller, he was lying on the checkered tiles, sprawled untidily on their clean pattern. Gardiner bent over him and picked up the Armalite rifle, checking it expertly.

"Which way out—the back way?" he snapped. Latymer's brain was still clogged by the noise and the dying.

"This one . . ." Latymer said slowly, opening the door to a sitting room he remembered overlooked the rear lawns which sloped down gently to a line of trees and the rest of the grounds. "Make your way down toward. . . ."

Gardiner heaved up the window.

"I'll make my own way," he said softly. Then, as if he remembered something forgotten for a long time, said, "I'll kill him for you—sometime, if not now." Then, as if in valediction, for the whole of his past, he asked, "Wish me luck?" It was something from the door in an aircraft fuselage or over a wartime dinner at the officers' club.

He lifted his leg over the windowsill, the rifle slung over his shoulder, and then he dropped onto the gravel path separating the house from the grounds. Latymer watched him running swiftly and warily, and it was as if he were watching a conscious performance of arts he had either forgotten or never used.

The door banged back on its hinges, and Constant entered the cool, airy room behind him, his face suffused with anger, a pale tinge to the dead skin; Aubrey was just behind him, and then Laker, a gun in his hand.

"Kill him—kill him now!" Constant ordered, his mouth working as if the words were filling it. "Kill him, Latymer!"

Laker, as if sensing something hidden in the situation, elbowed Constant and Latymer out of the way.

"I'll do it!"

He raised the .357 Magnum to his eyes, arms stiff, and carefully squeezed off three shots. Gardiner did not turn but broke the course he had been taking, beginning to weave erratically toward the trees, a stiff line of markers ahead of him. It was evident he was unhit.

"Get a rifleman!" Constant snapped. Laker left the room. "Get men after him—everyone!" Constant called after him. "I want him taken or killed!"

He turned to Latymer, still at the window. Gardiner was beyond the trees now and spotted only with difficulty, a shadow dwindling across the grounds. Latymer said, "I'm sorry, Deputy. . . ."

"Sorry?" Constant asked in his most austerely mocking tone. His eyes were bleak. "Why, what have you to be sorry for, Latymer?"

"I—should have shot him when I saw him coming into this room. I don't know why I hesitated."

"Yes, you should have. How could he have managed to escape?"

Aubrey saw a furious activity behind the unreflecting surfaces of Constant's eyes, as if a sequence of images through the wrong end of a telescope. Constant was beginning to panic. He knew why they had released Gardiner.

"Sorry, Deputy—but we'll have him again before night, I can assure you of that." Aubrey was brisk, officious. He saw Constant's eyes gleam, as if he had guessed the whole strategy in one moment of insight.

"Quite. It will, of course, mean a serious reprimand, if not worse." He nodded as if he had seen the challenge, his mind stooping to the cast gage. Aubrey saw that the last fragment of the puzzle fitted. He had read Constant correctly. But Constant, he saw, still believed he could win.

"I am leaving now!" he snapped. "Get things organized." He left the room, and Latymer looked at his watch. Then he looked out of the window. A figure ran toward the trees, but there was no sign of Gardiner.

"Has he time?" Latymer asked.

"I hope so. He's all that's left to us. Without him, the cupboard is bare." His face became grim. "He has to get him! I'm willing to bet the telephone is out of order."

Aubrey turned to the window, and the lawns down to the trees were empty. Gardiner was well ahead of the pursuit. He heard a car engine fire and the screech of tires on the gravel of the front drive. Constant was on his way, and suddenly Aubrey felt helpless. It required an act of faith to believe that Constant was driving to his death. He looked at Latymer's features and found no such faith there.

He wanted to look at a map suddenly—a failure of nerve.

Gardiner's chest heaved with the effort. The Armalite rifle, held in one hand, banged painfully against his thigh with each stride. He was in Wigtwizzle now, converging on the road that Constant's car would have to take. He was heading for the reservoir, praying that he would be in time and that doubts trembling in his mind would leave him. He wanted, with a choking desire, to be in time. His blood pounded in his brain, and his body ached from the beating they had given him.

As he ran, there was a sudden fusion of memory's circuits, prompted by pain, and it was as if his whole person had jolted in him and screamed at the perspective that was his life. He was running through the woods, from the train toward the river, and the SS were firing behind him. It was 1944. Without checking his stride, he squashed the memories bubbling through. In a moment, no more, he was calm, and he thought about nothing then. One nightmarish moment, and it was over, that tunnel of pain down which something horrid and misshapen made its way, and he afraid to look at its face, which was only a mirror. Now there was nothing but the path through the trees and the ears straining to pick up the first sounds of a car.

There was nothing to think about, except the hatred of Constant, which made his grip on the rifle sweaty with fearful anticipation; that was enough to substitute for the flashing imagery of the past, the bright fish beneath the surface of the blood, winking in and out of shadows.

He had to repay. The past had become a formula, a slim package of blood and bone and nerves and brain, with a name and an identity and a life that could be let out. . . .

The trees opened, and the stream of the Ewden, flowing into the reservoir, was just below him. He paused, breathing suddenly loudly in the silence of the racing blood, and then crossed the last yards to the minor road that crossed the stream by a narrow bridge humped over the water.

He was on the bridge when he heard the car. On one side of the bridge was the reservoir, a sheet of dark water under the cloudless, hot sky, and on the other the trees and the stream. And then the car, heading out of Wigtwizzle, two faces in the front seats, a driver's and the cadaverous patch of white that was Constant's.

It took no more than a second. He regretted, clearly and distinctly, not having reached the bank of the reservoir and the overlooking trees on the other side of the bridge, from which Olympian height he had designed the end of the drama. He regretted his suddenly turning body, the noise of the car, the untidiness and unfitness of it. . . .

He switched the rifle to automatic and squeezed the trigger. The windshield dissolved in a frosty gleam, then emptied back into the car under the awesome pressure and firing speed of the rifle. Then the car swerved into the side of the bridge, halting itself abruptly—with sufficient force to eject one of the occupants through the shattered windshield and onto the hood.

Then the car toppled, and the body slid onto the road as the car eased itself down the bank toward the stream, where it slid with a drowning gurgle into the Ewden.

The magazine was empty, and the deafening din silence again before the body popped comic and doll-like through the shattered windshield. Gardiner's hearing came back, and he could apprehend the drowning of the car, distantly. Then he walked over to the body and looked down at it. He turned it over with his foot.

The head had been lying in a pool of muddy water, and the white shirt and neat collar had become soaked and stained. One manicured hand was outflung and the nails were dirty. The head flopped stupidly in a way its owner would not have allowed in life as the body turned onto its back.

There were four holes in the thin, dead face, and lacerations, more vivid in places than the small blue holes, from the flying glass of the windshield. There were tears in the cloth of the jacket and a red patch, beginning but stemmed, on the shirt, near the breastbone.

The man had been wiped out, swept aside.

Gardiner stood there for a little time, as if paying some final valediction to the crumpled thing that was growing cold and that now, even to him, was less than nothing.

And he was satisfied. Pleased with the complete reduction of the living Constant to this nameless, breathless, stained thing on a narrow bridge, riddled and erased. His satisfaction was complete.

ABOUT THE AUTHOR

Born in Wales, educated at grammar school and University College, Cardiff, CRAIG THOMAS began to write and send his work to British magazines while only in his teens. Everything was rejected. Undaunted, he started a constant flow of scripts to the BBC in the hopes that they might bite. They never did. However, one BBC editor gave him some very important advice. As Thomas tells it, "He told me that I wrote well but asked me why didn't I write a novel?"

This spurred him on. At the time, Thomas was teaching English, and he continued doing so until 1977, just after he wrote *Firefox*. This novel was actually his second book, the first being a novel called *Rat Trap*. *Wolfsbane,* his third novel will soon be followed by Mr. Thomas's fourth book.

Although Thomas claims he doesn't like doing research on his books, he does admit its necessity. "I research as well as I can. Its only fair to your readers that you do. These days you couldn't get away with a 'Bulldog Drummond' approach. My books are authentic. The minute details are less important than the convincing details."

Today, Thomas is married and lives in Lichfield, Staffordshire, England, in a house that is gradually becoming smaller. Before the success of *Firefox,* he used the staff room and his own kitchen table for his writing. Since last year, one bedroom has become his office and a second room is required for his wife who acts as his secretary and bookkeeper. He writes "during office hours —10 A.M. to 4 P.M.," dislikes editing his books and lives a life "as close to perfection" as he can imagine.

Thomas's novel *Firefox* is also currently available in paperback from Bantam Books.

A Special Preview of
opening pages from the ingenious new shocker

THE EVIL
THAT
MEN DO
by
R. Lance Hill

"Like THE DAY OF THE JACKAL a frightening, razor-slice thriller that holds the reader
hostage until the last shuddering climax."

DJAKARTA, INDONESIA. 3:53 A.M./17 June/1974.

There were two military vehicles and one black car parked beside the house.

The ensemble made a tidy row under the light, the black car in the middle, the other two as close as lusting escorts. All three appeared empty, and were, except for the panel truck nearest the house. Behind the wheel was a soldier in the uniform of the Indonesian army. His hands were clasped on his belly, his head back on the seat, his mouth an open hole.

He had been sleeping for two hours.

Outside, the temperature was 29 degrees Celsius, the equivalent of 84 degrees Fahrenheit. In the day it had reached 114 degrees Fahrenheit. Birds had plummeted from the trees. Humidity made snapping noises with radio waves. People waded in the *Kali*.

The house appeared cool despite excesses of climate. All windows were shuttered.

Heat oozing from the pavement beneath the black car made the confined space a boiling cauldron. If the man lying pressed between the asphalt and floorboards made the slightest slip in his labors, the space would become his crematorium. If he made a noise sufficient to wake the soldier, or if the others came out of the house before he finished, he would be delivered into the hands of a man who could kill him without his dying. His sweat ran profusely.

Assael Ganot was carefully and quietly affixing C-4 plastic explosive to the entrails of the automobile. For Assael Ganot to be doing what he was doing required he be exceptionally courageous . . . or committed . . . or cavalier. Most members of the elite Mossad possessed varying parts of the prescription, though certainly the accent was on commitment. The Mossad was the deadly efficient Israeli intelligence organization, and Assael the demolitions expert in a commando squad of six members. His commander and one of the surveillance team were watching from a house across the street, the balance waiting in a freighter on the bay.

Assael lowered his arms to rest, letting the blood flow back from where it had thinned. He was young, only twenty-two, but cramps are hurried by heat. Even with the back of his head on the pavement there was little room to turn it. The sheet metal planed his face as he did so, prompting him to silently curse the nose he considered at other times his prized feature.

He normalized his breathing, rhythmically, each intake spreading his ribs against the underbelly of the car. Bathed in perspiration, the juice mingled with road grease and became rivulets speeding into his eyes and ears. His hands were wet and slippery. Pressing them against his shirt did not help; it was wet enough to be wrung.

The glow from the lightbulb skipped across the pavement, flickering ominously again. He knew what that signified. The knowledge chilled him, his sweat rearing up cold and clammy. Assael shivered in the heat.

The flickering meant that electrical current was being drawn from the house circuits to be passed through the bodies of human beings within. Each dimming of illumination meant a fresh charge administered. Sometimes the light quaked, nearly vanished, for long seconds. Dutch electrical standards had not been of a high order when the house was erected in their colonial era. Had they been, the lights would not dim.

Assael shut his eyes from the spastic sight. A harsh fetid odor from the canal hung heavy near the ground. To Assael, who had never smelled anything to rival it—not even Syrian cadavers baking in the deserts of the October War—the stench seemed caustic enough to rot the tires around him.

But, he knew he must finish, and soon. Four plugs of C-4 had been taped already, two on the transmission tailshaft housing forward of the front seat, and two more to the driveshaft just forward of the rear seat's proximity. A plug was fixed independently at both 45 and 315 degree angles on the housing and shaft. The charges were designed to kill one man, regardless of the location he assumed in the car. Such perfection was largely immaterial. There was enough explosive on the drivetrain to powder a small building, much less dismantle a common American sedan. . . .

The young commando's preparations had been thorough and meticulous. Once the surveillance team informed him of the type of automobile used to chauffeur the subject, the commander had rented an identical unit from Hertz. Assael spent hours under it, tracing wiring harnesses, measuring distances by hand-spreads, plotting points of placement, cutting wires to precise lengths, committing all to memory. He was a stone cold professional selected for a squad comprising the best the Mossad could cull from ranks. He knew explosives as he knew the roof of his mouth. The mission was one of the heart, and he in turn was the heart of the mission. His plugs of plastic would rend the subject into jelly. Assael would be a lion in the Mossad.

He slid his hand below his beltless trousers and into the dampness near his genitals. The shunning of a belt was just another precaution; belts snag and scrape at inopportune times. When he extracted his hand it held two coils of double wire. Each coil had a brass alligator clamp on one end, a small round blasting cap resembling a firecracker on the other.

The crucial part of the operation was now. Electrical blasting caps dictate respect bordering on fear. Caps are the fuse that fires first, thereby setting off whatever larger charge they are mated to; without them the plastic explosive being just so much inert putty. Caps must never fail and are assembled with a machined neurosis that makes a fuse *want* to fire regardless of appropriate inducement. In rash hands they often rebelled fatally.

Assael unravelled the wires, gingerly holding the closed cap ends between two fingers and slipping them inside his shirt so they would not be jostled while he worked. From between his teeth he took an object no larger than a fountain pen. This was a fiber-optics light, having a frosted plastic tube the size of a pencil projecting from one end, thus directing illumination down the tube to project in a concentration equal to the tube's diameter. Besides the intense convergence of light provided, the preeminent feature of the device was that it was undetectable until quite close.

The pencil-beam played on the automobile's starter solenoid a few inches from Assael's face. There they were, the three terminals jutting out. The larger one in the middle posed the threat; it directly connected to the car's battery and therefore was a constant source of current. If he were to so much as brush that terminal with one of the clamps, the caps would detonate. It would be all over. No, it was the smaller outrigger terminal he would have to fasten his clamps to, scarcely a thumbnail distance from the live terminal. His touch would have to be steady and sure. Once the clamps were fastened he could ease himself back to the plastic plugs where he would tuck the caps gently into the craters formed in the C-4. That would complete the exercise. He could then crawl back through the bushes to the canal.

After, it would be simply a matter of waiting. Waiting for them to come from the house . . . for the subject to get into the car . . . for his driver to turn the ignition key. Other members of the squad would conceivably hear the explosion all the way to the freighter. They would smile and cuff each other in the macho ritual of triumph.

Hinges squeaked on parched metal. Assael closed the light, his breath seized. He lowered his head and turned his eyes. A pair of army issue boots were a few feet to his right. The soldier was coming around to the car, near enough to reach out and touch.

Across the street the commander of the squad grew tense as he watched the drama from a second floor window, his eye to an infrared spotting scope that afforded a view as clear as though it were high noon.

"Aei," he whispered anxiously.

"What? What is it?" the man next to him wanted to know, moving to see what he could.

"The soldier woke up," the commander said tightly. "Next to the car."

"I see him," the surveillance man confirmed. Though he did not have benefit of an infrared instrument, he was trained to see in the night and could make out the form of the soldier between the truck and the car. The trick was in knowing that the center of the eye is a dead zone at night its nerves the ones used primarily to detect colors. By focusing ten degrees or so from the desired object and rotating the vision around this field, the more sensitive nerves were brought into play and a suitable image transmitted.

"Is Assael out of there yet?" he asked the leader.

"No." The man looked at his watch. "Six minutes more are required. Minimum." The commander dealt in absolutes, even in speech.

"What is the scrotum doing? I can't see enough."

"Pishing. Against the truck."

"Move, you pig," the surveillance man hissed, as if to will it by word. "Go back to your truck and sleep the long sleep."

The commander elbowed him away from where he was encroaching on the window. The man slumped against the wall.

They waited, only two in a room belonging to a teenage girl in an empty house. The occupants were on vacation in Japan.

The surveillance man fidgeted with his hands incessantly. For the past while he had been fingering a pair of the girl's panties. The rite annoyed his senior.

"His bladder doesn't stop," the commander marvelled.

"He's filling his boots so his feet will be cool," the other said derisively, stretching the silk bridge of the panties tightly over his fist. "Go back to your wet dreams in your wet boots, you scrote."

The commando leader was annoyed by the man's solitary bantering, considering it unbefitting a professional.

Then, as though heeding instruction, the soldier walked back to settle as he had been behind the wheel.

The commander lowered the scope in relief.

"He went back?" his companion queried.

The commander snatched the panties and sent

them flying into the darkness of the room. He had little patience for the inspirations resorted to in times of waiting. Surveillance men were a peculiar breed by any measure. His personal suspicion was that they would be peeping in bedroom windows of their own volition anyway. This way they at least had a worthy purpose. Still, the man deserved his respect. When assigning this mission the heads of the Institute had extended him full discretion in choosing his squad of four men and two women. Each of them had performed faultlessly thus far, all aware that promotions were for the taking on this one, knowing that entire careers had taken seed in less vital operations. The likelihood was that he himself would advance to the inner circle of the Institute.

In a house across the way was a man the Institute very much wanted dead. The briefing in Tel Aviv had been conducted in a mood of enmity more pronounced than that reserved for Black September, the virulence on display then causing him wonder. It still did. He did not know enough. Only that the man, thought to be named Clement Moloch, was known to most only as The Doctor. And that he apparently moved from country to country instructing various nefarious organizations in methods of interrogation.

Assael said he had heard rumors. Of unspeakable tortures, perpetrated by this Doctor. Of monstrous methods devised and imparted to others. Of service to the most barbaric of regimes. According to Assael's reasoning, it must have to do with the Israeli prisoners tortured by the Syrians in the aftermath of the October conflict.

Beyond the conjecture, the commander had only his orders to go on. The major-general had given him a passport photograph that had been altered by a skilled hand at some time, a date and some anticipated zones of interception in Djakarta, and a directive to remove the man from the face of the earth at all cost.

Costs thus far had been substantial. Members of the squad were registered as seamen in the employ of the Biscayne Traders Shipping Corporation, a Mossad front incorporated in Liberia's curtain of anonymity. A tramp freighter, part of the Biscayne apparatus, was chartered solely so that they would have legitimate endorsement to be in Djakarta. Ostensibly, the freighter was in port for repairs to her pumps, but the instant the mission concluded she would be blessed by a wondrous recovery and make straight for the congested shipping lanes.

In the eight days spent observing the house, any doubts of its function were quickly laid to rest. Too many trucks brought too many prisoners. Too many men and women were sent cowed and stumbling through the gauntlet of soldiers between the trucks and the house. Too many of them had been carried out prone and shrouded. The house was an interrogation center for political prisoners, a chamber of horrors.

The Grey Eminence known as The Doctor had been inside up to thirteen hours a day. His exit was usually made in the early hours of evening, in time to have dinner with his wife and children at the Commissioner's compound where they were quartered. This day was different. This day he had not left as darkness fell, and the commander had been quick to put into motion the only plan he deemed left him.

He raised the scope and scanned the scene again. The sweep of filtered beam detected no movement. In the truck the soldier's head lay back, his mouth open again.

Assael would have allowed four or five minutes for the soldier to reclaim his sleep. That meant the explosives would be set and primed inside of four minutes. In seven minutes the young commando should be clear of the car. The success of the mission was at hand. They were close.

Under the car, Assael closed the last clamp as gently as a caress, drew his hand away, and allowed his lungs to function once more. Wires from the clamps hung down, curling on his face and neck, leading to the blasting caps in the folds of his shirt. Artless wires. Umbilicals of death. Caution would have to be taken they did not nudge the clamps against the live terminal.

The soldier's urine had wormed under the car and formed a pool where his right leg rested. Moving rearward to place the caps in the plastic would necessitate a slide through the puddle. The prospect was a trifling incidental now that the clamps were set.

He reached into his shirt to extract the caps, holding them by the closed ends with enormous care.

From somewhere across the still air he heard the oriental timbre of a gamelan—the Indonesian xylophone. Late for music, he thought. Or early, depending on your reason of reference and level of discomfort.

He squirmed slowly toward the rear of the car, shifting a bit to center, full into the urine, playing out the wires as he went.

The pencil-light, now off, caught on the emergency brake cable and was pulled from his mouth, falling to the pavement with a clatter. Assael came rigid as a man on a blade. His ears took the attention of a blind man's. His eyes closed, the better to hear. At least the noise had been partially dispersed by the waiting urine pool. Small mercies. He waited.

Sounds were those of the night. Crickets. A

dog barking. The engine of a light plane far off. A screen closing somewhere along the lane.

If the soldier had stirred, Assael had not heard him. No squawk came from the door hinges. Boots had not appeared from the truck. The soldier could be listening too, and waiting, unsure whether his drowsiness had betrayed his ears. Assael deliberated, the pragmatic commando temper reckoning quickly. The eager blasting caps decided for him; counting risk was now a luxury to be jettisoned.

Both caps in one hand, he groped with the other for the pencil-light, his fingers making tracks in the wetness there. Where was the damn thing? There. There it was. He placed it, wet, back between his teeth.

The last few inches were taken on his back, bringing the deposits of C-4 into view above. His shoulder blades were raw and hurting, stung by the acidity on the ground. But the wires leading forward were lax and unhindered for placing the caps. The moment of truth. Once the caps were joined with the C-4 there was no turning back . . .

Outside, a grey Mercedes had swung into the drive by the house across the way, its headlights shining full in the face of the waking soldier. The beams flicked to high and back, spurring the soldier to start the truck.

"What are they doing?" the surveillance man wondered aloud, having taken up a position back of the window. "Is Assael clear yet?"

"Under the car," was the terse reply.

The truck was backing up, the Mercedes taking its place next to the house. When the truck stopped it too activated its headlights.

The commander stood, his attention fastened to the window, his chair knocked over by the reflex motion. The man behind caught it before it struck the carpet.

"What is that Mercedes doing there?" he demanded of the subordinate, more accusation than question.

"I don't know. Maybe—"

"Maybe a switch," the commander finished for him.

"It cannot be . . ." the man said in his imploring way.

"It is," the senior confirmed stiffly, watching their fears pantomimed for them.

The Mercedes halted so that its passenger doors were adjacent to the side of the house, scarcely a stride away. A man stepped from the house and opened both doors of the German car, glancing in at the driver. This man was recognized by the commander as having been at the house daily. He was a high ranking officer of the Indonesian security agency, named Epatj. Upon confirming the driver's identity, Epatj presented his back to the street and stood like a shield at the door.

Three men, all in batik shirts out at the waist, emerged and stepped into the rear of the Mercedes. An older man followed, thick in stature, white hair caught passing in the light, face lowered. The Doctor. The center seat in front was his. Epatj got in beside him, slamming the door in accustomed military manner.

With that the Mercedes backed into the street and in a single fluid sweep leapt away. Less than a minute passed from its initial appearance. The commander watched his quarry disappear untouched; taillights receding.

"How did this happen?" the commander snapped.

"They used the American car . . . always. . . ." the other defended haltingly, shaken by the realization their chance had slipped away and his surveillance team would be held largely responsible. Someone on the other side had been exceptionally clever. "He must have suspected," he said, grasping.

"Impossible. They did this purely as a precaution. You should have known."

"What if The Doctor wasn't with them? Are you certain you saw—?"

"Confirmed," his superior interrupted. He repeated, "How did this happen?"

"I don't know how it happened." Then he remembered Assael. "We've got to get Assael clear . . . before someone uses that car."

"The house still has a dozen soldiers, and the one outside," the commander said. "We can't help him. You could pray . . . and do it better than you did your reconnaissance."

His voice carried more optimism than conviction. The scope showed him the soldier, and the truck still with its lights on. Anticipating. Waiting on something.

A uniformed officer came from the house, walked briskly to the black car, nodded to the soldier in passing.

"Gott in Himmel!" the commander rasped, turning on his heel from the window and dropping the scope in flight. His companion sped after him.

Assael felt a frieze of hypnotic tranquility embrace him as he watched the wing-tipped shoes of the officer approach . . . as the door opened and the automobile grunted under the settling weight . . . at the sound of keys so close and sweet.

Assael Ganot never heard the snap of the starter solenoid. Instead he became, at 4:06 A.M., a swirling red dust shot from a hurricane.

C-4 plastic is not a selective exposive, as are

some. Of high velocity characteristic, its fury radiates indiscriminately in every direction. Where the black car had been—and Assael Ganot—the dense clay was pulverized to a crater of nearly two meters in depth. Most of the side of the house was laid open. The officer was reduced to a clump of pounded rags. Components of the automobile splashed down in the canal for a considerable distance. Even the soldier in the truck was killed, shredded by the imploding shards of glass.

The commander and his underling flew down the rear steps of their lair and into the night on silent crepe soles, the rooftops washed in fire flashes behind them.

To the freighter, where the celebration awaiting them was aborted as soon as the others saw their faces. Permission was granted to put to sea almost immediately.

Within forty-eight hours the Institute in Tel Aviv received a coded message that was not altogether unexpected. In it the United States Central Intelligence Agency curtly suggested the Mossad suspend all interest in The Doctor.

As has become the custom of most quasi-bureaucratic entities, merit is not necessarily a condition for advancement in the Mossad. Therefore the tainted commander went on to a somewhat more enhancing mission in the early days of July, 1976, at an obscure airfield in Africa called Entebbe.

The foiled operation in Djakarta signalled the last attempt made on The Doctor's life by any group or individual for the following four years. The prevailing consensus arrived at was dogmatically clear: The Doctor had too many patrons in too many towers, who had made him one of their own, and, like themselves, had pronounced him an untouchable. To try was not only futile, but presciently suicidal.

The word had come down. Everyone heard. . . .

By the time George was finished his swim Holland had banked a fire in front of the house and was heating butter in a cast-iron skillet. In a hole dug in the sand were two bottles of wine resting in sea water.

George helped him rinse fresh fruit in the ocean. The sun, half gone, had brushed everything in clarets of red. The water looked bloody and even the sand had the glow of a blast furnace as they squatted by the fire.

George looked around. "Like this, the sun reminds me of a line I read somewhere: 'Forged in the smithy of the mind.' "

"Uh-huh," said Holland.

"Would you live here if you felt differently about your country?" George said, the words chosen carefully.

Holland put the first few shrimps in the skillet, the butter singed to a mahogany where it ringed the metal. "Henry James said 'It's a complex fate being an American.' The man could lift his shit, I'd say."

George did not pursue it. He knew the reason why Holland, an American citizen by birth, felt he could no longer live there. His self-imposed exile was a condition of conscience and conviction; a protest so private and deep that George was the only one who knew.

He also knew that if one were to unjustly discredit the United States of America in the presence of Holland, that person had best move quickly.

"You didn't come for the sunset, George," Holland said quietly. "What brings you?"

George prepared his thoughts, squirming his

folded legs deeper into the sand, seeking stability.
To broach the subject so early was unexpected.

"Do you recall my mentioning The Doctor?"

"A time or two." Holland did not look up. "I
thought it might be that."

"It's what I've wanted for five years. I'm not
sure of the proper term. We—I'm not alone in this
—wish to have The Doctor disposed of."

"Hold this, will you?" Holland said, extending
the handle of the skillet. "Don't let it rest on the
coals just yet." He reached into the hole and filled
two tumblers with wine.

"Is that how you put it?"

"You want him killed, George."

"Yes. That is what we want."

"You want me to kill him."

"Yes."

*Holland, the professional killer, accepts the
challenge to stalk Clement Moloch, The Doctor of evil torture. Holland combines forces
with a beautiful woman who seeks revenge
for her husband's murder, and they become
full-fledged partners in love and death.*

(Read the complete Bantam Book, available
December 1st, wherever paperbacks are sold.)

DON'T MISS
THESE CURRENT
Bantam Bestsellers

☐ 11708	**JAWS 2** Hank Searls	$2.25
☐ 12400	**THE BOOK OF LISTS** Wallechinsky & Wallace	$2.75
☐ 11001	**DR. ATKINS DIET REVOLUTION**	$2.25
☐ 12997	**THE FAR PAVILIONS** M. M. Kaye	$2.95
☐ 12683	**EVEN COWGIRLS GET THE BLUES** Tom Robbins	$2.75
☐ 10077	**TRINITY** Leon Uris	$2.75
☐ 13286	**ALL CREATURES GREAT AND SMALL** James Herriot	$2.75
☐ 13287	**ALL THINGS BRIGHT AND BEAUTIFUL** James Herriot	$2.75
☐ 11770	**ONCE IS NOT ENOUGH** Jacqueline Susann	$2.25
☐ 13430	**DELTA OF VENUS** Anais Nin	$2.75
☐ 12386	**NEBRASKA!** Dana Fuller Ross	$2.50
☐ 13065	**THE IRON MARSHAL** Louis L'Amour	$1.75
☐ 12991	**PASSAGES** Gail Sheehy	$2.95
☐ 12370	**THE GUINNESS BOOK OF WORLD RECORDS 17th Ed.** The McWhirters	$2.50
☐ 13374	**LIFE AFTER LIFE** Raymond Moody, Jr.	$2.50
☐ 11917	**LINDA GOODMAN'S SUN SIGNS**	$2.50
☐ 12923	**ZEN AND THE ART OF MOTORCYCLE MAINTENANCE** Robert Pirsig	$2.75
☐ 10888	**RAISE THE TITANIC!** Clive Cussler	$2.25
☐ 12797	**STRYKER** Chuck Scarborough	$2.50

Buy them at your local bookstore or use this handy coupon for ordering:

RELAX!
SIT DOWN
and Catch Up On Your Reading!

Bantam Book Catalog

Here's your up-to-the-minute listing of over 1,400 titles by your favorite authors.

This illustrated, large format catalog gives a description of each title. For your convenience, it is divided into categories in fiction and non-fiction——gothics, science fiction, westerns, mysteries, cookbooks, mysticism and occult, biographies, history, family living, health, psychology, art.

So don't delay——take advantage of this special opportunity to increase your reading pleasure.

Just send us your name and address and 50¢ (to help defray postage and handling costs).